HER
EVERY
MOVE

Center Point
Large Print

Also by Kelly Irvin and available from
Center Point Large Print:

Tell Her No Lies
Over the Line
Closer Than She Knows

**This Large Print Book carries the
Seal of Approval of N.A.V.H.**

HER EVERY MOVE

EVERY

MOVE

KELLY IRVIN

CENTER POINT LARGE PRINT
THORNDIKE, MAINE

This Center Point Large Print edition
is published in the year 2021 by arrangement with
Thomas Nelson.

The text of this Large Print edition is unabridged.
In other aspects, this book may vary
from the original edition.
Printed in the United States of America
on permanent paper.
Set in 16-point Times New Roman type.

ISBN: 978-1-64358-938-1

The Library of Congress has cataloged this record
under Library of Congress Control Number: 2021932356

For Eileen Key, my writing mentor, my friend, my sister in Christ. Your departure has left a hole in my heart. Breathe easy now, sweet friend. One day we'll talk books again near God's heavenly throne. I can only imagine how many books He has in His library. We'll read them all!

ONE

Jackie Santoro checked her smartwatch for the fifth time. She needed to leave *now*.

She waved to catch her best friend Estrella Diaz's gaze. The City Council District 1 chief of staff stood next to her boss, Councilman Diego Sandoval, who was in deep conversation with the library foundation board chairman a few feet from the stage. Estrella offered a discreet fist pump. Jackie grinned and gave her a thumbs-up in return. Then she pointed at her watch.

Estrella nodded and cocked her head toward Sandoval. That meant she would shoo him and his entourage toward the doors shortly. Part of Estrella's job consisted of keeping him on message and on schedule. The woman loved being in charge and she loved being chin deep in local politics.

So far everything had gone like clockwork. Elected dignitaries, city officials, and citizens who'd plunked down their hard-earned money to watch a debate between a climate-change activist and author and an it's-all-a-hoax proponent crowded the Tobin Center for the Performing Arts.

The next step in this elegant special event waltz belonged to Jackie, who created programming as part of her position as adult collections coordinator at the Central Library. The library foundation had agreed to sponsor a more intimate reception for the authors, dignitaries, and VIP donors at the library only a dozen blocks away, and they were running late.

Adrenaline pumped through Jackie's veins and left a metallic taste in the back of her throat. Event planning added spice to a job she loved. It also kept her from sleeping much.

Intent on a quick getaway, she strode toward the back of the hall. Best friend number two, Bella Glover, waved from the reserved media seating. Jackie waved back. She'd scored tickets for herself and her friends to the Spurs game Saturday night. She could critique the *Express-News* reporter's story while the Spurs clobbered the LA Clippers. Spurs fans were nothing if not optimistic.

A steady stream of patrons stood and edged toward the center aisle. A low murmur swelled to the sound of hundreds of people all talking at once. Soon they'd be in front of Jackie, impeding her progress from the parking garage and on the narrow, one-way downtown streets of San Antonio.

"Great job, Jackie. Looks like your boss was wrong." Sandoval's constituent services director, Tony Guerra, sauntered up the aisle toward her. "Climate change opponents can coexist amicably in the same space. And so can city manager and city council staff."

"Thanks, but it took a whole host of partners to make this happen. And it's not over yet." Jackie stuck her hand on the door lever that would release her to the Tobin's massive lobby.

She liked Tony, which was a good thing since he'd asked Estrella to marry him. However, he wore his political ambitions like an obnoxious neon-pink tie.

"I have to go. I want to make sure there are no last-minute snags with the reception. Then it's back to fine-tuning the altars for the Catrina Ball. It's only a week away, and I'm behind because of the debate."

"You never let up, do you? Are we still on for the Spurs game tomorrow—"

A powerful force knocked Jackie from her feet.

Her skull banged on the hardwood floor.

Sharp projectiles pelted her face in a painful *ping-ping*.

What's happening?

Estrella? Tony? Bella?

Muffled screams and even her own moaning seemed strangely distant. "Estrella? Tony? Bella?"

If they answered, Jackie couldn't hear them. She dragged herself onto her hands and knees. Glass and sharp metal pierced both. She forced open burning eyes.

Heavy black smoke shrouded the hall. Metal and debris like deadly confetti showered her. She raised her arm to her forehead to protect her face from the remnants of folding chairs and electronics.

Warm blood dripped from her nose. The acrid taste of smoke and fear collected in her mouth. Her stomach heaved. Her pulse pounded so hard dizziness threatened to overcome her.

No, no, no. Do not pass out. People need help.

Shrieking alarms bellowed.

Water, like torrential rain, poured from above. Rain, inside? Her ricocheting thoughts made no sense. Jackie shook her head. Neither the smoke nor the clanging in her brain subsided.

Sprinkler system.

The smoke had triggered the sprinklers.

Where there's smoke there's fire. The old cliché ran circles in her mind like a children's nursery rhyme.

Estrella's mama and papa would never forgive Jackie if something happened to their sweet daughter. Mercedes and Mateo always saw Jackie as the instigator of trouble. And they were usually right.

Ignoring pain and panic, she crawled forward. Sharp metal bit into her skin. Where were her shoes?

Finally she encountered a warm, writhing body. "Tony?"

"What happened?" He struggled to sit up. Blood poured from an open wound on his scalp, his nose, and a cut on his lip. "I have to get to Estrella and Diego."

He might have yelled, but Jackie could barely make out the words. She leaned back on her haunches. "You're hurt. Does anything feel broken?"

"No, but I can't hear anything." He wiped at his face. Blood streaked his once crisply starched white shirt. "Why can't I hear?"

"It'll pass. We have to get everyone out."

With a groan, Tony leaned over and vomited on the floor. He wiped his mouth with his sleeve. "Okay, let's go."

"Everyone out. If you can walk on your own, evacuate." One of the contract security guards hired for the debate loomed over them. "The bomb squad is on the way. Go, go."

"We're fine. We'll help get the others out."

"Negative. Get out, there could be more bombs."

Bombs.

That word came through loud and clear. It hit Jackie with the force of a second explosion. People were hurt. People might be dead. People she cared about.

She grabbed Tony's arm and together they managed to stand. Around them others dragged themselves up. Frantic, bloodied faces with numb, shocked, baffled expressions. Screams and moans mingled in a horrible, muffled cacophony.

A woman knelt beside a man. She pressed her jacket against one leg. "Hang in there, hang in there." She repeated the phrase like a mantra to block out his agonized shrieks. "You're okay, you're okay."

A man carried a young teenager in his arms. Both her legs were mangled and bloody. "She needs help." Dazed, he seemed unaware of the blood pouring from a jagged wound on his arm. "Somebody, she needs help."

"Get outside. Help is on the way." Jackie guided him toward the door. "Take care of yourself."

People stumbled into her. She staggered and kept going. *God, please.*

A few more yards. She squatted beside a man's body facedown on the floor. He groaned, pulled himself to his knees, and crawled away. *Oh God.*

A few more feet.

There.

Jackie closed her burning eyes and opened them. "Oh Estrella."

"No, no, no." Moaning, Tony pushed Jackie aside. "*Mi amor*, I'm here. I've got you."

He collapsed next to her still body. Her lovely cocoa-brown eyes were wide and surprised in death. Blood matted charcoal-colored curls that surrounded her head like a jostled tiara. Her mouth was open as if caught in a perpetual *oh no.*

"*Por favor*, answer me, *mi corazón*."

"Tony, let me." The grotesque smell of death in her nose, Jackie swallowed against vomit in the back of her throat. Her stomach rocked. It took every ounce of strength left in her body to raise her hand. She touched Estrella's throat and found no pulse. "*Mi amiga*."

"No." Tony shoved Jackie away. "She needs a doctor. Get a doctor. Hurry."

Jackie fell backward in a heap next to the woman who had gone with her to a Britney Spears concert in the fifth grade. Estrella colored Jackie's hair with henna before her first date. She held Jackie's ponytail while she retched into the toilet after her first keg party. She managed Jackie's student council campaign for president her senior year in high school. She held Jackie's hand at Daddy's funeral.

Tony's sobs sounded more like screams. Jackie fought the urge to scream with him. She clasped her hands over her ears. *God, God, God, God. You brought Jairus's daughter back to life. And Lazarus. Why not Estrellita?*

A run-of-the mill doctor couldn't bring back this woman who had celebrated her thirtieth birthday Memorial Day weekend. One moment she was arguing social justice issues like the path to citizenship for Dreamers. The next she lay shattered and still, in the aftermath of a bomb, alongside her boss.

13

Part of the councilman's face was missing.

Jackie rubbed Tony's back. "She's gone on ahead of us, Tony. She's dancing with Jesus right now."

Estrella's unflinching faith offered the one silver lining in this dark, unfathomable moment.

Tony wiggled closer. She put her arm around his shoulders and held on as if they could buoy each other up on a storm-lashed sea. They were both drowning.

"Get out, get out." An SAPD officer in bomb gear lurched toward them. "Evacuate now."

"I'm not leaving her." Tony struggled to free himself from Jackie's grip. "I'm staying right here with her."

"We have to go." Jackie released him.

"Sweet dreams, my friend." She kissed Estrella's still-warm forehead and gently closed her eyelids. "We have to go, honey, but we'll make sure they take good care of you. We have to help the police find who did this."

Find them and make them pay.

TWO

Only a coward would look away.

Jackie fought the urge to rip her gaze from the body bags on gurneys in the triage tent set up on Municipal Auditorium Way across from the Tobin Center. The bomb squad had cleared the building without finding another incendiary device, and the removal of bodies had begun.

One, two, three, four, five. Five body bags. Estrella occupied one of those bags awaiting transport to the Bexar County medical examiner's office. By now crime scene investigators had photographed and videotaped her body from every angle. An ME investigator had done a preliminary review of her body and injuries. The final indignity of an autopsy still awaited her. Who were the others who faced the same ignominious procedures?

Head down, cell phone to his ear, Tony stood next to Estrella's gurney. The bandage on his brown forehead shone white. His face was red and swollen from crying. His free hand patted the bag every few seconds as if to comfort his fiancée.

Bella hovered close by. Whether as a friend or a reporter remained to be seen. Life became even more complicated in the aftermath of an explosion that ripped their lives into tiny pieces and scattered them across eternity.

Only a coward would refuse to look. Just as only a coward would detonate a bomb in a crowded auditorium.

Focus. Jackie tightened her grip on an elderly woman who wore a pink suit splattered with blood. Together they hobbled on punctured bare feet to the triage tent. The woman kept saying the blood didn't belong to her. She was fine, she said, but she wasn't. The gash on her rouged cheek needed attention.

An EMT took the handoff with a murmured thanks. He held out a blanket. "You look cold."

It would take years to shake this chill. Jackie settled the blanket around her shoulders and headed back into the fray. They wouldn't let her inside the building, but she made the rounds to the other victims who'd been deemed able to wait while the more critically injured were transported to area hospitals. She offered them what little she could—a kind word, a hug, a blanket, a cup of hot coffee made by Victim Assistance.

She pulled the blanket tighter, turned, and bumped into City Manager Jason Vogel. His normally perfectly coiffed black hair stuck out in tuffs on what had always struck her as an absurdly oversized head. The knees of his navy pinstriped suit were torn, his tie askew, and his hands caked with blood. His lips were blue. His teeth chattered. "Do I know you?"

Technically he was her boss. Ultimately all twelve thousand-plus city employees worked for him.

Jackie introduced herself. They'd met numerous times at library special events, but he couldn't be expected to remember all of the employees in his charge, especially in the aftermath of a traumatic event.

"Sam Santoro's daughter, I remember now."

Even a bomb with multiple fatalities couldn't erase that fact from Vogel's mind. The man had had the audacity to attend the funeral as if he'd forgotten his role in her father's untimely demise.

"A lady is a lady no matter the circumstances." Her mother's voice shouted in her ears. *"Only Jesus is perfect. Forgive, seventy times seven."* "Yes, sir."

He nodded, but his gaze shifted over her shoulder toward the command center set up by Alcohol, Tobacco, Firearms and Explosives and shared by the FBI, San Antonio Police Department, and Homeland Security Investigations. "Are you all right?"

"Yes, sir. Are you?"

Surprise flashed across his face. He probably thought his Teflon coating made him Superman. Couldn't a lowly librarian see that? "Of course. I have to go. Take care of yourself."

17

"You too, sir." It was nice of him to stop long enough to say the words. He managed a city of 1.3 million citizens, and ultimately he was responsible for their safety. "Here, take this blanket. You're freezing."

His hands remained at his sides. Jackie arranged it across his beefy shoulders. "It's okay, I'll get another one. Go."

"People are dead."

"I know, sir. Do the police have any idea who did this?"

"Lots of ideas. All conjecture." Vogel reached for the blanket. His hands were shaking. "Rest assured, we will get whoever did it. My wife could've been killed. Bill was my friend . . ." His voice trailed away.

Chief of Police Bill Little? "Is the chief—?"

"I have to go." He brushed past her and trudged, head down, toward the command center.

"This is all your fault."

Jackie whirled at the familiar, shrill voice. Meagan Nobel. Her immediate boss. Meagan's black silk blouse gaped open, revealing a lacy camisole. Either the explosion or a fall had ripped her tight, narrow skirt up to midthigh on the right side. Her shoes were intact but one heel was missing, so she meandered toward Jackie in a hip-hop, drunken fashion. "This debate was your idea. It's your fault."

"What? What are you talking about?" Jackie

staggered back from Meagan's pointed forefinger with its long nail lacquered in blood red. Her tone blasted the words for everyone in a one-block radius to hear. "Are you hurt?"

"Oh no, I'm fine and dandy." Meagan swiped at a straggling strand of red hair that covered her hazel eyes. "Milton is dead. Dead. You said it would be fine. You said it would be a great fund-raiser. I told you it was political dynamite. I never thought it would be actual dynamite."

Milton Schaeffer, San Antonio Library Foundation board chairman and number-one donor recruiter, lay in one of those body bags.

Her fault. All her fault. Jackie threw her hands up, but she couldn't stop the spewing words. Would Mercedes and Mateo Diaz hold her responsible for their daughter's death too? *Was* she responsible? "His wife . . . is his wife okay?"

"Injured. On her way to University's trauma center right now. The downtown hospitals are full." Meagan projected her ire with such velocity, a fine spray of spittle landed on Jackie's face. "Thank God the director is at an ALA conference this week. At least he's safe. Wait until he hears about this. What was I thinking to trust you with this?"

"I never thought—"

"Of course you never thought. We had our hands full with the Catrina Ball next weekend, and yet you bulldozed your way through every

19

objection because you want what you want and you're always right and you have no respect for the opinions of others. You love the limelight. You're never satisfied with simple signings by local authors. You want the big names, the controversy. 'Intellectual discourse,' you said. 'Civilized conversation,' you said. All along you wanted to make a big splash. You never should have become a librarian."

Of all the accusations spewing from Meagan's mouth, only the last sentence held no kernel of truth. Meagan stopped abruptly. Even she knew she'd gone too far.

Jackie's best friends—aside from Estrella and Bella, who grabbed on to Jackie and refused to let go—were books. She never went anywhere without at least two—one for backup. Church, camping, fishing, basketball games, the bathroom. Everywhere. Her now-lost bag contained Laurie R. King's newest Mary Russell novel and *Strands of Truth*. "Libraries are meant to be places of intellectual exchange."

"People died."

"I know. My best friend died." To her horror Jackie's voice cracked. She swallowed back tears. "I'll never forgive myself for that."

"You shouldn't. If I could fire you, I would."

Another piece of Jackie's world crumbled. She'd known since she was eleven that she would be a librarian. It defined her. Going to the library every day to work among thousands of books gave her life not only meaning but joy. "Do what you think is best, Meagan."

"Have you seen either of your guest speakers, by any chance?" Meagan's voice rose so high it hurt Jackie's ears. The pounding in her temples spiked. Her boss didn't seem to notice Jackie was hanging on by a thread. "Have you even looked for them?"

She had but to no avail. "There were more than eight hundred people in there. I'll keep searching for them."

"You'd better pray they weren't hurt. They could sue us, the library director, the city, you, me—"

"Meagan Nobel, are you saying you know who the bomber is?" Bella stepped between them, her back to Jackie. "Bella Glover with the *Express-News*. Are you saying you think it's a city employee? One of your employees? Are you willing to go on the record with that statement?"

Meagan's face blanched. She stuttered for a few seconds, then drew herself up to her full height— not quite to Jackie's shoulders. "Of course not. You misheard. Don't you dare quote me. All media requests to city officials are being referred to the city hall PIO—"

"I don't want a watered-down news release quote from the city manager. I want the real story from people who were here." Bella swiped at her face with a sodden tissue. "People like me."

Meagan backed away. "I'm not authorized to talk to the media." She pointed at Jackie. "Neither is she."

"She's my friend. I only want to make sure she's okay." Bella wrapped her arm around Jackie and squeezed. "I'm sure HR would love to know that she was being bullied by her superior on the worst day of her life."

The two women locked gazes. Meagan whirled and hip-hopped toward the command center. "If I pick up tomorrow's paper and see you quoted, Jackie, you're gone. Fired for cause." She threw the words over her shoulder, stumbled, regained her balance, and hobbled away.

Meagan always had the last word.

"You didn't have to do that. I'm capable of holding my own with her." Jackie entwined her arm with Bella's. "But thank you."

"I know, honey, you're fearless. You're my hero. I just despise a bully." Bella sank against Jackie. "I can't believe Estrella is dead. My brain—my heart—refuse to accept it. Why? Why her?"

Meagan could suck a lemon. Jackie guided Bella to a folding chair in the Victim Assistance area. Bella had been her roommate at UT–Austin. They'd navigated the collegiate world of keggers, campus politics, and college boys together, and pulled all-nighters at the library. No way would they abandon each other now.

Bella had skinned knees and puncture marks on her hands, bare legs, and arms. Her beaded braids, normally bundled in a ponytail at her neck, lay askew around her face. Her round, sturdy body shook. Tears streaked her mocha-brown cheeks. Jackie draped a blanket around Bella's shoulders and hugged her. "It's okay. Give yourself a minute to recover." She rubbed the other woman's back. "I can't believe you were able to hang on to your backpack throughout the explosion."

"The laptop belongs to the newspaper and I have a job to do." Having served with Bella on the high school newspaper staff, Jackie knew nothing stood in the way of the born-to-write reporter getting her story and finishing it on deadline. She took her Fourth Estate government watchdog responsibilities seriously. "I can't believe I'll never hear Estrella's laugh-snort again. Or hear her screaming, 'Go, Spurs, go' again. Or hear her stupid puns again."

They had been the fearsome threesome in high school. Debate, school newspaper, basketball team. The Three Amigas, as Mateo liked to call them. Jackie drew a shuddering breath. "It's surreal. I keep thinking she'll come bursting out of the building and start giving orders. She would've taken charge of the whole rescue operation."

"I feel terrible, but I have to get the story.

People have a right to know what happened and whether there could be more attacks coming." Bella clutched her backpack to her chest. "I can't mourn right now."

"Estrella wouldn't want it any other way. We'll have time to mourn later, when we've figured out who did this."

"Jack, I know that look on your face." Bella shook her head so vigorously the braids flopped and rearranged themselves. "The entire law enforcement community will run with that ball. Whoever did this doesn't have a rat's-behind chance of getting away with it."

"I saw her. I was with Tony when he realized she was dead."

"It's beyond unfathomable." Bella closed her eyes and heaved a tear-laden sigh. "Okay. This was supposed to be a climate-change debate story. Now they want a page 1, above-the-fold story about a bombing. Sig can't get inside the crime scene tape to interview people. The PIOs aren't answering their phones. The city editor says it's on me. My thought is extremists who are angry that safeguards designed to slow climate change were dismantled during an earlier administration. Or extremists who support the contention that climate change is a hoax perpetuated by Democrats that's hurting industries and big businesses."

"That's a decent theory. You can do this. You'll

share the investigation with Sig." Sig was the crime reporter and Bella's beau. Sometimes it seemed all Jackie's friends were engaged or in long-term relationships. Everyone except her. Not even close. "He has the sources you need. Together you'll be a formidable team. Have you interviewed witnesses who were inside?"

Bella nodded and winced. Her free hand went to her temple. She likely had the same concussive headache as Jackie. "But I couldn't get close to the command center. Everyone's there—the city manager, the mayor, the federal agencies, the cops."

"Something this big, they'll hold a news conference. They won't want to give individual interviews with every media outlet in the city, let alone the country."

"I know you, Jack. If you want to know something, you don't let up. At least confirm what I've got. Off the record."

"As a friend or as a city employee?"

"Either. Both."

As a city employee Jackie had no authority or permission to speak to the media. In most circumstances she would be expected to refer a reporter to the library systems' public relations manager, who would run it up the flagpole with the director's office. An arduous and lengthy process. Most reporters—not all—could be trusted when it came to speaking off the record. Bella's integrity, like her honesty, was impeccable. "I'll make you a deal. I tell you what I know and you keep me in the loop."

"Deal. It's not like you work for a competing media outlet." Bella opened her laptop. "This is what I know or think I know. At 3:05 p.m. Friday—today—a bomb went off in the Tobin Center for Performing Arts' H-E-B Performance Hall. At least five people were killed. I have the names of four. I need the fifth one." She ran down a list of four names. The names coincided with the ones Jackie could confirm. All except the last one.

The fifth body bag held a vivacious and smart climate-change expert named Laura Peterson, who was also a journalist and international bestselling author of a book on the global climate-justice movement. She carried around her cell phone, showing a photo of her first granddaughter to anyone who would look.

Guilt tightened its noose around Jackie's neck. "I arranged for her to speak here today. I convinced Meagan to go to the foundation to secure the funds to pay her fat speaker's fee, her travel expenses, her hotel. She was worth every penny, but now she's dead. Because of me."

"A psycho killed her, not you." Bella's fingers flew across the small keyboard. "You're not responsible for her death any more than you're responsible for Estrella's. They were doing what

26

they loved and what they believed in. I tried to get the name of the fifth person, but the cop I talked to—off the record because he didn't have the authority to talk to the media—said they weren't releasing it until the family had been notified."

Pain so acute it took her breath pierced Jackie. Estrella's mother and father knew she was involved in this event. Word of the bombing would spread like the common cold. The media were already camped out down the street, held back by crime scene tape and uniformed officers. No doubt onlookers who joined them behind the tape were recording the scene and posting on social media. So would those who had been inside but escaped unscathed.

She and Tony needed to tell Mercedes and Mateo about Estrella before they turned on the TV and saw the news. The TV stations would break into regular programming for this. Or one of the Diazes' dozens of extended family members could call them to report seeing something on social media. *"Have you heard? Have you talked to* su hijita*? Is Estrellita okay?"*

They would call her, their message would go to voice mail, and they would start to worry.

So would Jackie's mother, her brother, and her sister. They'd lost so much already. She could call her mom but not Estrella's parents. A person didn't tell parents over the phone that their daughter was dead. Thankful she always kept her phone in her jacket pocket and not in her purse, Jackie wrapped her fingers around it. "I need to call my mom. We have to tell Estrella's parents. Have you told yours?"

"Mama called me, freaking out. She saw a special report in the middle of *Judge Judy*. Call Aimee. She'll be scared to death if she hears it from my mom. She's probably calling her right now."

Jackie made the call with trembling fingers. "Mom, it's me."

"I know, honey. I have that funny ringtone Tosca set up for me, remember? Al Yankovic?"

"Mom, listen. Have you been watching the news?"

"You know I never watch the news. After school we went out for Mexican food to celebrate the end of another week and I—"

"Mom, listen to me." Once Mom started to describe what she and her best friend and teaching colleague managed to accomplish in a few hours' time, she was almost unstoppable. "There was an explosion at the Tobin Center. I was there, but I'm fine."

No response. Just jerky breathing.

"Mom, I'm okay. Did you hear me? Call Cris and Tosca for me. I don't want them seeing it on the news and worrying."

"I'll come get you." Her mother's tone turned determined. "Where are you?"

"I can't leave yet. I'm here with Bella. She's fine too. I have to talk to the police. Mom, Estrella was killed."

"Sweet baby Estrella is gone?" Mom's voice broke. "I can't believe it."

No one could. "You'll be there for Mercedes and Mateo?"

"Yes. Of course. I'll send an email to my Sunday school class. We'll get the prayer chain and the meals going." A half sob punctuated the words. "Are you sure? What about Tony? Does he know?"

"He was here too. She's gone, Mom. Don't call Mercedes yet. I have to get to them as soon as I leave here."

"I'll call Bella's folks. We can go over to Mateo's as soon as you give us the go-ahead. I'm so sorry, honey."

"Me too."

"She's with Jesus."

"I know."

"Good. Keep that tucked in your heart, baby."

"I'll try."

Jackie disconnected. Bella, her hands poised over her keyboard, jumped in. "I've been asking the other witnesses these questions. Did you see anybody or anything suspicious before the event began, or during it, for that matter?"

Jackie forced herself to rewind her day to midmorning on a record-breaking cold day

29

in October. The Tobin Center staff had been perfect. Everything went like clockwork. She grabbed a quick lunch at Boudro's on the River Walk, most of which butterflies in her stomach forced her to leave on the table. She returned to wait for Meagan to arrive with their guest speakers. Estrella called. They discussed parking and reserved seating for the councilman and his entourage.

Jackie's head pounded and she rubbed her temple. "It's all muddled right now. Honestly, I can't think straight."

"What about as you were preparing to leave? Right before the explosion?"

"Surely the culprit wasn't inside the hall . . . unless you're thinking suicide bomber. Why would terrorists target a relatively small event in San Antonio?"

"I don't know, but that's why the FBI, Homeland Security, and ATF are here. They have to consider all possibilities. They have all the intel on any chatter that might have been heard in the last few weeks. Did you see anyone or anything that seemed out of place?"

Jackie rubbed her eyes. The memories fast-forwarded past her chat with climate activist Laura Peterson, who asked for a bottle of water and two Tylenol. She was jet-lagged. Hoaxer Robert Mitchell helped himself to fruit and cheese in the green room and asked for a Big

Red soda. The dignitaries started arriving shortly after that. Jackie led them to their reserved seats. She chewed her lower lip. Polite chatter, chatter, chatter.

Then what? "Meher."

"Meher? The catering manager?"

Jackie shot from her chair and did a 360-degree turn, her gaze bouncing from one survivor to the next. "I need to find Meher."

"Why? What did she do?"

"She didn't do anything. It's what I did." Jackie caught a glimpse of a black hajib wrapped around a woman's head. In San Antonio the sight was rare. The woman stood talking to a man in a Tobin Center catering polo. "There she is."

Jackie wound her way through the metal chairs set up in meandering lines that suggested a drunk person set them up. Her event planner persona chastised whoever had done this. Didn't they know to leave adequate space between chairs for oversized men who needed to spread out their legs? Didn't they know about adequate space in the aisles?

Aware of Bella's exasperated breathing behind her, Jackie plunged forward. "Meher, hey, over here."

The petite chef swiveled and waved. Her grave expression blossomed into a relieved smile. "You're okay. I'm so glad you made it."

"I need to talk to you." Jackie drew the much

shorter woman into a quick hug. Meher's dark eyebrows arched, but she returned the hug. Jackie took a breath. "What did you do with the backpack?"

The smile disappeared. Meher excused herself from her coworker and moved away from the tent. "I gave it to a security guard. He saw me with it and demanded I turn it over. I thought he was going to arrest me or something."

"What backpack?" Bella barreled her way into the conversation. "What are you talking about?"

"I had found it before everyone started coming in." Jackie swatted away the defensiveness that threatened to overwhelm her. "I figured it belonged to one of the workers. Meher said she would check for me."

An obscenity popped from Bella's mouth. She'd claimed her penchant for colorful language came from working in a newsroom. Jackie reminded her twenty times a day that cussing was the result of a weak vocabulary—something no journalist wanted. "Neither of you opened it?"

"I was in a hurry."

"So was I." Meher's face crumpled. "You think it was the bomb. I had the bomb in my arms? The security guard will tell the police. They'll be looking for me."

"You turned it over. You did the right thing. Just tell them the truth."

"They'll take one look at my name and all

they'll see is Middle Eastern, Muslim, terrorist."

"Seriously? You're a Saudi American. That doesn't make you a terrorist. I work with a woman whose parents are Iranian. She was born here. I work with a Kuwaiti man who immigrated here with his family when he was six. They're Muslim, just like Bella and I are Christians. They're Americans just like you and me."

"It doesn't matter." Bella glanced around. "You two need to find a cop and tell him about this. The backpack might have held the bomb."

Jackie clasped her hands to her pounding head. "You're saying we could've prevented this?"

Fear etched deep lines in Meher's lovely face. She backed away. "You can't tell them I was involved. You can't tell them I was the last person you saw with the backpack."

"We'll talk to them together. Just tell the truth. I'll have your back."

With a little snort of disbelief, Meher shook her head. "I love that you're so naive. You live in such a small, secure world. DHS will take me in before I have a chance to even say good-bye to my children. Under the Patriot Act they can hold me as long as they want."

"Meher, wait. I'll be—"

"I can't. Leave me out of it. Please, keep me out of it. Promise!"

"We have to tell the police. It will help them find the monster who did this."

"No it won't. They'll be too busy investigating me, my family, and my friends." Meher whirled, dodged a cluster of survivors, and ducked behind the tent to parts unknown.

Shivering, Jackie wrapped her arms around her chest and tried to think. Meher had reason to be afraid. Muslim Americans still faced profiling, discrimination, and hate-mongering every day thanks to 9/11.

That didn't change the situation. "I have to tell."

"Yes, you do. I feel for Meher. Wrong place, wrong time, but if she didn't do anything wrong, the police will figure that out." Bella slid into a chair and opened her laptop. "Go. I have to file the website story, but I'll be waiting right here for you. I want a blow-by-blow account."

For a reporter Bella had far more faith in the system than Jackie did. Her teeth chattering, ears ringing, hands shaking, she headed for the command center. Maybe Bella would be right. Maybe this time justice would prevail.

THREE

Finding a cop was no problem. Getting him to stop long enough to listen proved more challenging. Jackie approached the uniformed officer standing guard outside the command center. He had his spiel down. "Wait. They're interviewing everyone. They'll get to you as soon as they can, ma'am."

"I may have important information—"

"Everyone is anxious to get out of here, ma'am. Have a seat. They'll get to you as soon as they can. They've got more than eight hundred witnesses to process. Have a cup of coffee. The Red Cross is bringing in sandwiches."

He was trying so hard to be kind. Jackie stuffed a sock in her impatience. First responders and law enforcement saw the worst of the worst—just as she had this day.

She trudged toward the chairs again. A lanky, scruffy-looking man in street clothes and a windbreaker emblazoned with SAPD across the back brushed past her, headed the same direction. "Excuse me, are you interviewing witnesses?"

He glanced back and stopped. The irritated expression faded. "If you've been triaged, ma'am, you can wait in the area set up by Victim Assistance. We'll get to you as soon as we can."

"I know that. Please listen to me." Jackie fought to bring her voice down a notch. He didn't need a hysterical witness right now. "I have information that might be important to give to you now rather than later."

"Who are you?"

"Jackie Santoro, the adult collections coordinator at the Central Library. I helped plan this event."

"You don't look like a librarian."

Jackie got that a lot. She didn't understand it. Librarians came in all shapes and sizes. "Sorry I don't meet your expectations."

"Don't apologize. It's been a day for everyone."

His assessment of the day was spot-on, even if he didn't catch her sarcasm. "Do you want to take my statement or not? Officer—"

"It's detective. Detective Avery Wick. SAPD Homicide Unit. I'd be happy to take your statement." He glanced around, then took her arm.

Surprise washed through Jackie, followed by sudden warmth. He had a steely grip—one a person could count on—and he hadn't hesitated to reach out. It had been a long time since someone did that for her.

He guided her to the curb. "Someone who volunteers to share information is either innocent or trying to look that way."

So much for warmth. Detective Avery's prickly-pear persona reasserted itself.

Anger could be a tonic under the right circumstances. Jackie's bubbled up. She tugged her arm free. "I was one of a team of people who planned this event. One of my best friends died in there." She pointed to the Tobin Center. "What possible motive would I have to set off a bomb in the middle of my event?"

"Sit down, please." Detective Wick's assessing gaze ran over Jackie from head to toe and back. A shiver ran through her that had nothing to do with the cold. It felt as if he could see through her. He smiled—a grim, sardonic half smile. "Give me a minute. I'm sure I can come up with a motive."

Before Jackie could introduce herself, he walked away, leaving her with her mouth open and her entire body shaking.

He returned a minute later with a blanket and a cup of coffee. Jackie wrapped the blanket around her hunched shoulders automatically. It wouldn't help, but his offer was so unexpected in light of his last words, she couldn't refuse.

"Here, drink this." He held out a Styrofoam cup filled with steaming liquid. "You look frozen."

Did this man have multiple personalities? "Bless you." Her words came out in a croak. She cleared her throat and tried again. "Thank you."

Her hands shook so hard the hot liquid spilled over the edges, burning her fingers. "Ouch. Sorry."

"Stop apologizing." Detective Wick cupped

his hands around hers and steadied them. Again, with the touch. "You're in shock. Why weren't you transported to Baptist or one of the other downtown hospitals?"

"I'm not hurt, not physically." Her voice didn't quiver. For that small victory she was grateful. "I refused to be transported. Or treated."

She wasn't leaving until Estrella did.

"Not smart."

"Not hurt. They're overwhelmed as it is."

"We're doing preliminary interviews . . ."

His big hands covered Jackie's completely. She closed her eyes, concentrating on how real and firm they were. He had a callus on his thumb. His fingers were strong. Finally the shaking stopped.

"You're not going to pass out on me, are you?"

She opened her eyes to find him leaning so close his scent of cinnamon gum and citrusy aftershave filled her nose. After the stench of blood, excrement, and burned rubber, it was comforting. So was his angular face filled with a mixture of concern at war with barely tethered impatience.

Jackie leaned away from his space. "Absolutely not. I've got it—the coffee, I mean."

His hands dropped. The warmth dissipated. She swallowed against sobs. No more tears. Estrella would not want tears. She would want action. She deserved action. "Did they find the remnants of the explosive device? Do they know how it was triggered?"

Detective Wick looked up from the narrow notebook he'd tugged from the hip pocket of his Dockers. "You said you had important information. Let's start with that."

Once she told him about the bag, her opportunity to get information from the detective would be gone. "Were there any unexploded devices found?"

Impatience spread across his face, his effort to muzzle it obvious. "The bomb squad cleared the hall before search and recovery began. Let me ask the questions, if you don't mind."

Everyone knew that. The other first responders wouldn't have been allowed in otherwise. Search and recovery. "One of the victims is—was—my best friend Estrella Diaz."

Detective Wick's pale-blue eyes studied her so intently he squinted. "I'm sorry about your friend. This has to be the worst day of your life. The faster we get all the facts, the faster we can track down the monster who did this. Okay?"

Another day came close, but Detective Wick didn't need to know that. They were on the same page, even if he chose not to share information with her. "Won't the ATF and the FBI have jurisdiction? How does SAPD figure in?"

"You ask a lot of questions." The crow's feet around his eyes and the lines around his mouth deepened. He sucked in a long breath and let it out. "Contrary to what you see on TV, the Feds don't come in and take over. They assist. There'll be a joint task force. But you can be sure we'll be leading the charge with one of our own dead. Chief Little—"

"Chief of Police Little is dead?" Confirmation of the city manager's words. Body bag number five. The chief, dressed in street clothes, had been sitting near the front with his wife—right behind the city manager and his spouse. The Littles had four kids, all still young enough to live at home. "I'm so sorry for your loss. Did his wife survive?"

"Yes, but she's in critical condition. We want the monster who did this for the sakes of all the victims, but this one is personal."

Estrella would be relegated to the *also killed* paragraph of every news story written about this incident. After the biographies and quotes collected from the peers of Councilman Sandoval, Chief Little, and Milton Schaeffer. That was fine if it meant law enforcement went after the killer with every resource available to them because of the intense public scrutiny that came with the victims' lofty status in the community.

"You said you had something important to tell me."

She held the coffee close, concentrating on its warmth. "There was a backpack left on the front row. I found it."

Any hint of cordiality disappeared from his rugged face. "You found it? When?"

She repeated the facts she'd shared with Bella. "I didn't give it another thought until I was talking to Bella and she asked me if I saw anything unusual before the event started."

"Bella Glover, the reporter?"

"She's also my friend."

"You told a reporter before you told law enforcement?" Anger rippled through his words like a current in a downed electrical line. He let go a string of obscenities under his breath. "You just compromised the investigation of five murders and more than 120 people injured in a bombing. The worst since San Antonio's founding in 1730."

"It wasn't my intent to c-compromise anything," Jackie stuttered. "She was walking me through the day when it hit me. I'd completely forgotten."

"Do you know the name of this catering person?"

Here we go again. Jackie again explained about Meher. "She said a security guard demanded the backpack. She gave it to him and went back to work."

"You talked to her after the bombing?"

"Yes."

Scowling, Detective Wick glanced around. "Where is she then?"

41

"She declined to come with me. She was frightened, in shock, and wanting to go home to her family. You can understand."

"Meher Faheem. Muslim?"

"Yes, but—"

"I'm not profiling. I'm following the evidence." Wick blew out air. His overly long bangs rose and descended. He might be trying not to draw conclusions, but his expression told a different story. "Describe her for me."

"She has brown skin, brown eyes. About my age. Medium height, medium build. She was wearing a hijab and an abaya, the black cloak they wear." The description fit more than half the women in San Antonio—until Jackie got to that last sentence. A mixture of various Arab nationalities accounted for less than 1 percent of San Antonio's population. "She's pretty."

"Okay." Wick stretched the two-syllable word across the length of a football field. "What did the backpack look like?"

Jackie closed her eyes and imagined the moment when she'd picked it up from the seat. "Dark-blue or black nylon. Heavy like it was full of a bunch of books. A typical backpack like a college kid would use."

"You didn't think to report a suspicious package?"

A rush of blood made her ears ring, and nausea rocked her stomach. "Are you saying I could've

42

prevented this? I never thought . . . It never occurred to me."

"You walked your way through the day with Bella Glover. Now do it for me." All compassion and concern had disappeared, replaced by a valiant attempt to contain his anger. "You gave the backpack to Faheem. You went about your business. You were inside when the incendiary device detonated?"

Jackie clasped her dignity around her like a shredded shawl. "Just barely. I was at the door, ready to go to the Central Library to prepare for the book signing and reception, but Tony stopped me."

"Tony Guerra, who works for Sandoval?"

"Yes."

"Why did he stop you?"

"To congratulate me on how well the event went." The dark irony of that statement added burning salt to her wounds. "He and Estrella were engaged. They were planning a Valentine's Day wedding."

Why had she volunteered that information? It would not help this detective find the animal who rained hell down on innocent people this afternoon.

In fact, a faintly sardonic look flitted across the man's face before he shut it down. "Was Mr. Guerra injured?"

"No."

"Where is he now?"

Jackie forced her gaze from the detective to the triage tent. His cell phone firmly planted to his ear, Tony still stood next to the gurney that held Estrella's body. He didn't understand. The woman he loved was no longer there. Bella stood next to him, one hand on his back. She might be a reporter, but she was also a steadfast friend.

"He's with Estrella's body. He wants to make sure her remains . . ." Jackie's throat clogged with tears. She heaved a breath. *"Chin up, chin up,"* that's what her dad always said. *Chin up.* "Her remains are treated with respect. I imagine he's figuring out what's next. His boss is dead. The council seat will have to be filled. The political fallout will have to be dealt with."

"Sandoval's body isn't even cold yet." Detective Wick's sarcastic tone matched Jackie's feelings about politics. So many of the politicians she knew had no soul. He stared at Tony. "I'll talk to him later, to confirm your story."

"It's not a story."

"Who else was seated in the first row where you found the bag?"

"The city manager and his wife were supposed to be seated in the same row, but they arrived late and I was dealing with some library donors so Meagan—my boss—seated them a few rows back."

She cradled her head in her hands. *God, what have I done?*

Something . . . fingers . . . brushed against her hair. "Look, no one thinks a bombing will happen to him." His voice was hoarse.

She forced herself to raise her head. Detective Wick ducked his head, but not before she saw the hollowness of his expression. "I'm cynical and suspicious by nature. And because of the job I do. It was only a question."

"Who do you think did this?"

"Who do you think did it?"

He changed personalities like a chameleon changed colors. "The possibilities are mind-boggling, aren't they?"

Detective Wick ran his free hand through long locks of hair the color of lightly toasted bread highlighted by an occasional silver strand. His scowl deepened. "Santoro. Are you related to Samuel Santoro?"

There it was. Most people made the connection sooner. In his defense the detective had a lot on his plate. "He was my father."

Detective Wick unfolded his long legs and stood, but he didn't walk away. He paused a moment longer, as if processing the information and weighing his options. "Get up, please."

"Excuse me?"

"You need to come with me. You likely had the explosive device in your hands. You handed it to a person of Middle Eastern descent. You gave that information to the media. And you're Sam Santoro's daughter. We need to talk some more, more formally."

"My father's death has nothing whatsoever to do with this."

"Your father took his own life after being accused of crimes by your boss. You have every reason to want the city manager dead. Didn't Vogel lead the charge to have him fired before his case went to trial?"

Jackie stood. Not because Wick ordered her to do it. But because she wanted to look him in the eye when she responded. Unfortunately he fell in that category of men taller than her five eleven. He had to be at least six two. "Maybe you're the kind of person so lacking in morals that you would kill and maim innocent people, including your best friend since second grade, in order to exact revenge on a few, but I assure you I am not."

"I'm sure you'll forgive me for not taking your word for that." Wick held her gaze. Jackie refused to avert her gaze. The air crackled between them in a strange push and pull of currents she couldn't identify. The emotion faded from the detective's face, leaving a carefully neutral businesslike facade. "I'm sorry for your loss. But I do need to follow the facts where they lead. Period."

"Hey, Wicked!" Another plainclothes officer yelled from the command center.

Wick's eyes narrowed, but he looked away from Jackie. The other officer waved a pocket-sized notebook to indicate the detective was needed.

"Again, I'm sorry for your loss—both of them." He ducked his head and swept his arm out in an *after-you* fashion. "Time for you to meet some of my associates."

Her feet so numb she couldn't feel them, Jackie did her best to obey. She stumbled and Wick took her arm once again. Jackie shrugged off his touch. "That's not necessary. I'm sure you don't touch your male prisoners."

"You're not a prisoner." He paused. "Not yet, anyway."

FOUR

Avery did a gut check. No way this good-looking, well-spoken, nosy librarian could be a mass murderer. His gut was never wrong.

Regardless, she'd screwed up the investigation by speaking out of turn to the media, and by setting aside the effort not to profile, she had spoken with one possible suspect in the bombing and allowed her to leave without talking to authorities. And she was Sam Santoro's kid. Avery pointed to a chair. "Sit."

Ms. Santoro didn't blink. "I'm not a dog. Don't speak to me like one."

She was right. Days like today brought out the worst in him. "Please have a seat, Ms. Santoro."

"Jackie. Ms. Santoro is my mother."

"Jackie."

Without further ado, she sat.

Avery brushed past Detective Scott Heller, aka Scotty, his partner, and moved far enough away that Jackie wouldn't hear the conversation, but not so far that Avery couldn't keep an eye on her.

"Who is she?"

"A librarian at the Central Library."

"She doesn't look like a librarian."

It didn't speak well of either of them that they noticed this woman's attributes in the aftermath of the worst bombing in San Antonio's history that dated back to the Spanish missions. Everything about Jackie Santoro, from her curves to her long legs to her tangled black curls and sapphire eyes that snapped when she was angry, caught and held a man's attention. "Moving right along."

"Just sayin'." Scotty didn't seem the least bit repentant. He was a happily married man, which made him all bark and no bite. "Why bring her over here? Aside from the fact that she is attractive?"

"She's also Sam Santoro's daughter."

Scotty's bushy gray eyebrows popped up. With his handlebar mustache and bulbous nose, he looked like a cartoon character come to life. "Huh. I'd say that moves Ms. Santoro up a few notches on the persons of interest list."

"He was as crooked as the day is long. Rather than going to prison, he took the cowardly way out and offed himself." Wick contemplated Jackie from afar. Her eyes glassy with unshed tears, she stared at the triage tent. Avery followed her gaze. Tony Guerra stood next to a body bag on a gurney. The ME investigators wanted to move the gurney, but Guerra wouldn't let go. Bella Glover was trying to cajole him into releasing his hold.

Avery let his gaze travel back to Jackie. She swiped at her face with a sleeve. Everything about her dejected pose made Wick want to fly to the rescue, but he wasn't the knight-on-a-white-horse type. Not anymore.

He recounted her story to his partner, including the backpack and Meher Faheem. "She stuck around to tell a cop her story. To cast suspicion elsewhere? My question is, why would she blow up the H-E-B Performance Hall with herself in it? She's no radicalized suicide bomber. She's wearing a cross, for crying out loud. Even if she could stomach killing Estrella Diaz, Tony Guerra, and Bella Glover, whom she claims are her closest friends?"

"She intended to get out before it went off." Scotty smiled a wolfish grin that showed off narrow canine teeth. "She was at the door when Guerra stopped her. She miscalculated. Maybe she cared more about getting back at the city manager who fired her father before he'd been adjudicated than she did about her friends. Maybe she had a secret grudge against them for working for Sandoval. Didn't he lead the charge against Sam Santoro after the accusations surfaced that he was for sale?"

"I thought the same thing, but it's not like Santoro was a crime boss. He took bribes from some developers who needed permits and inspections."

"He made money at the expense of citizens who bought homes built by cutting corners and in subdivisions stripped of heritage trees." Scotty's disdain turned his tone icy cold. He was the son of a career U.S. Army man. He didn't like dishonorable people. "It's not like he was hurting for money. He was a Santoro."

The grandson of one of the richest men in San Antonio, Santoro had chosen a life of public service as a lowly Development Services Department inspector who worked his way up the food chain to director. He didn't need the money. He wanted to thumb his nose at his father. So the story went.

"The apple doesn't fall far from the tree, even when it tries." Avery studied his person of interest. Was he barking up the wrong tree here? "Why tell me about the backpack then? She sought me out and she told a reporter about it. Why didn't she fade into the crowd and slip out in the first wave before the cavalry arrived? You know some people did. They started running and never came back."

"Maybe she is planting a red herring. A Middle Eastern woman in a hijab would definitely serve that purpose. Santoro is smart enough to know we would've tracked her down. She helped plan the event. She was in the hall before the crowd arrived. Plenty of opportunity to plant the bomb with the intention of detonating it after she left the building." Scotty excelled in creating worst-case scenarios, but he hadn't interviewed Ms.

Santoro. He hadn't seen her agony. "She could be lying through her teeth. You only have her word there was a backpack at this point. We need to find the catering manager, as well as the security guard, and corroborate Santoro's story. When the explosive experts get done sifting through the debris, we'll know more about the bomb."

The job demanded they trust no one. Yet. Avery stuck his pen behind his ear and rubbed the two-day-old stubble on his chin. Jackie Santoro's angst had been so real. The thought that she should've handled the backpack differently had shaken her to the core.

Or not. Avery had investigated murders for a living for nine years. Mothers who killed their babies. Teenagers who killed one or both parents. A sleeping eight-year-old killed in a drive-by shooting because the gangbanger got the wrong house. A drunk old man who got into a fight with his best friend over a card game and stabbed him to death with a butcher knife. Nothing surprised Avery anymore.

Jackie Santoro moved him. *Get over it. She's young and pretty and way out of your league.*

Not to mention a person of interest in an investigation.

"What's the matter with you?" Scotty flapped his notebook at Avery. "Earth to Wicked."

"Nothing." Avery cocked his head toward the command center. "I need to pass this tidbit up the chain of command. Do you want to see if Meher Faheem has a record? Get her address."

"Will do. I'll see if she's been interviewed by any of the other officers and ask for a background check."

Avery nodded, but his gaze was riveted by the scene playing out at the RV that served as the mobile command unit.

The ATF special agent stood in fierce conversation, his finger occasionally jabbing in the air, with FBI Agent Petra Jantzen, who would serve as their case agent. The Homeland Security Investigations rep had his arms crossed. His head turned side to side like he was watching a tennis match. Avery's path had crossed with Jantzen's on a missing child case a few years earlier. She was a good agent and a good person.

Chief Little should be right there in the middle of it all. Instead he was on his way to the morgue for the final indignity of an autopsy. City Manager Jason Vogel rubbed his forehead every few seconds while adding nothing to the conversation. Avery turned back to Scotty. "What do you think's going on there?"

"They're not telling a lowly detective like me anything, but I heard from one of our civilian PIOs that they're huddling up before they do a press conference. They want to feed the beast." His acne-scarred face filled with contempt, Scotty tugged on his mustache so hard it had to hurt.

"All the PIO types from every agency are holed up inside drafting news releases so everyone and his uncle can approve the language. That'll take at least a week."

Avery snorted. He would never move up the chain of command for reasons like this one. "Or a month. In the meantime we should find the scum who did this and end him."

"Yep. You and me, brother, you and me." Scotty let loose with a string of obscenities meant to show his support. "Little was straightlaced, but even the police officers' association liked him. Ruiz is dumb as a doorknob. He won't last five minutes as the interim."

"Rogelio is the interim?" The desire to puke overwhelmed Avery. Operations Support Bureau Assistant Chief Rogelio Ruiz had memorized the playbook and never deviated from it. They had graduated from the same class at the academy. While Rogelio flew up the chain of command, Wick chose to stay close to the streets. "That didn't take long. Is LT moving up too?"

As head of the Homicide/Attempted Homicide Unit, Lieutenant Deke Carmichael was their direct supervisor. A good guy who worked to get them the resources they needed while he gave them the space they required to do their jobs.

"As far as I know. The ripple-down effect isn't over, but they had to move fast." Scotty lit a cigarette and stuck his BIC back in his pocket.

"The city manager probably figured he needed someone familiar with the SWTFC to stand in front of him at these task force meetings."

The Southwest Texas Fusion Center was a multiagency task force that handled intelligence and technology for fighting both terrorism and violent crime.

"So far we have international and domestic terrorism on the table." Avery glanced at Jackie. Her face a study of impatience, she scowled in return. He turned back to Scotty. "Or, it might be something as simple as revenge."

"Environmental terrorists are pretty crazy. They're just as likely to resort to violence as the Aryan Nation." Scotty wrinkled his oversized schnoz. "Some gun-lovers don't like the climate-change peddlers either."

"So you think the climate-change lady was the real target?"

"I wouldn't put it past the hoax people to take out an opponent, thinking it'll make points with some political leaders."

"Wicked & Hell. I guess we're getting the old band back together." Despite an obvious attempt at joviality, Rogelio Ruiz approached with all the signs of a man under enormous stress. "What are you doing here?"

Ruiz's use of the tongue-in-cheek nicknames thrown around in the Homicide Unit did nothing to improve Avery's mood. Scotty could be aggressive, but he was a crack detective and their solve rate was excellent.

Ruiz's questioning gaze remained on Avery, so he stepped into the line of fire. "I was up next."

Detectives rotated as lead detectives on murder/ attempted murder cases. Avery and Scotty were next in line. This was more than a murder investigation, but five people had been murdered, one of them his chief. Nobody was taking this case from him.

If Rogelio had other ideas, he didn't express them. "I just came from the hospital. Bill's wife is in surgery. They asked us to wait until she comes out to tell her the news." His eyes reddened. His Adam's apple bobbed. "Bill's brother elected me to be the one to tell her."

"Tough gig."

"Four kids are fatherless. They could be raised by their grandparents if their mother doesn't pull through. Our families live daily with the fact that their loved ones might not come home, but he was off duty at a library event, for crying out loud." Rogelio cleared his throat and spit on the sidewalk. "I better get to the meeting. They want me to lay the groundwork with the media and then introduce the Feds."

"Do you need anything from us?"

"Did you learn anything from interviews you've done?"

"Too early in the game to draw conclusions,

but we've got persons of interest out the wazoo."
Avery ignored his partner's raised eyebrows.
They did way too much talking. "It could
be environmental terrorists. We've got a
catering manager who's Muslim. It could be
the people who think climate change is a hoax.
We have a witness who saw an unaccompanied
backpack shortly before the event began. We
can't even discount domestic violence at this
point."

Avery didn't need to remind them that the
worst mass shooting at a church occurred at First
Baptist Church of Sutherland Springs, only a
few miles southeast of San Antonio, and it had
resulted from domestic violence.

"You have eyes on this Muslim?"

"Not yet, but—"

"Then get on it. And find out everything you
can about the backpack. It could be our bomb."

The guy was a regular Sherlock. Avery kept his
surly comments to himself and offered his new
boss a half salute. "Yes, sir. Good luck with the
news conference."

"Thanks, but if good luck existed, I wouldn't
be interim chief right now."

No one wanted to get a promotion—even a
temporary one—by stepping on the body of a
fallen comrade in arms. Avery nodded. "We'll get
the guy."

"Or woman," Scotty added. "You never know.

This might be the day the stats on mass murderers even out. Ain't that right, Wicked?"

Scotty claimed to never be wrong—about anything. A puzzled look on his face, Rogelio—Chief Ruiz—trudged away. Avery waited until he got close to the command center to smack Scotty's arm with his notebook. "Seriously?"

"Why didn't you tell him the witness is Miss Bodacious?"

"Because we'll get cussed out by LT if we jump over him in the chain of command. We need to tell LT first. I'll call him and see how he wants to handle it."

"Don't you think the Feds will want to know about the backpack ASAP?"

"I don't answer to them. It'll be LT's responsibility to report up the chain of command. We're just grunts on this one."

"When do you ever care about chain of command?"

Avery didn't, but something about Jackie Santoro had burrowed under his skin. Until he knew more about her, he wasn't giving her up to the Feds. If it turned out she had anything to do with the bombing, he would be on the front row to watch her get the needle.

FIVE

Avery stationed himself on the perimeter of the news conference between the media and the crowd that had amassed behind the crime scene tape. Tourists, citizens, and even the homeless who frequented the Methodist church across from Travis Park were drawn by the sirens and dozens of law enforcement vehicles. Out-of-town media outlets were starting to arrive—CBS Southwest, Associated Press. In the next few hours the national media would swarm the location. This would be the Super Bowl of crime investigations.

He nodded at a patrolman assigned to monitor the tape. The guy looked barely old enough to shave. "Keep an eye on the crowd. There's always a possibility the bomber will return to admire his work."

The patrolman's eyes widened. "What am I looking for?"

"You'll know it when you see it." Avery squeezed past him and stopped where he had a good line of sight for Bella Glover. He needed to move quickly.

Two uniformed officers had been assigned to transport Jackie Santoro to the PD headquarters a few miles across town. He wanted to do the interview, but first he wanted to check out her buddy. Bella had a unique position in this mess. She witnessed the explosion, but she was a reporter. She would write a firsthand account of the event. As perverse as it seemed, the other reporters probably envied her.

She stood with another reporter Avery knew better. Sig Ritter had the crime beat for the *Express-News*. He might be an obnoxious jerk or he might simply be doing his job. Either way, he irritated Avery. He had to be freaked that his girlfriend had been in danger and that she would have the story of her career because of it.

Acting Chief Ruiz stepped in front of the portable podium. He tapped the microphone. It squealed. He winced and cleared his throat. Anyone who knew Bill Little couldn't help but draw comparisons. Ruiz had sweat rings around his armpits despite the record low October temperatures. He didn't just look nervous . . . he looked petrified. Chief Little always said never let them see you sweat. That applied to criminals, politicians, the media, and civilians. He was a class act.

"We lost five individuals today to a senseless act of violence. The current count on injured is 120, several in critical condition with missing limbs. We took immediate action to set up a task force . . ."

Avery half listened as Ruiz listed the names of the victims, where the injured were taken, and the agencies involved, and then talked about what the bomb squad had discovered so far—very little—and outlined next steps. Very succinct.

Then the questions started. Was it terrorism? Did they have any suspects? Didn't the FBI take the lead? Rogelio was surprisingly deft at the thrust and parry of media interaction.

After allowing reporters to attempt to pry more information out of him, Rogelio called it and soothed the savage beast with the promise of another news conference as soon as they had more information that could be shared.

The photographers dismantled tripods while reporters grabbed mics from the podium. The mass exodus happened quickly. The TV stations would do live shots here with the Tobin as a backdrop. Radio could call in their sound. The *Express-News* reporters didn't have far to go to their office at Third and Avenue E a few blocks away. They still had plenty of time to file for the Saturday morning paper. Avery followed Bella and Sig across Municipal Auditorium Way to a ground parking lot.

"Bella."

She glanced back, halted, and did an about-face. Her eyebrows rose. "Detective Wick. Did you have something to add?"

"Can I talk to you for a minute?"

His curiosity plain on his face, Sig edged closer. "Are you sure you want Bella? I'm the crime reporter."

"It'll just take a minute."

Sig patted his girlfriend's arm. "I'll see you at the office. We have a lot of work to do before we can write our stories. They'll want this up on mysantonio.com ASAP."

Bella wiped at her face with a torn sleeve. She was a pretty woman, but the day had done some damage. Her eyes were red, her lip was split, and her face was dirty. She placed her hand on top of Sig's for a second. "I'm right behind you. Make a fresh pot of coffee."

"Will do." He withdrew his hand, but still he lingered. "Are you sure you're all right?"

Did he mind sharing the biggest story of his career with his main squeeze?

"I'm fine." Her voice strengthened. "I'll call you when I'm on my way."

Sig shot Avery a fierce look, but he left.

"Do you have some additional information for me?" Bella shifted the backpack to her shoulder, unzipped it, and withdrew a digital recorder. "I was surprised that the chief didn't mention the backpack or a certain person of interest, but I suppose you need to keep those details close to the vest until you have more information. You don't want the catering manager bailing—if she hasn't already. Did you find anyone else who remembered seeing the backpack?"

"Ms. Santoro's account of events is still under investigation. We want to verify it before we make it public. That's what I wanted to talk to you about. Can you hold off publishing what she told you until we can verify her story?"

"Are you suggesting she made it up? Jackie is one of the most honorable, moral, honest people I've ever met." Bella's deep-brown eyes spit fire. Her round face hardened. "If she said she found a backpack and handed it off to someone else, that's what happened. As for holding off, that won't happen. Did you interview the catering manager? Can I call you later to see if you have her in custody?"

"You love having a piece of the story that the rest of the media doesn't."

"True."

Avery edged a few steps closer. He knew she wouldn't agree. Why had he bothered? Because she knew the librarian. "What else can you tell me about Jackie Santoro?"

"Like what?"

"Her father was Samuel Santoro."

"Yes, how is that relevant?"

"Right now everything is relevant." He was about to interview the man's daughter. "How long have you known her?"

"Since grade school."

"Has she ever expressed anger over the way her father was treated by the city manager?"

"Seriously?" Bella turned the recorder off. "If you make this about her, a mass murderer, maybe a terrorist, will get away with killing five people and injuring 120 more. Don't be an idiot."

She didn't mince words. What had he expected? "Don't worry. We'll look under every rock for this scum of the earth. We'll follow every lead. What about other friends? Does Ms. Santoro belong to any political organizations? Is she married? Does she have a significant other? Does she live alone?"

"No, she's not political, and no, she's not married. Yes, she lives alone with her cats. What does that have to do with anything? And why don't you just search your databases for her?"

"She's a cat lady? Socially awkward. Withdrawn." Avery filed the cat thing away for further review. He preferred dogs. "I'm building a profile."

"She's outgoing. A total extrovert." Bella stuck her recorder in her backpack. "She doesn't need a man to be happy. You really are a dinosaur. You're ridiculous. I have a story to write."

She whirled and left him eating her dust.

He likely did sound ridiculous. Investigating a suspect meant building a file on him or her. "You just keep telling yourself that, Wick."

He didn't usually talk aloud to himself. The horrific scene had blasted through his defenses. Not an anguished librarian with sapphire eyes.

You just keep telling yourself that, Wick.

SIX

Am I under arrest?"

Avery didn't answer. He sat a bottle of cold water and a sandwich he'd filched from the Red Cross in front of Jackie Santoro and took a seat at the HQ interrogation room table. Her anger was understandable. Being hauled across town in the backseat of a cruiser only made a horrible day worse. "Eat. Please. You look like you're about to pass out."

"Thank you, but I'm not hungry. These plastic water bottles are bad for the environment. I hope you recycle." Pushing it away, she winced and touched her forehead. A smudge of dirt on her cheek and mascara under her eyes didn't keep her from being beautiful. "If you were worried about my well-being, you wouldn't have forced me to come here. Estrella's family needs me."

"The acting chief decided he wanted to make the notification himself with a community service officer and a chaplain."

"All the more reason for me to be with them now." Her voice faltered for the first time. Pain carved lines around her full lips. "I didn't want strangers to tell them. That's exactly what I was trying to avoid."

"I know and I'm sorry." He really was sorry.

Inflicting more pain on a hurting human being wasn't Avery's idea of fun. "I'll get you out of here as soon as I can."

If he could. When the task force found out about the backpack and Meher Faheem, every agency would want a piece of Jackie and the other woman.

"I thought the good cop–bad cop shtick was supposed to be done with two cops. Or is that only in TV shows?" Her expression puzzled, Jackie cocked her head and studied him. "It's as if you have a split personality."

"I don't know what you mean." She had a melodic voice that reminded Avery of something. He couldn't put his finger on it. "I'm just doing my job."

"One minute you're concerned about my health and offering me a sandwich." She pushed the wrapped bundle of turkey on rye with swiss cheese toward him with one finger. Her nail was broken and had dirt under it. "Earlier you gave me a blanket and brought me coffee. You say you are sorry for my loss. But then you go back to being a jerk."

"A jerk? Is that the best you can do?" She was good. She'd made him feel guilty. "Why not call me what you really want and get it over with?" He cursed.

"Do you kiss your mother with that mouth?"

"My mother enlisted in the Army at the tender

age of twenty. Where do you think I learned it?" His father was career Army as well. Avery was a military brat from birth. He'd lived in nine states by the time he enrolled in his sophomore year at San Antonio's O'Connor High School. "Let's stay on track here. Let's talk about the backpack."

"We've been through it three times already. Do I need an attorney?"

"That's up to you. Call one if you want."

She pulled her phone from her jacket pocket and laid it on the table. Her fingers stayed on it, but she seemed torn. "I'd like to tell him what I'm doing here. You haven't explained that clearly."

"As I told you before, this is the formal interview. We need to record your statement and give you a written copy to sign."

"Then why did you read me my rights?"

"In case something comes up in this interview that makes me decide you should be arrested."

Jackie rolled the water bottle across her forehead and set it back on the table. "What about the other agencies involved? Won't they be peeved that you didn't give them first crack at me?"

She was a tough cookie. Even after the day she'd had, she had her wits about her. Avery filed those thoughts away and tried to appear nonchalant. He shrugged. "You don't have to worry about them."

LT had instructed Avery to bring his person of

interest to headquarters for a formal sit-down. Scotty had reported back that Catering Manager Meher Faheem was not among the injured. Nor had she been interviewed by anyone at the scene. She had no police record.

Tobin admin staff could provide a little more information. Ms. Faheem was a Pearl School of Culinary Arts graduate with a husband and two small children. She'd worked for the Tobin's catering company since the Municipal Auditorium, now known as the Tobin Center for the Performing Arts, reopened in 2015.

No one had come to the family's door when Scotty and Petra Jantzen knocked. So far no judge would give them a warrant to search the woman's house. Not without something more to tie her to terrorist activity than her presence at a bombing that seemed more likely connected to the climate controversy. They needed more. Petra would do a deep dive of all the databases to garner more information on the woman.

In the meantime Scotty moved on to bring Tony Guerra down for questioning since he'd been the last person to talk to Jackie before the explosion. Petra was compiling a list of Tobin employees who worked the event setup so they could be interviewed to see if any of them had talked to Faheem about the backpack or seen the alleged handoff from Jackie to the catering manager.

Avery sank into the chair across from Jackie

and laid his notebook in front of him. "I had a couple of minutes of free time, so I hopped on social media. Turns out you have quite strong opinions on the subject of global warming."

"If you mean I care about God's creation and what we're doing to it, then yes, I have an opinion. Don't you, or don't you care?"

"I'm not a person of interest in a bombing." He dutifully recycled. Did that count? "You're a member of the Evangelical Environmental Network, Young Evangelicals for Climate Action, and a supporter of the National Religious Partnership for the Environment. You sing Greta Thunberg's praises every chance you get."

The exhausted, sad woman sitting across from him transformed. She sat up straight. Her sapphire eyes darkened and her cheeks turned crimson. Shaking her head, she leaned in closer. "Those are all faith-based organizations undergirded by Scripture that tells us to honor and respect God's creation. They're made up of people from every Christian denomination, Roman Catholics, Jews, and other faiths. We work to educate people, to remind people of faith that they have an obligation to care for and love the earth. We send out resource kits, we compost, we plant trees and gardens. We write letters to our elected officials. We support the Paris Accord and strive to reduce our carbon footprint. Surely you don't think these organizations secretly engage in terrorism?" She laughed, but she looked and sounded disappointed in him.

"Greta Thunberg gives me hope for future generations. She's a teenager who has Asperger's syndrome and she's addressing the United Nations. Regardless of where people stand on climate change, they should respect that. They must see what a role model she is for other kids. She not only cares, she's doing something about it. I'm absolutely in awe."

"Got it, got it." Kind of like his awe of Jackie, especially when she showed such passion for a topic he only knew about because his ex-wife was similarly passionate about it.

Avery studied his notebook to avoid looking at her. She would see his awe. How could she not? "I'm sure you'll understand if we continue to delve into them and to your participation."

"Delve away. Maybe you'll learn something. Maybe you'll be moved to action." She opened the bottled water and took a long drink. "It's really warm in here."

Could her passion for the topic translate to obsession? Anything was possible. "Let's go through your story again."

"We've been through it three times now. The facts aren't going to change." Jackie recapped the water bottle and pushed it away. "I'm calling my attorney."

"You're not under arrest, so you can call whoever you want. If you want to call an attorney, do it."

"I'd like some privacy."

"Fine."

Fighting the urge to bang his head on the wall, he stepped from the room into the hall. Scotty greeted him. "I've got Guerra next door. Do you want to do the honors, or should I?"

"I'll do it. I want to compare their stories. Can you keep an eye on Jackie—Ms. Santoro? She's calling her attorney. She's already told me everything she knows. At least I think she has. It's no skin off my nose if he jerks her out of here."

Scotty's gaze held amusement. "You're dying to be on a first name basis with her, aren't you? Be careful, tiger. Keep it professional until you know if she's a mass murderer or not."

Good advice even if it came from a man who never knew when to shut up.

"To be honest, I don't think she did it." That might not be Avery's brain talking, but his partner didn't need to know that. "I've gone at her from every direction and she hasn't varied one detail in her story."

"Just means she's a cool cucumber. It doesn't mean she's innocent."

Avery's cell phone vibrated in his jacket pocket. He pulled it out and glanced at the screen. "You got her? It's Chandra. I'd better grab it."

73

Scotty rolled his eyes the way he always did when the subject of Avery's ex-wife came up. The detective didn't think much of Chandra, his version of being a loyal friend. "No sweat."

Avery connected and walked toward interrogation two. Chandra's timing sucked, but in the interest of postdivorce civility, he always made it a point to take her calls. "What's up, sweetheart?"

"I saw the news. Are you there?" His ex-wife's East Texas accent deepened whenever she was concerned about something. Right now the Fulbright scholar and Harvard Law School graduate sounded like a hillbilly. "Are you okay?"

"I was, but I'm at headquarters now, interviewing persons of interest. I wasn't there when the bomb exploded." He ducked into the observation room so he could keep an eye on Tony Guerra. As usual, the man jabbered on his cell phone. "I'm fine."

As long as he didn't examine too closely the images of the maimed victims that rose to the surface every time he paused long enough to think.

"Channel 12 carried the news conference live. You're not fine. Your boss was killed. You saw dead and injured, maimed people. You like to pretend it doesn't bother you, but it does. I'm sorry about Bill Little. I always liked him."

"Yeah, me too." He leaned against the wall,

took a deep breath, and let it out. Chandra was married to another man now and had a child with him. She and Avery had now been divorced longer than they were married. Even so, she still had a calming effect on him. Even when her yoga and her meditation drove him nuts, she had a way of centering him in the early days of their five-year marriage—before her career took off and his took him into places where nightmares were made. "His wife is critical. They have four kids."

"Councilman Sandoval will be missed too. He was a champion of the sanctuary-city designation and he pushed for more funding for migrant services."

"His chief of staff was young and engaged to get married on Valentine's Day."

That detail from Jackie's story would float to the top. He and Chandra had married on the Fourth of July. Appropriate given the fireworks that had exploded when she asked him for a divorce. Chandra never raised her voice. She didn't have it in her. She simply went her own way. The same could not be said for Avery. He'd been pathetic in his attempt to hang on to her. It had been like trying to hug a shooting star.

"Estrella Diaz. Such a pretty name." Sadness reduced Chandra's voice to a wispy thread. "I met her once at a debate when Sandoval was running for reelection. She should've been running. Smart, articulate, informed, passionate, photogenic. She would've gone far, given time."

"She didn't get time."

"You'll get the monster who did this."

"That's the plan." He studied his dirty loafers. One of the things he missed most in the early days after his divorce was being able to use Chandra as a sounding board on his cases. As an attorney she offered invaluable insight. "Do you remember the Sam Santoro case?"

"Sure, who doesn't?"

"I have his daughter Jackie in an interview room right now. Estrella Diaz was her best friend."

"You think she's involved?"

"Keeping an open mind. She had motive and means."

"Why would she kill her best friend?"

"Just letting the marbles roll around in my brain."

"It's early."

"The whole world will be breathing down our necks on this one."

"You'll nail the offender."

"So was there some reason you called me?" Chandra's optimism was kind, in keeping with her overall compassionate soul. "Or did you just want the behind-the-scenes scoop available only to ex-wives of cops?"

"Avery, I was worried about you." Her breathing was soft, sweet. "We've had this conversation before. I didn't stop caring about you when I divorced you. I love you like I would a good friend. We both let work become more important than our marriage."

She was right. They were better friends than they had ever been spouses. When Chandra had decided to resign from her high-powered law firm and go to work for an agency with the unwieldy name of The Refugee and Immigrant Center for Education and Legal Services, Avery had no idea the beginning of the end neared. He was too busy catching bad guys to notice.

Now she worked high-profile immigration cases, cared for a growing brood, and still found time to make her marriage to a doctor work. Avery simply worked. "How's Julio?"

"He's fine." Her husband was a widower with three kids of his own when they married, and they quickly produced a fourth one. He worked for Doctors Without Borders. "I respect your dedication to your job, Avery. Don't ever doubt that."

"Yeah. And I respect yours." Even if the two combined had sounded the death knell for their marriage. He pushed off the wall and straightened. "I better get to it."

"Be careful, please."

Her words joined a chorus that echoed through time. Chandra had said them at the beginning of his shift for five years. "Take care."

She was already gone.

That usual restless feeling of nostalgia mixed with loneliness bombarded Avery. It happened every time he talked to Chandra. It wasn't her specifically, but rather what she represented. A relationship. Someone to whom he could come home at night. A partner in life. Her leaving left a big hole in him. After six years, he still hadn't figured out how to fill it. He'd tried drinking. All that did was give him a headache and a beer gut. He'd taken up jogging. It made his knees hurt. He'd dated. He was too old, too tired, and too impatient for inconsequential small talk.

So he worked. Avery stuffed his phone in his pocket and went to grill a man who'd lost the love of his life and his boss on the same day.

SEVEN

The surprised look on Detective Wick's face when he walked into the interrogation room made the long wait worth it—almost. Jackie relaxed in her chair next to Lee Drucker, an on-the-rise hotshot criminal defense attorney and her sister Tosca's boyfriend. He wore a tailored navy suit and red silk tie cut to fit his muscle-bound body perfectly. He cut an imposing figure that made the small room seem crowded. "Thanks for joining us, Detective. It's about time."

"Sorry, I had another interview to do first. So he's your lawyer?" Wick's sardonic tone and his choice to speak to Jackie first was an obvious ploy to irritate Lee. Wick slapped a folder on the table and slid into the chair across from them. "I should've known. Your family can afford his daddy's firm."

People liked to assume Lee's reputation stemmed from his father's. Big mistake. The older Drucker preferred white-collar crime, but he never stood in his son's way when he went after murder cases—particularly capital punishment cases—that captured the media's and the public's attention. He won cases that couldn't be won.

"If you're trying to insult one or both of

us, don't bother." Jackie dug deep for some semblance of civility. None to be found. "My father's family might have money, but I make a public servant's salary, much less than police officers who have a union to negotiate high-dollar contracts that leave nothing in the city's general fund budget for libraries, parks, and other so-called 'nonessentials.' "

Two could play this sarcasm game. Her facts were right on target. She waited for a sense of pleasure from delivering the comeback. None came, only shame. Wick had dark circles under his eyes. His shirt was wrinkled and his tie had coffee stains on it.

To his credit, he didn't bite. "So you've had a chance to confer with your attorney. Is there anything you'd like to change about your statement?"

"Jackie's statement stands. She's been generous with her time in an effort to assist in your investigation into today's horrific event." Lee's even tone matched his bland expression. "If there's nothing else, she's been through hell today. We need to make this quick since you've also requested the presence of Jackie's sister, Tosca. I also represent her. She's my fiancée."

"A move I totally don't understand. You're wasting your time with us—especially Tosca—when you could be searching for the real killer." Jackie drew a breath. "Tosca is a landscape architect. She designs butterfly gardens and earth-friendly xeriscape yards with native plants."

"Your family was involved in a high-profile scandal that ended in your father's suicide. I'm sorry to be so blunt, but we'll take a close look at every member of your family as potentially having motives for wanting to kill city officials. The victims deserve a thorough investigation." Wick's tone was even but firm. "We'll make this as quick as possible. While you were getting legal advice, I spent some time with your friend Tony Guerra—"

"You couldn't give the man a break? He lost his fiancée this morning. His boss is dead—"

"Believe or not, I took no pleasure in hauling him in here." The muscle in Wick's jaw twitched. "He wants the murderer to be found, so he's willing to do whatever it takes."

"So am I."

"Good. Guerra confirmed your story about the conversation that occurred right before the explosion. He was surprised you didn't mention the backpack to security."

"It was innocuous. It had Spurs patches on the front. Parker, Duncan, and Ginóbili's numbers were stitched on it." Jackie pulled the sweater Tosca had sent up for her tighter. Her body wouldn't stop shivering. She didn't dare drink any more coffee. "I remember thinking someone loves the Spurs as much as I do."

"You didn't mention that before." The exhaustion faded from Wick's face. He sat up straight. "Interesting."

"It's taken some time for the shock to wear off." That time before the explosion felt a million miles and days ago. Did it even happen? "All three of these players are retired now. Someone is a longtime fan. Like me and anyone who grew up watching the Spurs play. Those three players were the big three for several years."

Stop blathering. Blackness crept along the periphery of her sight. She bit her lip until it hurt. "Sorry. Sorry. None of that has to do with anything."

"Not true. You never know what tiny detail might unravel the entire thing."

That almost sounded like a compliment. Jackie wanted to smile, but she couldn't imagine being able to smile ever again.

"We're done here." Lee pushed back his chair. "She's told you everything she knows. Let's move on."

"Every lead, every detail has to be followed up and investigated." Wick didn't move. "This backpack is huge. You know it and I know it. Whether she's a person of interest or a witness who had a critical piece of evidence in her possession for a split second, Ms. Santoro—"

"Jackie."

"Jackie will be in the middle of this investigation to the bitter end." He shoved his business card across the table. "If you think of anything else, please call me."

Lee held out his business card. "You want to talk to her again. Call *me*. I'll arrange it."

Wick accepted the card. He studied it for a second. "Just so you know, FBI agents are interviewing Tobin Center staff as we speak. So far they haven't found anyone who remembers being asked about the backpack or seeing it." He glanced at a black sports wristwatch. "Chief Ruiz will share what we've learned from Jackie with the task force in the next few minutes. It's likely your client will be interviewed by one or more of our federal colleagues shortly."

Lee put his hand on Jackie's arm and steered her around the table. "Like I said, they can call me."

Wick held the door for them. Jackie brushed past him. She could feel his gaze on her. She glanced back. "I hope you get some sleep soon, Detective."

"I'll sleep when this scumbag is in jail."

His gritty tone and scowl were strangely comforting. "Me too."

In the hallway Lee offered a hug and Jackie took it. "Thanks for bailing me out. Go be with Tosca. She needs you."

The Santoro free spirit, Tosca, had a childlike sensitive soul. Lee would protect that. He rubbed

Jackie's back. "Can you wait here for us? It won't take long. It's a fishing expedition, and anyone who talks to Tosca for five seconds will see that."

"Do you mind if I wait in your car? I can't take another minute of this place."

And she didn't want to run into Detective Wick again. She couldn't dwell on the reasons why. Lee slipped his car fob into her hand and explained where he'd parked.

Feeling ancient, Jackie stumbled to Lee's gleaming black Jaguar on the third floor of the parking garage. Exactly thirty minutes later, Lee and Tosca followed. Jackie shoved herself from the car and opened her arms for the hug. Tosca burrowed in tight. Neither spoke for a few seconds.

"Are you okay?" Jackie eased back and gave her sister a once-over. "Do I need to kick some detective behind?"

"I can't believe they had the audacity to even consider the possibility that any of us had something to do with this." Tosca brushed Jackie's hair from her face. Looking at her baby sister was like staring at herself in the mirror—except that Tosca stood five inches shorter and was not quite as well endowed—a fact that didn't bother her in the least. "I'm fine. Detective Wick was surprisingly courteous. He was very sweet, actually. I think he's had some hard times in his life."

Tosca also served as the family's empathetic sibling. She could be counted on to see the best in every person. Jackie tried to emulate her but often fell short. "It's possible. Probable."

"You look awful, Sissy." Tosca patted Jackie's cheek like a grandma. "We need to get you home. A hot shower and a nice bowl of Mom's chicken noodle soup, ten hours of sleep, and you'll feel human again."

As if Jackie ever slept even five hours back-to-back. "I have to go to Mateo's."

"Not looking like that. You'll only make it worse. Besides all the *tías* and *tíos* and *abuelitas* and *abuelitos* have descended already."

Tosca was right. Jackie slid into the backseat, leaned her head against the velvety soft leather, and closed her eyes. Every part of her body ached. Images etched on her psyche flashed on a continuous loop in her head. Estrella's mangled body. Sandoval's misshapen face. Tony's anguished screams. People with missing limbs.

She forced her eyes open. When crisis smacked her in the face, she always ran to Estrella. Never again.

Pain gutted her. *Estrella, I need you. I will miss you every minute of every day until I see you again.*

"Where to then?"

Jackie cleared her throat. "Home, please."

Lee started the engine and pulled from the parking space.

"You're not spending the night at your house alone, Sis." Tosca slid around in her seat so she could see Jackie. "Stay with Mom. She'll take care of you. She's worried about you."

"I need some quiet time. I don't want to rehash the day right now. There will be time for that tomorrow. Right now I need to feed my kitties. I need to pet them and listen to them purr." Estrella had been certain Jackie was turning into a cat lady. She hadn't had a date in almost two years. Most of her after-work conversation took place with Mr. Darcy, who was missing an eye, Jane, who allowed no one but Jackie to touch her, and Don Quixote—Don for short—who seemed to forget how to find the litter box at least once a week. "I need to just breathe in the silence for a while."

"Mom couldn't get ahold of Cris. He's not returning her calls."

Jackie stared out the window, watching the other cars' lights flash as they passed by. "Did she try the big house?"

That's what they called Nonno's house in the Dominion, a far northside subdivision that housed the richest families in San Antonio, where people like actor Tommy Lee Jones, former Spurs David Robinson, country singer George Strait, and other celebrities had homes. Where Jackie,

Tosca, and Cris had played hide-and-seek in the thick stand of mesquite and live oaks or swam in the infinity pool before wolfing down Grandma's lasagna followed by tiramisu or, in the summer, gelato. If it rained, they watched movies in the home theater or bowled in the basement bowling alley.

Until the falling out between Daddy and Nonno.

"Nonna said she thought he was at work. She hadn't seen him all day."

The rift that had opened when their father took his own life a year ago grew wider with the passage of time. They didn't talk about it. They simply drifted. Jackie dug her phone from her pocket and texted him.

Cris, I need to talk to you. Please text me. Or call.

More than likely he wouldn't, but at least she'd tried.

Jackie loosened her seat belt so she could lean forward. "Was that the first time you've dealt with Detective Wick?"

"No, he's testified in a couple of my trials."

"What do you know about him?"

Lee eyed Jackie in the rearview mirror and smiled. "Got your attention, did he?"

True, Wick had an intensity that reminded her

of sticking a bobby pin in a socket—something she'd done as a child. Once had been enough, but Wick ran like boiling water and Arctic cold. A decent human being peeked from behind his cop persona at odd times.

The feel of his hands on hers returned to haunt her. It had been a long time since she held hands with a man. Had she imagined his fingers caressing her hair? A shiver ran through her. *Shake it off, Santoro.* That's what Coach always said when a play didn't go her way. "I want to know what I'm up against. And whether he'll get the job done."

"Don't let his rough-around-the-edges demeanor fool you." Lee chuckled. "He's smart, he's tenacious, and he's experienced. He's well respected by his peers. He's cool under fire on the stand. I couldn't shake him."

That said a lot. Lee's AR-15 style of cross-examination had decimated more than one veteran police officer. "What else?"

"From what I've heard he's not above taking a half step over the line if it serves the so-called greater good."

Like Lee. "Which is why his peers respect him."

"As far as chain of command is concerned, his solve rate absolves his less-than-desirable tactics. But some folks see him as a loose cannon. Especially in the last six years or so."

"Why the last six years?"

"His wife quit her job at Martinez, Salazar, and Lewis to work for RAICES. Then she divorced him after only five years of marriage. He was blindsided."

Apparently cops were worse gossipers than librarians. Wick's wife had worked for one of the best corporate law firms in town. Refugee and Immigrant Center for Education and Legal Services was a nonprofit, which would mean a huge cut in pay. Why had she divorced her public servant husband? That was no one's business, least of all Jackie's. "How do you know all this?"

"I make it a point to learn everything I can about the assistant district attorney's witnesses. He's forty, has a degree in criminal justice from UTSA, and plays basketball in the police department league."

A basketball player. No guy who still pounded the court at his age could be all bad. Jackie forced the thought aside. "I don't care about his personal life. I don't care that he steps over the line. Well, I do, but in this case, I'll give him a pass."

Her attitude was wrong and she knew it. Somehow she couldn't bring herself to care. Not today. Surely God's grace would cover her on a day like today. "Did you see any of the news conference?"

"Nope, we were busy coming to your rescue." Tosca responded before Lee could. "TV stations have preempted regularly scheduled pro-gramming for hours. I don't think I could take any more of the images. I can't imagine what it was like for you being there. When I think of what could have happened to you . . ." Her voice broke.

Rustling sounds told Jackie her sister was hunting for a tissue in her purse. "Sis, I made it through it. I'm here—"

"Seriously, Lee, you don't have tissues in the glove compartment. You should always keep tissues and napkins in your car."

"Console, sweetie." Lee's deep, soothing voice held nothing but love. "We'll get through this, I promise."

The two clasped hands over the console. Jackie looked away. Most of the time she determinedly embraced her singleness. Tonight it would have been nice to be embraced by a man who loved her.

EIGHT

The Feds were waiting on Jackie's doorstep—along with Detective Wick. The guy was everywhere.

"Long time no see." She was too tired to rein in the sarcasm. "I thought you'd had enough of me for one day."

Wick had the good grace to look chagrined. "Sorry. It's hard to know sometimes how a joint investigation will take shape. My superior asked me to accompany our task force members in the search of your home."

"I understand." Not really. She took the search warrant from Wick's FBI colleague and handed it to Lee. His expression tense, he perused it, frowned, and let it slip through his fingers. It landed on her secondhand coffee table amid half a dozen literary magazines filled with short stories and poems, an ugly alien amid beauty and creativity. "They basically have carte blanche."

The contingent of agents in FBI and HSI jackets swarmed her tiny house. With an apologetic nod, Wick followed. Trying to remember if she made her bed and hung up her wet towel in the bathroom that morning, Jackie sank onto her couch. At least she hadn't left dirty dishes in the sink. Her head pounded and small cuts on her face and arms burned. Had she actually performed all those mundane tasks like showering and brushing her teeth this same day?

The same day Estrella died?

"Can they really do this?" Tosca squeezed onto the couch next to Jackie. "She's the victim here. Somebody tried to blow her up today."

"Not me specifically." Jackie grabbed a pillow and hugged it to her chest. Her sister's proximity and scent of sandalwood and citrus comforted her. "They're only doing their jobs."

"It's garbage. They should be out there trying to find the real bomber."

Wick paused in her arched living room door. "We need to take your computer. We'll give you a list of items confiscated as a receipt."

"Will I get it back?"

He was already gone.

Fine. She still had her laptop. Unless they took that too. They were making such a ruckus, poor Don had taken refuge in his favorite hidey-hole among Jackie's shoes in the closet. Darcy and Jane sat on the top level of their six-foot scratching post, huddled together, keeping guard for her.

"We have a few questions for you." FBI Special Agent Petra Jantzen strolled into the living room. She was a petite silver-haired woman with lovely light-brown skin. She settled onto the glider rocker that had belonged to Jackie's great-grandmother. "Why didn't you immediately report the backpack?"

"She already answered these questions at PD. I'm sure Detective Wick made the recording of her interview available to you." Lee eased from his spot in front of the stone fireplace and came to stand next to the sofa. "What can you possibly expect to gain from replicating his efforts?"

Jantzen's smile was pleasant, her voice soft. "We're simply fleshing out a few of the answers in support of local law enforcement. That's our role in these situations."

"Ms. Santoro has been through a horrific experience and now you're harassing her."

"We're deeply sorry for your loss, Ms. Santoro." The agent's gaze swiveled to Jackie. "Believe me, it's not our desire to make it worse. Our goal is to find the culprit and give everyone the closure they need in order to find some peace."

Everything about the agent assured Jackie of her sincerity. "Are you about done searching my home?" Jackie clasped her arms close to her body and shivered. Strangers were touching her belongings, invading her privacy. "I'd like to clean up, if you are."

"It's a small house. It didn't take long."

The cottage home built in the 1950s fit Jackie perfectly. It had been hard to find one she could afford on her librarian's salary. "Then you can go and report back to your superiors that you found nothing because there's nothing to find."

"Tell me about the backpack."

Exhaustion blurred Jackie's vision. She rubbed her eyes. Only a good upbringing kept her from rolling them and uttering, "Whatever," like a recalcitrant teenager. She dutifully repeated everything she'd reported to Detective Wick. Jantzen occasionally nodded, and once she tut-tutted, which made her sound like a grandma.

"So you handed a backpack to a caterer who happens to be Muslim with connections to Saudi Arabia and walked off without another thought?"

"I don't live in your world. My first thought isn't of incendiary devices. Meher is a professional colleague. My first inclination is not to profile a woman because of her dress or her faith."

"We have a warrant pending for your cell phone records and your finances. If you've received large sums of money recently, if you've made contributions to terrorist organizations, if you've spoken to anyone on our watch lists, we'll know."

"Good grief. You know that cliché, 'Don't make a federal case out of it'? That applies here. I'm a librarian. I have twelve hundred dollars in my savings account and enough in my checking account to cover next month's bills with a little left over for Spurs tickets and the new Elizabeth

George Inspector Lynley novel. My phone records will show I talk to my mother and sister every day. Until today I texted my friend Estrella even more often. Her and Bella Glover. My life is books, family, and church—not in that order, of course. I teach third graders about Jesus in Sunday school. I haven't had a date in eons. Maybe that's something I have in common with terrorists. I don't know."

Her expression sympathetic, Jantzen leaned forward in her chair. "I have a granddaughter who's in the third grade—"

Wick strode into the room. He held a moleskin notebook in one hand. "This is interesting."

Jackie jolted to her feet. "You're reading my journal? Seriously? Give me that. Have you no shame?"

Jantzen stood and slipped between them. "Take a seat, Ms. Santoro."

Lee took her arm. "Easy, Jackie."

"That's private. Extremely private." They'd violated every corner of her snug, cozy sanctuary. Now this. Her therapist had urged Jackie to try journaling to work through her father's suicide. "Is this how you get your jollies? Reading a woman's journal?"

"You say in here you considered approaching the city manager at your father's funeral and slapping his face." Wick tapped the notebook with one gloved finger. "You wrote about feeling as if he deserved a fate worse than death for the way he treated your father."

"Does it say anything in there about me wanting to blow him up?" Jackie swallowed a barrage of angry words. She drew a long breath and eased from Lee's grip. "The purpose of the journal is to release angry feelings instead of letting them stew and build up. My therapist suggested it."

"I understand seeing a therapist in such an awful situation." Wick's tone softened. He smoothed his hand over the cover. "The issue here is that you state the city destroyed your father's reputation before he had a chance to defend himself in court. He took his own life as a result. You hold them responsible."

"We all do." Tosca's voice trembled. "We suffered a catastrophic loss. You would too."

Jackie breathed. *Never let them see you cry.* She'd learned that from her mother during the long media siege after Daddy's arrest. "Does that make us all bombers? You think this is some big conspiracy? The situation drove our father to kill himself. That leaves a mark that never goes away. That doesn't make any of us raging lunatics who indiscriminately bomb innocent people.

"Besides, those entries were written almost a year ago. I've come to grips with what happened." It still hurt. Jackie still had a chasm in her heart where the man who taught her a left-handed hook and how to make a good cup of coffee had resided. "I've moved on. The fact that I still work for the city speaks to that."

It also spoke to her love of the Central Library, her hometown, and her family. She could never leave.

"I'm afraid we'll have to take it with us." Wick slid the slim notebook into a paper bag. His fair skin mottled red.

Furious embarrassment burned through Jackie. She gritted her teeth and summoned calm. Her innermost thoughts were recorded in that journal. Her hopes and dreams. Her fears. At thirty she was no closer to motherhood than she had been at twenty. No soul mate had appeared. She loved her house and her cats and her job, but in her heart of hearts, she wanted more. "Please don't do that. It's personal."

Wick's face turned a deeper crimson. "We'll get it back to you as soon as possible. I'll see to it."

Jackie stood and marched past them into the kitchen. A small square of real estate that hadn't been invaded by strangers couldn't be found. She shuffled through her coffee stash, trying to find something that would soothe a pain that burrowed into every corner of her body. Wick followed.

"Look, I'm sorry."

"Please get out of my kitchen."

"I know you're hurting, but you have to understand, the sooner we investigate every possible lead, every possible avenue, the sooner we'll catch the animal who did this."

Willing tears not to fall with sheer stubbornness, Jackie chewed her lower lip. She poured water into her large coffeepot, normally reserved for company. "You're wasting your time with me when you could be out there finding the real culprit."

"You'd be surprised how often we hear that from people who turn out to be the culprit." Wick picked up her package of Italian coffee beans. "Stop with the coffee already. This isn't personal. Everyone here is doing a job. We're trying to do it well out of respect for the dead, the victims."

Jackie sucked in a long breath. He was right. "Then go do it. Don't waste one more minute on my journal."

"We don't enjoy invading people's privacy—at least I don't."

"Then don't."

"It doesn't work that way." He handed her the package of coffee beans. His warm fingers brushed against hers. "I wish it wasn't necessary."

"Me too." The two syllables came out in a croak. If this was necessary in order to get law enforcement to move on, so be it. "But it's okay. I'll live."

"That's good." A fleeting smile made Wick look years younger. "That's what I want to hear."

Held by his intent gaze, Jackie didn't move.

His phone rang.

Phones rang in the living room.

Everyone answered at the same time.

Wick disconnected. "We have to go."

"What's going—?"

Jackie's phone burst forth with Gloria Gaynor's "I Will Survive."

Watching Wick shoot out the door, Jackie took the call. "Bella."

"I have to hurry. The cops are on the way."

Bella's whispered words faded away. Her tortured breathing filled the line. She sounded scared. Nothing scared her. Fear did a number on Jackie. "What is it? Are you all right? Are you hurt?"

"Yes. No. A guy who claimed to be the bomber called me."

Jackie clutched the phone to her ear, trying to hear over the buzz that filled her head. "What did he say?"

"Jack, he's not done yet."

NINE

Avery didn't know whether to be disgusted or thankful.

The bomber had decided to chat up a member of the media. His call would give them more information, more leads, but it also put the newspaper in the driver's seat.

Avery picked up his pace. His escort, the managing editor, trotted ahead of him. The alphabet soup brigade of ATF, FBI, and HSI followed them through the halls of the *Express-News*'s historic art deco building that had housed its operations since the day the stock market crashed in 1929. Avery never expected to find himself in a newsroom in the line of duty. He wasn't as mediaphobic as many of his colleagues, but he treaded cautiously with them.

Bella Glover sat at a long table in the conference room. Gathered around her were Sig Ritter, the publisher, one of the newspaper's lawyers, the city editor, and now the breathless managing editor. They clustered together like a pack of salivating junkyard pit bulls. Whatever happened next was fair game for tomorrow's front page. Everyone here knew it.

Avery came with his own pack, but they were more like wolves. ATF Special Agent

Michael Chavez, Petra, and Homeland Security Investigations Special Agent Nathan Wilson. Petra nodded. Her smile was terse but acknowledged their past work together.

He managed a quick smile, but his stomach tightened at the job ahead. Having Petra on the team helped. She was solid. Even so, Avery didn't bother with introductions, too many words in those titles. Between the two groups it would take an hour.

"Walk us through it." Avery spoke at the same time as Chavez.

The ATF agent frowned and busied himself opening his Mac. Wilson from HSI did the same.

Ignoring Chavez, Bella held up Avery's card. "You told me to call you if anything came up. So I did."

Her insistence that she speak with him had garnered Avery this spot at the table. However, he would not be running the show. Anything that involved media involved the chief.

"I appreciate that." His impatience to hear the recording barely in check, Avery tried to look encouraging. The clock continued to tick. "Go ahead. Tell us what happened."

Bella glanced at the publisher. The older woman nodded. Bella picked up her notebook but didn't glance at it. "I had most of my story written. Sig and I were comparing notes when my phone rang." The reporter touched her split lip, likely an injury suffered in the blast. "It sounded like he was using one of those voice changers—"

"It was a man?" Chavez jumped in.

"What time was that?" Jantzen added.

"Look, folks, this will go a lot faster if we let the woman tell her story." Avery held up his hand like a stop sign. "Go on, Bella. How quickly did you realize who was calling?"

"It was about eight thirty. It sounded like a woman, but like I said, a voice changer could mask a man's voice as well. I have friends who use them to prank each other—and as party favors. I knew almost immediately it was something weird. The speaker said she was sorry for my split lip but I got off lucky."

Her boyfriend grabbed her hand and squeezed. She smiled at him but tugged free. No female reporter—or librarian—worth her salt wanted to seem weak in this situation. She and Jackie had the same mindset, no doubt. "He or she knew I was there. He knew I hurt my lip. I wasn't sure what was going on exactly, but I knew it could really be the bomber. I put him on speaker, grabbed my digital recorder, and hit Record."

"Could we hear the recording?"

Bella once again glanced at her superiors. The beanstalk lawyer in the high-priced suit nodded. She pushed Play.

The recording wasn't great but understandable. The speaker didn't mess around.

"I'm glad you survived the explosion, Bella."

"Who is this? Do I know you?"

"No, but I know you. I saw you outside the Tobin. Working hard as usual."

"Who are you?"

Avery had to hand it to Bella. She stayed cool under pressure. Her voice didn't waver. She might have been talking to one of her subject-matter experts about global warming.

"My organization is responsible for today's call to action."

"Explain to me how a bombing that killed five people and injured one hundred twenty is a call to any action other than hunting you down and making sure you get the death penalty."

Nice. She had guts.

"We have to stop the terrorists who are preying on innocent citizens' fears. We have to match their extreme actions with our own inside of buying into the drivel they're pushing. They use arson and bombings to disrupt businesses. The bombing was step one. We need help from you and your newspaper for step two."

"You killed a close friend of mine. Why should I do anything for you? Tell me who you are and what you want, and I'll talk to my bosses about whether we can even consider your request. I can tell you right now, we don't bow to pressure any more than the government does when it comes to terrorists."

"I'm deeply sorry for your loss." The speaker's voice was altered in such a way that the words were cold and stilted. Which likely matched his true emotions. "Collateral damage cannot be avoided."

"Estrella was a beautiful human being. Don't you dare call her collateral damage. She was a living, breathing person who loved and was loved."

A pause. Avery leaned forward. So did his colleagues. Had she surprised the guy with her counterattack? Had she scared him off?

"This is war. We're being attacked. We need to fight back." The self-confessed killer's voice become more strident. "The *Express-News* supports the mayor's climate-action plan. You're wrong. You're influencing your readers, filling their minds with bunk, pseudoscience. You're part of the problem. Don't play high-and-mighty with me. We want your newspaper to make amends by fairly presenting our side of the story. Be our mouthpiece for a change."

"The *Express-News* doesn't act as a mouthpiece for anyone or any organization. Especially a domestic terrorist organization. We serve the public with factual, fair, objective reporting on a wide range of important topics. You should write a letter to the editor or an op-ed piece if you want your opinion to be heard."

The city editor and managing editor pretended

to high-five without making a noise. Their feature writer turned crime reporter was scoring points with her bosses. She was also pushing back against a dangerous criminal. She trod on thin ice.

"Spoken like a true puppet of the government. You're a mouthpiece for the city manager, the city council, and their lackeys." The caller half snorted, half laughed. "They feed you their stinking PR pap and you accept it like milk for a mewling kitten. You're in no position to be righteous or indignant with us. Ignore our demands and more people will die. Do you want that?"

"No, no, I don't." Bella's voice held the first hint of fear. "What organization are we talking about? What demands?"

"United San Antonians for Prosperity."

"I've never heard of it."

Neither had Avery. His compadres from the federal agencies were furiously typing on their laptops. Digging into the databases and sending alerts to their buddies. If there was any intel on this organization, they would know soon.

"We want our local officials to back off on their green initiatives. They're perpetuating a hoax on the citizens of this community. They're costing businesses millions of dollars with their rules and regulations."

"So you thought you would kill a bunch of

them in one fell swoop rather than waiting for election day?"

Bella had let the scorn rip. Weren't reporters supposed to be objective? Still, she deserved the benefit of the doubt, having been a victim of that same bombing. Avery glanced at her face. She looked as if she were hearing the conversation for the first time. Sick to her stomach. No doubt she wasn't used to being stuck in the middle of her story.

"It's not a bad way to go, but no, we wanted to get people's attention. If we don't eliminate the putrid pus that calls itself leaders now, the city will die a slow, painful death."

"So what do you want to say to the people who read our newspaper?"

"Tell them that the city manager, the mayor, the city council, the police—they're ignoring science. Fossil fuel is not responsible for melting glaciers. It's a naturally occurring phenomenon. They're hurting business. They're hurting the economy. They need to be replaced immediately."

"Why not work through the system to initiate change? Why resort to extreme measures?"

"In Bexar County? It's a stronghold for the liberals. The mayor is leading the charge with this so-called San Antonio climate-action plan. They control the left-wing media. A left-wing city manager hires liberals in all the key director positions. They'll do anything to maintain their power. Everyone knows that. We're tired of waiting. We want change now."

"Change to what?"

"A responsive elected body that appoints city officials who answer to the people. We're tired of being ignored, our rights trampled, and our voices snuffed out."

"Snuffed out?"

"Bella, I don't have time to educate you right now. Here's the bottom line: If they don't step down immediately, there will be more events like the one that happened today at public buildings throughout the downtown area. We won't confine ourselves to buildings primarily involving local citizens. The USAP will demonstrate that we mean business. Bombs will be detonated, one after the other, in places like Market Square, the River Walk, the Alamo, Hemisfair Park."

In other words the USAP planned to cripple San Antonio's number-one industry—tourism. Even though this might be considered the off-season, millions flocked to the Alamo City year-round.

"Why hurt all those innocent people?"

"It's the only way to get their attention and make change happen. It was a perfect opportunity considering the organizers brought us a climate-change shill and government hacks in the same room. I have to go now. I'm looking forward to reading your story in the paper tomorrow. I assume it'll be posted on your website before then."

"How can I get in touch with you if I need more information?"

"You can't."

"I need your name. I have to attribute your statements to someone. I need to be able to corroborate your information regarding the USAP."

Avery gave Bella a thumbs-up for her concerted effort to draw the caller out. It wouldn't work, but it had been worth a try.

"Media use unnamed sources all the time."

"But the reporters know the names of their sources."

"Run with this story or be responsible for the deaths of many more people. Those are your choices."

He hung up. Bella turned off the recorder and leaned back in her chair. Her eyes were glassy with unshed tears and fatigue. Her lips quivered.

No one spoke for several seconds.

"You can't publish this story." Chavez closed his laptop. "You'll create a public panic."

"You heard what the person said." The publisher placed her tightly clasped hands on the table. She wore a huge chunk of diamond on her wedding ring finger. Her knotted knuckles suggested rheumatoid arthritis. "More people will die if we don't. We have an obligation to warn the public."

"Agreed. The problem is how to frame it." The managing editor scratched his freckled, bald head. "We don't know where or when. Are we going to tell all of San Antonio to stay home from work? Not to go into public buildings to do business? To stay away from Spurs games and events on the River Walk? For how long? Based on the first bombing, I assume y'all consider this a credible threat."

"I'm not stepping down. Neither is the mayor." City Manager Jason Vogel burst into the room, followed closely by Mayor Peter Cavazos and their security details. The room became far too crowded. Vogel settled into a chair between Petra and Wilson, across from Bella. "My chief of staff delivered your message, young lady. Here is your quote: Be assured the leadership of this city will not be bullied by an anonymous person who likely fabricated the entire story about this fictitious USAP. We can find no evidence that such an organization exists. I doubt our law enforcement partners will either. Whoever you are, show your face. Don't be a coward hiding behind voice changers and anonymity. Work with us to address the issues that concern you. Don't be a coward who kills innocent people. Be assured our police force will hunt you down and arrest you. Our district attorney will prosecute you. You will receive the death penalty. Count on it."

Vogel was on a roll. He'd likely scripted that entire tirade with a PR flack on the ride over to

Avenue E and Third Street. He glanced sideways at the mayor, his boss, along with the city council.

Cavazos was a thirtysomething Latino with his sights set on a big, bright future. His aspirations included the governorship, the senate, or even acquiring 1600 Pennsylvania Avenue as his address. He nodded, leaned back, and steepled his fingers. He probably thought the pose made him look sage. Mostly he looked constipated. "As the only elected official in the room and as someone being asked to give up a seat given to me by the people of San Antonio, I can see both sides of this coin."

Way to sit on the fence, buddy.

"We must keep our citizenry safe. By the same token we can't let a man with blood on his hands tell us how to run this city. I answer to the citizens of San Antonio, not a mass murderer. I think my constituents would agree with me. You don't push around Texans. They fight back. They would want us to flush out this killer and make sure he gets what is coming to him."

He nodded at Bella, who was busy writing furiously on a skinny reporter notebook. "You can also quote me on that."

Posturing for the media. That's what he and Vogel were good for.

"You're wrong about one thing." Wilson glanced down at his laptop. "There's a national think tank called Citizens for Economic Prosperity that espouses the opinion that science doesn't support global warming. This could be a local chapter, so to speak."

"It's as if this organization, if it really exists, took a page from the extreme fringes of the ecoterrorism organizations like the Earth Liberation Front." Petra picked up the theme. "The less radical groups tend toward vandalism, like the valve turners that stopped the flow of oil through the Keystone Pipeline or putting spikes in the ground to halt the logging trucks. But the extremists resort to criminal acts that result in loss of life, like pipe bombs and arson. We've not seen an anticlimate-change organization do that."

"There's a first time for everything," Wilson said. "We'll get into it. In the past the radical ecoterrorists have worked in small, loosely organized cells. They don't show up at public demonstrations or make public declarations—until that first act of violence. They're usually well educated and frequently they're women. They tend to get better at acts of violence as they get more experience. The model fits no matter which side of the political equation they fall on."

"We just haven't seen that in San Antonio." Sig Ritter stirred the dregs of his coffee with a plastic spoon. "The conversations around the climate-action plan have been ubercivilized. Both sides have come to the table and tried to come up with strategies that can quickly address the problem of carbon emissions while not being so onerous they cause businesses to fail."

"The few protestors have been from organizations who want more change more quickly, not the hoaxers," Bella added. "The big businesses here in finance, wholesale and retail groceries, the tourist industry, the medical complexes, and the high-tech folks have been all about being good corporate citizens."

"Or they're putting on a happy face for the public while working to dismantle any regulations that will impact their bottom lines." Sig's journalistic cynicism was showing. "We need to dig deeper in the people and organizations on the conservative side of the table."

"I've done a massive search and I can't find any mention of a local organization by that name." Bella shifted in her chair. Her hands were clasped so tightly her knuckles were white. "This could be a red herring. Why would an organization that claims global warming fixes are stymieing the economy turn around and destroy said economy?"

"We'll get into it." Wilson shut his laptop. "We have more resources than you do."

"So is this enough to cross Jackie Santoro and Meher Faheem off your persons-of-interest list?" Bella picked up her pen and repositioned her notebook. "If ISIS was involved they'd take credit for it, but why would they attack a small gathering of people interested in the environment in South Texas?"

"We're not eliminating anyone at this point. Many times Americans are radicalized through the internet without direct contact with ISIS. They act with no forewarning to anyone and they do it where they are. ISIS encourages that."

"We're including the call, the caller's demands, and city officials' response, as well as the possibility that the caller is perpetuating a hoax on us." The managing editor glanced at his publisher for confirmation. She nodded. "Like the bomber said, if we choose not to do it, we'll be responsible for more deaths, or we can print the story and warn the public."

It would take a court order to gag the press, and many judges were leery of doing that—particularly in this case where public safety likely was at stake. The managing editor had a strong argument. "You can print the story, but these guys aren't stepping down. The city manager is correct. He can't bow to the demands of a psychotic individual or ask his bosses on the council to step down. There will be more bombings either way."

"Running the story could have lasting harmful effects." Vogel rubbed his face with both hands. "Stepping down is not an option. It sets a precedent."

"I do understand that." The managing editor

pushed wire-rimmed glasses up his narrow nose. His expression held pain, sorrow, and determination. The newsman didn't like being pressured into this course of action either. "But imagine if it gets out that you knew of this demand, coerced us into not publishing the story, and more people die. The court of public opinion will massacre all of you. You'd be out of your jobs anyway. It's a no-win situation."

It was also the biggest story of his career—of the newspaper's history. And the *Express-News* had an exclusive.

No one responded. He was right. Writing about this whack job would at least help citizens understand what had happened and why. They would empathize with city leaders and abhor the bomber.

"Don't worry, we'll give it context." The publisher patted Bella's hand. "I have absolute faith in my reporters. They will write the whole story. People will know what happened and why, and that law enforcement is doing everything it can to find the perpetrator before more people are killed."

Bella rubbed her eyes. She scooted her chair back and stood. Sig joined her.

"Where are you two going?" Wilson shook his head. "We need to—"

They turned and left the room.

"Where are they going?"

"To finish writing their stories." The managing editor glanced at his watch. "We have deadlines. They have work to do. I imagine you do too."

Avery reached across the table and snagged the recorder. "We need to keep this."

"Sig recorded it too, so we're good with that. The room is yours for as long as you need it."

"My people are drafting a release about this development as we speak, just so you know." Vogel threw the statement down like a gauntlet. "The rest of the media will eviscerate us if we don't."

"Do what you have to do. It's too late for the ten o'clock newscasts. We'll have it up on our website before midnight. Papers will be delivered between five and six in the morning. We still broke it first—not that we had anything to do with that." The managing editor paused at the door. "Find this psycho before someone else dies."

"That's the plan." Avery pushed back from his seat. That wouldn't happen in this room. "Let's huddle up at our place. The war room was already set up."

No question about it. They were at war.

TEN

Not even an hour of sweeping, straightening, and scrubbing with bleach wipes could erase the sense of violation. Jackie took a shower so hot her skin glowed red. She donned her favorite UT-Austin sweatshirt and baggy flannel pajama bottoms. She drank two cups of Sleepytime tea with lemon and honey. Still the images on endless loop in her head wouldn't cease and desist.

Usually she read when she couldn't sleep. Jackie ran her fingers down the spines of her favorite books on one of the dozens of floor-to-ceiling shelves that hugged two full walls in her living room. She'd constructed the built-in shelves herself, which allowed her to indulge in something she'd always wanted—a library with a sliding ladder. She wanted a good home for her friends. *Gone with the Wind, Little Women, The Hound of the Baskervilles, Anna Karenina, To Kill a Mockingbird, The Complete Works of William Shakespeare, I Know Why the Caged Bird Sings, Cry, the Beloved Country, Cien Años de Soledad*, and hundreds more.

Her eyes were gritty with exhaustion. As much as she wanted to escape, she couldn't possibly read now. Instead she crawled under her favorite fleece blanket on the couch.

Darcy kept her bare feet warm. Don kept watch from his post on the back of the couch, and Jane did what she did best, purr and snuggle against Jackie's chest. They were trying to help her relax, but sleep still refused to come.

Every time she closed her eyes, the faces of the dead and injured reappeared. Better to keep them open. She was still waiting for Bella to call her back. Their conversation had been cut short after Bella's cryptic statement that the bomber wasn't done yet. Surely she would call when she finished her story. It was ten—past deadline. Jackie had tried calling her. Voice mail.

Come on, Bella, come on.

The phone trilled, but it wasn't "I Will Survive." The first notes of Lady Gaga's "Shallow" sounded. Jackie sat straight up, dumping Jane and Darcy onto the hardwood floor. The stack of books that comprised Jackie's TBR pile on the end table tumbled in a series of thumps. Jane yowled and scurried away, tail straight up in the air. Darcy followed. Don hopped down from his perch in solidarity. "Sorry, my sweets."

She scooped up her phone from the coffee table. Cris's photo appeared. The one she took on the Fourth of July two years ago, the last time they'd spent together as a whole, complete family. Her brother was a carbon copy of their dad with his sculpted nose, high cheekbones, almost-black curly hair already beginning to thin, and blue eyes. "Cris, how are you?"

"Are you okay?" Panic made his voice shake. The only other time she'd heard him sound like that was when Daddy died. "Are you hurt?"

"I'm okay." Her big brother still cared about her. Some of the tension seeped from her knotted muscles. "Just shook up. And sad."

"I'm sorry."

Of course he would think he was somehow at fault for not keeping her safe. He had Mom's sweet spirit—until he found Daddy's body in the garage. His decision to move in with their grandparents had been intended as a slap in Mom's face, but Mom always thought the best of people, particularly her only son. She wanted what was best for him. They all did. "It's not your fault."

He didn't respond for a few seconds. When he did, his voice was hoarse. "I know. I'm sorry you had to go through this."

She had to tell him. She hated to be the one. *You're not a coward.* "Estrella's dead."

Silence. Finally he cleared his throat. His voice grew deeper. "I know. I'm sorry about that. I always liked her."

Liked? Liked!

Cris was a year older than Jackie. He'd had a crush on her best friend for years before the two had a fierce, tempestuous three-year relationship in high school. The flame finally burned out after a horrific screaming match the night of his senior prom. Estrella said Cris was too jealous and too controlling. Cris hadn't taken well her decision to walk away.

"Come on. You loved her once. Is that the best you can do? Don't you want to stop by and pay your respects to her parents?"

"It was a long time ago. I got over her. We both moved on."

"She still cared about you. She cared about what I care about."

"And I followed her career. I always knew she would get mixed up in politics. She loved to debate. She loved to argue."

"She was happy and she always wanted you to be happy."

"I am."

He was thirty-one, single, and living with his grandparents. Did that really make him happy? *Don't judge.* Her grandparents doted on their only grandson, especially now. They had every reason to want to spoil him. "I'm glad you're happy. Mom would love for you to come home now and then."

"I am home."

"You know what I mean. She could use some TLC from her son."

"Mom made Dad feel guilty. She shamed him.

We were his family. We should've stood behind him no matter what. All of us."

"He never offered an explanation or an apology when the media descended on us like a modern-day plague. How does it make you feel to know kickbacks paid for yours and my and Tosca's college education?"

"All that assumes he was guilty."

"He was guilty."

"How do you know? His case never went to trial."

Old, much-trodden territory. Jackie had spent many sleepless nights tossing and turning over this point. "If he was innocent, why did he kill himself? Why not go to trial and defend himself?"

"Aren't you going to ask how Nonna and Nonno are doing?"

He didn't have the answers either, so he deflected to another sore point between them. Jackie took a shaky breath. "I talk to Nonna all the time. So does Tosca."

"But you don't visit."

"Nonno was the one who had the falling out with Daddy. You've conveniently forgotten that."

"Nonno forgave Dad. He's letting me step into the business where Dad would have been if he hadn't decided to take a job as a bureaucrat."

Nonno had his fingers in many pies. Real estate. Fine jewelry. Import-export. Dabbling in the stock market. Whatever he did, he did well. "Which business is that?"

"What do you care?"

Stalemate. "Please call Mom. She's worried about you."

"I will. I promise."

"Good. She wants what's left of her family back together."

"I'd like that, too, but she doesn't seem to recognize she played a role in tearing us apart. She encouraged Dad to take a job with the city. If she hadn't, he'd still be here today."

Jackie hung on by the skin of her teeth to her determination not to fight. "That's one side of the story. You have to know that."

"I'll call her. I'm glad you're all right, Sissy. Love you." He hung up.

"Love you too."

Jackie clutched the phone to her chest. Her head pounded. Her father's decision to leave his fully restored classic 1972 Oldsmobile Cutlass running and close the garage door had changed them all. But especially Cris. He found Daddy slumped over in the front seat of the Cutlass. How could he do that to his son? What if it had been Mom who found his body? Much as she hated it, Jackie agreed with those who said he took the coward's way out and left them to pick up the pieces.

Cris had been a typical big brother who teased her mercilessly when she bought her first bra years ahead of her friends. He'd also spent hours helping her perfect her jump shot one miserable night after her attempt at the buzzer spun around the rim and spiraled out, ending the game with her team's defeat.

Now he lived across town, but it might as well be on another planet.

Jackie grabbed her pillow, closed her eyes, and curled up on the couch. Her heartbeat began to slow. Cris had a way of getting to her. She wasn't his little sister anymore, but she missed him. She could use a big brother right now.

The doorbell dinged. She jumped. "Get a grip, girl."

That's what Estrella would've said.

She glanced at her watch. Eleven fifteen. She shuffled to the window next to the front door and pulled the curtain back an inch to peek. Her heart squeezed in a painful hiccup.

She opened the door. "Nonno."

Looking as fit and trim as ever, her grandfather removed his fedora and bowed. "In the flesh. May I come in?"

"Yes, yes, of course."

He'd never been in her home before—not even when Daddy died. Jackie glanced around, trying to see it through his blue eyes, still as sharp and steely as ever at seventy-three. The entire structure would fit in the foyer of his grand Spanish Mission–style mansion. He stepped inside and wiped his gleaming Italian leather shoes on her WELCOME I'M MAT rug. His thin lips widened in a faint smile under his neatly trimmed silver-and-gray mustache. He got the joke.

"May I take your coat?"

He paused in unbuttoning the black lamb leather jacket. "I can't stay long. I only wanted to make sure with my own eyes that you're all right. Your grandmother sends her love. She would've sent a pot of her *zuppa Toscana* but she was out of sausage and I didn't have time to wait."

Nonna thought soup could fix everything. "Oh Nonno. Estrella died."

He held out his arms and she slipped into his hug. It was quick and efficient, just like everything else about him. "Let me look at you." He nudged her away. His stare encompassed everything about her, from her baggy pajamas to her bruised face to her broken heart and lacerated soul. "I'm thankful you didn't."

That was Nonno. Straight to the point. No room for sentimentality.

"Won't you sit down a minute? I can make a *caffè macchiato*."

"I had to give it up in the evenings. Sleeping when you're old is hard enough."

When a person was young as well. "I have *deca*. I'll make you a *caffè latte*."

"I'm not that old. I haven't entered my second

childhood yet." Nonno punctuated the statement with a snort. Just as Daddy would've. He sounded like Daddy with his husky voice and careful diction. Or Daddy had sounded like his father. Neither would drink warm milk with a dash of decaffeinated coffee. "Stop trying to play hostess. I simply wanted to see for myself that you are fine."

She had no choice but to feign bravery. The Santoro family expected it. Stiff upper lip and all that bull. Even as a little girl she'd known that. A Santoro didn't blink. As a youngster she'd dispatched more than one bully with a kick in the behind or a black eye. She ended up in the principal's office, but her father never punished her. Which led to impassioned yelling behind closed doors. Her mother didn't agree with the Santoro code. "I'm fine."

Nonno flipped his fedora onto his silver curls with the fluid motion he always used. "Then I'll be off. Make the warm milk for you. Then go to bed. Tomorrow is another day."

The speech had the flavor of Scarlett O'Hara to it. Jackie had always imagined Nonno as her grandmother's Rhett Butler. In another age he might have been a swashbuckling pirate or a bootlegger. "Thank you for coming. It means a lot to me."

"Don't get maudlin on me, child." He patted her cheek. "You have no father to protect you, and your mother . . . Well, enough said."

"I'm a full-grown woman. I don't need a man or my mother." Almost. They'd almost made it through a visit without this topic arising. Nonno never hid what he thought of his son's choice of wives. A woman with no ambition who urged her husband to strike out on his own. Mom had made the terrible mistake of valuing happiness over family loyalty. "It would mean a lot to Mom if you and Nonna would come to the house. Or invite her out. And Cris too."

Nonno opened the door without acknowledging Jackie's words. No one would've been good enough, but a woman who supported his son's decision to leave the family business had done the unforgivable. "Nonno."

"Cris is his own man. What he does is up to him. I work hard to forgive your mother for her attitude toward us when your father . . . did what he did." His voice softened. "Parents should go first. A man should not have to bury his son. Give your nonno a kiss."

She dutifully pecked his cool cheek. "Thank you for coming."

"No matter what you may think, I love my grandchildren." His tone turned fierce. "Even when they continue to disappoint me." He strode through the doorway.

Disappoint him? By being her own person?

"Nonno."

"Go to bed, child." He stopped at his elegant silver Mercedes and lifted his hand in a farewell wave. "Make good choices in your life."

"What choices?" She pushed through the door and tap-danced down the cold cement steps in her bare feet. "Nonno, what choices?"

He blew her a kiss and drove away.

ELEVEN

The silence reverberated in Jackie's ears. She leaned against the door and took a cleansing breath. One of the drawbacks of living alone was that she had no one with whom she could commiserate after such an earth-shattering event as a visit to her home—which now looked cramped and shabby in her eyes—by her grandfather. Maybe she should have the *caffè latte.* Nonno made her feel like that little girl.

Maybe all grandparents were like that. Mom's parents lived in Minnesota and rarely visited before Grandpa's death of a heart attack at sixty and Grandma's two years later from an embolism.

The doorbell rang. Maybe Nonno came back. She whirled and opened the door. "Nonno?"

"Your grandfather was here? I thought I saw hell freeze over on the way here." Bella shoved past her into the foyer. She held up a reusable grocery bag. "I knew you'd still be up. Ben and Jerry's. You have your choice of Chunky Monkey, Chocolate Chip Cookie Dough, Cherry Garcia, and Chocolate Therapy."

"All of the above. I'll get the spoons."

Jackie led the way to her newly DIY renovated galley kitchen. She didn't need a big kitchen or a chef to prepare her meals. So why did it seem small now? Bella followed and settled at one of the bar stools at the granite-topped peninsula. She set out the pints in a row. Jackie joined her with a pile of four spoons for each of them. She lit a s'mores-scented candle and inhaled. The pain in her chest eased.

Jackie clinked spoons with Bella. "Here's to Estrella."

Cherry Garcia had been Estrella's favorite. They started there.

"How many gallons of ice cream do you think we've eaten together over the years?" Jackie closed her eyes and savored the cold, creamy sweetness. "How many study nights, how many boyfriend-breakup nights, how many dreams-about-our-future nights?"

"Hundreds? Thousands?" Bella moved on to Chocolate Therapy. She smacked her lips, but her eyes shone with tears. "Not enough. I always thought there would be more."

Jackie took another bite of Cherry Garcia. Estrella hadn't even known who Jerry Garcia was. Jackie had to explain the name to her. Giggling and teasing, Jackie had asked Alexa to play Grateful Dead's "I Will Get By" while they ate their first pint of the luscious ice cream filled with fudge chunks and cherries. Tonight the ice cream did nothing to ease the ache in her throat. "I know you're exhausted, but I have to know what the bomber said. What are the cops doing about it?"

"Why was your grandfather here?"

"I'm still processing why. The bombing is much more important right now."

"It's bad. He's—"

The doorbell dinged again. They both jumped. "Who shows up at your house at almost midnight?" Bella rolled her eyes. "Besides Estrella and me." Her face crumpled. "I mean me."

"It's okay. It'll take some getting used to." Jackie squeezed her hand and slid from the stool. "Somebody who knows I never sleep."

Tony stood on her porch. He'd changed into faded jeans and a wrinkled Baylor sweatshirt. She'd never seen him in anything but *GQ* clothes. He ran his hand through his tousled brown hair. "I was driving around, trying to think, and I ended up on your street. I saw Bella's car and I thought . . ."

His normally clipped enunciation was slurred. His breath smelled of whiskey.

Jackie grabbed his hand and tugged him inside. "Have you been drinking?"

"The mayor cracked open a bottle of Crown Royal. We hoisted a drink in Diego's memory. It was his favorite."

Tony probably weighed 150 pounds sopping wet. He was too much of a health fanatic to drink, unless under extreme duress, it seemed. "You thought it would be smart to drive home?"

"I couldn't think at all."

"Come on. We're eating ice cream in Estrella's honor."

She offered him a seat at the peninsula and gave him his own spoons. Tears trickled down his face. "It's like a faucet I can't turn off." He used a napkin to wipe his runny nose. "It's embarrassing."

"That you cared so much for the love of your life that you can't stop crying? No way." Jackie plopped a box of tissues next to the pints. "There, in easy reach for all of us."

He blew his nose hard. "The mayor insisted we all go home to sleep for a few hours. We're to be back at eight for another news conference."

"So you know then." Bella commandeered the Chunky Monkey and dug a fresh spoon into it. "Do you think we're making the right decision to publish this maniac's demands? Is the city doing the right thing in refusing to bow to those demands?"

"Whoa, what demands?" Jackie laid down her spoon. "Start at the beginning."

Bella went first, recounting the phone call and the subsequent meeting with law enforcement. With the proviso that anything said over Cherry Garcia was off the record, Tony filled them in on City Hall's response.

"So Laura Peterson, Vogel, and Sandoval were the targets, if we accept that the caller was legit." Jackie took their dirty spoons to the sink.

Her own stomach protested so much sugar and so little nutritious fuel. "We gave the bombers exactly what they wanted. They'll be on the national stage with such a direct hit."

"The national media are all over this." Bella leaned on her elbows, her chin on her palms. Her eyelids drooped. "They'll all be here for the news conference tomorrow. I would agree with you if I thought the caller *was* legit, but I couldn't find any mention of USAP in our archives. I think it's an attempt to camouflage the real motive. I could be wrong, though. My head is about to explode and this ice cream is the only thing I've eaten today."

"Which brings them back to their theory that I was somehow involved." Jackie snorted. "My father's been gone for two years. Why would I wait this long? Why would I keep working for the city?"

"I'm sure they're asking themselves those same questions."

Tony tried to pat her hand and missed. Jackie moved closer in case he fell from the stool. He wiggled and righted himself. "Your dad was a good guy. I always liked him, but he should've stuck around. He shouldn't have done that to you."

The dad who came to all her basketball games, all of Tosca's dance recitals, and all Cris's baseball games couldn't have wanted this.

Surely he had thought about the consequences of suicide for them. He chose to finance her college education with ill-gotten gains. According to the DA, he accepted kickbacks from developers to shortcut the permit process. He looked the other way when they violated city ordinances.

Municipal Integrity had video of him in a bar having a drink with one of the biggest residential developers in town. Dad claimed they ran into each other purely by accident. Dad didn't go to bars. He didn't drink.

Or had he?

She hadn't really known him.

"Politicians and government officials make enemies. Many people think they have reasons to want revenge." Bella's gaze dropped to the counter. She plucked a tissue from the box and dabbed at a drop of melted ice cream. "If they think you have motive, they'll also take a hard look at Tosca and Cris, your mother, and even your grandparents."

"That's crazy." A spurt of anger fueled Jackie's derision. "You have to be kidding me. Tosca is a pacifist. She doesn't even eat meat. My mother prays for forgiveness every day. My grandparents are in their seventies."

"You said yourself Cris refuses to concede your father was guilty of the alleged offenses. Your grandparents lost their only son before they could be reconciled to him." Bella's gaze begged

134

forgiveness. "I'm just saying that's how they'll see it."

"It doesn't have to be your family." Tony rubbed his eyes, which only made them redder. "What about Marcus Camacho? He lost to Diego in the District 1 race not once but twice. The second time by only a handful of votes. He hated everything Diego stood for, but especially his stance on sanctuary-city status and LGBTQ rights."

"It's worth checking out. Tomorrow I have to cancel my cards and apply for new ones. I need to go to the bank to get some cash until I have a debit card to use. I have to go to work. I still have a ton of final prep to do for the Catrina Ball." Life would go on, wouldn't it? Hard as it was to imagine. The library foundation's biggest fund-raiser of the year had to happen or many of Jackie's educational activities for patrons would not.

"I'll try to find time to do my own research on USAP, Meher Faheem, and the victims. You see what you can find out about Camacho's whereabouts yesterday, Bella. See what you can find out about threats Vogel and Sandoval have received in recent months."

Bella patted her split lip with a napkin. She had chocolate syrup on her bruised cheek. "Sig and I already did that. We got zilch."

"Does he know where you are?"

"He called me three times on his way to his apartment." Bella smiled for the first time all day. "He's so sweet. He's a keeper."

The image of Wick's kind face as he handed Jackie a blanket and a cup of steaming coffee waltzed through her mind, the way he cupped her hands, the way his fingers touched her hair. "You are blessed."

"I pray every night that you'll meet your Sig soon." Bella wiped her eyes with the napkin. "You will. I know you will."

Maybe she had and just didn't know it. Maybe she'd blown her chance by being too bossy, too opinionated, too tall, too wrapped up in her job. Who knew? "I still have to do what I can to come up with something that helps the investigation."

"Moving the backpack doesn't make you responsible for the dead and injured, Jack. You have to believe me."

"She's right." Tony slurred the words. "You couldn't have known."

"Why didn't I recognize the possibility? Why didn't it occur to me that this could be a threat? I don't understand how I could be so clueless. I'm not normally stupid, am I?"

Scowling, Bella pointed her spoon at Jackie. "Don't do this to yourself. You live in an Atticus Finch world. You don't give a rat's behind about politics. You don't even watch the news. When you're planning an event, you have blinders on.

136

You work the details to death. The backpack wasn't germane to your plan, so you discarded it. That's you."

"We have a security plan at the library. We've done active shooter drills. If you can flee, you flee. If you can't, you hide. If you can't hide, you fight. Why didn't any of what we'd learned surface when I saw the backpack?"

"I know you. During those drills, you made sure everyone fled. Then you ran over to Madison Square Park, settled onto a bench, and read a book until they said you could come back. Or you wrote in your journal. Or you made a to-do list for your next program. You're the world's greatest multitasker. But you also believe in the innate goodness of people."

Bella knew Jackie all too well. But her explanation didn't make her failure to act okay. "If you'd found that backpack, you would've immediately called 911 and rushed it outside. Admit it."

"Journalists' cynicism is second only to that of people in law enforcement." Bella's smile was long gone, replaced by a longing for innocence. "It's one of the reasons I moved from straight news to feature writing, so I could get away from some of the ugliness and focus on good people doing good things. Sig couldn't understand it. He lives for diving into the sewer and coming up smelling like Woodward or Bernstein. He dreams of winning a Pulitzer for enterprise reporting. I'd rather win for literature."

"Someday you will. I've read your short stories. You're a Toni Morrison in the making." Jackie loved writing book reviews, but she had no interest in writing a novel. "I'll have the champagne chilled and ready."

"You're the best bestie." Bella's smile reappeared. "Even if you're a liar."

"I better go." Tony slid from his stool, teetered, and grabbed the peninsula. "Gotta be up early in the morning."

"You're not going anywhere. The last thing you need right now is to be driving." Jackie tucked her arm under his elbow. "*Mi casa es tu casa*."

"I don't want to put you out . . ." His voice trailed off.

It took all of five minutes to escort him to the guest bedroom, remove his shoes, get him into bed, and cover him with a fleece-lined comforter. He was snoring by the time Jackie cracked the door so her cat friends could keep an eye on him and returned to the kitchen.

Bella had stowed the ice cream. She swished a washcloth across the countertops.

Jackie stuck the dirty spoons in the dishwasher. "Sleepover?"

"I thought you'd never ask."

Jackie brought out blankets, pillows, and her

sleeping bag. After some argument, Bella agreed to take the couch. Jackie snuggled with Jane in her sleeping bag next to the couch. Don joined Bella. Her light breathing was comforting in the dark.

"Do you think you can sleep?" Bella was always coming up with new "cures" for Jackie's insomnia. "Do you want me to sing you a lullaby?"

They both giggled the hysterical hiccups of two traumatized friends.

Jackie closed her eyes and tried to summon sleep.

"Detective Wick asked me about you after the news conference this afternoon."

Jackie opened her eyes. "I'm not surprised. He was unhappy I told you about the backpack. He wanted to see if my story stayed consistent."

"Sure, but he also asked me if you were married, if you had a significant other, and if you lived alone. I asked him how that was relevant, and he tried to pass it off as building a profile, that you might be an introvert with antisocial tendencies. A cat lady. I laughed my head off. I told him he was full of baloney."

Knowing Bella, *baloney* had not been the word used.

Jackie wiggled around in her sleeping bag and stuck her hands under her cheek. "Why else would he ask?"

"You made an impression, of course, you dope."

Neither of them spoke for a while. Jackie stared into the darkness. The purring of three cats serenaded them. "I asked Lee about him."

"Aha." Sleep softened Bella's voice. "Why would you do that?"

Why indeed?

"It's definitely not good looks. Or the way he dresses. It must be his personality. Nope. Spill. What did Lee say?"

Detective Wick had his moments. And he wasn't bad looking. Just not terminally handsome. His face had character. His body looked lived in. Jackie ran through the pertinent details.

"Divorced." Bella ruminated on the word aloud. "He's probably in his late thirties, wouldn't you say?"

"Go to sleep."

"To be continued."

A few minutes later classy Bella began to snore. Jackie hugged her pillow and closed her eyes and waited for daylight. Getting through another day would be her way of honoring Estrella. She would stop to check on Mateo and Mercedes, then head to the library. She wouldn't let the bombing stop her from doing her job. Estrella would expect that. The Catrina Ball would go on. She could also delve into USAP and the lives of all five victims. Leave no stone unturned.

Explore every possibility. Make no assumptions without all the facts. Librarians knew how to do research.

They also knew how to avoid thinking about the pull of a man who, on the surface, was all wrong for her. She'd always imagined herself with a man who liked the same things she did—riding bikes on the Greenway trails, community theater, old black-and-white movies, and traveling. She couldn't see Wick on a mountain bike or at a community play at The Public Theater in San Pedro Springs Park.

Then again, her last boyfriend had been all those things, and look how that turned out.

Jackie wiggled onto her back and stared into the dark above her. A Trinity University librarian, he loved to talk books, theater, movies, politics, and religion. He loved to talk, period. He was cute in a Jude Law way, wanted kids, recycled, and even made compost for a vegetable garden in his tiny backyard. And he liked cats. He'd been known to shed a tear over a good book.

He was perfect.

Until he stopped returning calls and ghosted her on social media. Right after Daddy was fired.

TWELVE

The faces of the dead stared at Avery.

He straightened the photo of Estrella Diaz hanging on the murder board next to Laura Peterson, the two female victims. Then Bill Little, Milton Schaeffer, and Diego Sandoval. All except Diaz were public figures. The bomber had hit the mother lode. The list of 120 injured included the chief's wife, but no other names of note. Hoaxer Robert Mitchell had escaped completely unscathed. So had the city manager and his wife. The mayor and his wife. None of this held significance, because a bomb couldn't discriminate.

Why not go after a specific target? Why kill innocent people? These questions would keep Avery up for many nights to come.

He slid into a chair next to Interim Chief Ruiz and prepared to keep his mouth shut. He was fortunate to be in the room thanks to his interview of Jackie Santoro and the powwow with the newspaper folks.

The ATF's special agent Michael Chavez went first. "We're still reconstructing the scene, but we've identified the seat of the blast." He hung a photo on the second board. "Just below the stage on the left." Another photo went up. A black handle attached to a patch of black nylon material. "We've also recovered part of an electronic circuit board, a pressure cooker lid, and a piece of the backpack that likely contained the bomb. It matches Ms. Santoro's description."

"We've determined the explosive device consisted of a simple pressure cooker bomb that contained metal, nails, ball bearings, and black powder likely from fireworks." ATF Explosives Enforcement Officer Gene McNamara jumped in. "Our guys ran it through BATS—the Bomb Arson Tracking System. It's a common signature. The most notable incident, of course, being the Boston Marathon in 2013 when brothers Tamerlan Tsarnaev and Dzhokhar Tsarnaev detonated two pressure cookers hidden in backpacks twelve seconds apart just as the first wave of runners hit the finish line. They claimed they used al-Qaeda bomb designs found online. There's been some discussion that those two kids couldn't design a bomb that sophisticated with remote detonation. It had to have been someone more knowledgeable, but the investigation never turned up a third party."

"In that case, we were fortunate to have street cameras that allowed us to capture the faces of the brothers quickly," Chavez pointed out. "We saw them place the backpacks. In this instance we're going through the footage of people parking their cars in the garage and entering the Tobin, but so far nothing. Ms. Santoro's story is that she moved the backpack from the first row and gave it to the catering manager, a Muslim American of Saudi descent named Meher Faheem, who left the scene allegedly after Ms. Santoro spoke to her about the backpack. She claims Ms. Faheem said she gave the backpack to a security guard. Ms. Santoro may be trying to cast blame in another direction, however."

If that were the case, it was a good pivot on Jackie's part. Fifteen of the nineteen 9/11 hijackers were Saudi Arabians sent by al-Qaeda on suicide missions to destroy the Twin Towers, the Pentagon, and the White House.

"Let's finish the what and come back to the who. How was this bomb detonated?" Chief Ruiz directed the question to the SAPD bomb squad commander. "Do we know?"

"Again the bomber took a page from the Tsarnaev brothers' notebook." The commander straightened the papers on the table in front of him. "The perpetrator used a remote control from a toy car. He chose to let the debate occur and wait until people were preparing to leave the hall before detonating."

"So now we know how. The question becomes why." Ruiz twisted his pen in his hands. If it were the bomber, he'd be strangled to death. "What do we know about USAP?"

"Nothing. The organization doesn't exist. If it

did we'd have intelligence on it. There's nothing in BATS." ATF Special Agent McNamara joined his colleagues in holding court in front of their buddies in the FBI and Homeland. "Our guys at the Bomb Data Center and the folks at SWTFC haven't heard any chatter either. It's dead silence. Our guess is somebody is planting false clues to throw us off track."

"Which brings us back to Santoro and Faheem. We need to find Faheem and get her side of the story." Chavez tapped his pen on the table in an annoying *rat-a-tat-tat*. "A preliminary background check shows Faheem is American born, grew up in San Antonio, and has never been out of the country. She's married to another American of Saudi descent who is a well-respected neurosurgeon specializing in spine trauma. Meher Faheem graduated from the Pearl School of Culinary Arts. No known ties to fanatical organizations. The one red flag in her dossier is a brother who left the U.S. to live in Saudi Arabia ten years ago. He's seeking Saudi citizenship. The parents have been to visit him several times. We'll need warrants to access her phone and computer. Right now we don't have enough cause to get them."

"Maybe the two of them were in it together and Santoro threw Faheem under the bus. If Faheem isn't involved, why did she leave the scene without talking to anyone? Until we know the answer to that question, she's high on the person-of-interest list." Ruiz's pen tapped in an equally annoying duplicate rhythm. "Wick, fill us in on what you know about the victims, their enemies, any skeletons in their closets. We need to dig our way out of the rabbit hole and eliminate some of these potential red herrings."

Startled at being allowed to contribute, Avery schooled his expression, stood, and went to the board. The FBI had been working around the clock investigating the possibilities. Ruiz's desire to exert control over the investigation would not win him friends. "Estrella Diaz, thirty, squeaky clean. Loved by all. Engaged to be married to Tony Guerra, Councilman Sandoval's constituent services director. Guerra is expected to be appointed to fill Sandoval's unexpired term and likely will run for the seat when elections roll around. Diaz had a degree in public administration. She was interested in local politics and likely to run for office herself at some point. Or manage future hubby's campaigns. Churchgoer, active in charities, liked to dance.

"Which brings us to Councilman Sandoval. Anybody who runs for public office has enemies. Sandoval won reelection by less than a thousand votes. His opponent asked for and received a recount. Marcus Camacho is an ultraconservative who hammered Sandoval for supporting San Antonio's sanctuary-city status and funding an assistance center for new migrants. Sandoval voted in favor of paid sick leave for workers in small businesses. Camacho favored the businesses who opposed the policy and have taken the city to court over it."

"Lots to work with there." Petra broke in. "We're doing a deep dive on Camacho. If he is so conservative, he may have ties to anticlimate-change organizations like the one our caller claims is responsible for the bombings. We're also delving into Guerra's background. We appreciate the transcript of your interview. We're happy to do those additional interviews with you, Detective Wick."

The formality spoke to the professional nature of the meeting. Off the books, she called him Wicked, same as Scotty did. Avery inclined his head in agreement. "We appreciate your help. Now about Laura Peterson—"

"That's us." Petra interrupted a second time. "We keep track of both sides of the fence. Peterson has a plethora of enemies. She was a climate-change expert, journalist, and columnist with a *New York Times* number-one bestseller. She wrote about global climate justice and made a case for a new Green Deal. All the conservative think tanks blast her for what they call fake science. She's received hundreds of death threats since publishing her book. Most of them are harmless crazies. We're digging through the list, verifying the whereabouts of the more plausible suspects."

"What about the think tank that employs hoaxer Robert Mitchell?"

Petra touched her iPad screen and stared at it briefly. As if she didn't have every fact carefully filed in her brain. The woman was a walking crime encyclopedia. "Mitchell was a commentator for one of the networks. He wrote several books critical of climate change science and the alleged risks of greenhouse emissions. At one time he was executive director of climate control for a coal company. Forty percent of his funding now comes from the oil and coal industry. Most recently his speaking tour was sponsored by an antiscience think tank. We're collating everything we have on them. They reek of respectability. A bombing would not be their style. Especially if it might kill one of their own."

"They might be willing to sacrifice one of their own in order to take out a well-spoken, well-liked opponent and a bunch of city officials who are working on a green city plan that will require companies to build clean energy buildings." Out of habit, Avery played devil's advocate. "And the library foundation was willing to pay her way from New York to San Antonio to speak and sign her book."

"Anything's possible, of course, but it's not their style." Petra's tone was gentle. She steepled her fingers and gave Avery an apologetic look. "They don't get their hands dirty. They use social media as their weapon of choice. They do letter-writing campaigns. They send out people like Robert Mitchell to speak all over the country. They have the ear of some high-ranking politicians. They would see this as beneath them."

"Understood." Avery moved on. "San Antonio Library Foundation board chairman Milton Schaeffer, age sixty-nine. Not even a parking ticket in the last thirty years. Retired banker. Member of the Rotary Club. Sunday school teacher at Northwest Hills UMC. Married to the same woman for forty-six years. Three children, nine grandchildren. One of the best fund-raisers in town, which is why the public library system was so pleased to snatch him up for their 501(c)(3). The library has a substantial city budget, but all programming is paid for through donations raised by Friends of the Library and/or the foundation."

Petra didn't look fazed. "Nobody gets out of this life without skeletons. We'll keep digging."

"Finally, Chief of Police Bill Little." Avery eyed Ruiz. The interim chief nodded. Avery plunged ahead. "He was generally well liked by the rank and file. Not so much by the Texas attorney general and the Feds."

Papers rustled. Chairs squeaked.

"He refused to turn his people into immigration officers who had to check immigration status when dealing with people who 'appeared' to be or 'might' be of another nationality. He supported our status as a sanctuary city. Chief Little was less popular when our contract was being negotiated by SAPOA—San Antonio Police Officers Association. He ran interference for the assistant city manager, Jason Vogel, who is now our city manager, in those negotiations. At issue was free health insurance benefits for every officer and his or her immediate family—"

"Nice."

"It's been a hallmark of our contract for many years." Avery plowed forward. "The city manager called it a legacy cost that would eventually drive the city into bankruptcy, claiming that's what happened to Detroit. Chief Little supported the city manager. He also took some heat for releasing a dozen illegal immigrants in a human-smuggling case to Catholic Charities instead of HSI. Some people thought the victims should've been treated as criminals because they entered the country illegally. Chief Little followed protocol for human-smuggling cases. HSI had the option of taking them into custody throughout the day and chose not to."

HSI Special Agent Wilson scratched his scalp with his pen. With his floppy chocolate-brown hair, he looked like a Labrador with fleas. He leaned back in his chair. "I'm aware of this incident. It's always possible that this was a hate crime and Little was the target."

Anything was possible.

"That's a quick synopsis for each victim."

"So let's talk about the others involved, either survivors or potential perpetrators." Petra peeled the paper from her water bottle, her forehead wrinkled in a frown. "The backpack was on the front row. Santoro claims to have handed it off to a Muslim American who suddenly can't be found. No indications either woman is involved in terrorism, domestic or international. Not yet. As requested, HSI and FBI folks are searching Faheem's house now. We've checked the homes of all her relatives locally. Nothing. Her absence doesn't bode well for her."

"What about Santoro?"

"We searched her house. Which took all of ten minutes. It's less than twelve hundred square feet." Petra typed something on her laptop in rapid-fire keystrokes. "Her journal had some fairly incendiary passages regarding the city manager and other city officials she blames for her father's suicide. That gives her motive. On the other hand, if she planted the backpack to exact revenge, why would she move it at the last moment? The city manager and his wife came in late. Maybe he was the intended target and the universe conspired to save him. Your girl helped by moving the backpack."

Jackie wasn't Avery's girl. Not in this universe. "Blowing off steam in a diary she never expected anyone to read isn't really evidence. There's no indication whatsoever that she acted on those feelings. Did you find bomb-making materials in her home?"

"No." Petra shrugged. "She did lawyer up immediately when you guys took her in. Why would she do that? What's your take on her, Detective Wick?"

Avery bit his lip. *My take? The first time I saw her she was limping, barefoot, dirty, wounded, and trying not to cry. Still, she knocked my socks off. I haven't been able to stop thinking about her since.*

He squeezed the dry erase marker until his fingers hurt. "She's thirty, an adult collections coordinator at the downtown library with a master's in library science from UT–Austin. Never been married. Her mother teaches second grade at San Antonio Christian School. Her father, as I mentioned previously, had just been indicted for accepting bribes as director of developmental services for the city of San Antonio when he killed himself. Ms. Santoro has one brother, who works for the Santoro family business empire, and one sister, a landscape architect who works for a local firm and dates the lawyer representing

Ms. Santoro, Lee Drucker. Out of an abundance of caution, I interviewed the sister, Tosca, as well. Nothing obvious there. She was at a site meeting with several coworkers on a City of San Antonio park project when the bombing occurred."

Avery dropped the dry erase marker on the board's rack and moved to pick up his water bottle. "Interviews with other family members, including the brother and grandfather are pending."

"Ms. Santoro's journal paints in vivid color what it was like when her father was charged." Petra cast the first stone. "It was ugly when the story broke. Reporters camped out at the library where she works and her family's home. It was all over the front page of the newspaper and on the ten o'clock newscasts. They got the video of him being interviewed by Municipal Integrity, which routinely releases the videos to the media in order to make an example of city employees who break the rules and get fired. They wrote about his suicide even though media don't typically cover suicides. They intruded on his funeral. The family has to have some hard feelings."

"Jackie Santoro continued to work for the city. I keep coming back to why would she plant a bomb that had a high probability of killing her closest friends." Wilson consulted his laptop. "Bella Glover was slightly injured. So was Guerra. Estrella Diaz was killed."

"I interviewed her less than two hours after the

bombing. She was devastated over Diaz's death." Avery took a breath. *Easy.* Objectivity served as a detective's most important tool. Despite her purported devastation, she had asked him several questions about the investigation. She gathered information from him instead of the other way around. "She volunteered the information about the backpack. Why would she do that?"

"Maybe there was something going on between her and Guerra." Ruiz's tone was matter-of-fact. "Maybe it was the perfect opportunity to take out Diaz, the city manager who fired her dad, and Councilman Sandoval, which gave Guerra the perfect opportunity to step in and take his boss's job. An interim councilman has a much better chance of being elected to a full term in the next election."

Ruiz was good at worst-case scenarios.

"Pure conjecture." Thankfully Petra was equally good at shutting them down. "We don't even have circumstantial evidence to support your theory."

"Agreed. Moving on." Avery added Vogel's name to the list. The smell of the marker was giving him a headache.

"Jason Vogel, forty, took over the top spot two years ago. He's a hometown boy with a master's in public administration from Trinity University. Ten years as deputy city manager with oversight of police and fire. Married to an accountant. They have two kids. They're Catholic and attend mass regularly. He's a registered firearm owner who likes to practice at the shooting range. He's the city manager. He has plenty of enemies. A bombing might be the best way to take him out. He has a driver who is a member of SAPD's Executive Protection Detail. On the street a shooter would have to get through his bodyguard to get to him."

"We've got a lot of work to do." Ruiz cranked his head side to side. He glanced at his watch, stood, and tossed his coffee cup into the trash can. "But first, get some sleep. It's past 1:00 a.m. Go home, hit the sack for a few hours, shower, change clothes, whatever you need to do. Kiss your loved ones. It'll be a while before you see them again. We'll reconvene at 8:00 a.m."

Prove it or disprove it. Avery leaned toward the latter, but the investigator in him insisted he go after the truth. Having scruples sucked.

THIRTEEN

Shots fired. Every time the wind blew, it knocked down acorns from the live oaks in Avery's backyard. When they hit the tin roof of the dilapidated corner lot house he'd bought after the divorce, they sounded like shots fired. Usually it struck him as funny in a morbid cop-humor sort of way. Not tonight.

He rolled over and stared into the darkness above him. Ace whined from his bed on the floor next to Avery's. Deuce continued to snore. Unlike his buddy of mixed origins, nothing bothered the arthritic elder statesman German shepherd. Unless someone rang the doorbell. Then he went full throttle until Avery verified to the dog's satisfaction that the guest was welcome. Knowing he only had a few hours to sleep made it that much more difficult to succumb to exhaustion. His brain refused to cooperate with his body.

"This is nuts." He threw off the comforter and padded barefoot to the kitchen, where he dumped out the day-old grounds in the trash can and started a fresh pot of coffee. He'd never lost the habit of making a big pot, even though he was the only one drinking it. Ace joined him, but his worried expression suggested he knew his dad was off his rocker. "Don't look at me like that. I'm an adult. If I want to drink coffee in the middle of the night, I will."

Ace subsided on the ratty rug in front of the kitchen sink. He thought it was a great place to nap. It also meant Avery had to stay on his toes or he'd step on the dog's tail.

The aroma of freshly brewed coffee filled the air, stifling the scent of Chinese takeout, a full trash can, dust, and loneliness. Avery tossed Ace a doggie treat and helped himself to a mini chocolate-covered donut. Breakfast of champions—if a person ate breakfast at two in the morning. He grabbed the guitar lying on the table and strummed three chords—the only ones he knew. His plan to teach himself to play progressed slowly.

It gave him something to do in the middle of the night when he couldn't go out and shoot layups in the driveway or perfect his jump shot and free throw. His basketball-sized hands should make playing a guitar easier. So far, it hadn't. His arsenal of insomnia activities had grown over the years. Eventually he'd graduate to jigsaw puzzles and crosswords like his dad.

Pounding on the front door brought Avery straight out of his chair. He dumped the guitar on the table and shot into the bedroom where he'd left his service weapon on the stand next to his bed. Deuce lumbered to his feet, wide awake, his bark deep, hoarse, and loud enough to scare the bejeebers out of an unwanted visitor.

"Who is it?"

"It's me, dude, open up."

Deuce's barking reached a fevered pitch. "Good job, buddy, good job, but it's friend not foe." Avery patted the dog's noble head. Deuce brought it down a notch. "Atta boy. It's Theo. You know Theo."

Both dogs knew Theo Beretta well. He'd spent more than a few nights bunking in Avery's spare bedroom. They were two sorry sons of guns. Avery unlocked the door. "What's up, dude?"

A duffel bag in one hand, Theo ducked his head and sighed. "The usual. Katie kicked me out. Again."

"You'd been drinking?"

"No more than usual."

Avery pushed the door wider. "Get in here. You're letting a cold draft in."

Theo edged inside and dropped his bag on the oak floor. Ace launched himself at the visitor and licked his caiman belly cowboy boots. The guy had a weakness for expensive footwear. He sighed some more, knelt, and gave the dog a thorough petting.

"So what's the story this time?"

"No story. Katie gets tired of me pacing the floor ranting and raving as she calls it." Theo rose and followed Avery into the kitchen. "I don't understand how she can be so calm when the animal who killed our kid is still out there walking around free while Caleb has been six feet under for more than a year."

"Her way of coping is different from yours." Avery admired Katie Beretta. A pediatric nurse, she filled her life with her patients in a hospital pediatric intensive-care unit after a drive-by shooter gunned down her ten-year-old son and only child during a Little League baseball game. Unlike her husband, who filled his with booze and attempts to solve the crime himself over the objections of SAPD and his wife. "Obviously her coping mechanisms work better."

"I just want justice for my boy. It's not too much to ask. No one is doing anything. It's a cold case through and through. Nobody will talk to me. The detective on the case won't even return my calls. I wish it was you. At least then I'd know you really tried."

Avery had been thankful he hadn't caught the case. He didn't want to look into the eyes of a man he'd known since high school and see disappointment at Avery's inability to give him the satisfaction of seeing his son's murderer go to prison. To give him closure. "They're trying. Every homicide detective in our unit tries. Every single one. We live to catch the bad guys and put them away. Don't think otherwise."

"I didn't mean to offend." Theo slumped into

a chair at the kitchen table and stretched out his long legs. He ran his hands through thick, curly black hair allowed to grow too long. He needed a shave. His blue eyes were bloodshot. Avery set a cup of coffee in front of him. "I have a different perspective than you do. Caleb was my kid. He was a murder victim. Even after a year I wake up in the morning and for a second I don't remember he's gone. Then it hits me and the rage starts building all over again."

"I can only imagine."

"I hope you never have to find out for real."

Avery and Chandra never could agree on the right time to have children. He wanted them sooner, she said later. Maybe that was for the best, given that their marriage had imploded. Now time was his enemy. "Me too."

"Sometimes it seems like I'm the only one who cares that the gangbanger thug who killed my only child is still out there. The chief doesn't care. The city doesn't care. The city council doesn't care. That was a municipal park. They didn't allow park police to make sure it was safe for kids to play baseball. *Baseball.* Americans' favorite pastime and we can't even keep our parks safe enough so our kids can play ball in them. What kind of city is this? What kind of world?"

Avery had heard Theo's lament many, many times. Yet each time he allowed his friend to vent. The man had desperately tried to save his own son's life on that warm May day. Caleb had bled to death before the first responders arrived. Theo deserved to be heard. "I'm sorry, man."

"Caleb deserved better."

"You're right. Every kid deserves better."

"I keep thinking I could've done more. If I were better trained—"

"Don't do that to yourself. Park police are well trained. You had no warning. You did your best. An SAPD officer couldn't have done more."

Theo hadn't made the cut for the PD academy, despite his military record as a first-class sniper. Competition for those spots was fierce and Theo didn't have a college degree. He wasn't good at test taking. So he applied for the park police academy and got in. Park police received less training, earned less, received fewer benefits, and the requirements were less stringent. They also had no right to collective bargaining. A constant source of frustration and friction for the one hundred-plus officers responsible for patrolling more than two hundred fifty parks, community centers, swimming pools, and recreational ame-nities across the sprawling city.

They sat in silence for several seconds. Theo swiped at his five o'clock shadow with a shaky hand. "Sorry. Didn't mean to get mushy on you."

"Don't apologize. I don't know how you manage to stay sane."

"I'm not sure I am."

"Any luck on the job front?"

The Park Police Division commander had cut Theo as much slack as possible, but a year of chronic absenteeism, on-the-job outbursts, and obvious signs he'd arrived for his night shift on the River Walk inebriated had earned him a forced leave of absence that likely would become permanent.

"I'm doing security for a chain of hotels." He sipped his coffee and grimaced. "You could remove tooth enamel with this stuff. Why are you drinking coffee at this time of night? Won't it keep you up?"

"I'm an early riser."

Theo rolled his eyes. "How about a brewski?"

"Sorry, bud, I'm fresh out."

"Fireball?"

"Nope."

"I can remember when you were a lot more fun. What happened?"

"I grew up."

"What good are you?"

"I have an empty bed you can sleep in." Avery pointed to the door. "You know the way. The sheets are clean. I think. Tomorrow make up with Katie, please. She needs you and you need her."

"Look, I know you stayed out of the investigation because you didn't want to step on your compadres' toes, but maybe you could talk to them, light a fire under them, or check out the file yourself. Maybe they missed something."

The ragged plea stopped short of begging. Avery pushed his Spurs coffee mug around on the scarred wooden table. "I'll see what I can do, but don't expect miracles. These guys are good, probably better than me."

"Thanks, amigo. 'Preciate it." His Adam's apple bobbed. Theo stood. Then he sat back down. "I'm a jerk. Your day probably stunk too. Were you on the explosion at the Tobin Center? What was that all about? Katie mentioned it, but I wasn't home to see any of the if-it-bleeds-it-leads news coverage."

Theo had been living in his own little world for the last year. It wasn't surprising he didn't know what was going on. That he asked at all about Avery's day was a step forward. Avery gave his friend an abbreviated rundown. "We need to find this sucker before he does it again."

"So the city manager, the mayor, District 1 councilman, and the chief were all in the hall and the bomber only managed to take out two of them?" Theo's sardonic smile didn't touch his eyes. "I bet he was disappointed."

"It depends on who the intended target was."

"Maybe he wanted to take them all out." Theo took his coffee cup to the sink and dumped its contents. "Extremists look for opportunities of maximum damage."

"The guy claims to represent anticlimate-change folks. We're still working that angle."

"San Antonio is a liberal stronghold. You won't find many hoaxers here." Theo shuffled to the door. Ace, sensitive to a human in need, followed. "It's more likely someone with a grudge against the city. Vogel and Sandoval have enemies up the wazoo. People who want revenge for real and imagined slights. Maybe he'll do everyone a favor and frag them all."

Shades of his thought processes post-Iraq were showing. Avery schooled his tone. "Innocent people were killed."

"Whoever it is will consider that collateral damage. That's what it's called during wartime."

"This isn't wartime."

"You wouldn't know it from the way the gangbangers are shooting up our town." He picked up Ace and turned toward the door. "Thanks for putting up with me."

"Hey, Theo."

He looked back.

"You can't keep this up. You love being a park police officer. Get your act together. Ask your boss for another chance."

"Oh man, stop looking so worried. It's not like I'm suicidal. Just tired. Sick and tired. Thanks for letting me crash here. I promise to be out of your hair when the sun comes up."

"No worries." Better Theo crashed here than

kept drinking and driving. He might not be suicidal, but he sounded like a man on the verge of exploding. Avery stood and saluted. "Get some rest. Tomorrow's another day."

Another day that Caleb would still be dead, along with the victims of the bombings. They all deserved to know who had killed them. Avery went to get dressed. He would sleep when the thugs responsible for their deaths were under lock and key.

FOURTEEN

E strella was dead. A sleepless sleepover hadn't changed that.

Jackie dragged herself from her sleeping bag and tiptoed to the kitchen. Darkness still prevailed outside the window over the sink. Her broken heart still limped along. From the crick in her neck to the ache in every muscle, she hurt. Between sleeping on the pine floor and being knocked around by a bomb, her body protested. The bruises on her arms and legs had turned an alarming purple and red color. She didn't want to know what her face looked like. Bella didn't stir. No signs of life from the guest bedroom. Jackie started a double shot of espresso and opened her laptop.

She pulled up the *Express-News* e-edition. Bella's first-person account had top billing on page 1 along with Sig's story outlining the facts, the law enforcement efforts, and the usual quotes from elected and city officials. A sidebar urged people who saw something or knew anything that might help police catch the perpetrator to call a hotline set up for this purpose.

The photos told the story. An EMT escorting a bloodied man from the Tobin. A second photo showed the ATF, FBI, HSI, and SAPD agents and officers congregated in front of the ATF's mobile unit. The third featured the triage area and the gurneys that held body bags.

One glance took Jackie right back there. She forced herself to start reading. Bella and Sig did an incredible job under extraordinarily difficult circumstances. Their simple, straightforward narrative allowed the corrupt and evil nature of the bomber to be revealed with no histrionics. His demands would not be met. There would be consequences. San Antonians were asked to stand with the city in refusing to be bullied. The mayor even invoked the statewide antilittering campaign Don't Mess with Texas adapted to Don't Mess with San Antonio.

A drop quote from the alleged bomber read, "It was a perfect opportunity considering the organizers brought us a climate-change shill and government lackeys in the same room."

The event Jackie helped organize offered a perfect opportunity to kill people in an indiscriminate act of domestic terrorism.

Her empty stomach roiled in painful spasms. Bitter bile rose in her throat. Hands shaking, she plopped onto a bar stool at the peninsula. She closed her eyes. The image of Estrella's broken body and Councilman Sandoval's missing face assailed her.

"Good morning."

Jackie forced her eyes open. Tony trudged into

the kitchen. He looked worse than she felt. She summoned a smile. "How are you feeling?"

"Like a semi ran over me."

She slapped the laptop shut. Tony didn't need to see the half-dozen photos that accompanied Bella's stories. He already had the images burned on his brain and his heart, never to be forgotten. "Coffee?"

"Can I mainline it?"

Jackie hopped up and proceeded to make more titanium-strength coffee, scrambled eggs, and toast. Her breakfast repertoire might be small, but she found it dependable. Bella joined them just as Jackie plated the food. "How are you this morning?"

"I feel like I've been put through a meat grinder."

"So it's agreed. We all feel great. Ready to take on the world."

They all laughed, the sound of hysteria early in the morning.

Jackie waited until they'd eaten and Tony went to take the first shower in her simple abode's one full bathroom. She turned to Bella, who was the oldest of six kids, washing a skillet with a practiced hand. "Why didn't you tell me what the caller said?"

"What are you talking about?"

"He basically thanked me for planning the perfect event for his bombing."

"He did not." Bella grabbed a dish towel and dried the skillet. "Besides, you didn't plan that event by yourself. It was a group effort."

"It was my idea." Meagan's tirade about her stubborn refusal to accept no for an answer ping-ponged inside Jackie's head. "I begged to do the event. Now people are dead."

"It's not your fault."

"I'm betting Detective Wick and the Feds will take it as another sign that I'm somehow involved in this."

"They won't. They'll do their jobs. They'll follow the evidence." Bella's tense face relaxed for a second. "Detective Wick will do his job."

"What if he thinks that involves pinning it on me?"

"Pinning what on you?" Despite his rumpled clothes and the stubble on his face, Tony looked marginally better with his damp hair slicked back and the dregs of the previous day washed from his face. He wore the same wrinkled, stinky clothes. "Shower's open."

"We're just rehashing the rehash." Jackie scraped plates into the garbage disposal and stuck them in the dishwasher. "Bella, you're next. I'll finish up here."

"I have to run home and change. I'm late." Tony accepted a hug from Bella, who then disappeared down the hallway. He shrugged on his coat. "I'm sorry about last night. I was out of my mind."

"You had a right to be." Jackie enveloped him in another hug. "Just promise me you won't drink and drive again. No matter what. Call me. I'll come get you. So will Bella. We can't afford to lose another friend."

He ducked his head like a repentant child. "Promise."

Pain bloomed in a face filled with the noble remnants of his Aztec ancestors. "Their family is pouring into town. They want me to meet all these people who would've been *my* family. They're hoping to have the funeral Thursday, if her . . . body has been released by then. Did you know Estrella had made all her own funeral arrangements?"

"I didn't, but it doesn't surprise me. She was an organizer, a planner, and she never liked to inconvenience other people. She probably had a living will and medical directives."

"Those I knew about. She made me read them. She had a Do Not Resuscitate. I fought her on that, but it turns out it didn't matter." Tears dribbled down his face and dripped from his chin. He didn't seem to notice.

Jackie snatched a tissue from the box on the counter and blotted them. Tony stilled her hand with his. "Thank you."

He wasn't talking about the tissue. Unable to speak, Jackie nodded. She walked him to the door and watched him stumble down the sidewalk to his svelte BMW. It was hard to imagine his life ever being the same. People didn't get over tragedies like this one. They simply learned to go on.

They all would.

An hour later Jackie and Bella shoved through the front door, hair still wet but ready to face the day. Bella, ever the intrepid reporter, kept a go-bag with a change of clothes in her car. Neither of them mentioned their earlier discussion.

Bella stopped at her ancient yellow VW Bug and looked back. "I'm sorry if my story upset you."

"It didn't. The situation upsets me. You did your job." Jackie leaned against her Rogue and contemplated the beautiful fall day. It seemed so incongruous against the backdrop of yesterday's events. "We need to stick together, no matter what happens. Stay in touch during the day?"

"Absolutely."

She blew Bella a kiss. Her friend returned the favor. Loath to face the day, Jackie watched her drive away. Time to get on the road. Jackie hit the unlock button on her car fob and turned.

Meher Faheem stood behind the Rogue. "You got me into this. You have to help me get out of it."

FIFTEEN

Jackie froze. Her keys slipped through her fingers. "Meher, you startled me. Where have you been? The police are looking for you."

"I know. Because of you, the FBI and Homeland Security are after me and my family."

"I didn't mean to do that." Jackie swallowed back regret and guilt. "I had to tell them about the backpack, which meant I had to tell them about you. If you didn't have anything to do with the bombing, then you have nothing to worry about. Just talk to them. Tell them the truth."

"You can't be that naive. My family is Saudi. I'm American, but that won't matter because I'm Muslim." Her gaze bounced from Jackie to the street. She scanned left and right. "I'm hiding out in my own country. They've raided my house, terrorized my parents, and scared my eighty-year-old grandmother."

"I'm sorry. Really I am." Jackie picked up her keys. Meher had a right to be scared. Watching the agents and Wick ransack her house and stare at her like lions about to rip apart the carcass of a gazelle had been a hundred times worse than the interrogations Jackie endured during the investigation of her father and his subsequent death. "I didn't have a choice. Look, let's not stand outside in the open. For all we know, they're watching me. Come in the house and I'll make you some coffee. You look exhausted."

The idea that the Feds were watching her was a new one but entirely within the realm of possibility. Indecision played across Meher's face, chased by fear. "If they were watching you, they'd be in your driveway by now. You won't call them?"

Not unless something the woman said indicated she was involved in the bombing. "Not if you're innocent."

"If? I have a culinary arts degree. I bake desserts and cater for a living. You handed me the backpack, not vice versa."

"Let's go inside."

"I read in the papers about the caller who claimed responsibility for the bombing. Why are they still after me?"

"They're not after you as a terrorist. They want to know what you did with the backpack. They want to know who you talked to about it. If you saw anything while setting up. It would've been a routine interview if you hadn't fled." Jackie paused. Meher didn't seem convinced. People accustomed to being persecuted because of historical events had a right to be skeptical. That Meher chose to hide out instead of coming forth didn't help her case. "The possibility also exists the caller may have been lying to create a smoke screen to hide the real reason for the bombing. A red herring."

"I didn't flee. I was out on the River Plaza when the bomb went off. If al-Qaeda or ISIS did this, they'd claim responsibility in a heartbeat. They would want the world to know what savage beasts they are." Meher chose to ignore Jackie's reassurances. "They don't hide their deeds."

"Law enforcement knows that, but they'll search under every stone and in every dark hole in their efforts to bring the culprit to justice. They don't want to miss something obvious because they're relying on the so-called normal practices of terrorist organizations to hold true. The longer you refuse to come forward, the more they'll question your motives. In other words the guiltier you look."

"I have no motives. I don't want to be railroaded because I'm Muslim."

"Come inside. Have some hot tea. I have decaf."

Meher scanned the street again. "Fine."

Jackie picked up her keys, fumbled them again, but managed to get Meher inside without further delay.

After making apple-cinnamon tea for them both, Jackie took a seat next to the other woman and slid a saucer of frosted gingersnaps toward her. "Tell me exactly what happened after I gave you the backpack."

"None of my coworkers claimed it." Meher cupped her mug with both hands. She hunched over the peninsula, elbows propping her up. "We had two events scheduled back to back. The second one was in the River Plaza. We had to move quickly. A security guard saw me with it and asked me what I was doing. His tone was very accusatory. I tried to explain. He didn't look as if he believed me. I heard a crash in the corridor, which is never a good thing, so I handed him the backpack and told him to see if he could find the owner. He was still asking me questions as I rushed away." She burst into tears.

"It's okay. You didn't know."

"In the rush to clean up my coworker's mess, I forgot about the backpack. He cut his finger on the glass. I put a bandage on it. We both swept up the glass. A few minutes later we were back in the kitchen preparing food for the next event. He can confirm that."

The LEOs would interview all the security guards on duty that day. Maybe the guy had already come forward. If he hadn't, why not? "Can you describe the security guard?"

"Tall, but everyone is tall to me. Dark hair and eyes. Mostly I remember how caustic his tone was. People immediately assume the worst after they see my manner of dress."

"None of your employees knew anything about it?"

"No. Sometimes they bring their lunches or dinners. They can't afford to eat lunch or dinner downtown. Tourist prices. The women will bring a bag if they have a lunch, a water bottle, and necessities—you know, things a woman might need. It would be unusual for them to bring it into the venue, though. We have lockers."

"Go to the Feds. Tell them that."

"You handed me a bomb. I held a bomb in my hands."

"I know. So did I."

The kitty clock with its swinging tail hanging on the wall next to the peninsula ticked in the sudden silence. What would have happened if one of them had thought to look inside? The bag was heavy. Too heavy to simply be books? Would it have blown up? Her ignorance of how bombs worked made her a perfect patsy.

Meher pushed away her cup of tea. "Why are they blaming me and not you?"

"They're not blaming you. They only want to talk to you. They're trying to find the truth." It did feel like blame. Everyone wanted an answer to the questions of who did this and why. "You have to talk to them. It's the only way to get them to leave you alone."

"I thought we were innocent until proven guilty in this country. If they think I had something to do with it, they should have to prove it. People already blame Muslims for everything. Since

9/11, people turn away from us, either in disgust or fear." Meher's words picked up speed. Her voice rose. Frustration and anger mingled. "They vandalize our mosques and denigrate our faith. People don't see us as people. They don't see our truth faith. They write off an entire nationality, an entire group of faithful believers, as bloodthirsty animals, terrorists, and killers."

"I know and I'm so sorry." Jackie scrambled for comforting words, for a solution, for anything that would help. "It's human nature to be afraid of that which we don't understand. And to generalize in our fear."

"My children are two and four years old. What do I tell them?"

"Tell them you have to do the right thing. You have to stand up for yourself. You have to tell the truth." Easy for Jackie to say. "Let's walk through your day at the Tobin and see if there's anything that stands out to you that might help the police track down the real killer. What time did you get there?"

Meher pressed her fingertips to her forehead just above her eyes. "We didn't have a lot of staff there yet since we were only doing beverages and finger foods for the first event. We arrived about nine. We prepared and decorated the serving stations and got the coffee, tea, flavored bottled waters, and hot chocolate started."

"Nothing seemed out of the ordinary?"

"We've done many events in the hall. We've done full meals there. Everything ran smoothly."

"You didn't see anybody out of the ordinary?"

"I wasn't looking for anyone. It's my job to supervise my team. That's what I did." She picked up the honey bear and added more honey to her tea. "So many people come and go. The Tobin is a huge facility. It has admin staff, custodians, delivery people. How am I to know who belongs there?"

"Nothing out of the ordinary?"

Meher's expression grew cloudy. She squinted as if staring into the distance. "A man in a brown uniform walked past me with a package under his arm."

"Like a delivery uniform?"

"I suppose. But why would he deliver a package to the grand hall? He had to walk past the administrative offices to get to it."

True. "Can you describe him?"

"Not really. It was a side glance and a passing thought as our paths crossed. White. Average build. Taller than me."

In heels Meher still wouldn't reach Jackie's shoulders. "Nothing else?"

"I called out to him, thinking I would save him some steps if he was lost. He didn't look back. He kept walking."

"What time was this?"

"We'd just started setting up. Around ten, I suppose."

"He just walked on by?"

"I assumed he knew what he was doing and went about my business."

"You need to tell the police about him."

"No." Meher's gaze met Jackie's. "You gave the book bag to me. Why aren't they focused on you?"

"They ransacked this place yesterday. I've been interrogated by three different law enforcement agencies. I'm still not off the hook."

If she was telling the truth, Meher was a dead end. The fact that she came to Jackie indicated she was being truthful. Why step out of the shadows otherwise? "What do you want from me, Meher?"

"I want you to help me convince Homeland and the FBI that my family and I had nothing to do with this." She stood and faced Jackie. "You owe me."

"I know I do, but you realize they would have gotten around to you eventually. Your name on the list of catering employees would have stood out like a red flag."

"That doesn't get you off the hook."

How could Jackie help?

Lee. Her future brother-in-law would know what to do. She picked up her phone. Meher snatched it from Jackie and held it behind her back. "You can't call anyone."

"I'm calling my sister's fiancé. He's an attorney. He'll help you."

"How do I know I can trust you or him?"

The ferocity drained away, leaving behind a scared wife and mother who loved and wanted to protect her family. Jackie bore her share of the blame for Meher's situation. "Please let me call Lee. He's a friend and he'll soon be family. He'll know what your rights are. He'll help you. Pro bono if money is an issue."

"My husband is a neurosurgeon. Money isn't the issue."

"But trust is. I understand that. You've come this far. It's my fault you're in this predicament. Let me help you."

The agony of indecision played across the woman's face. Finally her hand crept out from behind her back. She held out the phone. "If you betray me, you'll go to hell."

If Meher had anything to do with the bombing, the same could be said of her. "I have no intention of betraying you. As you said, I owe you this."

She dialed Lee's number. As was his habit, he picked up immediately, talked fast, and listened well. Thirty minutes later he arrived at Jackie's door, along with a woman who followed him into the house with a quick searching look at Jackie.

"This is a colleague of mine. Chandra Martinez. She works for RAICES—"

Meher edged away from the peninsula. "But I'm not an immi—"

"Let me finish. Chandra specializes in immigration, but she also handles social justice cases of all kinds. She's cut her teeth on cases involving racial or nationality profiling, minority rights, religious persecution, and LGBTQ issues. Your situation, Mrs. Faheem, is right up her alley. That's why she's here. To help."

Likely in her late thirties, the attorney was a slender yet voluptuous woman with a fierce mass of chestnut curls that touched her shoulders. A few silver and white strands had to be premature. Her jaw was too square and her lightly freckled nose too long to call her a beauty, but her large hazel eyes commanded attention. She wore a no-nonsense black suit with a creamy beige blouse.

Lee quickly led Meher through the same questions Jackie had asked her earlier. Meher wound and unwound the thin material of her abaya around her fingers.

"Are any of your family members in the country illegally?" Chandra had a distinct East Texas accent. "Have you or any members of your family been to Saudi Arabia recently?"

"No to the first. Yes to the second." Meher grabbed a tissue and dabbed at her face. "My father and mother visited my brother and his family in Riyadh last year."

"How long has your brother lived there?"

"Ten years. He's seeking Saudi citizenship."

Chandra and Lee exchanged glances. "Why?"

"Because he's been made to feel like a second-class U.S. citizen his entire life." Meher's voice rose. She tossed the tissue on the peninsula. "We all have. He's been spit on and called a terrorist and denied jobs because they don't want 'his kind' in their workplace. In Saudi Arabia he's respected. So is his faith."

"So he harbors ill will against the United States?"

"No. His heart is broken, but he's choosing to make a new life for himself in the birth country of our grandparents." Meher's venomous glare would've daunted braver women. "He wants to join the Saudi military. The Saudis are, after all, allies of the United States."

"How can you be sure he hasn't become involved with Islamic extremists in the last ten years? Al-Qaeda for example."

"Because he's my brother!"

"Chandra has to ask these questions, Meher. She has to think about what the Feds know and what they can use against you. It's hurtful but necessary." Jackie set a fresh cup of tea in front of her. "When was the last time you ate? Let me fix you some breakfast."

Meher shook her head. "The friends we stayed with last night fed me."

Lee shot Jackie a semiamused look. He knew how limited her cooking skills were. "Jackie's right, Mrs. Faheem. To protect you, we need to know everything about your family. What friends?"

"No, I'll not draw them into this. One more night and we'll move again."

"Stay here." Jackie ignored Lee's raised eyebrows. "The Feds would never think to look for you here. They've already searched the place."

"It'll make you seem like coconspirators," Lee objected. "Perception is everything."

"I agree." Her gaze sweeping the kitchen and living room, Chandra fiddled with the pen she'd been scribbling notes with. "You could stay with my family. We have a big house, lots of bedrooms and bathrooms. Your kids can play with mine."

They were both right. Jackie didn't have room for a family of four. If the Feds were watching her, she'd lead them right to the woman and her family. "Will she have to turn herself in?"

"We'll negotiate a meeting, but we'll set the terms." Chandra shoved her notebook into a leather satchel. "First we need to pick up your husband and the kiddos. We don't want to paint your friends with the same brush, so to speak. We have dogs. Do they like dogs?"

Avery liked dogs too.

"They do. We have a Pekinese. He's with my grandmother, though. I'd like to use the bathroom to freshen up first." Meher's voice broke. She slid from the bar stool. "I should call my husband, too, let him know we're coming. He's beside himself worrying about everything."

"By all means." Chandra stood as well. "Thank you for the tea, Jackie."

Jackie showed Meher to the guest bathroom and returned to find Lee on the phone and Chandra perusing the books in the living room. "You have eclectic tastes."

"I read pretty much everything, except erotica."

Chandra looked up from the copy of *The Collected Works of Walt Whitman* and smiled. "I hear you met my ex-husband, Detective Avery Wick. He's a sweetheart, isn't he?"

"How did you know that?"

"I called him to make sure he was okay. He mentioned it. I used to be his sounding board for all his cases. We're still friends even though we've been divorced forever."

"You didn't take his name?"

The attorney held up her hand. A diamond solitaire decorated her ring finger. "Remarried. Avery is a good friend. I never wanted to lose that friendship. I think he's the same."

Not the sentiment one usually heard from a divorced spouse. "I've only met him in his official capacity, but he had his moments—both good and bad."

"Oh, don't let his cop-tude fool you. The guy is a teddy bear."

Her smile and her tone said Chandra's words were genuine. Jackie ran her fingers down the spines of *Harriet the Spy* and then *A Wrinkle in Time*. What had it been like to be married to Avery Wick? This wasn't the time or place to ask. She glanced toward the hallway. No sign of Meher. "I know it's none of my business—"

Chandra grinned. "You want the sordid details of our divorce? Are you interested? That would be so wonderful. I could stop feeling guilty for divorcing him."

"I'm not saying I'm interested—"

"You should be. He's a catch. At least he would be if he didn't work so hard and so long. But that's who he is. He's passionate and he doesn't do anything halfway. Except maybe being a husband."

"Kind of an important failing."

"In this case I'm equally at fault." Chandra touched Steinbeck's *The Grapes of Wrath*. "I love this book. He doesn't read, you know. That might be a problem for a librarian. He's not averse to it. He just never has. His parents didn't so he doesn't. He doesn't have time, really. He brings his work home. He lives and breathes his cases. So did I. We hardly saw each other. One day I realized I was living with a stranger."

"Couldn't you have dedicated yourselves to getting to know each other again?"

"He tried. I tried less hard. We truly had little in

common aside from a fierce chemistry. The fire was out, for me anyway. I loved the man. I still do, but not as my husband."

"How did you meet?"

"I moved to San Antonio from Boston where I had a nice job as a junior partner, a condo, and season tickets to the Red Sox. Because of a boyfriend, can you believe it? I'm originally from Beaumont and I always said I would never live in Texas. The things we do for love. It didn't last and here I was in a town where I had no family and really didn't know anyone. I ran into Avery at a 5K fund-raiser for breast cancer. His only sister died from it. Anyway, we were both at an after-party. We hit it off and six months later we got married."

Amazing how much a person could learn from an ex-wife. Not that any of this was Jackie's business. "Thanks for telling me."

"May I borrow this copy of *Gaudy Night*? I've always liked Dorothy Sayers and it's been years since I've read it. I'd love to reread it."

"Absolutely. It's one of my favorite English detective stories too." Jackie took the book, a 1936 American first edition she picked up from a used bookstore, and handed it to Chandra. "Do you really think you can help Meher?"

"I do. It's obvious she's not the culprit. The Feds feel an obligation to delve into any potential international threats however far-fetched, but this

187

obviously is not that. It's homegrown terrorism, if not something of a purely personal nature."

Another person who'd heard of Samuel Santoro. "Like a person seeking revenge?"

After a shrug, Chandra patted the book. "Thank you for this. I'll be careful with it and faithfully return it."

"I'm ready." Meher strode into the room. She rubbed her hands together like she was washing them with soap again. "I talked to my husband. He is not happy that I slipped out of the house without telling him where I was going. He wants me back there immediately. I'm not sure he's convinced that we should trust you."

His phone still in his hand, Lee joined them in the living room. "Let's roll. I want to get your family situated, Meher. Then we'll set up a meeting time and place. My folks are putting together a dossier on everyone in your family that we can give to the Feds. It's better to go on the offensive. We can use it to show how ludicrous their concerns are."

Meher's gaze sought Jackie's. She nodded. "You can trust them, I promise."

At the door Jackie watched them go and prayed they were doing the right thing. She trusted Lee and Chandra Martinez.

Could she trust the Feds?

SIXTEEN

Their daughter's murder had aged Mateo and Mercedes. They were two silver-haired peas in a now-shriveled pod. Jackie's visit with Estrella's parents after leaving Meher in Lee and Chandra's capable hands had been a short one. Relatives overran the house, all engaged in some activity meant to help—cooking arroz con pollo, pressing tortillas between their hands, cleaning the modest four-bedroom house down to the baseboards, and waiting on the grieving parents' every need. The scents of *comino* and garlic sent Jackie reeling back to a simpler, sweeter time in her life. A time of innocence.

After a quick hug and a kiss, Mercedes pled a headache and fled to the bedroom. Mateo soon followed, after thanking Jackie profusely for stopping by. The unadulterated pain in his faded brown eyes left no doubt. Jackie's presence reminded them of the undeniable truth—that their beloved had died in the bombing. That Jackie had survived eased their suffering, but for now they needed time to overcome the reality of life going forward.

She'd fled the Diaz home for the comfort of her favorite place on earth—the Central Library. The bank, closed by the time Lee and Chandra

189

left with Meher, would have to wait. The library was hopping as usual on a Saturday afternoon. Clutching her travel coffee mug in one hand, Jackie strode up to the enchilada-red building with its giant red marbles posed to roll away from it, through the neon Blue Room, and into the first-floor lobby. One of their regular homeless men waved as she passed him. Someone had given him a ratty faux leather coat and a plaid scarf he wore knotted around his neck that made him look quite rakish. She waved back. The banks of public computers were full, mostly with people experiencing homelessness. They came to the downtown library to get out of the cold, wash up in the restrooms, and fill their days reading newspapers and watching videos on YouTube.

People who thought libraries were book warehouses hadn't visited in a long time. They were community centers with librarians helping patrons who were in need of social services. Over the years she'd helped seniors learn to email and taught technology classes, desktop publishing, and social media. More recently, much of the programming focused on social issues such as the opiate crisis.

Libraries were more vital than ever. All that programming cost money and the budget stretched. Which brought her back to today's critical mission—the Catrina Ball. Eager to get to her desk, she double punched the elevator button and stepped back when the door opened. One of the weekend librarians stepped out. Jackie smiled at her. "How's it going?"

"I just explained to a little old man that I have no idea what the growth on his hand is." She chuckled. "He thought I should be able to look it up. He wasn't very happy with me."

Jackie shared a grin with her and slipped into the elevators. Over the years she'd been asked to diagnose a variety of ailments, file complaints on vacuum cleaners, and listen to teenage girls' love life woes. Librarians were like bartenders without the booze.

The doors closed. Jackie leaned against the wall and closed her eyes. An ordinary backpack. She'd moved a backpack and Estrella had died.

God, forgive me.

The *ding-ding* forced her to open her eyes and exit the elevator onto the library's fourth floor, home of the administrative offices. Jackie trudged to her office, where she plopped into the chair behind her crowded desk with her back to the window that gave her a view of downtown San Antonio—a coup that was the envy of her coworkers.

Don't think. Do.

She logged into her computer. Three dozen emails and a dozen voice mails. Questions from the caterers, copies of contracts for the musicians to be reviewed and returned to the foundation staff, AV requirements for each musical group as well as the dignitaries' ceremony, and her blessing of the news release from the PR folks. It still had to go to Meagan and up the chain of command before it could be released.

Emails regarding upcoming programming—Slammin' the Stacks in honor of National Poetry Month in April, homeless and veteran assistance with housing and job hunting, a panel of mental health experts discussing suicide prevention, and a workshop by a local published romance writer for beginning writers would wait a few more days. Then she'd be full speed ahead on the library's contributions to Fiesta—San Antonio's annual massive ten-day party in April, which featured hundreds of events across the city, including parades, pageants, oyster bakes, concerts, art fairs, etcetera.

Juggling events was her forte.

Their next Catrina meeting was scheduled for Tuesday afternoon. She needed to walk staff through the stations that would be set up throughout the building. Hundreds of potential donors dressed in costume would visit those stations. Staff—including Jackie—would spend the coming week decorating and setting up *ofrendas* for famous people throughout San Antonio history. The altars were the center of the Mexican Día de los Muertos celebration.

Maybe they should do an altar honoring Milton

Schaeffer. Would that be in good taste? She'd have to run it by the library's public relations manager. Let her feel out the foundation board.

To suggest they cancel the event because of Milton's murder would be met with a resounding no. The event helped fund the programming done at the public library system's twenty-nine branch libraries as well as the Central Library. Program planning and implementation also comprised the bulk of Jackie's job. Literacy programs, history programs, LEGO clubs, computer literacy workshops, debates on important issues like immigration and climate change.

Her thought process came to a screaming halt. Jackie turned her chair back to her desk and opened the search function. She typed in *United San Antonians for Prosperity*. Nothing. The closest was a think tank called Citizens for Economic Prosperity.

For the next hour she delved into San Antonio organizations on both sides of the climate debate. She dug deep into Marcus Camacho's political history. The only finding of note was one law enforcement would already know. Camacho's biggest donors were oil and gas companies, followed by conservative organizations that opposed San Antonio's sanctuary-city designation. They were anti-immigration. They also supported the city's decision not to allow Chick-fil-A a slot at San Antonio International Airport because of the restaurant owner's contributions to certain conservation groups. City Council said the exclusion was necessary because Chick-fil-A restaurants weren't open on Sunday—a big travel day.

A Michael Bublé tune burst from her jacket pocket. Startled, she fumbled for her phone, dropped it on the floor, snagged it, and answered. "Mom, are you all right?"

"I'm fine, sweetie. Why do you sound breathless?"

"No reason. What's up? What's all that noise?"

"Mercedes wants to create an altar in Estrella's honor. Victoria and I are shopping for Día de los Muertos stuff at Market Square. The mariachis are serenading us outside Mi Tierra. I just had the most scrumptious huevos rancheros—"

Victoria was not only her mom's best friend, but she had aunt status for Jackie and her siblings. They went everywhere together. Neither one of them should be at Market Square today. Jackie stood and attempted to pace between her desk and the door. Tourists and locals alike flocked to the historic Market Square, known as El Mercado to the old-timers, with its plethora of shops filled with authentic Mexican wares and less-than-authentic, cheaper knockoffs. Some of the best Mexican food in San Antonio was served at Mi Tierra and La Margarita. Tejano bands performed in the open air on the weekends, along with mariachis and Mexican *folklórico* dancers. What a perfect place for a madman to wreak havoc.

"You need to go home right now—"

"Last time I checked, I'm the mom and you're the daughter, dear." Mom proceeded to repeat everything Jackie had said, presumably to Victoria. "We can't stop living. In fact we need to celebrate living. Starting with celebrating Estrella's life. Mercedes has photos picked out and some of her favorite jewelry. Her prom dress and those cute leather boots she liked. Mercedes wants to include her baby blanket, and her Girl Scout sash, and her college diploma, among other things. We have the *calaveras* and the *papel picado*—I bought purple, but I also think I should get pink for celebration and white for hope. Oh, an artisan is making beautiful red candles that smell like candied apples. Estrella would love that. We'll wait until later to buy the marigolds and the *pan de muerto*, of course."

Finally she paused long enough to draw a breath.

"Mother, listen to me." Jackie pressed her forehead against the window's cool glass. When her mother got started, it took a tsunami to stop her. She had the lungs of a long-distance swimmer and the staying power of a marathon runner. "Have you been paying attention to the news at all? The bomber is still out there. He promised to keep setting bombs at places like Market Square if the mayor and the city manager didn't step down. Obviously they can't do that."

"Honey, the world is full of wackos. If we stayed home every time there's another act of terrorism in this world, none of us would ever go anywhere . . ."

Noise boomed over the line. Followed by screams.

"Mom? Mom, are you still there?" Was that her screaming? "Mom, answer me. Answer me please!"

Nothing.

SEVENTEEN

Having a two-track mind in the middle of a firestorm required supreme concentration. Avery sucked down an energy drink to top off the three cups of coffee he'd already consumed since coming out of the shower to find Theo already gone. His heart banged in his chest and his head pounded.

His Homicide Unit colleague Dale Wheeler didn't look up from his computer. His desk was covered with files on open cases. Like everyone in the unit, he had plenty to do in a city with more than a hundred murders a year and many more attempted homicides, assaults, suicides, threats, resisting arrests, and missing children. Even curfew violations fell into the unit's bailiwick. "Come on, Dale, anything new on Caleb Beretta's case?"

"You're a hotshot on the bombing task force now." Dale sipped some kind of snooty iced green tea and set the cup on the perfect wet ring on his desk. "You have enough to do. You know Eric and I have done everything possible to find the kid's killer. We're not giving up. Someone will come forward. Someone saw something that day."

"I'm not faulting your work. Believe me. I told

Theo the same thing, but the man's hanging by a thread. Have you talked to him lately?"

"He calls me at least once a week. Sometimes he shows up here."

"Then you know the guy has gone off the rails."

"It happens." The words sounded callous, but Dale's grimace suggested the situation bothered him plenty.

"What can it hurt for me to take a look?"

"You're a family friend."

"With sixteen years on the force."

"Fine. But I want it back ASAP. Like tomorrow. No matter what happens with the bombing."

Avery snatched the bulging accordion file from Dale, whirled, and fled to his desk before his colleague changed his mind.

"I saw you making nice with Dale. Whatcha got?" Scotty dropped his phone receiver back on the base. I talked to—"

"Market Square just blew up!" Lieutenant Carmichael bolted from his office. "We need all hands on deck."

Everyone moved. Avery dumped the folder on his desk, grabbed his Smith & Wesson M&P40, and headed for the stairs. It would be faster than the elevator. Market Square, home to every imaginable south-of-the-border trinket possible, lay one block north of HQ.

Outside he and Scotty joined the burgeoning stream of officers racing toward the market.

Smoke, a gloomy harbinger of destruction, spiraled into the blue sky. Ambulance and fire department sirens screamed. Traffic cops spilled into the street to direct traffic.

The bomb squad van rolled into place ahead of the officers on foot. The Feds had farther to come but no doubt were en route. The stench of burned wood, rubber, and human flesh in his nostrils, Avery stuck his arm over his nose and tried to breathe through his mouth.

Because of trips to the market for Fiesta music festivals and shopping for Christmas presents with his mom, Avery had always thought of El Mercado as a big, never-ending party.

The party was over. The Mexican artisan shops in historic wood-and-brick buildings had taken the brunt of the blast. Blackened, smoldering ruins replaced brightly colored yellow, turquoise, and pink walls.

The racks filled with cowboy hats, serapes, leather goods, and jewelry were gone. So were the outdoor tables that lined the patio of Mi Tierra Restaurant, the planters, and the old-fashioned streetlight poles. Yet a single string of delicate pink, yellow, purple, and red *papel picado* still fluttered over their heads.

A man with blood gushing from a cut on his head stumbled through the debris calling, "Sandy, Sandy, where are you?"

A woman hugging a baby to her chest sat on

the curb. She sobbed and rocked, seemingly oblivious to the baby's screaming. Firefighters and EMTs surged forward. The bomb squad was already inside, searching for any remaining explosives.

Avery stifled the desire to run in behind them. Everybody had a job to do. Right now he'd only be in the way. "Where do you want me, Boss?"

"You and Heller spread out. Eyeball the crowd, the rubberneckers. He had to be close to detonate the bomb or bombs. We'll have camera security footage eventually. Right now see if anyone seems suspicious. Taking pictures or video."

Everybody shot video these days. They loved sending it to the TV stations and having it show up on the six o'clock news. They posted it on social media, becoming instant de facto journalists. Only they reported unverified rumors. Often before police could notify victims' families.

"Got it."

He waded into the mass of humanity already gathered behind hastily strung crime scene tape on Santa Rosa Avenue. Normally a heavily traveled thoroughfare that skirted the downtown business district, the street was empty for a block on either side of the main entry to the market. Beyond that traffic was gridlocked. Drivers honked. People yelled. Curious pedestrians congregated in Milam Park and on the other side of Santa Rosa Avenue. Cell phones held high.

No one looked familiar. Avery stopped and took his time. He studied faces. What was he searching for? Their killer, if he was still here enjoying the fruits of his labor, would keep his expression neutral or go for a horrified grimace. He might wear the infamous hoodie with the hood up and sunglasses to disguise his features. Neither would be out of place on a cool October morning bathed in sunlight. Nothing like profiling based on clothes. On stereotype.

Avery dug his phone from his windbreaker pocket and started shooting video in a panoramic sweep. No one seemed to notice or care. They were too busy doing their own recording.

A man in a gray hoodie and aviator sunglasses that glinted in the light squeezed between two mothers with strollers. He crossed Santa Rosa and veered toward Milam Park. Avery followed with Scotty close on his heels.

It could be nothing. It could be something.

Please, God, let it be something.

The man paused for a red light. Avery grabbed his shoulder and jerked him around.

"Hey! What are you doing?"

The man shoved back his hood and whipped off the glasses. "What am I doing? What are you doing?"

Avery heaved a breath. Sig Ritter, *Express-News* crime reporter. "Sig. Sorry."

"Doing a little profiling, Detective?" Sig stumbled back two steps. "A black guy in a hoodie must be up to no good."

"Leaving so soon?"

"My phone is dying. I need to charge it in my car. I'll be back."

"You better get going then."

"You stepped in some doo-doo there." Scotty chuckled. "And wasted valuable time."

"Shut up."

"Yep."

What seemed to be too good to be true always was.

EIGHTEEN

Fear made track stars of even the worst couch potato. Pain like a dagger in her side accosted Jackie with every breath. She hadn't thought. She simply bolted from the library, pelted down Soledad, raced up Martin Street, and hung a left on Santa Rosa Avenue in her version of the track-and-field mile to El Mercado. Her lackadaisical approach to exercise came back to haunt her as she sprinted past Christus Santa Rosa Hospital and then Milam Park. By the grace of God, she'd worn jeans and her favorite sneakers on this unofficial workday, but her Spurs sweatshirt was too warm for careening on foot through downtown on a sunny October day.

God, please. God, please. God, please.

No other words of supplication would form. God knew what she needed even when she couldn't formulate a thought. The Holy Spirit heard her groanings.

God.

Sirens screamed. Traffic stood still. Horns honked. People slid from their cars stopped in the middle of the road, hands to their foreheads against the sun, as they squinted at the smoke billowing from the market. The stoplight turned red. Jackie halted, gasped, and bent over, one hand to her side. Light-headed, she sucked in air.

Her heart concussed against her rib cage. Purple lights pulsated in her vision.

Don't pass out. Don't you dare pass out.

"What's going on?" A guy in an Amazon delivery van stopped at the light yelled at her. "Is it a fire or that bomber dude?"

She shook her head and took off again. Her calves burned and her thighs had gone numb. Her head floated above her body in a surreal world where they were no longer connected. If she didn't collapse and die of a heart attack before this was over, she would return to the gym again. *I promise, God.*

Fire trucks, ambulances, and cop cars clogged the street at the main pedestrian entrance to the market. Traffic Unit officers set up a detour onto Houston Street heading east and west. Uniformed officers unrolled yellow crime scene tape and set up barricades. An EMT raced across the street toward Jackie pushing a gurney. Faster to do that than stick the victim in an ambulance and fight traffic one block to the hospital. A woman lay on it. Her hair was silver.

"Wait. Wait." Jackie swerved into his path. "I need to know who she is."

The EMT didn't stop. "Move, lady. She needs medical attention stat."

Jackie stumbled out of his way. She reached for the gurney and missed. "Mom, it's me, Jackie. Is that you? Talk to me."

The woman moaned and raised her head. She was Latina. *"Fue una bomba. No se, no se . . ."* Her head sank back on the pillow.

Jackie whirled, stumbled over the curb, and collapsed to her knees. Head down, she caught herself with both hands. *Not Mom. Not Mom. Keep going.*

A hand gripped her arm and pulled her to her feet. She raised her head.

His eyes wide and fierce, Detective Wick stared down at her. "What are you doing here? Were you in the market when the bomb went off? Are you hurt?"

His voice had gone hoarse. She sank against him. His arms wrapped around her and tightened. "Jackie? Are you hurt?"

"No. I'm okay." The effort to suck in air stung. His heartbeat sounded in her ear. Steady and strong. The momentary desire to let him hold her overwhelmed Jackie. *Get a grip.* She pushed him away. "I have to get in there."

"You can't go in. They're sweeping for additional bombs. What are you doing here?" Detective Wick's arms hung at his side, but his hands fisted. Frustration mixed with concern on his rugged face. "Better yet, when did you get here?"

"My mom is in there. My mom and her best friend Victoria. She's like an aunt to me." Jackie dodged to his right. His arm shot out and stopped her. She tried to rip free and couldn't. "Either let me go or get me in there."

"Wick, did you need help?" Huffing and puffing, Wick's partner did a fine imitation of running in place. "You want me to cuff her?"

"No. Head back. I'll catch up."

He didn't seem to find Scotty's suggestion that she be cuffed as ludicrous as Jackie did. "I don't have time for this, Detective."

"No civilian is getting in there." Emotion that looked like profound regret clouded his pale-blue eyes. "I'm sorry. It takes time to clear a three-block area. The bomb squad is working its way through. First responders are triaging the wounded right behind them."

In an eerie, grotesque moment of déjà vu, he led her to the curb with a gentle tug. "Please sit down. You look like you're gonna pass out. If you promise not to move from this spot, I'll try to get more information on the . . . wounded. How do you know they're in there?"

His reluctance to say the word *dead* only added to Jackie's precarious hold on her sanity. Dead or wounded. Or maybe Mom and Victoria walked away without a scratch. Only Jackie's life hadn't been like that for a few years now.

She sank onto the cement. "I was on the phone with her when it happened. I heard screaming. Then the phone went dead. She and Victoria were shopping for an ofrenda for Estrella. Papel picado, candles, calaveras." She was babbling.

Wick squatted next to her. "What are their names? Do you have photos?"

"Aimee Santoro, age fifty-nine, and Victoria Zocchi, age sixty-one." Jackie tugged her phone from her back pocket and thumbed through the photos stored there. She held out a picture of Mom and Victoria dressed to the hilt before a Children's Shelter fund-raiser. "That was a few months ago."

Wick took the phone and held it closer, then farther away. After a second, he pulled a pair of reading glasses from his windbreaker pocket and stuck them on the end of his nose. "My arms are getting too short."

He studied the photo and handed her phone back. "You know I have to interview you. I don't believe you're a criminal, though. So prove me right and stay put. Please."

That Wick still had an ounce of trust for the human race was a small miracle, but Jackie couldn't care at this moment. Not with her mother possibly injured, maybe even dead. "If you aren't back in three minutes, I'll find my own way in."

"You'll end up getting arrested. Let me do this for you."

He stuck the glasses back in his pocket, whirled, and trotted into the controlled chaos a few hundred yards away.

The kindness in those words nearly undid her.

Jackie swallowed again and again. No tears. No tears. Instead she studied her watch, counting the seconds. After two minutes she stood and took a wobbly step. "Sorry, Detective, I lied."

Déjà vu all over again. Avery tried not to breathe the foul-smelling smoke as he held up his badge for the uniformed cop manning the barricade. He didn't know this woman. She glanced from the badge to his face, shrugged, and made space for him to squeeze through.

A few yards ahead, the mass of EMTs triaged dozens of people, some prone, others sitting, and a few bloodied but unbowed who stood. Firefighters raced back and forth, ferrying more victims to the triage area while their colleagues sprayed down any remaining hot spots.

Avery sucked in a breath and regretted it. His throat and nose burned. He covered his mouth and slipped into the triage area where Scotty stood talking to the lieutenant.

"How many victims so far?"

"The number keeps climbing. Right now we're at seven dead and twenty-two injured."

Avery didn't try to suppress the string of obscenities. *Sorry, Jackie.* "Jackie Santoro's mother and friend were in here."

LT's eyebrows shot up. "Seriously? Bad luck? Coincidence? Targets? This doesn't get any easier."

"The perpetrator said the USAP would do this if their demands weren't met." Scotty joined Wick in displaying his prodigious ability to cuss. "Can we start interviewing the victims at least?"

LT nodded. "The ATF's mobile unit is on the way. We'll set up on the southwest plaza next to the Farmer's Market building. Damage is minimal there."

Avery edged his way toward the triaged patients. An elderly man thrashed and moaned. A middle-aged woman clasped her hands to her bloodied head. A mom with three crying children huddled around a stroller. Mom offered him a tearful glance. "Do you know what happened?"

"We're working on it, ma'am."

She clutched a screaming newborn wrapped in a giraffe-covered blanket to her chest. "We're alive, so that's good, right?"

"Yes, it is."

"Praise God."

"Yes, ma'am."

"My husband is on the way."

"That's good."

Row after row of hurt, bewildered people waited for help and answers. Not one looked like Aimee Santoro or Victoria Zocchi.

Avery stood back to let firefighters deposit a woman on a gurney where personnel from Christus Santa Rosa helped EMTs set up tents. The hospital had called in all off-duty employees.

Hospitals across the city were in the process of doing the same thing. It would be a horrendous few days followed by more counseling sessions for most of the first responders and medical professionals who'd thought they'd seen it all until they encountered the mangled bodies of people caught in a blast filled with nails and ball bearings.

He wouldn't resort to therapy, but he understood the need.

"Get back here now! Miss. Miss!"

Wick whirled. Jackie ran full tilt toward triage. The uni from the barricades gave chase.

"Whoa. Whoa. I've got her." Avery stepped into Jackie's path. She swerved. He shot after her. "Come on, Jackie. Give it up."

"You said you'd find her. You said three minutes." Gasping for breath, she dodged an EMT pushing a gurney and slipped past a man holding a wad of paper towels to his bleeding leg. "Time is up."

Scotty popped in from the other side. "Come on, Ms. Santoro. This isn't kosher. Give it up."

She slammed to a halt, caught between two old geezer cops, injured folks on either side. "I just need to know if my mother is alive." She did a dance like the one Avery had seen a slick Texas Ranger rookie do when caught in a box between a Los Angeles Angels' third baseman and catcher. "Help me look. Please."

"I can't help someone bent on contaminating a crime scene." Avery closed the gap. She had long legs and anguished fear on her side. He had the knowledge that she'd end up in jail if she didn't desist. "Stop and I'll go back to searching for your mother like I said I would."

She feinted, twisted the opposite direction, and tried an end run around Scotty. The aging detective and former Baylor University power forward made a Herculean effort to grab her. His long reach corralled her around the waist.

"I already lost my dad." She immediately stopped struggling. "Don't you see?"

"I know." Avery nodded at Scotty. His partner let go. Jackie swayed but didn't go down. Avery slid between her and the biggest crime scene he'd ever worked. "Not knowing is worse than death itself."

"Jackie! Is that you? Everything is muffled and I lost my glasses."

Jackie whirled and staggered toward an SAFD firefighter carrying a slim woman dressed in blood that dripped under contrasting silver hair down her forehead and from her nose. More blood decorated her ripped cardigan sweater and once-white slacks. Her shoes were missing.

"Mom? You're alive. Oh, thank You, Jesus, thank You." Jackie's knees hit the brick pavers. She scrambled to her feet and hurled herself the remaining few yards. "Are you all right? How bad are you hurt? Where's Victoria? Is she all right?"

"I'm fine. They found us in the rubble and dug us out. This kind man insisted on carrying me." Despite her injuries, Mrs. Santoro's voice was strong. Her rescuer looked like a pro-football linebacker with shoulders as wide as the woman was long. "I told him I could walk, but he nixed that idea. Victoria needs more help than I do."

Two more firefighters approached with a well-rounded woman in jeans and a navy, silver, and white Cowboys sweatshirt on a stretcher between them. Unlike Mrs. Santoro's, Zocchi's body sagged against the stretcher, her arms limp. Her head lolled to one side. Her eyes were closed.

Jackie let go of her mother's hand and shot toward them. "Is she . . . is she all right?"

Avery caught the first firefighter's gaze. His chiseled features were grim. Avery took a closer look at the woman. Part of a pole like the kind used to hold up an umbrella on an outdoor patio table extruded from her abdomen.

Mrs. Zocchi didn't look all right. She looked dead.

NINETEEN

Two best friends in two days. First Estrella, now possibly Victoria. Jackie held on to her mom. She kept trying to get up to go to Victoria. Mom had lost Daddy in what she saw as an incomprehensible act of cowardice. She couldn't lose her best friend too. Victoria had stood with the family through the investigation into Daddy's alleged crimes, through the media glare focused on his family and what they did or did not know, through his suicide and that investigation, and finally, in the search for some vestige of normalcy after the public glare died away.

She was family in the best sense of the word.

"She'll be okay." Mom struggled, but the firefighter didn't release her from his grip. "Let me down. I'm fine. Go tend to her. Vicky is tough. She teaches English to fifth graders. She'll be fine if you take care of her."

"Ma'am, the best thing you can do is let the EMTs transport your friend so she can get the medical care she needs." The firefighter set her gently on a folding chair next to an intake table. "Let them take care of you too. You're in shock. You're not feeling anything right now, but you will, I promise."

Mom attempted to stand. Jackie pressed her

hands on her shoulders, forcing her to stay seated. "He's right."

"Jacqueline Rose, let me up. I have to go to her."

"Wait here." As if she would obey any better than Jackie had. They were already loading Victoria into a waiting ambulance. Jackie relinquished her hold and scurried toward them. "At least tell us if she has a chance. Is she stable? Where are you taking her?"

"She's alive. Her breathing is shallow and her pulse thready. Leaving the pole in place allows us to transport her without major blood loss." The EMT shut the vehicle's doors. "She'll go to University's trauma unit."

Jackie trotted back to Mom, who stood, one hand on the table to balance herself. She relayed the information. An EMT went to work on her mother, who protested the entire time. "We have to go."

The EMT ignored her.

She had cuts and abrasions on her scalp, forehead, nose, cheeks, neck, and arms. At least three needed stitches. Her thumb and two fingers on her left hand appeared fractured. The EMT catalogued the injuries as he examined Mom. She might have broken ribs. "She likely has a concussion. She'll need X-rays, a CT scan, and possibly an MRI." He applied pressure to a cut on her arm and then bandaged it. "She needs to be transported."

"My daughter can take me."

"I can't. My Rogue is at the library."

Mom groaned. "I don't need an ambulance."

"You do." The EMT motioned for his colleagues to take over. "You're alive, ma'am, count your blessings."

"He's right, Mom. Do what you do best. Pray."

Tears trickled down her mother's face, leaving tracks through the blood and dirt that turned her peaches-and-cream complexion dark. She sniffed and bowed her head. So did the EMT. The lump in Jackie's throat threatened to choke her. She closed her eyes and let Mom's words wash over her. Not for the first time since the news broke of Dad's alleged crimes, the unbelief threatened the stronghold of her faith. She refused to let the doubt in. Without faith, she had no weapon big enough to stand against this enemy.

God, please.

A puny prayer, but it would have to do. She climbed into the ambulance and held her mother's hand. They prayed all the way to University Hospital.

In the emergency room Jackie clawed her way through hordes of people searching for relatives, seeking answers, crying, or staring into space, looks of horror and disbelief on their faces. Finally it was her turn to talk to the triage nurse.

When the nurse asked Jackie if she was family, she lied. "Daughter."

So close to being the truth, it could be the truth.

The nurse reviewed a list in front of her. The moment she found Victoria's name was obvious. Her expression grew resigned. "Let me get the doctor who worked on her."

"That's not necessary. She's gone, isn't she?"

The nurse nodded. "I'm so sorry. She coded in the ambulance. They were unable to resuscitate her. Can I call someone for you?"

Jackie shook her head. "I have family here."

Shoulders hunched, Jackie trudged to the spot in the hallway where the EMTs had temporarily parked Mom's gurney with several others.

Her mother's head sank against the pillow. She turned her face to the wall. "She's gone, isn't she?"

"She didn't make it to the hospital. They couldn't bring her back." Jackie smoothed her mother's silver hair. Her hand shook. She swallowed against mounting tears. "I'm so sorry, Mom."

"Me, too, baby. I don't know how I'll tell her kids."

Victoria's three now-grown children lived out of state, another reason she embraced her students and the Santoro kids so closely.

A man whose name tag identified him as a hospital chaplain approached. He clutched a black leather Bible in one hand. "Anything I can do for you ladies?"

"Can you give God a good scolding for me?" Jackie rubbed her cold hands together. Once again, she couldn't get warm. "I know all about in this life there will be troubles, but this seems excessive. Assure Him we're thoroughly honed now."

"You can have that conversation with Him yourself. He'll understand your pain and your anger." The chaplain's gentle tone, free of chastisement for her attitude, was galling. "He knows what it feels like to lose a loved one."

"The plan was always for Jesus to return to the throne." Why was she arguing this? She believed with her whole heart, but right now her heart writhed in agony. "He knew His Son would be all right in the end."

"If you're a believer, so will you."

Victoria was a believer. No more pain, no more sorrow, no more tears. "I'm sorry. It's been a horrific few days."

Few years.

His understanding gaze only made the tears harder to manage. He patted her shoulder with fingers gnarled with arthritis. "Like I said, God knows."

"I have to make some phone calls. Can you wait with my mother?"

He nodded and held out his hand. "I'm the hospital chaplain on duty."

She shook his hand and made the introductions.

Then she shared the loss of a woman who'd been more an aunt than a friend. His hand was warm, his shake firm. "Go make your calls. Remember, this life is only a season. The good stuff is still to come."

Truth to hang on to until the perpetrator of this terrible season was found and punished. Then the new season could begin.

TWENTY

The final body count totaled twelve dead. Thirty-eight were injured, some in critical condition. The hours ran together in a bloodbath of battered bodies and shattered psyches. Avery interviewed witness after witness, victim after victim. They couldn't remember much after the powerful explosion knocked them from their shoes. A little girl cried for her mommy. An elderly woman answered every question with, "Do you know where my purse is? It has my blood pressure medicine in it."

A man wondered how the police could let this happen. Most stared into space, foreheads wrinkled, trying to remember what they'd been doing before their world shattered.

Avery fist-bumped a ten-year-old and left him huddled next to his mother. She had a bandage on her forehead and a wrist wrapped in an elastic Ace bandage. They were among the fortunate. They would go home later, battered but not irrevocably broken.

"How many more?" Scotty shrugged off his windbreaker and swiped a bottle of water from the Victim Assistance cooler. "I'm starting to see double."

"We're winding down." Avery glanced at his

watch. Still Saturday. Hard to believe. ATF's Explosives Enforcement people worked side by side with the SAPD bomb squad. That the bomb was the same type used at the Tobin grand hall came as no surprise. The bomber had promised retaliation for not giving in to his demands. Avery wasn't seeing double yet, but he would see the eviscerated victims in his nightmares for the rest of his life. If he ever slept again. His chest ached, his knees hurt, and a spot behind his ears throbbed. "I'm hoping they find something that'll give us a lead. Anything."

"Wick, get over here."

The investigative division's deputy chief stood with the chief near the command center. He shoved his phone in his pocket and waved Avery over a second time. "Hurry up."

"Uh-oh, somebody's in trouble." Scotty's effort to look supportive only made him appear more squirrelly than usual. "Godspeed, my friend. What kind of coffin do you want?"

"Shut up."

Donning his best *there's-no-I-in-team* demeanor, Avery strode toward them. "What's up, Boss?"

"What do you know about the Feds interviewing Meher Faheem this afternoon without us?"

"The catering manager? I know they've been pulling out all the stops to find her. They'll share the intel as soon as they get done."

"And your ex-wife didn't give you a heads-up?"

What did they think? That Chandra kept Avery posted on her every move? That didn't happen even when they were married. "What does Chandra have to do with it?"

"She set up the meeting to bring Faheem in." Ruiz's lips were pinched like he had a bad case of the runs. "She's representing the woman. I would've thought she'd come to you first."

"Chandra's a free agent. We haven't been together for five years." Even when they were married, his wife went her own way. She'd decided to quit corporate law and take a massive pay cut without consulting him—not that he had a problem with that. Only the divorce part. "Chandra doesn't ask my permission or advice on anything. She never has."

"She knows you're working this case. She doesn't trust you to bring this woman in?"

"I'm a homicide detective. If this woman is a terrorist, her case is way above my pay grade and Chandra knows it."

"Guess how she connected with Faheem."

Avery wasn't in the mood for guessing games. "I have no idea."

"Through Jackie Santoro and her attorney. Drucker brought your ex into it, but Faheem was at Santoro's house. I smell conspiracy and an attempt to cover it up."

"What's Faheem's story?"

"Who knows? We weren't invited to the party."

Ruiz pointed his hairy index finger at Avery. "Get in your ex's face. Find out. We can't get to Faheem, but we can get to Santoro. Run her down."

Jackie was at the hospital with her mother and quasi aunt, who probably had died from her injuries. "Wilson and Jantzen will give us the details at the briefing."

"I'd rather be on the offensive."

Avery nodded. Ruiz was like a spoiled kid who didn't get to the swings first and had to wait his turn. "I'll see if Chandra picks up."

"If she doesn't, hunt her down. And Santoro."

They didn't know Chandra. If she wanted him to know, she'd have called him. Jackie was tough, but tougher people had crumbled under the weight of what she'd endured in the last few days. *Sorry, Jackie.*

Avery ducked into the Victim Assistance area and hit Favorites on his phone. Chandra picked up on the second ring. "I wondered how long it would be before you called."

"Y'all hurt my boss's feelings." He kept his tone light. Chandra didn't respond well to petulance. "They're surprised you didn't call me first before the Feds."

"But you know better. So do they. She's an American Muslim of Saudi descent. She has relatives in Saudi Arabia. If she doesn't cooperate, Homeland Security and the FBI are the ones who can make her life miserable."

"I know."

She stayed quiet. So did Avery. Chandra always had her clients' best interests at heart. She championed underdogs, disenfranchised, and anyone she perceived as persecuted. She didn't care about religion or politics, only fair and just treatment.

Avery nudged an acorn with his shoe. "I understand your position. Is there anything you can tell me that will help us in our investigation? Or assist us in helping our partner agencies in finding the monster who has now murdered seventeen innocent souls?"

"Nicely done." Her approval always made him feel like the smartest guy in the room. "First, let's agree that Meher had nothing to do with this. She was being interrogated when the second bomb exploded—"

"That doesn't mean she's not involved in an organization that is doing this. The real one, not the one that claimed credit."

"Neither ISIS nor al-Qaeda is shy about taking credit. Why let some anticlimate-change group do it instead?"

"That's an unknown at this point."

"It's a fact. Here's another one. Meher is a witness. She corroborates Jackie Santoro's story about the backpack. The important new fact is she gave it to a security guard. At least he appeared to be one. She also saw a deliveryman with a package—in the wrong place."

"She gave descriptions?"

"She did. So vague as to be almost useless, but she tried."

"Where is Faheem now?"

"Safely tucked away with her family. That was the deal. She'd sit down for a conversation as long as they agreed not to hold her without additional evidence. We're also not taking any chances. If either the security guard or the alleged deliveryman was involved, she could be in danger if either knows she's still alive and talking to the Feds."

"Tell me she's not at your house."

"Okay, I won't."

"Stay out of the line of fire, please."

"You're sweet, but I know how to take care of myself."

"Thank you for sharing."

"It's always been one of my strong suits."

"I'd better—"

"Wait, wait." Her voice reminded him of warm evenings on the Gulf Coast. Better days long gone. "Aren't you going to ask about Jackie? I know you know that's where I picked up Meher early this morning."

"Why would I ask about Ms. Santoro?"

"You never were good at dissembling, my friend." She laughed, that full-throated laugh that used to make his brain fuzzy. "She's awesome and she asked me about you and not because you're investigating her. You made an impression."

Not in his wildest dreams. "What are you talking about? I dragged her downtown and interrogated her on one of the worst days of her life. She despises me. Why did my name even come up?"

"She brought it up. She wanted to know about you."

"Probably planning a lawsuit for violation of her civil rights. She'll probably ask you to do the honors and you'll feel duty bound to accept the job."

"No way. She likes you."

"I have to go."

"Time to get back in the saddle, buttercup."

"I'm not having this conversation with you."

The sound of her laughter still tickling his ear, Avery rang off and slid in next to Scotty to catch the tail end of the mayor's contribution to the latest news conference. Following the big guns didn't make him any less popular with the media. Like every good politician, he knew how to wind up and let it rip. "El Mercado is a historic icon. It has been part of the fabric of this city since the Spanish missionaries settled here in 1718. The chili queens sold their delicious chili here. Hundreds of thousands of people, San Antonians and visitors, have shopped and eaten and danced here over the years. We won't let a spineless, faceless mass murderer take this place from us. We lost vendors here today. We lost visitors. We lost friends and loved ones. Every family mourning a death right now, I'm speaking to you. I promise you we will find and apprehend the animal who did this. You will have justice. You have my word."

Scotty dug his elbow into Avery's side. "That's our cue."

As they walked away, Avery told his partner about the conversation with Chandra—the part pertinent to the case, not the Jackie part. "Shall we start with tracking the security guard?"

"You don't want to start with Ms. Bodacious?"

"Scotty."

"Ms. Santoro?"

"She's at the hospital with her mother. Let's give her two minutes to gather her wits before we attack her again."

"Going soft on me, huh?"

"Security guard."

Scotty offered a thumbs-up. "The question being why wouldn't a security guard come forward to report that he'd been given a backpack by a Muslim Saudi?"

"A Muslim American of Saudi descent."

"Do you think he knew that?"

"Then we have the lost package-delivery guy."

226

"Any idea what company he allegedly worked for?"

"We'll know more when the Feds cough up the interview at the briefing." Avery glanced at his watch. "Which should be in twenty minutes. Fortunately it'll only take three minutes to hoof it back to HQ."

"Speak for yourself." Sweat matted Scotty's stringy bangs to his forehead and soaked the pits of his white button-down collared shirt. The afternoon sun had turned his face ruddy. Even his handlebar mustache drooped. "I can do it in two."

"How are you holding up?"

"Good. You?"

"Good."

Pep talk over, they went to work.

TWENTY-ONE

Victoria's favorite seat in the Santoro living room—a hickory Amish-made glider rocker—sat empty. Turning away from the bay window where Victoria liked to sit in the sun that warmed the room on winter days, Jackie added another pillow behind her mother's back. She handed her the TV remote. "Find something to watch while I make you a grilled cheese sandwich."

Preferably something without a laugh track.

"I've got dinner covered," Tosca yelled from the kitchen. "I'm making patty melts and tater tots."

The Santoro sisters were not known for their culinary prowess. Apparently it wasn't genetic. The remote nestled against her chest, Mom settled back. The bruises under her eyes had blackened. A bandage hugged her jaw on the right side. Her eyes were red from crying. "I'm really not hungry. Hand me that box of tissues, will you?"

A grilled cheese might've been comfort food when Jackie and Tosca were little girls and home from school sick, but nothing would bring comfort to a woman who'd just lost her best friend. Jackie had firsthand experience in that arena.

"The doctor said you should eat something and drink lots of fluids." Jackie complied with her request and followed up with a glass of lemonade. "You're lucky he released you."

The tests revealed no concussion, but Mom did have two broken ribs, two broken fingers, and abrasions and contusions galore. That didn't begin to cover the broken heart.

"I still can't believe it. It doesn't seem real. One minute we're buying papel picado and the next minute she's gone." Mom handed the glass back without drinking. "I know all about sudden death. I know about tragedy and suffering. It's not an intellectual or theological discussion for me. I've lived it. Yet the words that keep running through my mind are so patently stupid."

"It's not fair."

"Exactly. It's not fair."

"Why do we think life should be fair?" Jackie tucked a blanket around her mother's thin legs. "I feel like a second grader. It's not fair. We've had more than our share."

"Is there such a thing? Look at the Kennedys. I'm sure they think the same thing." Mom closed her eyes. Tears escaped and rolled down her temples into her hair. "Her kids will be here tomorrow. I'm so thankful they have spouses to support them through this."

Mom had delivered the news with far more aplomb than Jackie could ever have imagined doing herself. Their own family—from Mom's side—had descended as soon as they heard the news. They had to see for themselves that their Aimee was still in one piece. Blessedly, they didn't stay long. Jackie's aunts would bring soup and pasta in the days to come. They'd help with the housework and do laundry. They were like that.

No word from the big house. Not even Cris had responded to her text.

"Me too." Jackie sat on the cherry coffee table where she'd scarred her nose as a child, falling into the edge while chasing Cris. She leaned forward and smoothed Mom's silver curls away from her forehead. "And you have all of us. Especially Tosca and me."

They were taking turns spending the night. "You're good girls." Mom's eyes closed again. "So is Cris. He'll be by soon. You'll see."

Maybe.

The doorbell trilled. "I bet that's him now."

Cris had a key.

"I'll get it." Tosca passed through the living room long enough to hand off the patty melt, nestled beside raw veggies and yogurt dill dip. "I'll tell whoever it is you're not up to company."

"I'm fine." Her wispy voice belied the protest.

A second later Tosca was back with Bella, who went straight to Mom. "I had to see for myself you're okay. I'm so sorry for your loss." She hugged the older woman with care and kissed her forehead. "I loved Victoria. I can't believe she's gone."

The same words again and again. Nothing else fit.

"I'm fine. Just sad." Mom's voice quivered. "Are you holding up, sweetie?"

Bella took off her jacket and laid it on the ottoman at the foot of Dad's chocolate-brown easy chair. No one ever sat there anymore. "Angry. I'm so angry."

"Me too." Jackie and her mom spoke in unison.

"Me three," Tosca added. "Can I fix you a patty melt? I'm in cooking mode."

"I've eaten more fast food the last three days than in the last year." Bella clutched her ever-present laptop in both hands. "I can't bear the sight of food right now. But thank you anyway."

"Lemonade—"

Bella's phone blasted an Alicia Keys song. "Sorry." She put the phone to her ear and scurried toward the kitchen. "This is Bella." She halted, whirled, and mouthed, *It's him.*

Jackie stood and moved toward her. "Him, him?" she whispered.

Bella nodded and motioned toward the kitchen. "I'm putting you on speaker so I can take notes. How did you get this number?"

Jackie dug her phone from her jean pocket, hit Record, and followed Bella into the kitchen.

They laid the phones side by side on the granite countertop. Bella opened a new document on her laptop. "Are you still there? Tell me, how'd you get my cell phone number?"

"I'm a computer nerd." The strange he-she voice chuckled. At least it might have been a mangled chuckle. "Don't worry, I'm not stalking you. I called the newsroom. You didn't answer. A little digging and voilà, I had your number."

"I already turned in my story."

"Too bad."

"Why?"

"You need to go back. You need to write a new story about how the mayor and the city manager are responsible for twelve more deaths and all those injured victims. They're killing the citizens they serve because they're too stupid and bloated with self-importance to do the right thing."

Jackie opened her mouth. Bella shook her finger and mimed zipping her lips. "You're wrong. You and only you are responsible for these deaths. You almost killed the mother of a good friend of mine. You killed a wonderful lady who taught grade school. You're a monster."

"Sticks and stones will break my bones, but words will never hurt."

"You hurt people who are loved, who leave behind grieving friends and family. How can you be so cavalier about it?"

"Again, collateral damage."

Tosca slid her hand over Jackie's mouth. Jackie gritted her teeth. The bomber's words were like firecrackers in her own head. She brushed Tosca's hand away.

"These are people. They are loved." Bella's tone didn't change. "They are living, breathing people."

"The city manager and the mayor and all their sycophants must be taught lessons. This is the only way they learn."

"What do you want now?"

"The same thing I wanted before. They must resign. The so-called climate-action plan must be rescinded. They must admit publicly that they're responsible for not only these deaths but many more."

"What do you mean . . . many more?"

How did Bella manage? How could she keep her cool while interviewing a psychopath? She simply kept him talking and kept writing. Jackie hunkered down on a bar stool and took her own notes. Anything to keep from reaming the caller.

"Look at the city's murder rate this year. Take a look at the crime stats. What are they doing about the safety of the citizens who live here? They're so worried about the fake science of climate change they don't have time to solve real problems, like crime and gang violence. They don't even deal with white-collar crime adequately. They can't get potholes filled or drainage at low-water crossings fixed."

The caller knew his city, but so did Bella. "You're ignoring the fact that you and your so-called organization contributed seventeen deaths to that murder rate. How can you criticize law enforcement when you're contributing massively to their workload? Instead of focusing on solving other crimes, they have to focus on investigating your crimes."

"What do you mean so-called organization?"

"We can't find any indication USAP exists."

"It does. Try harder. If they want to avoid more bombings, they'll fulfill my—our—original demands."

"How will the city manager and the mayor resigning help your cause?"

"New blood."

"Do they do anything right?"

"Not that I can name offhand." The bomber apparently missed the sarcasm in Bella's voice. "They abuse the taxpayers' dollars, funneling them into their pet projects like building a bridge over Wurzbach Parkway so wildlife can get from one side of Hardberger Park to the other. Or building zip lines at Pearsall Park. They work city employees to death and then lay them off to save a buck so they can pay themselves more."

Not far from the truth. But no excuse for bloodshed. Most people simply made themselves heard in their polling place or by writing a letter to the editor.

He-she paused. Jackie leaned forward. Had he hung up? Jackie glanced at Bella. Her friend stared at the phone, her expression full of loathing.

"We're off topic. Deliver my ultimatum. I expect to see their resignations in the paper tomorrow." A *tsk-tsk* floated on the air. "You don't want to see the Alamo or the River Walk destroyed along with hundreds of visitors do you?"

He hung up.

Tosca plopped into a chair at the kitchen table. "How do you do this for a living?"

Bella closed her laptop. She grabbed her phone and made a call. "He called again. Yeah, yeah, I'm on my way. Yeah, you call them." She stuck the phone in her jean pocket. "I have to go back to the newsroom."

"Did you hear what he said?" Jackie picked up her own phone. She had the urge to wipe it down with bleach wipes. "He fumbled the words."

"He said *my* instead of *our,* you mean?"

"Yep. He also realized he'd said too much."

"This person doesn't care about climate control or lack thereof. This is personal."

"All that means is the cops will be on your tail again." Bella raced into the living room, where she grabbed her coat and slid it on. "Yours too,

Tosca. They think your whole family is holding a grudge. Don't let them push you around. Get Chandra Martinez to help you."

"How do you know about Chandra?"

"I'm a reporter. I have sources." Bella squeezed Jackie in a hug. She leaned back and stared at her face with such intensity Jackie blinked. "Where's Cris? He should be here for your mom and for you. You need his help. He's your big brother."

"Tosca and I have this covered. Cris will be here when he gets here." Now she was making excuses for her brother just like Mom. "I texted him. He hasn't responded."

"Don't let Detective Wick push you around."

"I won't. You be careful too."

Bella opened the door. Cris stood on the porch. Bella screeched.

"I know I'm an ugly bum, but really?" Cris held out a large plastic container. "Nonna sent some of her soup for Mom. Nonno suggested it."

In times like these, families came together. No matter what came before. "Mom will love it." She took his offering. "Maybe she'll call and tell them so."

"It's about time you got here." Bella brushed past him. "Get it together. Your sisters and your mom need you."

Cris simply watched her progress. When her Bug sputtered and then fired up, he turned to Jackie. "I'm sorry it took me so long. Being the boss's grandson is more responsibility than I realized. I can't believe Aunt Victoria is dead."

Jackie walked into his hug and hid her face in his shoulder. He smelled of Irish Spring soap and Polo aftershave, just like Dad. "Me either," she whispered.

God could use every situation for her good. Cris was home. That was something.

TWENTY-TWO

Tracking down Jackie Santoro wasn't as easy as Avery anticipated. The briefing had been anything but brief. It mostly consisted of inter-agency squabbling. Chief wasn't pleased with the decision not to bring Meher Faheem in. And why hadn't they brought Jackie Santoro in for questioning after she colluded with another person of interest in the bombings, including hiding that person in her home?

Mostly because Jackie hadn't been at her home. She'd been at Market Square looking for her mother amid the ruins. And then the hospital.

Only, when Avery arrived at the hospital, she and her mother were already gone. Victoria Zucchi's name had appeared on the list of deceased victims. DOA.

Instead of tracking down the security guard who allegedly took the backpack from Meher, Avery was sent to bring in "his" witness. Ruiz wanted an SAPD interview. Or he wanted to spite the Feds.

Avery punched in Jackie's number. His call went to voice mail. He left her a polite message to call him at her earliest convenience. Then he drove to her house. The porch light was on at her Craftsman-style cottage in the Five Points neighborhood. As a uniformed cop, Avery had patrolled this area, then best known for decaying and abandoned homes, drug traffic, gangbangers, and other sordid businesses. Then a few brave souls had ventured into rehabbing one of the oldest neighborhoods in town, home to the second-oldest park in the country—San Pedro Springs—and one of the oldest elementary schools still in use in the country.

They'd done good. The result was many millennials were staking their claims, mostly in rentals, so they could be close to jobs downtown.

Jackie's car wasn't under the carport. Probably at her mother's home. He glanced at his watch. What would it hurt to give them until tomorrow to recover? Or he could track down Aimee Santoro's address. Likely her daughter would spend the night with her.

His phone dinged. An unknown number. He drummed his fingers on the wheel. Whatever. He picked up. "Wick."

"It's Chuy over at the Ball and Cue."

Theo's favorite hangout. Avery leaned his head on the headrest. "So what's up?"

"I tried calling him an Uber, but he won't leave. He had been drinking when he got here. I cut him off after two beers, so he's throwing a fit."

"I'm on my way."

Ten minutes later Avery pulled into the parking lot at a near northside pool hall and beer tavern frequented by law enforcement. The last place Theo should be making a scene. He would never get his job back with park police. An old Garth Brooks song, "Friends in Low Places," blared over the click of ball against ball and hooting and hollering of a good-size crowd.

Avery nodded in passing to a few guys he knew. One or two gave him a curious glance. He hadn't been here in at least a year. Finally he spotted Theo chatting up a Vice detective who had a pained expression on her face.

"Hey, Theo, your ride home is here." Chuy slid a bottle of water onto the bar in front of Theo. "Take this with you. Hydration helps with the hangover."

Theo's glassy, unfocused gaze meandered from the woman on the stool next to him to Avery. "Dude, what are you doing here? I thought you swore off beer."

"I came to get you."

Avery gave the detective an apologetic smile. She shrugged, picked up her Modelo, and moved away.

"Have a drink with me." Theo slid around on his stool and waved at Chuy. "Bring a Heineken for my friend. It's on me. And bring me one more for the road while you're at it."

Avery shook his head. Chuy went back to washing glasses.

"Let's go, mi amigo."

"I can't go home."

Avery plopped onto the stool next to him. "I thought you were headed home to apologize this morning."

"I did. Katie said I have to go back to therapy with her or I have to find another place to live. I left."

"Seriously? Your wife loves you. She wants to help you."

"I'm not taking ultimatums from anyone." Theo hiccupped and excused himself. "And I don't need any more head shrinking."

"Even if it makes Katie feel better? Your wife needs you."

Theo pushed the bottle of water aside and laid his head on the bar.

"Theo, come on." Avery stood and touched his friend's arm. "Let me take you home. Tell her you love her. Tell her you'll do whatever she wants. She's been hurt enough. Don't hurt her more."

"I couldn't save him."

"I know." Avery gripped Theo's arm and helped him stand. "You did your best. No one could've done more."

He slid his arm around Theo's shoulders and guided him to the door. A couple of motorcycle patrol officers gave Avery a thumbs-up. He nodded and moved on.

Getting Theo into the truck took a bucket of patience. Avery sang, "He Ain't Heavy, He's My

Brother," while he buckled Theo's seat belt. By the time he shut the door, trotted around to his side, and slid in, the man was snoring.

Avery breathed and studied the stars overhead. Theo smelled like stale beer and BO. Avery opened his window. The cool night air felt good on his warm face. His phone rang.

Katie.

"Just the person I wanted to talk to."

"Do you have him?" Katie's husky voice always seemed incongruent with her slight build. "Is he okay?"

"Yeah, I have him. He's passed out in my truck."

"I'm sorry, Avery."

"He's a friend."

"One day he'll wear out that get-out-of-jail-free card." Her sigh hummed along the imaginary line that connected them. "Bring him home, please."

"Are you sure?"

"There's something I want you to see."

That didn't sound good. Avery hopped on I-10 West and headed for the medical center area northwest of downtown. The Berettas lived in an old one-story ranch-style house near the hospital where Katie worked. Despite the late hour, traffic was snarled at the I-10/Loop 410 interchange. Par for the course. By the time he pulled into the driveway, Theo's snoring had reached the level of a supersonic jet taking off.

Katie opened the door before Avery could jockey her husband from the truck. Light spilled from their house, silhouetting her tiny frame and leaving her face in the shadows.

"Let's get him into the guest bedroom, if we can." She grabbed Theo's other arm and slung it over her shoulders. "He's not as heavy as he used to be."

"I haven't been able to talk him into Bill Miller's in a long time." Theo had a thing for brisket with all the sides washed down with a bucket of sweet tea from his favorite barbecue place. Avery had eaten there with him many times—but not since his son's death. "I think he's adopted a liquid diet."

In the bedroom Katie tugged off Theo's ostrich-skin boots and tucked him under a plaid flannel blanket. "He used to love my cooking. We haven't eaten a meal together in weeks."

Avery followed her from the bedroom back to the living room. "You said you had something for me to see?"

Without a word she kept going to the kitchen and out the door that led to the garage.

Her sturdy Honda was parked on one side. Tools, a workbench, a mower, and gardening implements crowded the other. Katie stopped at the long homemade workbench. Avery paused next to her. She didn't have to explain. A collection of weapons lay neatly arranged across the back of the bench. Mostly handguns, but several rifles joined them, along with an AK-15 and an M4 carbine.

"How long has he had these?" Avery ran his hand over a Ruger, then touched a Sig Sauer. They didn't surprise him. Theo liked his guns. If he had more discretionary income, he'd collect them. The AK-15 and the M4 carbine, on the other hand, were unexpected. Avery picked up the AK-15 and checked to see if it was loaded. Thankfully, it wasn't. "This isn't really his style."

"I asked him about the other weapons when he brought them home. He claimed the rifles were for hunting, the handguns for safety." Katie pulled her pink cardigan tighter around her body. A pretty woman, she didn't ordinarily need makeup. Tonight her face appeared washed out. She'd been crying recently. "I didn't know about the assault rifles."

"He hasn't asked me to go hunting in a long time." Given his experience with his son's death, it wasn't surprising that he felt unsafe or a need to protect Katie. "Has he been talking about security a lot?"

Prior to Caleb's death, they'd hunted frequently. Deer, javelina, dove, quail, wild turkeys. Chandra and Katie hung out, watched movies, and commiserated about being married to LEOs, while their husbands brought home wild game for the barbecue pit. Under a starry night, the four of them sat around the chiminea in the backyard and solved the world's problems while Caleb slept. After Avery's divorce, he didn't have the heart for it anymore. Theo eventually stopped asking.

"He upgraded our security system and added cameras in the front and back of the house." Katie edged away from the bench and then turned her back on it. She wore shaggy Elmo slippers that were endearing on a thirtysomething woman. "He wanted me to get a license to carry. I refused."

"I can see why he might want you to do that."

"I've seen firsthand what damage guns do. I don't need any more of that in my life." Katie had insisted on seeing Caleb before the medical examiner began the autopsy. "I'm good with my pepper spray."

"Assault rifles can be modified to be used for hunting deer." A case of overkill without a doubt. "The problem is he hasn't been hunting."

"The problem is he drinks too much. He shouldn't be handling any guns. I was happy when they put him on medical leave so he wouldn't be carrying around his service revolver. Now this. Can you take them?" Her calm facade slipped for a second. A frightened woman filled with agonizing pain peeked out. "Do something with them? Get rid of them?"

"I'll need the paperwork to show they're legit. I don't want to get pulled over with a stash of somebody else's guns." Avery pushed the button to open the garage door. "Why don't you see if you can find it while I load these into my truck?"

Katie's face filled with relief. Her shoulders sagging, she started toward the door that led to the kitchen.

"He'll come after them."

"I know, but it'll give him time to think about what he's doing." Hopefulness warred with uncertainty in her voice. "It'll give me time to convince him to go back to therapy."

"Have you thought about a temporary commitment?"

Her hand on the doorknob, she bowed her head. "Do you think it's that bad?"

"It isn't good." Avery cocked his head toward the stash of weapons. "I'm also worried about you."

"He'd never hurt me."

"He's hurting you now by not getting his act together." Avery contemplated the weapons. "I'll give it another try tomorrow. My pastor is a good guy." Manny was easier to talk to than the departmental shrink. Maybe it was the tattoo on his forearm or his endless repertoire of jokes. "Maybe Theo will agree to talk to him."

"You're a good friend." She pulled the door shut behind her.

Avery loaded the stash into the truck bed. His stomach lurched with each step. The wind picked up. Clouds snuffed out the moon. A shiver rolled through Avery. After a day knee-deep in bloody mayhem, this discovery only made it harder to believe daylight would bother to come. His best friend had amassed an arsenal. What was going on in his traumatized brain? Did he really want the guns for protection, or did he have another use in mind?

No. Theo hadn't staggered that far from the straight and narrow.

No way.

"Here's the paperwork." Katie jogged up to the truck. "Get some sleep. I'll put off taking him to get his truck for as long as possible tomorrow."

"If he refuses to get help, send him to stay with me." Avery started the truck. He leaned out the open window. "Or go stay with a friend for a while. You don't need this, and I don't want you getting caught in the line of fire if we can't get him straightened out."

Her gaze held his. "My leaving will only make his state of mind worse."

"Sometimes you have to hit rock bottom."

The clouds parted. The moonlight shone on her white face. She hugged her arms to her chest. "I thought we already did that."

Head bowed, she turned and trudged back into the house.

Sometimes even rock bottom wasn't enough.

Avery touched the accordion folder on the seat next to him. Time to lay his friend's ghosts to rest. He drove home, parked in the garage, unloaded the cache of guns into a lockbox, and took the folder inside. Every muscle in his body ached for sleep. His throat hurt from inhaling smoke. His clothes were dirty and he smelled.

Fortunately Avery lived alone. He scrubbed his face in cold water and made a fresh pot of coffee.

No more procrastinating. He opened the folder. Caleb's toothy grin was frozen in time. He had Theo's dark curly hair and blue eyes. Given the chance, he would've been tall like his father.

He didn't get that chance. Deeper into the file resided less pleasant photos. Crime scene photos. Caleb's eyes mercifully were closed. His face had gone slack. Blood soaked his baseball jersey. The Broncos. Number 4. A smudge of dirt decorated his cheek.

Autopsy photos. Bullets entered his body near his heart, below the sternum, and through his belly. Two kids from the other team were injured and one spectator, a dad, but they survived. They would never be the same, but they lived.

Avery touched Caleb's photo. He still had a photo of the boy in his Cub Scout uniform on his fireplace mantel. That's the way he wanted to remember him. The kid loved to camp. They'd gone to Big Bend a couple of times. At barbecues, Avery played H-O-R-S-E with him and taught him the teardrop, Tony Parker's signature shot. He had another photo of them eating watermelon at the Woodlawn Lake Fourth of July celebration.

That's how he would remember Caleb. After he found the thug who killed him.

He poured more coffee and went to work.

TWENTY-THREE

Nonna's *minestra d'orzo*, ibuprofen, chamomile tea, and sheer exhaustion finally did their work. Jackie gently tugged the remote from her mother's limp hand and turned off the TV. She cocked her head toward the kitchen and headed that direction. Cris's booted tread told her he followed. They'd spent the last hour and a half laughing and crying as they traded memories of Victoria with Mom. Tosca gave in and went to bed in her childhood room about halfway in. Jackie's own exhaustion refused to be daunted. Her head buzzed and the room swayed like an inebriated reveler, but still she couldn't summon slumber.

Instead she put together the ingredients for cocoa. "Marshmallows?"

"Are you kidding?" Cris slid onto a bar stool and laid his phone on the island. "Put some cinnamon in it too. Nonna does that and it's tasty."

"Is that where you were tonight? With Nonna when Mom needed you?"

"Here we go."

"Yes, here we go. After all Mom's been through, you couldn't come to the hospital to be with her in her grief and her pain."

"I was late because Nonna was making the *zuppa*. That should count for something. I'm here now."

"Mom loves you best." So did her grandparents, no matter what Nonno said. "You know that, right?"

"I'm the favorite? You want to throw that in my face? You have impeccable timing."

"Nonna and Nonno are replacing their son with their grandson. You remind them of Daddy. She clings to that memory."

"You say that like it's a bad thing. It alleviates some of the pain of losing their only son. Surely you can see that."

"I simply think you need to be you. Loved for you and not a remembrance of a man who hurt them because they had to concede he had human frailties. As much as Daddy hurt his parents by leaving the family businesses, they still idolized him as their only son. Do you want to spend your life living up to the lie that was our father?"

"He wasn't a lie." Cris slammed his fist on the granite. His chest heaved. He shook his head. "He wasn't."

His anger seemed preferable to his usual cool neutrality. Jackie leaned into her own anger. It gave her new energy and swallowed up the grief of the past few days. "How can you make excuses for him after what he did?"

"How can you not forgive him?" Cris's mouth

twisted into a sardonic smile. "Isn't that a big no-no with your God?"

Jackie paused with her mug halfway to her mouth. Carefully she lowered it. He was right, of course, about the forgiveness. She'd been trying for two years to forgive her father. At this point she could only hope for an A for effort. She had to answer for her own sins. The plank in her eye. Something else about his statement stung more. "Don't you mean *our* God?"

"Let's just say He's proven Himself unreliable recently."

Like Tosca and Jackie, Cris was never allowed to miss church as a child. Sunday school, choir, Christmas programs, youth group—they did it all. They never questioned it. Invariably when someone asked her about when she had come to Christ, she felt a pinch of disappointment because she couldn't point to a high-on-the-mountain moment of acceptance of her Savior. *"I have always believed,"* she would say awkwardly. It seemed better than *"I don't know."* Cris had accepted Christ as his Savior at age sixteen while on a mission trip to the Tenderloin District in San Francisco. He came back walking on air and ready to do battle against Satan.

"Daddy would never want his actions to cause you to lose your faith."

"Sometimes actions have unintended consequences."

An irrefutable statement. "I'm so sorry you had to go through that. It must have been horrific. God is still here. He's walking through this with you. He wants you to turn to Him."

They'd never talked about it. Cris bolted every time she brought it up. Mom suggested therapy. He fled. Tosca suggested their pastor. Cris shook his head and ran away like a mugger was chasing him.

"If it's a test, it's a sadistic one. If it's meant to toughen me up, again, sadistic. If He's all-powerful, all-knowing, all-wise, why didn't He stop Dad? Was He busy with the Palestinian-Israeli conflict? Or trying to overturn *Roe v. Wade*? What?"

"I won't lie. I struggle to understand too. Kids getting cancer or getting blown up with landmines, SIDS deaths. How much honing does our character really need? Why do some get healing or relief in this life and others have to wait until the next?" Those were simply a sampling of questions Jackie planned to ask when she saw God face-to-face. Many believers said their questions would fade away in the excitement of basking in God's glory around the throne. Jackie was far too stubbornly curious to believe she would fall into that category. "I just know my minuscule brain can't begin to fathom—"

"If you tell me God has a plan and He's working for our good, I swear I'll walk out that door."

Cris stood. "Sunday school talk falls easily from the lips of other people who've lived in cocoons all their lives. Surely you aren't still mouthing them like a parrot who has no idea what she's saying even in the aftermath of the slaughter of your best friend and Vicky's death."

"I know what Scripture says. Unlike the words of Sunday school teachers, the truth of the Holy Bible is indisputable."

Cris sank back onto the stool. He closed his eyes. He looked sixty instead of thirty-one. His summer tan had faded. Thinning hair left his forehead exposed. Dark circles like bruises ringed his eyes. Jackie's heart cracked. Her brother looked defeated.

He looked like Daddy did when he had invited all of them to dinner and waited until dessert to tell them what the ten o'clock news would report. The media had already gathered in the street in front of the house where they grew up. His cell phone rang so many times he finally turned it off. After hearing his story Mom stood and left the room. He followed.

Neither returned, leaving Cris to comfort his younger sisters. They huddled in front of the TV, watching the news stories in which a few thirty-second sound bites turned their father from hardworking city employee into a criminal tried and convicted in the court of public opinion. After they played the video released by Municipal Integrity of Daddy sitting in a bar with a well-known developer, Tosca cried. Cris turned off the TV and reminded them both that TV news was an oxymoron. It hadn't helped.

"God didn't slaughter our friends. Evil did that."

"For someone so smart, you're so dumb." Cris opened his eyes. They were red and filled with tears. "Wasn't it enough that the city manager bowed to pressure and fired Dad before he had a chance to defend himself? You're still working for that slug and his cronies."

She had considered walking away from a job she loved, but it seemed a great deal like cutting off her nose to spite her face. She would have to leave her hometown to get another job with similar responsibilities and pay. The city manager would never notice her absence. Estrella worked for one of the "cronies" who led the witch hunt against her father. Her friend had always argued that it was easier to change the system by working inside it. She would've made a stellar elected official one day.

None of this came close to being as important as Cris's tattered faith. "Why don't you spend the night? It's too late to drive all the way to the Dominion. You're tired. In the morning I'll make waffles." Dawn was only an hour away. "We'll go to church together as a family."

Maybe they would find some modicum of peace there. Mom would like it too.

"Did you hear anything I said?" He picked up his mug and took it to the sink, where he rinsed it and stuck it in the dishwasher. Ever the neat, industrious Santoro sibling. "I'd better get back to the house. Nonna is a light sleeper. She worries until I come home."

"Don't you care how Mom feels?"

"Mom has you and Tosca."

He strode past the living room on his way to the front door without glancing toward the living room. Jackie followed. "Be careful."

"I'm sorry."

A landslide of pain crushed Jackie. "Me too. Please stay."

A fleeting but hard hug served as his response.

She closed the door and leaned against it. *God, I've been too self-absorbed to notice. Cris needs You. Forgive me for not noticing how lost he is. I don't deserve it, I know. I'm sorry.*

Sometimes sorry came too late.

Her phone buzzed. No, no, no, she couldn't speak another word, couldn't hear another word. Like a Pavlovian response, she couldn't ignore it either.

Nonno.

A call she couldn't ignore. "Nonno?"

"How is your mother? I called her number, but there was no answer, so I left a message."

"I put her phone away. So many of her friends were calling." Jackie sank to the floor and sat cross-legged, her back against the door. "Tell Nonna thank you for the soup. It helped Mom relax and sleep."

"Minestra d'orzo has medicinal qualities." He sounded weary. Unusual for him. "I'm so sorry for your loss. Victoria was a good friend to your mother during a time of trouble."

"At all times." Fatigue married with grief made Jackie's voice tremble. She closed her eyes. *Do not cry.* "I'm sure Mom will call you back tomorrow."

"And Tosca? How is she taking it?"

"She's cooking patty melts."

"If she's cooking, she must be truly traumatized." Nonno chuckled. "Give her our love."

The knot in Jackie's voice grew. "I will," she whispered.

"Get some sleep. You've had a traumatic day. At least Aimee wasn't more badly hurt. It is a miracle."

"You get some sleep too. You sound tired."

His sigh filled the line. "No rest for the worried. Godspeed."

Eyes closed, Jackie sat on the floor for a long time mulling his words. The fissure in their family had begun to close. She would never have chosen this method to bury the past, but she would have to learn to accept it as a tiny light of hope in the midst of darkest night.

She had her nonno back.

TWENTY-FOUR

No rest for the wicked meant no rest for the weary. Bright and early Sunday morning, Avery returned to PD where he met up with Petra Jantzen. In the interest of restoring harmony, the FBI case agent had suggested the agencies share interviews. Avery was lucky to get Petra as his ride-along. Scotty had another agent from her squad. They were trying to suss out the deliveryman Meher Faheem claimed to have seen wandering around the Tobin grand hall before the first bombing.

Avery and Petra's mission was to find the security guard who allegedly took the backpack from Faheem. Petra settled into the unmarked Charger's passenger seat. "Nice ride."

"We were fortunate to get a new one when they made the changeover from the Crown Vics. Patrol units are driving SUVs these days. How have you been?"

Petra held up her cell, allowing him to see a chunky toddler with a gaping mouth that revealed two tiny teeth sprouting from his bottom gum. "Grandchild number three."

"Nice."

"I keep thinking I'll retire and go spend time with them."

"Yet here you are."

"Thrill of the chase, I suppose. I have two years left before the bureau makes the retirement decision for me."

Thankfully police officers weren't required to retire at fifty-seven. Although some should. "Retirement must look good in the middle of this mess."

From there the conversation turned to hash and rehash of the current "chase." They headed for the corporate offices of Alamo Security. They were open seven days a week in the Colonnade on I-10 West, no doubt because the need for people to feel secure had never been higher. The cramped office smelled of floral air freshener and somebody's lunch. A retired PD captain sat at one of the metal desks behind the front counter. Chuck Hausman, former traffic motorcycle cop, had never been one of Avery's favorites, but they had an immediate connection that might prove useful in extracting more information than the Feds were able to get from his bosses.

"Wicked. You're the last guy I expected to see walk through those doors." Hausman rose and lumbered to the counter. He wore a Glock on his hip and a polo with an Alamo Security logo on it. "And who's this lovely lady? What happened to Heller?"

Avery made the introductions. "Scotty's had different marching orders this time."

Hausman cocked his head and gave Petra an unabashed once-over. "FBI? Huh. I guess you're not looking for work. We hire plenty of washed-up cops."

"I'll keep that in mind." Avery matched Hausman's just-joking grin. The guy made his teeth grind. "We're working the bombings."

"Oh yah, so they sent the Feds to babysit you?"

"It's a joint operation." Petra's tone remained cordial. She even smiled. "We need to talk to your personnel who worked the event. All of them."

"We already gave the list to HSI. We're only talking about four guys. Nobody was expecting a terrorist attack in a little hoity-toity arts center."

Even though climate change was one of the most hotly debated topics of the century with an enormous chasm between the believers and nonbelievers—particularly among the politicians on both sides of the aisle. Hausman's provincialism was showing.

"They're having trouble running down a couple of names on the list." Avery sought to match Petra's evenhanded approach. "We thought maybe you can help with that."

"No problem, but I can save you some time." Hausman leaned on the counter on both meaty arms. "Get you home in time for Sunday supper."

Oh boy. Likely a Whataburger with cheese and fries for Avery. Petra's husband, a retired customs officer, on the other hand, specialized in pot roasts for Sunday dinner. "How's that?"

"I emailed the guys who worked the event to see if anyone saw anything suspicious." Hausman straightened. "Nobody did."

"Based on an email response?" Avery's irritation threatened to breach the bunker. "Is that how you conducted investigations when you were on the force?"

"These are all guys who've been background checked. They come from law enforcement backgrounds. They're certified peace officers."

"Which begs the question, why are they working security?"

Petra shot Avery a cease-and-desist scowl. "What my colleague means is we'd like to walk through the interviews ourselves."

"Not everyone makes the academy cut." Hausman shrugged. "For minor health reasons, a misdemeanor violation, something small disqualifies them. A lot of them are retired cops from the school districts or the universities. It's a diverse group."

And some didn't pass the psych evals.

"So tell us about the two our guys haven't been able to run down." Avery glanced at the sticky note on his notebook. "Ethan Richter and Charley Brunswick. What can you tell us about either of those men?"

Hausman jerked his head toward the desk.

"You might as well come in, have a seat while I look them up."

Thirty seconds later Avery and Petra squeezed into cheap plastic chairs across from Hausman while he employed a hunt-and-peck method of typing to look up the two guards in question.

After a silence punctuated by the snap of his wad of gum, Hausman leaned back and scratched his balding head. "Brunswick, I know. He's a decent guy but kind of wussy. He left before the event started, claimed he had a stomachache, according to a supervisor on duty. He's called in sick every day since. But that's nothing new. His attendance is spotty at best. He's always got something wrong."

"Why does the company keep him?"

"He's up for review. He won't be around much longer."

"Any red flags in his behavior—other than chronic absenteeism?"

"Nope. No complaints on his record. He'd worked for mall security and neighborhood security. Basically he's made a career of being a rent-a-cop."

Avery glanced at Petra. She raised her shapely eyebrows and nodded. "We'll need his address."

"I imagine management gave it to your buddies already."

"We're following up." Avery offered a conspiratorial wink. Hausman liked to think of himself as part of the inner circle even though he'd never been a particularly good cop and dumped his shield as soon as he could retire. "What about Richter?"

"Him I don't know." Hausman returned to the computer screen. The chair squeaked under his weight. "Huh. Interesting."

Avery waited. Nothing. Making them beg for it? "What?"

"Richter was a new hire. The Tobin gig was only his second." His jowls quivering, Hausman tapped the keyboard with his index finger. "The guy was a no-show for a gig this past weekend. After two no-shows and two no-calls, the boss fired him. Richter didn't respond to our emails or phone calls."

"So he worked the Tobin event and walked away."

"Yep."

"What's his background?"

"Peace officer certification. His file shows he hired out to a paramilitary firm in Kuwait after he got out of the Army. He's done security jobs in Vegas, mostly celebrities."

"Anything there about his military service?"

A smirk on his clean-shaven face, Hausman rocked in the chair. *Squeak, squeak.* "Bomb detection and disposal. Iraq."

Somebody with more than a passing knowledge of how bombs worked.

"Did HSI know this?"

"As far as I know, they didn't ask, but I assume they did their own background checks."

"Got a photo of him?"

Hausman slid the monitor around. Meher Faheem had described the security guard who took the backpack as tall, dark hair, dark eyes. Richter definitely fit the bill for the last two. "How tall is he?"

Hausman squinted. "Hmmm. Same height as me, if I remember right."

The retired cop looked to be around six feet tall. He would seem tall to Meher.

"What about Brunswick?"

Hausman did more hunt-and-peck. "Here you go. Brunswick is about the same height, maybe a little taller. Richter is muscle bound, but Brunswick is just a beanpole."

Both would be giants to Meher.

"We need addresses."

"You got it." Hausman printed the information and handed it over. "Don't say I never did anything for you."

Outside, Petra stretched and cranked her head side to side. "Do we try to call them first? See if they're around? Or drop in before they have a chance to rabbit?"

"Knock and talk."

"*Vamonos.*" Petra's attempt to speak Spanish made him smile. She was a Dallas native with a drawl as long as Avery was tall. "Right behind you."

Charley Brunswick's small house with its peeling paint and lackluster landscaping was closer, but no one answered the door. "Must not be too sick," Petra opined. "He's probably wining and dining his girl right now."

Avery peeked in a front window. Living room looked lived in. Mail strewn across a coffee table. Empty beer bottles. A jacket slung over the back of a couch. "I don't think he's been gone long. Likely coming back."

They traipsed through a fence gate into the backyard. A charcoal grill and some broken-down lawn chairs. Not much else. Back windows revealed a bedroom with an unmade bed and a kitchen with a sink full of dirty dishes. From a distance nothing seemed suspicious, but not even a rent-a-cop would leave a stash of weapons or bomb-making materials in plain sight. Would he?

"The guy left before the bombing on Friday morning. That's suspect. But is it enough for a search warrant?" Avery kicked at a dirty baseball lying next to the grill. "Being a chronic wuss isn't a crime."

"Considering the stakes, a judge might be inclined to allow it." Petra tried the doorknob. No dice. Not that she was thinking of entering without the warrant. She knew better. "We don't have time to sit on this place. Let's try Richter's place. If we can rule out one of them or connect the two of them, we might have better luck with the judge."

"Agreed. We better get out of here. Somebody will see us and call the cops to report two Peeping Toms."

That would be the crowning glory of a long day getting longer.

Avery led the charge back to the car just as a woman pushing a double stroller filled with two sleeping toddlers trotted toward them. She had a canister of pepper spray in one hand.

"What were you doing in Charley's backyard?"

"We're law enforcement officers." Avery produced his badge. The woman's gaze flicked to it and back to his face. Her scowl darkened. Avery pointed at Petra. "I'm PD. She's FBI. We just want to talk to him."

"That doesn't give you the right to waltz onto private property like you own the place. Where's your search warrant? Texas is a stand-your-ground state. You could get shot, you know. Call the man and make an appointment, why don't you?"

"Have you seen Charley—?"

"No and I wouldn't tell you if I had." The canister's aim bobbed from Avery to Petra. "I will tell him that a guy who claimed to be a cop showed up and messed around on his private property. Go now."

It seemed prudent to go, so they went.

TWENTY-FIVE

From rags to riches. Ethan Richter's home turned out to be a duplex off Loop 1604 and Highway 281. Not a cheap area. With its fresh white paint and manicured lawn, it looked like someone had prepared it for Zillow.

"Pricey neighborhood." Avery clomped up three steps to the tiny porch with its chiminea filled with red and purple pansies. The welcome mat sported a sunflower pattern. "Feels like it has a woman's touch, but it's really small. Probably couldn't afford anything bigger out here."

Petra pushed the doorbell. When nothing happened, she knocked. No response.

Two for two. Time was not on their side. The bomber, irked that the city manager hadn't stepped down, would strike again. Avery stepped in and knocked harder. "Anybody home?"

"You can shout all you want. He won't answer." A middle-aged lady in a pink sweatshirt and leggings, which made her look like a bunch of cotton candy on two sticks, hollered from the yard next door. "He's not there."

"Do you happen to know where he is?" Avery took a shot. People could be walking calendars for their neighbors or totally oblivious. "Or when he'll be back?"

"His schedule varies, depending on his case-load. He works a lot of night shifts. When he has to be downtown, though, he's usually out of here around six fifteen." The woman introduced herself as Richter's landlord, Marie Castaneda. She had that self-important air people assumed when they knew something others don't. "He even works Sundays when he's undercover. Why?"

Meet the walking calendar neighbor. Undercover? Avery held up his badge. "SAPD. We just want to talk to him."

"That's funny." She poked her blue-framed glasses up her skinny nose. "Can't you just catch him at the station?"

"What do you mean, undercover?" Petra's eyebrows got a workout. "What station?"

"Your station. He's an undercover officer. Vice." She chortled. Her double chin wobbled. "He tells some whopper stories about the crazy things people do."

"Huh. Someone must've gotten their wires crossed." Avery backpedaled. "We'll check our info. When was the last time Officer Richter was home?"

"I took him some brownies Friday night. I do that sometimes, being he's a widower and all." Her sugary tone suggested she deserved sainthood for this mission of mercy. "He said he might be undercover for a while and asked me to take care of his pooch. Pogo. He's a Dalmatian—

like the one in *101 Dalmatians*, you know?"

Avery didn't know, but he nodded anyway. "Does he do that a lot?"

"Sure. It's okay with me. Pogo and I get along great."

"We'd like to take a look around his duplex."

"I watch *Blue Bloods* and *Law & Order*. Don't you need a warrant for that?"

"Not if you're the property owner and you give us permission."

Scowling, she thought it over, probably comparing it to the many cop shows she'd watched throughout the ages. "Why would you do that to another cop?"

"We just want to make sure he's all right." Petra offered a solicitous glance. "Something may have gone wrong with his undercover gig."

Ms. Castaneda didn't seem convinced.

"It's a matter of life and death."

Not a lie. Many people's lives were at risk.

"Oh, of course, of course. I know how dangerous undercover work can be." She tugged on the chain around her neck and a house key appeared from behind her sweatshirt. "I'll let you in, but I can't leave you alone with Ethan's property."

"We're law enforcement, ma'am."

"There are plenty of crooked cops."

Indeed. And fake cops. More knowledge culled from the boob tube.

They followed her into the duplex. Richter had nice leather furniture, warm wood floors, and a taste for Ansel Adams prints. He was also a much better housekeeper than Avery.

"He's a good tenant. He never makes messes." Ms. Castaneda smoothed a pillow on the recliner facing a big-screen TV. "He always takes care of any minor repairs himself."

Avery had nothing to say to that. "Could you just hang here a minute while we look around?"

The faint shuffle of footsteps sounded from the house's interior.

"Ethan? Is that you? I thought you were gone or I would've knocked."

The shuffle turned into a scramble.

Avery shot toward the hallway that presumably led to the kitchen. Petra followed. "Richter? We just want to talk."

Something banged.

"Police. Stop!"

Too late for that. "Take the front."

Petra reversed directions.

Avery raced to the kitchen in time to see the back door close with such force its window cracked.

His heart banged in his chest. His breath screaming in his ears, Avery jerked the door open and hurled himself into the backyard. Like most new developments in San Antonio this one had a six-foot wooden privacy fence that surrounded a postage-stamp-size backyard. It was split from the yard that belonged to the landlord. His harried sweep of the yard caught a few dog toys, a lawn chair, and a portable ashtray.

And one sneakered foot hanging over the fence that connected with Richter's neighbor on the back side.

"Richter, don't make us chase you."

The foot disappeared. Avery darted toward the fence. Getting more exercise should be at the top of his New Year's resolutions.

Pop, pop, pop!

Bullets.

One whizzed by so close to his face that he felt its heat.

Cussing a breathless steady stream, Avery hit the ground with a thud that shook his entire body.

Now it was personal. He slid his S&W from his holster and crawled to his feet. Hunkered low, he approached the fence, weapon ready. A quick peek over it revealed a twin yard and no Richter.

If it was Richter. Had someone else been lying in wait for the fake cop?

More cussing. Avery attempted to scale the fence. They made it look so easy in the movies. The second time he hoisted himself to the top and straddled it.

"Avery! Talk to me!" Petra's shout echoed behind him.

"I'm good. He booked over the fence. He's

headed north." Avery dropped into thick, soft St. Augustine grass and raced across the yard. A resident stuck his head out the back door. "Police. Stay inside. Lock the doors."

The resident withdrew.

The squealing of tires spurred Avery on. He squeezed past thick flowering bushes to peek around the front of the house. A deep-blue late-model Chevy Silverado hauled butt down the street.

Petra's obscenities were more colorful than Avery's. She called it in to the dispatcher. Everybody and their uncle would come running.

They both bent over, hands on their knees, breath heaving.

"I guess he's our guy." Petra gasped. "Why would he tell the landlady he was out of town?"

"Too noisy? Too chummy? Or it wasn't him."

"Our info says he drives a Chevy Silverado. A security guard with a military background. What happened to him in Iraq?"

"That's what we need to find out." Avery sucked in air. "We need his military records, his financials, and his telephone records."

Which could take weeks to get. They didn't have that kind of time.

"I'll get on it. You need to go to the hospital."

"No I don't."

"Yes you do. You're hit."

"You're nuts." The shakes rocked Avery. They

always did after the adrenaline started to fade. Something warm dribbled down his cheek. He touched it and stared at his fingers. Blood. Suddenly the pain registered. It stung like a son of a gun. "Okay so I got hit a little. But you're still nuts."

Sirens sounded in the distance. The cavalry. Avery's legs wobbled. *God, don't let me embarrass myself by falling on my behind now that everything is over.*

God was probably thinking, *Yeah, sure, now you wanna talk.*

Petra chuckled and clapped him on the back. "I'm sticking close to you, bud. You're one lucky dude. A little more to your right and that bullet would be lodged in your brain. Lucky for you it was too small a target for Richter."

When Avery didn't respond, Petra grinned. "Too soon?"

"We were that close to him and let him get away."

That would be the story of the day when the cavalry arrived.

TWENTY-SIX

The light at the end of the tunnel flickered and went out. Avery braked and stopped the truck at the curb in front of his house. Theo's presence in his driveway at ten o'clock on a Sunday night couldn't be a good thing. Even if he was shooting baskets, a healthy, innocent pastime—one Avery frequently indulged in after a rotten day. This day certainly qualified. After being treated by an EMT, Avery had joined in watching the CSU rip Richter's duplex to pieces, then the debrief that followed. After satisfying himself that Avery's injury was minor, LT proceeded to nitpick the way the encounter went down. Which was what superiors who'd been off the streets for a while tended to do.

Everyone was on board with finding Richter. They thought he was the bomber.

Avery was withholding judgment. The FBI's deep dive into Richter's background had revealed no motive for such attacks. While he knew how to disarm bombs, he had no real connections to San Antonio. He had no reason to hate San Antonio city officials. He had no known connections to any terrorist organizations, not even environmental ones.

He was divorced. His ex-wife lived in his home state of Kentucky.

So why do it? On the other hand, why run if he hadn't?

Theo dunked the ball and whirled to chase it. His hand went to his forehead as if shielding his face from the truck's light. "Are you coming in, dude, or what?"

His shout carried over the engine's rumble. Avery turned off the engine, hopped from the truck, and slammed the door—sometimes it had a mind of its own. Theo pivoted and dropped a basket from three-point range. Nothing but net. "It's about time, dude."

A box containing a semihot large supreme pizza from a shop four blocks over balanced in one hand, Avery trudged up the driveway. He was too tired to move any faster. A rousing game of twenty-one was out of the question. The dogs barked in unison from the backyard—Ace's anxious yelp on the higher end of the range, while Deuce's provided the bass. The neighbors wouldn't be happy about the chorus.

Avery set the box on an empty planter under the front windows and went to let them through the gate that divided the two yards. They shot around the house, yipping, jumping, and singing Avery's praises. "Good boys, good boys, it's nice to see you too. No, you can't have my pizza."

"Come on, dude, are you afraid I'll whip your behind?"

"Normally I'd wipe up the driveway with your behind, but it's been a long day and I'm beat." Avery finished petting the dogs, opened a ratty lawn chair, grabbed his pizza, and sat. "How did you get here?"

"Uber."

"Do me a favor and Uber on home."

"I want my guns." Theo rolled the ball around in his hands, then let it spin on his index finger. He always had good hands. Deuce begged for a pet. Theo tucked the ball under one arm and obliged. The odor of unwashed body wafted from his faded jeans and wrinkled Jason Aldean concert T-shirt. "Katie had no right to give them to you like I'm some crazed lone gunman out for revenge."

"Pizza?" Avery held out the box. "It still feels fairly warm."

Theo grabbed a slice and hunkered down cross-legged in the grass. "Where's the beer?"

"There's cold tea in the fridge. I don't know how long it's been in there, but I drank some of it yesterday—or maybe it was the day before."

"What happened to your face?"

"Cut myself shaving."

"Come on. Fess up."

"Leaned in too close to a passing bullet."

"That's not smart."

"Life in the fast lane."

"Wanna talk about it?"

"Nope."

"Where are my guns?" Theo spoke over a mouthful of crust, cheese, mushrooms, black olives, and Italian sausage. "Also you owe me a ride to the bar."

"You owe me thanks for saving your life the other night."

"You exaggerate." Theo sounded unrepentant. "I was doing fine."

"You were hitting on a Vice cop."

"I was not. I love my wife."

"You have a funny way of showing it."

"Katie's a worrywart."

That made Avery one too. Not even the most fervent survivalist or Second Amendment supporter-slash-big-game-hunter amassed an arsenal of weapons of this magnitude without nefarious intent. "Why do you need all those weapons?"

Theo snatched a paper napkin from the pizza box. "No reason. Collecting them. It's something to do."

Alcohol had killed too many of Theo's brain cells if he thought Avery would buy that line of bull. "Do you really think I'm an idiot?"

"I'm not planning to hurt someone if that's what you're inferring."

"I'm not inferring anything. Why have an

AK-15 in the house if you're not planning to use it?"

"For hunting."

Avery dropped his slice in the box and wiped greasy hands on his napkin. It didn't do much good. "Get out of my yard. Go home. Get your act together. The guns are locked up."

"Okay, okay. Just chill out." Theo picked up another piece of pizza, then tossed it back in the box. He wiggled, took off his Missions ball cap, smoothed his hair, returned the cap.

"I'm tired, Theo. Really tired."

"Okay, okay. They make me feel . . . safer."

"In control, you mean."

"Something like that."

Now they were getting somewhere. Avery took pity on Ace and tossed him a chunk of sausage. The dog caught it in midair, then sniffed the ground, looking for more. "I understand the urge, believe me, but guns won't help in your situation."

"They won't hurt."

Apparently Theo lived in an alternate universe now that he was no longer a park police officer. Guns hurt people every second of every day. "What if you have too much to drink one day and decide to confront Vogel or your boss or the detective who hasn't arrested the guy who killed Caleb? You'll end up in prison for murder or dead yourself. Do you want to do that to Katie?

She doesn't deserve that. She's been through enough."

Theo ducked his head. He cleared his throat. "It won't happen."

"I can't take that chance."

"What if I call the police and report them stolen?"

"Good luck with that." For the first time in days, Avery wanted to laugh. Not that it was funny. It had to be exhaustion. "Katie said you have a new security system. A good one."

"Katie moved out."

So she'd taken Avery's advice. "She's scared. I don't blame her."

"My own wife is afraid of me. She wouldn't even give me a ride here first."

"Think about that."

"I just want justice."

They all wanted justice. The image of Jackie Santoro's terrified face after the Market Square bombing brushed up against Avery's memory. "We can't always have what we want." He stood and picked up the pizza box. "Let me put this stuff away and I'll take you to get your truck."

"Maybe I'll go see Katie."

"That's a good idea. She needs you."

And Theo needed her.

Together they clomped up the steps to the door. Theo talked sweet nothings to Ace while Avery unlocked the door and stepped inside. A few seconds later the murmuring ceased. Avery glanced back. His friend had dropped onto the sofa. His eyes were closed. Relief blew through Avery. He would be safe here and so would the people he demonized. "Theo?"

"Hmmm?"

"Why don't you take the guest bedroom."

A few seconds later his snoring cut the air like a buzz saw.

"Or you could just sleep right there." At least for tonight Avery wouldn't have to worry Theo might take justice into his own hands. One way or another, those weapons would remain out of the man's reach. He might not consciously consider exacting his own form of justice, but Theo's actions suggested that the idea festered just below the surface. Having the means and the ability to justify them were a tragedy waiting to happen.

His friend needed professional help. Katie needed to make that call. If she didn't, Avery would have to do it.

Avery went to bed. But not to sleep.

TWENTY-SEVEN

Zero for two.

Wired to the max with caffeine and sugar consumed far too early on a Monday morning, Avery fired up the Charger and let it idle in the HQ parking garage slot. His eyes burned and a headache loomed. Theo wanted to argue some more about his arsenal. Avery refused. Instead he came to work to find Petra waiting for him.

"That eliminates the deliveryman."

Petra, who looked far too perky with her Starbucks travel mug and whole-wheat bagel slathered with cream cheese in her hands, shrugged. "At least Scotty and Nathan tracked him down."

Indeed. The delivery guy had turned out to be a newbie who started working for UPS the day before the Tobin bombing. He really was lost.

Sometimes there was no felonious intent. As hard as that was for an experienced detective to believe.

"Maybe we'll do better with the Santoros." Petra looked as philosophical as a woman could with cream cheese on her upper lip. "My money's on them anyway."

She could be right, but that didn't make Avery any less grumpy. He popped onto I-10 West and fought morning gridlock, erroneously known as rush-hour traffic, to the Dominion. Forty-five minutes later they clomped up the winding sidewalk to the senior Santoros' home. The early morning sun warmed Avery's neck as he pressed the doorbell. It was one of those bells that let the homeowner see who stood on their front porch.

Not that this house in San Antonio's ritziest neighborhood had anything so mundane as a front porch. The limestone walkway led to a massive foyer with enormous arched wooden doors that dwarfed Avery and Petra. The upper half of the three panels consisted of frosted half-circle glass etched with intricate leaves. Stunning and not a little intimidating. The historic-looking stone house sat high on a hill surrounded by majestic oaks, which gave it a secluded air even though it was part of one of the fastest-growing cities in the country.

"Ready?"

Petra grinned. "Absolutely."

Avery pushed the button. Bells tinkled. He studied his scuffed loafers. His cheek throbbed. He ignored it. A little scratch was nothing to what a head shot would've been. He'd downed two ibuprofen with coffee Theo had made before he left at the crack of dawn, according to the note he left next to the pot. His plan was to Uber to his truck and then go see Katie. The big question was, would he stick to it?

The other big question: Where had Richter gone? No hits on the APB or the BOLO. His military record was spotless. They had warrants for his financials and the phone records, but they were slow in coming.

Petra shuffled her shiny black flats. "Push it again."

Avery obliged.

The middle panel opened. A woman with shiny white hair that curled around her shoulders looked him up and down, then proceeded to do the same with Petra. "What can I do for you?"

Avery made the introductions. "May I ask who you are, ma'am?"

"Lucia Santoro, the lady of the house."

It was eight fifteen and Mrs. Santoro wore white slacks, a red silk blouse, and red slip-on shoes. A slash of red lipstick stood out against her flawless white complexion. So did her sapphire eyes. Jackie's eyes. If Jackie aged as well as her grandmother, she would be as striking at seventy as she was at thirty.

"Again, what can I do for you?"

"Could we come inside?" Avery moved closer. "We'd like to speak to your husband as well as your grandson."

Mrs. Santoro stood firm. "What's this about?"

"We're following up on issues related to the bombings. I'm sure you've seen the news about them."

"It's preposterous to think my husband, Daniel Santoro, or our grandson had anything to do with those bombings. They work together in my husband's businesses." She paused as if to let the name sink in. Some would call Daniel Santoro a philanthropist, a smart businessman, or a successful entrepreneur. Those who dabbled in stereotypes might suggest he was San Antonio's answer to the Mafia. "Cristian lives here with us. He's never had so much as a parking ticket in his life."

"His sister Jackie was there. She's a person of interest. In fact all the Santoros are." Avery held her gaze. She didn't blink. "Because of what happened to your son. Revenge is a powerful motive for murder."

Mrs. Santoro laughed, the sound like tinkling bells. "You must be seriously deranged. Jackie might have been a little wild in high school and college, but she grew out of it. She wouldn't hurt a soul. She has a degree in library science. She teaches Sunday school. Her idea of a party is Scrabble, Ben & Jerry's ice cream, and peanut M&Ms. Tosca's happiest digging in the dirt, planting flowers and trees, and creating butterfly gardens. My grandson has a degree in business administration. He's good with numbers. None of them have ever been in trouble."

There was a first time for everything. "We're sorry to bother you so early in the morning, but it's necessary for us to cross all of you off the list so we can move on."

"My husband has already left. He had a business breakfast. I doubt Cristian is up yet. He was out late last night."

"Where was he?"

"He decided to rearrange the displays at one of our stores. That's how my grandson deals with loss. He works. Much like my husband does."

The sudden tightening of the lines around her generous mouth suggested Mrs. Santoro understood too well the nature of that loss.

"I'm sorry for his loss and for yours. I've left your husband and your grandson several messages. Neither has responded. We need to talk to them now." Petra's tone was pleasant but firm. "We can haul Cristian downtown or we can have a nice conversation in the comfort of your home."

Mrs. Santoro pulled the door back and waved them in. "Don't be so dramatic, Special Agent Jantzen. We certainly want to do our civic duty, even if it is a wild-goose chase. As soon as you get done here, you can go find the real bomber."

She turned and led them past a sitting room where everything was white except a shiny, black grand piano. On the right side Avery caught a glimpse of a huge alcove under a spiral staircase with a wrought-iron railing. A jungle mural reached toward the sixteen-foot stained coffered ceiling from which hung an enormous birdcage. Parakeets, canaries, and cockatiels chattered from their perches.

They passed a massive kitchen with a marble-topped island bigger than Avery's guest bedroom, then another sitting room-slash-library. An elderly, ornate pool table filled one corner.

Finally she pushed through glass doors to an outdoor terrace that overlooked a kidney-shaped pool, hot tub, and rushing fountain surrounded by thick, tropical vegetation that gave the entire back side of the house a green shroud of privacy. "Have a seat. I'll ask Debby to bring you coffee, or would you prefer orange juice?"

"Coffee would be great." Avery raised his eyebrows at Petra. She politely declined.

With a gracious incline of her head, Mrs. Santoro left them alone.

"This is an amazing place. Like something you would see on that show about lottery winners." Petra sipped her coffee and shook her head. "It's a long way from the Dallas neighborhood where I grew up. I think it's giving me hives."

"I wouldn't mind the pool table or the pool." Avery stood and paced the length of the terrace. It featured a full kitchen, a bar, and a barbecue pit the size of his truck. Bigger was better in Texas. "Imagine growing up here. Sam Santoro gave up all this to become a public servant. He could've made four or five times his monthly salary working with his dad. Why choose to take a graft from developers instead? It doesn't make sense."

"Pride? He couldn't come back, but he was sick of living like the rest of us peons?"

Avery leaned on the black wrought-iron fence and stared at the pool's shimmering turquoise water. "I bet they have some gorgeous sunsets."

"I bet they think they own the sunsets."

The glass doors hummed open and a woman, presumably Debby, appeared with a tray filled with a coffee carafe, dainty cups, an assortment of *pan dulce* and fresh fruit as well as a cut-crystal pitcher of orange juice. "Mrs. Santoro said to make yourself comfortable. Young Mr. Cristian wants a shower before he meets with you." Her smile made her round cheeks dimple. "You're to help yourself to some pastries and fruit. Or I can make you some breakfast. An omelet, toast, bacon, whatever you might like." Still smiling, she poured a cup of coffee.

"How long have you worked for the Santoros?" Avery went to the table and took the cup from her. "What's it like working here?"

"Since I was sixteen." Debby picked up the tray. "Ten years. Mr. and Mrs. Santoro are kind and fair." She deftly parked a period after that last word, then trotted back toward the house.

"Please tell Mrs. Santoro we'd like to speak to her in the meantime."

Debby didn't respond.

"A bit like royalty, aren't they?" Petra sounded less patient now. "Keeps law enforcement waiting while he showers. Who does that?"

"He's sending a message, no doubt." Avery took a seat and selected a croissant, which he slathered with peach preserves. It wasn't a convenience store chocolate-covered donut, but it would do. "He wants us to know he's in control of this situation."

Fifteen minutes later Mrs. Santoro returned. "I asked Cris not to keep you waiting too long." She sighed as if greatly perturbed by their inconvenience. "You wanted to speak to me as well?"

"What was on your schedule on Friday?"

Amusement flickered in her eyes. "In the morning I attended a planning meeting for a Junior League fund-raiser, followed by lunch with friends, and then a doctor's appointment. I returned home, swam for thirty minutes, did another thirty minutes of yoga, followed by an hour of piano practice with my teacher. Then I fixed dinner for my boys. Daniel likes it when I cook."

"And Saturday?"

"I had a spa day with several friends. We were celebrating two birthdays. I was home in time to make supper and play for Daniel in the evening. We watched a movie in our home theater. It was a quiet evening."

"How do you feel about the way your son's alleged crimes were handled by the city of San Antonio?"

Bam. Petra might have a genial facade, but she knew when to go for the jugular.

Mrs. Santoro's jaw tightened. She straightened in the rattan chair. Her long, thin fingers that ended in manicured fingernails painted a pearly gray tapped on the glass tabletop. "It was disgraceful." Her throaty voice turned hoarse. "They allowed Samuel to be tried in the court of public opinion. We never stopped trying to convince him to come back to the family business. Instead he chose public service. In return he received a paltry paycheck and scorn heaped upon disdain, shame, and unsubstantiated claims."

A nice rewrite given the recordings of him clinking glasses with a well-known real estate developer in a swanky far-northside watering hole. "It must have bothered you and your husband that Jackie continued to work for the city after your son's death."

"Number one, Jacqueline is her own woman. She always has been. Two, if she quit her job with the library system, she likely would have to leave the city in order to get another one. Unless she could get hired by a university library system. It's a surprisingly small world. We don't want our family moving farther away."

"You want them to come closer, like Cris did."

"Cris is a stellar accountant and has a head for business. He's an asset to my husband's sundry operations."

"And what exactly are those?"

"I'm sure you've done your research on that subject."

She was a tough old broad. She surely had to be to hold her own with Daniel Santoro for fifty years. According to the FBI's dossier, she and Santoro were high school sweethearts. Santoro was the son of poor Italian immigrants while Lucia's parents owned a mom-and-pop Italian restaurant on the west side. While she obtained a degree in music from St. Mary's University, he worked his way up at a locally owned check cashing-slash-pawn shop operation, quickly making a name for himself as an astute money manager and entrepreneur. Everything he touched turned to gold. Real estate, import-export, jewelry stores, and electronics. His competitors complained that he was ruthless and uncompromising. Rumors flew about his business practices, but he'd never flagrantly crossed the line into prosecutable offenses. His net worth neared a billion dollars.

"Cris is an asset where his father was not?"

"My son wanted to be his own man. I respect that." Cracks in Lucia's facade appeared for the first time. "Where do you think Jackie got it? Samuel might have been misguided, but he was no more a criminal than my husband."

"But you and your husband harbor ill will toward Jason Vogel and the mayor for their treatment of your son."

Her eyes reddened, but she raised her chin. "Do I think they're idiotic miscreants? Yes. But I also think a quick death in an explosion is too good for them. If I could choose a punishment, it would be long and agonizing torment. I'd cover them with small cuts, chain them to a wall in an abandoned warehouse, and let the rats eat them. Or cover them with honey and release a horde of fire ants on them."

What did a police officer say to that?

"Purely a fantasy, Officers." Cris Santoro made his entrance dressed in tan slacks, a long-sleeve, pale-pink cotton shirt, and a mauve tie. With his dark, curly hair and sapphire eyes, he could've been Jackie's twin. Strong genes. With a murmured good morning, he went directly to the carafe of coffee and helped himself. After settling into the chair next to his grandmother, he nodded as if to say, *Go ahead.*

"You know why we're here." Avery sipped his coffee and waited.

Cris sipped and shrugged. "I can't believe you came all the way out here. I'm a businessman, not a bomber. I'm apolitical. I'm interested in dollars and cents, not the climate. I'm sure my sister told you all this."

"After your father's suicide, you were vocal about your anger over how he was treated by the city."

A faint grimace. Nothing more. "So you think I bombed an event my sister put together, ignoring the fact that she and her closest friends could die in the explosion? You're not very bright if you even consider that scenario."

"Maybe you resent the fact that your sister and your ex-girlfriend kept working for the city after the way Vogel and Sandoval treated your dad." Petra's tone was gentle, but her gaze icy. "Maybe you decided to make Estrella Diaz rue the day she met you."

"You don't get to talk to me about Estrella." Cris smacked his cup on the glass tabletop. Hot liquid spilled over the side. His grandmother grabbed a napkin and sopped it up. "Ask your questions and then get out of my house."

It took his facade less time to crack than his mother's.

"Number one, it's not your house. Number two, we decide when we go and whether you go with us." Having laid down the rules, Avery went to work. "Give us a play-by-play of your movements, starting with Friday."

Cris leaned back in his chair. The icy cool

returned. "Nonna, don't you have a parks foundation meeting this morning?"

"I do." She stood and kissed her grandson's forehead. "I spoke with my husband about your desire to interview him. He suggested you call the downtown store and make an appointment with his administrative assistant."

"Wait." Avery kept his tone courteous but firm. "One more question for you, Mrs. Santoro."

Eyebrows raised, she paused.

"Do you know a man called Ethan Richter?"

She frowned. Her gaze bounced out to the pool and back. "I don't believe that name rings a bell."

"Are you sure? He hasn't worked for your husband?"

"If she says she doesn't recognize the name, then she doesn't." Cris waved at his grandmother. "As the attorneys say, asked and answered."

Lucia nodded and smiled. "Have a good day, Officers. Don't be late for supper, Cristian." With that, she sauntered back into the house.

Did they teach that sort of nonchalance in music school? Avery focused on Cris. "How about you? Do you know Richter? Does he work for your grandfather?"

"Honestly? It sounds familiar, but Nonno has hundreds of employees in various different locations and in various different capacities. I couldn't begin to know them all. I really don't know if Richter is one of them. Why? Who is he?"

"A person of interest." Avery made a show of examining his notes. "You were saying about your schedule Friday?"

"Friday, I rotated between our jewelry stores at The Rim, the Quarry, and downtown—"

Rotating among the stores in two of San Antonio's high-end shopping centers would give him leeway to be other places in between. Daniel Santoro's employees wouldn't keep track. Neither would the elder Santoro. If questioned, Cris could shrug it off with a fictitious stop at a coffeehouse or for lunch. "Times, please."

"I don't keep track of my time. I'm not punching a clock." Cris's cool resurfaced. "I also made a stop at the warehouse. I had lunch with Nonno at Schilo's. I know that was about one because he had to be at a meeting with an investor for our real estate project at two, so we had to hurry."

Depending on traffic, it would take about twenty minutes to get from The Rim to the Alamo Quarry Market, less to travel from the Quarry to the downtown store in The Shops at Rivercenter mall on the River Walk. Schilo's was less than two blocks from the mall. And two blocks from the Tobin Center—a brisk five-minute walk.

"No, you wouldn't punch a clock, being you're the grandson." Her tone dry, Petra studied the young man like a grandmother would her grandchild. "You get paid either way, plus I don't imagine you're paying rent to live here. Does your grandfather make your car payment too? By the way, what car do you drive?"

"What's wrong with her?" Cris directed the question to Avery. "Does she hate all rich people or just my grandparents? My grandfather earned every penny. He's a perfect example of pulling yourself up by your bootstraps. No one handed him a fortune. His parents were Italian immigrants. I benefit from their hard work, it's true, but I work for my paycheck. And I make the payments on my Mercedes."

"I assure you, I have no problem with wealthy folks." Petra didn't wait for Avery to answer the question. "I'm only trying to get to the truth. What did you do after that?"

"I went back to the warehouse on César Chávez Boulevard to review shipments received and the invoices to make sure they matched. You know, I worked."

"After that?"

"Seriously?" Cris leaned forward and poured more coffee. "I went to the gym—"

"Which one?"

"Gold's on Prue Road."

"Why? I imagine you have one here."

"I like people-watching and the camaraderie. It's boring doing it by yourself."

Avery preferred the exercise room he'd set up

in his garage. Weights, a bag, a treadmill. Not that he used them much. "And then?"

"Don't you have real suspects to interrogate?" Cris steepled his fingers and stared at the pool as if seeking inspiration. "I came home and had dinner with my grandparents. Nonna made my favorite: spinach-mushroom lasagna."

And of course, she would alibi her only grandson and her husband.

"Weren't you worried about your sister? You had to have heard about the bombing."

His expression darkened. "Nonna told me. My mother left her a message about Estrella and said Jackie was fine. There was no need to rush over there. I told Nonno I would meet him at a wine-and-dine thing with those same investors, so I went. Afterward I called Jackie."

His voice quivered slightly on that last word. Avery examined his words. For a guy who claimed not to keep track of his whereabouts, he was able to give a blow-by-blow of the entire day. "All things considered, you had time to pop over to the Tobin Center and leave a backpack in the hall."

"But I didn't. Why would I?"

"Let's go back to your feelings about your father's suicide."

"My feelings are none of your business."

No man wanted to talk about his feelings. It was in the Universal Code of Manly Conduct.

"Let's approach it from a different angle. Why did you give an interview to the *Express-News* in which you blamed the city manager for your father's death?"

"In this country people are innocent until proven guilty. Vogel ignored a bedrock principle of our justice system. My father dedicated himself to public service for twenty years. He worked his behind off for Vogel and that nasty woman who served in the position before him. He survived her and then Vogel got rid of him. He deserved his day in court."

"He killed himself before he could get it. What does that tell you?"

"Shame killed him. My father was a proud man. He chose to make his own way rather than capitalize on his father's wealth. After working his way up the ladder, he was accused of being dishonest. That's why he took his own life. He couldn't look his kids in the eyes. He taught us to be honest, hardworking citizens."

"After your father died, you moved out of your mother's house and went to work for your grandfather." Petra picked up the thread. "You distanced yourself from your sister Jackie. Did you hold a grudge because she didn't join you in your war of words with Vogel? Did it bother you that she remained close with Estrella Diaz after she broke up with you?"

"Jackie and Estrella had been friends since the

301

second grade. Estrella always loved Jackie more than me. I could live with that." The muscle in his jaw jumped. Cris sat up straight. He tossed a business card on the table. It landed in the spilled coffee. "I have to get to work. If you have any more questions, contact our lawyer."

"Do you need a lawyer?" Avery helped himself to a juicy chunk of cantaloupe. "We're just talking right now. We haven't even touched on Saturday."

"I worked Saturday, same as Friday, only more so." He pushed back his chair and stood. "Same rounds, except I had pizza at Grimaldi's with a friend and then I took Chick-fil-A to the employees at the store."

"We'll need the name and number of the friend."

"She'll love that." He turned his back and went to stand at the railing. "Nothing better than getting a woman you're trying to date involved in a police investigation."

Trying to date. Or laying out an alibi.

"Your mother was injured in the explosion at Market Square. A woman who was like an aunt to you died." Avery went to stand next to him. "Did you go to the hospital when you got the call?"

"Actually I didn't pick up when Jackie called. I figured she wanted to continue the discussion we had the night Estrella died. I wasn't up for it. After I heard what happened, I went by my mother's house. She's hurting, but she assured me she would survive. We've been through worse." Cris glanced at his watch. "I really do have to go. I'm opening the shop downtown."

"You don't seem too broken up about Estrella or your family friend."

"Mom got us a counselor after Dad died. He said people process grief differently. He said not to let people tell us how we should grieve."

His stare grazed Avery and moved away, but not before anger sparked, sizzled, and turned to ash.

"Point well taken." Avery leaned his elbows on the railing and clasped his hands together. "My sister died of breast cancer. She was thirty-one. Mostly I was furious. I wanted to beat the snot out of someone. Mostly the doctors who charged all that money and couldn't save her. So I get it. I have a friend whose son was killed in a drive-by a year ago and he's still spiraling out of control."

"I remember seeing that one in the paper." Cris's hands gripped the railing. His knuckles turned white. "He understands what it's like to have the entire town watching your grief on the six o'clock news and all over again at ten."

"People also deal with perceived injustices and anger differently." Avery straightened. "They bomb a crowded event or an iconic historical landmark filled with shoppers enjoying Day of the Dead altars."

"I told you. I was working."

"Okay." Avery patted the railing. "But it would take a lot of resentment not to race to the hospital after your mother's nearly blown up and her best friend dies."

"I told you I didn't listen to Jackie's voice mail until later. I spent two hours reminiscing about Aunt Vicky. And another hour letting Jackie pick at me." He backed away. "I'm going. If you need anything else, call my grandfather's lawyer."

"What did Jackie pick at you about?"

"She's another one who thinks she should tell me how to grieve. My sister doesn't know when to give it up. She never has."

Avery waited until Cris neared the door. "You'll be hearing from us."

Cris waved over his shoulder. "Enjoy your breakfast. I'll send Debby out to get you some fresh coffee. Make a day of it. The water's too cold for a swim, but you could hop in the hot tub. Enjoy the fruits of my grandfather's labor." His sarcasm floated on the air even as he disappeared into the house.

"That's one angry young man." Petra wiped cantaloupe juice from her fingers with a cloth napkin. "He's a smoldering volcano about to blow."

"Or maybe he already has." Avery picked the

business card from the puddle of coffee. He patted it down with a napkin and stuck it in his jacket pocket. "That kind of anger is the gift that keeps on giving."

"Nice how he set up alibis everywhere he went."

Avery liked a challenge. Entitlement babies like Cris only made him more determined to pull the golden diaper out from under them. "Let's go kick those alibi tires and see if they hold air."

Cris was Jackie's brother. She might not like the cop who messed him up, but she would be grateful to the one who collared the mass murderer who killed two people she loved.

Debby reappeared and escorted them to the front door. They walked down to the Charger parked in the roundabout driveway without speaking.

Avery's phone blared before he could start the car. LT wanted him at the library ASAP for a security briefing regarding an upcoming library foundation event called Catrina Ball. "They want to have a dance in the middle of—"

"Don't get me started. Chief spoke to the city manager. Vogel said to work with them. Whatever that means."

"And you want me to go?"

"Library. Librarian. Santoro. Do I have to spell it out for you?"

Jackie had said her duties included pro-gramming and special events. And he thought librarians mostly checked out books and did story hour. "On it."

"It's only nine o'clock and you already man-aged to anger one of Ruiz's hunting buddies."

"Santoro already called? He wasn't even there."

"Grandson called. And then Santoro Senior. Just get to the meeting. Keep your mouth shut and follow my lead."

LT was in a surly mood. Now Avery knew the true meaning of sitting duck.

One of Petra's squad agents was already at the library for the security meeting, so Avery dropped her off at HQ. Her mission was to work on paperwork requesting warrants for Cris's phone records. Avery didn't want to think about how likely a judge would be to sign that paperwork. He headed out.

Avery usually hated paperwork. Today he was jealous. Then he remembered. Jackie would be at the library. Maybe he would cross paths with her.

In fact, he would make sure of it.

TWENTY-EIGHT

I know it's been a rough patch."

Only Meagan would refer to two bombings and mass casualties as a rough patch. Jackie edged toward her boss's office door. She'd stopped in to remind Meagan she would need Thursday morning off for Estrella's funeral. Meagan hadn't stopped talking long enough for Jackie to squeeze in the request. The decision had been made to go forward with the Catrina Ball on Saturday. Meagan didn't seem to find that mind-boggling.

"They start building the altars tomorrow, and we haven't finalized the locations. The catering is coming by to walk the venue and discuss the food stations. Our PR folks are working with the foundation's communications director to finalize the news release and the media advisory. The sound folks are—"

If Jackie waited for Meagan to draw a breath, she would never get a word in edgewise. "With everything that's happened, we're still having the ball? Upwards of a thousand people will come through the library in the span of four hours during the event."

"I'm well aware of the numbers and the potential threat. The director is back in town.

He recommended to the city manager that we proceed with the event. The foundation board agrees. Our staff and the foundation's have put an enormous amount of work into the event. Even with our sponsors defraying most of the costs, the foundation will end up in the hole. Milton would want the show to go on. He knew how much the funds are needed."

It all came down to money. The Catrina Ball was the biggest fund-raiser of the year. The library's skimpy city-funded budget didn't cover needs like programming, community literacy outreach, the latest and greatest technology, development of special collections, and branch library development—all important to the community and to Jackie. The foundation's big push this year was raising funds to transform the Texana Resource Center into a state-of-the-art resource for San Antonio and Bexar County for Texas history. Jackie should care. She did care deeply. Yet she couldn't summon a morsel of enthusiasm for an event she'd always enjoyed. "Did anyone talk to Homeland or SAPD about the risk involved in having a major event right now?"

"We're not idiots." Meagan's huff hurt Jackie's ears. "The director is meeting with the foundation president and staff as well as the interim board chairman as we speak. Security is a top priority. We'll have a safe event."

No one could guarantee that. Not anymore.

"So were they the ones who reached out to law enforcement?"

"No, the interim chief of police ran to the city manager. Now everyone and their uncles are involved. Who knows what will happen? The city manager knows how vital our relationship with the foundation is. No one wants to alienate anyone. They'll work it out."

A piercing headache reared its ugly head. Jackie whirled and headed down the hall. To her dismay Meagan followed. "You don't agree, do you? Just remember, it's not up to you."

"People are dying."

"I'm aware. The director says we can't let a terrorist intimidate us. It sets a bad example." Meagan scampered to keep up with Jackie's long strides. "Just so you know, your PD officer asked for you."

Jackie laid her laptop on her desk and set the travel mug containing her double espresso next to it. "I don't have a PD officer."

"He said to let him know when you arrived." Meagan cocked her head toward the ceiling and licked her chapped lips. "Homicide Detective Avery Wick."

"He's here?" Jackie tried and failed to keep a sudden surge of interest from her voice. "He's welcome to come by my office if he thinks it's totally necessary. I have work to do. My assigned task was to finalize the locations of the ofrendas and start helping to build them. I'm also helping La Catrina with her costume this afternoon."

La Catrina and her companion El Catrín, both played by members of the foundation board, served as hosts for the event and as such required substantial support from staff.

"It's not good to avoid the police. It looks like you have something to hide." Meagan's questioning air coupled with a drop of drool on her chin left no doubt that she believed that was the case. "Of course you would know more about the police than I would."

Did she really go there? "You're right. I do know. That's why I'm certain he'll track me down if he's serious about talking to me. I'm meeting the artists who are creating the Don Pedro Huizar and the Rose Window altar on the first floor. They need to start today or they won't finish in time." Jackie knocked back the last of her espresso and brushed past Meagan. "Will you let me know if the powers that be decide to cancel? I hate for the artists to waste their time."

"If they decide to cancel, we'll have many people to notify." Meagan rushed to keep up on spindly heels. "The event has been sold out for over a month. All those sponsors. All the donors. All the board members. All the elected officials and VIPs. It would be a nightmare."

The exact reason the event should be canceled.

While the ball was technically open to the public, tickets started at three hundred fifty dollars. Members of San Antonio's social elite prided themselves on supporting worthy causes while showcasing to the world how generous they were. It was good for business and good for the city. A win-win as the city manager liked to say. Also another opportunity for the bomber to obliterate the city's top-tier officials.

The foundation handled the invitations and RSVPs. "Have you seen a guest list?"

"It's a veritable who's who." Meagan stopped short of smacking her lips, but she couldn't contain her smart one-two-three clap. "By the way, I guess you know your grandparents are sponsoring for the first time. A very generous donation at the Calaveras level, I might add."

Seriously? Caffeine and adrenaline combined to give the day a surreal feel. Trying to keep her expression neutral, Jackie gathered up her laptop. Her grandparents had never attended this event. Her mother, Victoria, and Tosca had cobbled together money from savings to attend the previous year in a much-appreciated show of support after a grim year. It had been fun to see their delight in the moving fiesta on the first floor, nibbling Mexican street tacos, enjoying the mariachis and Tejano performances and the reading by a celebrated national poet in the art gallery. None of them could afford the art on display for the silent auction, but it was fun to "window-shop." Tosca would attend this year with Lee. Their mother was busy helping Victoria's children plan her funeral.

Her grandparents liked to spread their wealth around, but Nonno would find this event too hoity-toity for his taste. Nonna managed to influence him enough to give to local charities such as Haven for Hope's mission to end homelessness in San Antonio, the children's shelter, and Habitat for Humanity. This had to be her grandmother's idea.

"I didn't know. It'll be fun to see them here." Maybe Jackie could convince them to leave early. Their sponsorship gave them rights to exclusive tickets to the DisglowTeca After-Party around the Dale Chihuly Fiesta Tower, a twenty-foot-tall sculpture of handcrafted, twisted glass orbs. Nonno and Nonna loved to dance. They made a dashing couple. "They may reconsider after everything that has happened."

"I doubt that. Jenn said they got the last two spots before the invitation closed."

Yet Nonno didn't mention it during his brief visit to her home—outside her home. He never quite made it inside. "Then I'd better get to work. My grandmother has experience with planning fund-raisers for the Junior League. She'll undoubtedly give me her critique of this one."

The elevator doors had started to close when

an arm belonging to Avery stopped them. He popped in as soon as the doors allowed. "Sorry. Hope you don't mind."

His tone said "even if you do."

"It's a public elevator."

"I was surprised to hear you were coming into work today." Avery punched the lighted button a second time. Everything about his body language suggested a bonfire about to combust, yet his tone was soft, almost placatory. The man was a study in contrasts. "You've been through a lot in the last few days. So has your mother. I thought maybe you would take some time off."

He was right. Jackie swallowed a lump the size of Texas and gathered her tattered courage. "I didn't have a choice. My boss is certain we'll go ahead with the Catrina Ball. If that's the case, I need to be here. It's a huge event and we're in the homestretch with all the details."

"Yeah, I just spent the last hour getting an earful about this Catrina Ball." He stood, legs planted, arms at his side, as if ready to engage some unseen foe. His suit was a tad less rumpled than the one he'd worn in the interview room at the Public Safety HQ. He smelled like soap and cinnamon gum. He smelled safe. "I don't get it. Lives are on the line and you folks act like the world will fall apart if this dance doesn't happen. All over town events are being canceled. Alamo Plaza is empty. The River Walk, empty. High school basketball games are being moved to out-of-town locations. Yet y'all can't see fit to cancel a dance."

"It isn't a dance."

"Isn't that what a ball is?" He tugged at his collar, causing the knot in his tie to give even more. "And who is Catrina?" He sprinkled both questions with the obligatory obscenities.

"This is a celebration modeled after the Día de los Muertos celebrations in Mexico. Catrina is straight from Mexican lore. Technically she's a tall female skeleton wearing a fancy hat. But symbolically she represents the way Mexicans see death. They choose humor and passion as they seek to send their loved ones on their way with everything they need." This was safe. Jackie could fill up the sixty-second elevator ride with a long-winded explanation of an important tradition in a multicultural city that was more than 50 percent Latinx. "They grieve and miss their loved ones, but they choose to celebrate the life and memories the person created while they were with them instead of focusing on the fact that they'll never see them again."

"And y'all turned that into a fund-raiser?"

"The foundation did. I would suggest you come, but it's sold out."

He shook his shaggy head. "Unfortunately, I can't afford three hundred fifty dollars for a ticket to look at dead people altars."

"We're making an altar for Estrella and for my dad. Don't you have anyone you would like to honor that way?"

The cop facade fell away for a split second, replaced with a grief so familiar it made Jackie's throat ache. Detective Wick had experienced a loss like her own. "My sister died of breast cancer. We used to hang out, even after we grew up. We played pool. Sometimes we just chilled and played one-on-one hoops. She had game."

"I'm sorry for your loss."

"It was a long time ago."

Time did not heal all wounds.

The elevator doors opened. Jackie stepped through them, made a left, and strode through the lobby to the long window next to the exit. The 22,722 teardrop-shaped crystals that hung on fishing filament five feet long between the double-paned glass sparkled in the sun. Detective Wick's grief followed her. He needed the same comfort she did. "Do you know what this is?"

Squinting, Wick studied the many-colored crystals. "Some kind of art?"

"San Antonio artist Jesse Amado did this. The 22,722 teardrops represent the days in the life of an artist friend of his who died." Jackie worked to steady her voice. "I would have to cry even more tears than that before I finish grieving for Estrella and Victoria and my dad. I know you must feel the same for your sister. We can't let this monster stand in the way of living. I won't let him stop this commemoration of our loved ones. Do you understand?"

He nodded, but his gaze remained on the art installation. He raised his hand and touched the glass. "This place doesn't look like any library I've been in."

"When was the last time you were in a library?"

His expression turned sheepish. "In college."

"The world has changed. Libraries have changed with it. I have to work." She turned and rushed toward the altar under construction for Don Pedro Huizar, eighteenth-century surveyor, property owner, carpenter, and alleged sculptor of the iconic Rose Window in the church sacristy at Mission San José.

"Wait." Wick's voice followed her. He sounded almost plaintive. "Stop."

"I have to work. You'll have to ask me questions while I work."

"Please don't go to this stupid fund-raiser."

Jackie plowed to a halt and whirled. Wick's long stride landed him in her space. "What?"

"Look, I don't know what you did or didn't do. You're still a person of interest. You consorted with a Muslim American. You called in favors to protect her." Somehow the words didn't match his expression. Wick's hand came up as if he might touch her, then dropped. "Your brother is a powder keg ready to explode. On the other hand, we have a bomb expert in the wind who might be able to tell us what really happened and whether either of you is telling the truth. Even with all that . . ." He lowered his voice to a whisper. "I'm concerned for your safety—the safety of anyone who comes to this dance."

Jackie stared at Avery. He'd come precariously close to crossing that barbed wire fence between professional and personal. Why? Did he feel that same sense that something else was about to explode every time their paths crossed? Then again, he also came close to calling Meher and her liars and Cris a suspect. The last bit of patience tried to skitter away. She grabbed it back. "Who is the bomb expert?"

"The security guard Meher claimed took the backpack. He also hired out as a mercenary after he got out of the service."

"You found him?"

"We know who he is. We just don't know where he is."

"So go find him and stop harassing me and my family." Jackie sought a conciliatory tone. He cared about the bombing victims. He cared about citizens in harm's way. That made him one of the good guys. "I promise you Cris has nothing to do with those bombings. He loved Estrella. He's moved on with his life. According to my grandparents, he's thriving."

Wick's hands fisted and unfisted. "You may be

in denial. Your grandmother is—about Cris and about your grandfather—"

"My grandmother is a very smart lady and tough. She runs that household. Don't underestimate her ability to size up a situation. If there was something going on, she'd put a stop to it."

"Sometimes we wear blinders when it comes to our loved ones."

Like they all had with Jackie's dad. "Surely you didn't just go there—"

"I'm trying to make you see reason, that's all." He stalked toward the exit. A few yards later, he whirled and returned. "Your mother has lost so much already. Why put her through it?"

He would bring out the big guns. As if Jackie wouldn't have thought of this. They agreed. So why was she arguing with him? "What makes you so certain the bomber will strike during the ball?"

His fair complexion turned ruddy. Both his hands came out, fingers wide, as he shrugged. "All the muckety-mucks will be here. It's a gut feeling. Sixteen years of dealing with scum and you learn to trust those feelings."

"Gut feelings don't make my mortgage payments." Jackie's stomach clenched. His head-on approach was doing a good job of scaring her. "I have a job to do. You deal with dangerous situations all the time. You get that."

"I'm not a librarian. I'm a homicide detective."

By now Jackie's coworkers behind the checkout and return counter had given up any semblance of working. Patrons openly gawked. The two artists working on the life-size skeleton in a black suit and top hat stood as if mesmerized by a tableau other than the one they were supposed to be building. This would get back to Meagan. "Then go detect. Catch the animal who's doing this and we won't have to worry. Let me do my work."

Wick's jaw jutted at a dangerous angle. "You're right. What was I thinking?"

This time he stomped past the security guard and through the exit scanner.

"There's nothing to see here, folks." Her face white hot, Jackie set her laptop on the counter and opened it. Her hands were shaking. What was his deal anyway? She accessed the list of items to be included in the ofrenda. "Let's get to work."

"Are you sure you don't want to go after *su novio*?" Joaquin Moreno, the lead artist, grinned and shook his finger at her. "Making up is the best part of an argument. Such fireworks so early in the morning. Such passion. I'm jealous."

"Don't be. He's not my boyfriend. Not even close." A chill shook Jackie. Wick was a hardheaded, bossy, overstepping cop. She didn't need that in her life. So why did every muscle in her body demand that she race after him?

To get the last word. That's why. Nothing more. "Do you have the narratives about Don

Pedro and the Rose Window we talked about? I'd like to compare notes with the *Handbook of Texas Online* entry. It really is a muddled story. I'm glad we're highlighting it this year. There's no way a carpenter sculpted that window. Oh, and the frames you needed are in my car. I need help bringing in the marigolds, calaveras, and candles."

She was babbling worse than a lovesick teenage girl.

Laughing, Joaquin held up both hands in surrender. "Whatever you say, *chiquita bonita*."

Would they be so tickled if they knew why Wick was so angry?

Should she tell them to stay away from the ball?

Those questions pricked her skin, demanding answers she didn't have.

TWENTY-NINE

Jackie, I need your help."

Phone to her ear, Jackie shut her car door and gave Meher her full attention. Suddenly the trip to the art supply store didn't seem like such an emergency. "What's the matter? Where are you?"

"I'm driving around in my car. I think someone is following me."

"Meher, what are you doing? You're supposed to be at Chandra's. That was the deal."

"My husband wants the children with his parents. He feels they are safer there. In all of this he has to keep working. He's not happy staying with a stranger." Panic reverberated in Meher's voice. "Besides, they're babies. They don't understand what's going on. They need familiar surroundings and faces. I stopped at the grocery store. I've been making lunch for Chandra and her children—"

"Go to the nearest police substation. There's one on Prue Road and another one—"

"No. I can't. They'll put me in protective custody. Don't you understand? My kids need me." Her voice rose. "I'm two blocks from your house. Can I go there?"

"I'm not at home."

"Please."

"Okay, I'll meet you there, but call Chandra and tell her what's going on. She can join us. We'll figure out what to do. There's a spare key under the chiminea on the front porch. Get inside."

She explained how to disarm the alarm. Meher promised to be careful.

Jackie disconnected. She started the Rogue but didn't put it in Drive. Meher had good reason not to want to involve the federal agencies, but Detective Wick could help. His outburst earlier in the day might have been painful, but it reflected how much he wanted to help. He could be trusted. She pulled his card from her purse and punched in his number, allowing Bluetooth to pick up the call.

"Wick."

"It's me. Jackie—"

"Look, I'm sorry. I overstepped—"

"It's Meher. She may be in trouble." Jackie recapped their conversation. "I'm on my way there. It may be nothing—"

"Or it may be something. I'm at the station. I can be there in under fifteen."

"I can be there in under ten."

"Call her. Get her back on the line."

"I'll try." She hung up and called Meher. No answer.

Spurred by a growing sense of dread, Jackie took the turns in the library's parking garage as fast as she dared. She got Wick back on the line.

The sound of his voice, terse and in control, assuring her help was on the way, filled the SUV. "When you get there, wait for me."

"It could be nothing. She might just be paranoid."

"That's possible."

But given the situation, not probable.

Jackie arrived first. Meher's gray Subaru was parked in front of the house. "Her car's here. I'll try calling her again."

"Wait—"

Jackie hung up and punched in Meher's number. The call went to voice mail. "Meher. I'm out front. I'm coming in."

She hopped from her SUV and surveyed the street. No unfamiliar cars parked conspicuously on the street of a quiet neighborhood known for block parties and National Night Out events. Her heartbeat slowed. *We're okay. So far so good.*

Jackie darted up the steps to the porch. The front door stood open. The air whooshed from her lungs. Light-headed, she leaned forward and peeked inside. Everything seemed normal. No sign of her kitties. They would never venture outside. They were fraidy cats when it came to the great outdoors. Jackie squeezed through door and looked around.

Meher probably brought her groceries in and didn't have a hand free to close the door. Logic allowed Jackie to breathe again.

"Meher? Where are you? It's not a good idea to leave the door open."

No answer. Jackie forced herself to take a long breath and let it out. "Meher?"

Nothing.

Groceries. Kitchen.

She kicked off her shoes and padded down the hallway in the eerie stillness. *Come on, Meher, come on, be all right, please be all right. God, let her be all right.*

Footsteps. Light, stealthy steps. A squeak of rubber on tile.

Adrenaline blasted through Jackie like a shot of mainlined caffeine.

She clutched her pepper spray in front of her and eased forward. At the kitchen door, she paused. The back door squeaked. The footsteps picked up speed. Jackie hurled herself into the kitchen.

The screen door that led to the tiny backyard slammed. Jackie careened across the room. Stumbling over a bag of basmati rice, she flung out her arms and managed to stay upright. She tugged the door open to an empty yard. Hand to her forehead, she squinted into the sunlight.

Nothing.

Gasping, she stepped outside and took a good look around. No one. He was gone.

Or she.

Jackie punched in Wick's number. He picked

up immediately. "I'm out front. Where are you?"

"Inside. A man—I think it was a man—was in here, in the kitchen."

"Get out front now. Come back through the house. I'm coming in."

"He left out the back door. Go after him. I have to find Meher."

"Get out—"

She hung up and tottered on shaking legs into her kitchen. *Please, God, let her be okay, please let her be okay.*

The knife butcher block, Jackie's beautiful arrangement of sunflowers, the pasta canisters—everything on the peninsula had been knocked to the floor. Her espresso machine reclined on its side.

A package of flatbread, a package of lamb, dried figs and apricots, pine nuts, peanuts, and sundry spices spilled across the floor next to reusable grocery bags. A carton of plain yogurt ended up in the tiny breakfast nook under the chair where Jackie usually sat to eat her granola, fruit, and almond milk.

A painful hitch in her chest, Jackie skirted the mess until she could see around the peninsula. Meher lay facedown on the floor. Her hijab had fallen away, revealing a mass of dark hair caught back in a tousled bun.

Jackie fell to her knees and leaned over her. "Meher, sweetie, come on. Talk to me."

The metallic smell mixed with human excrement gagged Jackie. She leaned in and touched the woman's exposed throat. Her skin was still warm, but she had no pulse.

CPR. Was it okay to turn her over? Would it hurt her? This wasn't a spinal injury. Dissonant thoughts banged around in Jackie's head. *Help me, God, help me.*

She tugged at Meher's arm, struggling to lift her weight. A wound gaped from her neck. Her eyes were open, distant, unseeing.

Oh God.

A hand grasped her shoulder. Jackie flinched, screamed, and jerked away. Gasping for breath, his face covered with sweat, Wick loomed over her. "It's me, it's me. Detective Wick." His voice went soft yet fierce with emotion. "She's gone, Jackie. Let her go."

"No, no, you're supposed to do CPR."

"Her throat has been cut. She's lost too much blood. She's gone."

Jackie stared at the blood on her hands and shirt. Too much blood. The man who did this had been within an arm's length. "Did you find him?"

"Whoever it was is gone."

Jackie shook her head, trying to clear the fog and pain. "Why kill Meher? Why?"

"I called for help. EMTs are on the way." Wick squatted next to her, just beyond the blood that pooled around Meher's torso. "Leave catching the killer to me."

Tears clogged Jackie's throat. Her stomach heaved. She scrambled to her feet and raced through the back door.

She made it into the grass before she vomited.

A few seconds earlier and Avery might have spared Jackie a future filled with this particular nightmare. Weren't two bombings enough? They were for him. Cussing under his breath, he edged closer to the spot where she crouched, shoulders hunched, head down. She didn't make a sound, but her body shook.

"Let me help you up, please." Avery touched her arm. She glanced up at him. Her lips trembled but she nodded. He gently tugged her to her feet. "Let's walk around front, okay? Help is on the way."

"It's too late for help." Her voice barely registered in a whisper. "I was too late."

"You shouldn't have been in there at all." Avery put a stopper in his frustration. It wasn't directed at her. She'd done a brave—if foolhardy—thing in trying to help a friend. A few minutes or even seconds earlier and she could've paid for it with her life.

The desire to comfort her warred with the need to do his job. He needed to know what she saw. Did the killer see her? His chest tightened at the thought. He squeezed her arm and let go. "I'm sorry I didn't get here sooner."

"You did your best too."

She stumbled and bumped into Avery. He slid his arm around her. Her body still shook. "Easy. Take it easy. We'll sit down on the porch and sort things out."

"Nothing to sort. She's dead."

"Her killer was in the house when you entered?"

"I heard footsteps. The door squeaked. The screen door slammed."

"You didn't see the killer?"

"No."

"He didn't see you?"

She shook her head.

As much as it would've helped them to have a description of the killer, Avery breathed a sigh of relief. The killer knew where Jackie lived. He left her alive, for now. At least he wouldn't come back and finish the job because he had been seen.

They exited through the white picket-fence gate to her front yard. Sirens blared. PD, a fire truck, and an ambulance filled the street. Avery guided Jackie to an Adirondack chair on the tiny front porch and then stood between her and the mass of first responders. "This will be hard, but you're tough. You'll get through it."

"I know." Jackie grabbed his hand and held on. Her fingers were icy cold. Startled, Avery tightened his grip and rubbed her hands between his. Her face white, eyes wide, she stared up at him. "You're not leaving, are you?"

"No. I'm right here. I promise. Let me tell these guys what's going on." Nothing said a cop couldn't also be a decent human being. Jackie was in shock. She needed his help. Still, he had to switch to homicide detective, whether he liked it or not. "Do you want me to call your sister or Cris?"

She shook her head. "I'll call them later. I'm okay."

"I'll be back."

She rose and started toward her front door. "My cats. I need to make sure my cats are okay."

Avery stepped into her path. "I'll check on them when I go inside. I promise. Please. Have a seat. I'll be back."

"You promise." She made it a statement, not a question. "They're family."

He nodded. Her gaze traced his face. Finally, as if satisfied, she sat.

Ten minutes and innumerable repeated explanations later, Avery made his way back to the porch. "The CSU folks are en route. They'll need to take photos of you and get your clothes."

Jackie nodded, but her hand went to her mouth. Her gaze plummeted to the ground. She would relive the scene in her kitchen hundreds, maybe thousands of times, in the coming days, months, and years. Nothing Avery said would change that.

He settled into the chair next to her and leaned in close. "Give yourself a few seconds to arrange your thoughts. Remember, you tried. That's all you could do. Start with the bags of groceries. Why was she shopping for groceries? She was supposed to stay put at Chandra's."

"She said she's been making lunch for Chandra and her children."

"She likely left the door open when she brought in the groceries. That's probably how the perpetrator got into the house. There wasn't any sign of forced entry, was there?"

"Not that I noticed. Not in the front, anyway."

"Wicked."

Avery looked back. Scotty stood at the base of the steps leading up to the porch. Avery gave his partner a hold-on sign. "I'll get the CSU investigator to work with you next. There will have to be a formal interview downtown. You know the drill, unfortunately."

"I'll call Lee."

"It'll be good to have him with you, even though there's no way you're a suspect in Meher's murder. I'll be back."

He walked Scotty through the events leading up to the discovery of Meher's body. Together they entered the house. Scotty waited while Avery poked around until he found all three cats under Jackie's cherry sleigh bed. One growled while the other two skittered into the corners. He hastily backed away.

Promise fulfilled. Thank God they were okay. Not another loss for a woman who'd had more than her share of tough breaks in recent days.

Ignoring the inquiring look on Scotty's face, he led the way to the kitchen where the ME investigator brushed past them with a low *tsk-tsk* that signaled his displeasure at their proximity to Meher's body. He knelt near her head. "Obviously I don't have anything to tell you guys, so don't ask."

"Yeah I know." Avery studied Meher's face. "You think a wire garrote did that?"

The ME investigator shrugged without looking up. "It's possible. Likely. It appears she bled out, but that's totally preliminary. I won't know for sure the cause and manner of death—"

"Until you do the autopsy," Avery and Scotty recited in unison.

"Stick it in your ear." The investigator grinned cheerfully. "I can always put her at the end of the line."

"No. Don't do that."

A uniformed officer stuck his head through the kitchen doorway. "Detective Wick, there's a Chandra Martinez out front, says she needs to see you. She's pretty insistent."

No doubt. Avery followed him out. In the living room a CSU investigator shot photos of Jackie from a dozen different angles. Her earlier chalky-white face had turned beet red.

"It's standard procedure," the other woman offered.

"That doesn't help."

"You'll need to change your clothes so I can collect them." The investigator held up several paper bags. "I'll stand outside the bathroom and you can hand them out to me."

Jackie swiped at her face with her sleeve. "Whatever you need."

"I'm going outside to talk to Chandra, but I'll be back." Avery drew her aside, avoiding the investigator's curious gaze. "I can take you to HQ for the formal interview and then to your mother's or your sister's. Wherever you want to stay tonight."

"I want to stay here in my house. How long will it be before . . . before it's my house again?"

"When the crime scene folks finish, that's it. The house is no longer a crime scene. But you might want to get someone to come in and clean for you."

Her arms wrapped around her middle. "I hadn't thought about that." Her voice faltered. "I don't think I can—"

"We'll get you some recommendations. Stay with your mom for a few days."

"My cats—"

"Are hiding under your bed. They're fine. You can take them with you." Maybe he shouldn't be lead on this murder. All he wanted to do was make the shock and grief on Jackie's face disappear. "We'll work out the details later."

He whirled and fled to the front porch. More shock and grief, this time on Chandra's face. He sat on the steps next to her while Scotty settled into a lawn chair. Chandra sniffed and blew her nose. Avery patted her back. "I'm sorry. I wish I could give you time to deal with this trauma, but I really need to ask you some questions."

"I understand." Chandra's smile was wan but still qualified as a smile. "I don't need kid glove handling."

For the first time in years, Avery longed for a cigarette. He inhaled and surveyed the street. The fire truck and ambulance were gone, replaced by the Bexar County Medical Examiner's vehicle and the CSU SUV. The media units lined the narrow street. It hadn't taken them long to congregate. "Why was she out driving around? Buying groceries?"

"She wasn't in prison, Avery." Chandra's shoulders drooped. "She wanted to make herself useful, so she cooked all the meals. She needed provisions, and no, she didn't consult me before she took off to the store."

Avery rubbed his forehead and tried to think in a straight line. "I thought the Feds had eyes on her."

"Not twenty-four-hour surveillance. They're like us, short on manpower." Scotty stood and lit a cigarette. The smoke wafted toward them. Ignoring Chandra's frown, Avery inhaled. Scotty moved to the edge of the small porch. "The bigger question is, why did the bomber decide to take out a single survivor?"

Avery cracked his knuckles one by one. Again he ignored Chandra's frown. Knuckle cracking didn't offer the relief that pounding someone's face would, but it was less likely to get him fired. "She had the backpack in her hand. She gave it to a security guard."

"Allegedly."

"She's dead." Chandra's voice shook. "Surely she can be eliminated as a suspect."

The ringing of Chandra's phone spared Avery from answering. Meher could've been an accomplice who was no longer needed. A loose end now tied up.

Chandra rose and walked down the sidewalk. She paced in front of her Prius. Finally she hung up. "That was Meher's husband. He was worried because he couldn't get ahold of Meher, so he called me." Her voice broke. "I had to tell him. I hated doing it over the phone. What an awful way to learn his wife is dead."

No good way existed.

"He's on his way here."

"It's okay. We'll deal with him together." Avery stood. Chandra rested her forehead on his shoulder and sobbed. He squeezed tighter.

This was the empathy that made her a great attorney for the disenfranchised. "We have some experience with this."

A silver Chevy Traverse rounded the corner, tires squealing, and roared down the block. Chandra stiffened. "It's him."

The SUV slammed to a halt at an angle outside crime scene tape that bobbed in a brisk fall breeze. A burly man in pale-green scrubs shoved open the door and ducked under the tape. The officer tried to stop him. The man shoved him aside. "Meher, Meher, Meher."

His hoarse screams grew more frenzied as he barreled toward the porch.

"Mr. Faheem, please, take it easy." Scotty waved the officer off and stepped into the man's path. Faheem thrust him aside with a stiff arm jab worthy of a wide receiver headed for the end zone. Scotty stumbled and landed on his behind. "Hey, you can't go in there. You don't want to go—"

"Shut up. Shut up. Where is she?" Faheem appealed to Chandra. "You said she'd be safe with you. You said it was better that she not go home. What have you done?"

"Mr. Faheem, I'm so sorry for your loss." Avery filled the space between the distraught man and his ex-wife. "If you'll sit down, we'll tell you what we know. We'll do everything possible to bring the perpetrator to justice."

Faheem opened his mouth. An earsplitting scream ripped the air. He dropped to his knees and covered his face with both hands. His body rocked. "No, no, no, no."

Avery squatted next to him. "Let me help you up."

The man's shoulders heaved, but his hands dropped. "Get away from me. Get away."

Some people were stunned into silence. Others simply walked away to grieve in private. Some lashed out. Some, like Faheem, imploded. No one reaction was typical.

Her expression hesitant, Chandra inched down the steps. She settled on the lowest one and placed her hand on his shoulder. "Can I call someone for you?"

"How will I tell the children?" His sobs dissipated. The initial shock had passed. Now reality set in. "Her parents."

"It will be hard. Are your parents here?"

"Yes."

"Can your father go with you to their home?"

He wiped tears and snot from his reddened face. Finally he nodded.

"Call him. He can come to get you. You shouldn't be driving."

"I want to see her."

Chandra glanced up at Avery. He shook his head.

"Later. At the funeral home. Or perhaps the

morgue once they've done what needs to be done."

He bent over until his head touched the grass. The man's entire body shook. Her face etched in a web of pain and regret, Chandra patted his back.

Avery had experience talking down loved ones, but his ex-wife did it much better. If he suggested it was a woman thing, she would scoff at his sexism. He had plenty of empathy but poor people skills.

Faheem stumbled to his feet. Chandra rose with him.

A shiny black SUV roared to a stop and joined the ever-expanding number of vehicles crowding what was usually a quiet residential street in need of repaving.

The Feds had arrived.

THIRTY

How many forces had to intersect, intertwine, reverse, then reconnect in order for a librarian and a chef to meet and play a part in a tragedy in a city of a million-plus people? Jackie and Meher's lives had intersected on only a dozen or so work-related occasions before the bombing. Yet her death filled Jackie with such deep sadness she could barely lift her head.

Meher's body had been transported. Meher's father-in-law had arrived to take her husband to her parents' house. That left a bunch of task force members. It seemed they might never leave. Until they left she couldn't meet Lee at police headquarters to make her statement and flee to her mother's house.

"Ms. Santoro, we need to talk." Special Agent Jantzen pushed through the screen door and let it shut gently behind her. "Had you and Ms. Faheem been in touch before she called you this morning? Any time since she went to stay with Ms. Martinez?"

"No."

"Nothing since? We have a warrant for your phone records. We'll be reviewing them shortly."

"Then why ask me?" Jackie rubbed burning eyes. "Just do what you have to do."

"We'd like to suggest protective custody." Special Agent Wilson stepped onto the porch. It was getting far too crowded. "Just until we resolve the situation."

"The situation? You call two bombings with multiple fatalities a situation?" Jackie stifled the urge to scream at him. It wasn't his fault. The person who did this had been in her house. He'd killed Meher. He'd escaped and was probably planning more mayhem right now. "You're no closer to resolving this 'situation' than you were four days ago."

"All the more reason for you to vacate the premises until we can detain the perpetrator."

"Fine. I'm happy to leave. As soon as I pack a bag and gather up my kitties." Jackie stood and measured the space between the two agents and her door. She should be able to squeeze by. "Feel free to brainstorm here in my home for as long as you like. There's a spare key . . ." Light-headed, she put one hand on the wall to steady herself. Meher had taken the spare key. Where was it now? In an evidence bag? "You can have my house key. I'll get it the next time you decide to harass me, which I'm sure won't be too far off. Close up when you leave."

She straightened, dodged the two agents, and grabbed the screen door handle.

Wick stood on the other side. "You can't just leave—"

"Am I under arrest? You haven't Mirandized me."

"You know you're not, but you still have to come downtown. Let me give you a ride."

Her stomach clenched. This day would never end. If her dad's death taught Jackie anything, it was that closure was a lightning-fast creature that careened out of reach at every corner. "I need my things."

He held up her purse. "Tammy—the CSU investigator—corralled your cats. Even the one-eyed guy came along peacefully. I found the carriers in the bedroom closet."

"I'm sure that's not in either of your job descriptions, but thank you."

"Our task statements have a line item called 'other duties as assigned.' You're welcome."

As another city employee, Jackie was all too familiar with the other-duties-as-assigned line item. She took her purse from Avery and waited for the investigator to pass between them carrying the two carriers that contained Jackie's precious cargo. Jane meowed piteously, but the other two kept a stiff upper lip. They didn't like to let down their guards in public. "Thank you," she called after the investigator, who simply nodded and trudged ahead.

Definitely other duties as assigned.

Without another glance at her federal friends, Jackie strode down the steps, along the sidewalk, and paused at her mailbox. When was the last time she'd checked it? Days? Weeks? Time had lost meaning. Here was another routine task she could perform. Do enough of them and perhaps life would resume some form of normalcy.

The box was full of fliers, bills, and magazines, but the pale-yellow envelope wedged on top caught and held Jackie's attention. The sender had employed simple block lettering to address it to her. There was no return address and no postage.

Hand delivered.

It could be an invitation to the neighborhood book club or a birthday party or a sympathy card for her loss. That would nice. Something personal in the midst of all this junk mail.

Gray clouds wafted over the afternoon sun. A chill tickled Jackie's spine. She shivered.

"What is it?"

Wick loomed over her. Jackie edged away from him. "A hand-delivered letter. Probably an invitation. We do a lot of socializing in this neighborhood. Block parties, book clubs—"

"No return address?"

He snatched the envelope from Jackie's hand and proceeded to slit the envelope with a pocket-knife.

"Hey, that's my mail. That's a federal offense."

"I'm confiscating it as potential evidence."

He pulled a single sheet of plain white

stationery from the envelope. Jackie leaned closer. Together they read:

> *Jackie,*
> *It has become necessary to find new, creative ways to contact your friend Bella Glover. Please share this message with her and her superiors:*
> *We're still waiting. How many people must die? Remove Vogel and Cavazos from power. Reverse the SACC Plan.*
> *Be assured that we won't shirk from our mission.*
> *Do nothing and you'll see the depth of our zeal.*
> *United San Antonians for Prosperity*

Jackie's stomach bucked with nausea. The edges of her vision darkened. She stuck her hand on the mailbox and closed her eyes. *Breathe.* Estrella's killer had stood on this very spot.

A letter instead of a phone call. Frustration wrapped itself around Jackie's chest, constricting her lungs. "He's cold-blooded, isn't he? Do you suppose he sashayed up here to leave the envelope before he entered my home and killed Meher?"

"You need to get a security system with cameras." His face dark with frustration, Wick studied the letter. He swore a steady stream. He probably didn't even realize it. "I'm betting there won't be any fingerprints either."

"He thinks he's so smart. He figures they've tapped Bella's phone."

"They have. It doesn't matter. He's using burner phones."

A phone call would still have been preferable. To be able to ask him why Meher had to die. She didn't know anything. She didn't do anything. Was she more collateral damage?

"How does Meher's murder track with this USAP charade? It's ridiculous." Jackie surveyed the block. As if he might still be hanging around watching. "He's worse than a monster. He's a psychopath."

"Meher saw something. She knew something."

"The security guard." Jackie fought to keep her voice steady. It rose in volume despite her best efforts. "Have you even tried to find him? Why not do that instead of hounding me and my family?"

"We will get whoever did this. For now I need to get on this. We need to tell the others." Wick held out his hand. Jackie stared at it and then at him. He was so solid, so sure, yet his expression was meek. Despite her best intentions, Jackie took it. His skin was warm against her cold fingers. His grip tightened. "We'll get him. I promise."

"When you do, I'd like first crack at him."

Wick shook his head. "You'll have to stand in line." He let her hand drop. The warmth receded. His gravelly voice held odd regret. Regret for taking her hand or for letting it go? "Someone else will have to take your statement downtown."

"I want to go to my mom's."

"I know. We'll get you there soon."

Avery—how could she think of him as Wick when he'd held her hand—did the talking to the agents while Jackie put as much distance between them as possible. She had liked holding his hand—too much.

Everyone moved at once. The letter went into an evidence bag. CSU returned a few minutes later. Special Agent Jantzen and her cohort left to canvass the block to see if anyone had seen someone other than a postal carrier in front of Jackie's home.

Avery stood in the front yard, his phone to his ear. After a few moments, he stuck his phone in his pocket. He and his partner conferred. A few seconds later Avery approached. "We have our marching orders. I'm to head with Petra to the *Express-News* to confer with them on how to handle the message—"

"Shouldn't I take the note? He left it for me. What if he's watching?"

"You can't go."

"Because I might have planted the note myself? Seriously?"

"No. Because one woman is already dead. You were simply a conduit for the message. The guy is smart. We'll take it from here."

"What will you tell Bella?"

"We don't get to tell the media much. We'll suggest that they report the note alongside whatever they're writing about Meher's murder. No expounding on it with comments from Vogel or the mayor or anything that might antagonize him more. Or whip up public concern."

"What about my formal interview?"

"My lieutenant is lining that up. I'm to head to the *Express-News*. Get Lee to meet you at HQ. Go to your mother's from there. Lay low."

"I still plan to finish the ofrendas. The Catrina Ball will go on." The bomber had taken so much. He didn't get to take this too. "If we don't, the programming this community needs will have to be scrapped. Early literacy programs. Homework assistance. Plans to expand and better utilize the Texana collection."

"Understood."

"Be careful." Jackie ignored Detective Heller, who stood within earshot, a knowing grin plastered across his face. She suppressed the urge to stick her tongue out at him. "Please."

"I'm always careful."

"Somehow I doubt that."

Fortunately he left before she gave in to the urge to hug him in front of God and everyone.

THIRTY-ONE

From a scene of death and unmitigated grief to the luxurious confines of a high-end jewelry store. The life of a detective. Avery wanted to be the one to drive Jackie to HQ, to interview her, and then see her safely to her mother's house. To protect her. To ease her grief and horror. Not here investigating her grandfather—an act that would surely push her away from him.

The moment she had told him she was in the house with the killer, Avery had known he was in over his head. His first gut instinct was to protect her. Not just as Ms. Citizen, but as a woman who somehow had begun to worm her way under his defenses.

Instead Avery and Scotty stood in Daniel Santoro's downtown store. Guilt at not telling Jackie the truth about where he was headed didn't improve Avery's mood. That he felt guilty only confirmed he was letting his feelings for her get in the way of good police work. She could not be privy to the investigation. Even so, Avery now wanted to pound someone to a bloody pulp. Preferably the bomber.

But he would have to be civilized. Santoro's administrative assistant insisted he would be available for a few minutes this afternoon. Thus

347

the pivot from the *Express-News*—left in Petra's capable hands. Santoro didn't have another opening in his schedule until Friday—not even for SAPD officers working on two bombings. LT instructed them to tread lightly with Jackie's grandfather. Neither order made Avery happy. Jackie was caught in the bomber's crosshairs. Her grandfather wasn't a suspect. His real value was in giving them insight to his grandchildren. Lee would deliver Jackie safely to her mother's.

The letter and envelope—as expected—offered no fingerprints. The stationery was run-of-the-mill, available at any discount store in town. Jackie had no security cameras. The FBI would do the handwriting analysis and add it to their profile. Other than that, no real forward progress.

The bomber was smart. He varied how and to whom he communicated. He used burner phones. Phone taps were useless.

The refrain *"no real forward progress"* rang in Avery's ears. He needed progress professionally but also on a personal level. This case needed to be over so he could figure out what to do with these stubborn, insistent feelings for one obstinate librarian.

A light-pole-skinny saleswoman with several examples of high-end bobbles strung around her neck and knobby wrists and hanging from her ears approached them with the care of a lioness stalking two wildebeests on the plains of Kenya.

Her pink painted lips drooped when Avery flashed his badge.

"How can I help two representatives of San Antonio's finest?" She flashed a smile containing a set of the whitest teeth Avery had ever seen. "We've already made a donation to Blue Santa."

SAPD didn't send out homicide detectives to collect donations for its Christmas charity. "We have an appointment to see Mr. Santoro." Avery moved past her, drawn to a glass display cabinet filled with matching sets of wedding rings. "Daniel, not Cristian."

Ms. Bleach Teeth teetered on high heels behind the counter. "See anything you like?"

With Scotty's snort ringing in his ears, Avery jerked his gaze from rings that cost more than six months' pay—gross, not net. "Is he in?"

"No, but I expect him any moment. Are you thinking of popping the question?" Bleach Teeth unlocked the cabinet and pulled out a plush velvet box lined with satin. It held half a dozen sets of diamond engagement rings matched with his and her wedding rings. "I see you eyeing these vintage-style sets. You have good taste."

Scotty laughed outright this time. "Once divorced, now mesmerized by a woman he can't have. Perusing rings he can't afford. That's my man Wick."

"Shut up."

He'd proposed to Chandra on bended knee

after a breezy springtime sixteen-mile bike ride—on a bike he borrowed—on the Leon Creek Greenway that left him almost too winded to speak. The ring, bought on credit, was a one-carat rectangular diamond surrounded by what the salesman called a multidiamond baguette set in white gold. The vintage-style design had the unfortunate name of "eternity" engagement ring.

"Really, I'm not in the market for a ring of any kind."

"You don't sound very convincing." She licked her lips in a feral, serpentine move. "This solitaire from Kobelli is gorgeous—"

"How much is it?" He wasn't in the market, simply curious. Really.

"You know the saying . . ."

"If you have to ask, you can't afford it." Scotty slapped Avery's back. "Maybe Chandra will return the one you gave her."

"Shut up."

Tinkly bells sounded. Avery turned. An older but just as fit version of Cris Santoro strode toward them. Tuffs of silver hair peeked from a black wool felt fedora over sharp blue eyes and a lined face. He wore a lightweight gray suit that fit him in a way that only tailored suits could. "You must be the homicide detectives my administrative assistant put on my schedule. She's always so stingy with my time. I apologize for that." He glanced at a smartwatch with a silver stainless-steel mesh band. "I'll make time for whatever you need. Let's talk in my office."

For a guy who hadn't returned their calls, he was Mr. Helpful now. "You're a tough man to catch up with. We'll take whatever you can spare."

Santoro kept walking. Avery and Scotty followed through a long, carpeted hallway that led to an office that could be described at once as minimally decorated yet exuding expensive taste. Simple but high-end furniture included a desk with a thin Mac laptop on it, a lightweight, black leather chair on rollers, and two black bookcases. A floral painting that someone other than Avery would no doubt recognize filled one wall. Floor-to-ceiling windows another. "I'm sure your wife or grandson filled you in on why we're doing these interviews, so I'll jump right in. Where were you Friday, starting in the early morning?"

Santoro opened the laptop and tapped on the keyboard. "I had a meeting with my contractor at the subdivision we're developing near The Rim. Do you know it?"

As hoity-toity as its neighbor, no doubt. "All morning?"

"No. I worked out with my trainer beginning at 5:30 a.m. and took a long run. I'm training for a half marathon. It's on my bucket list. Then I had a breakfast meeting at the Guenther, another meeting at Frost Bank, lunch with my grandson at Schilo's, visits to my stores in the afternoon, and dinner with my family."

Some of his family. "That's it? You were in for the night after dinner?"

Santoro's gaze flickered. He dropped his fedora on a spot next to his laptop. He cleared his throat but said nothing. Avery waited.

He leaned back and swiveled in his chair. "Later in the evening I drove to my granddaughter Jacqueline's home and briefly chatted with her before I returned to my house."

His voice held a thinly disguised sadness. Why hesitate to admit such a simple act of concern? No one would hold a visit to his granddaughter against him. "You didn't take your wife and son with you?"

"We have a complicated family dynamic." Santoro sighed. His gaze dropped to the laptop. "A private one."

"It was anything but private when your son was accused of breaking the law and then committed suicide." Scotty's lackadaisical tone belied his keen stare. "You didn't stop by your daughter-in-law's house as well, did you?"

"My son was a good man who wanted to make his way on his own. I respected that. I also felt— still feel—my daughter-in-law, Aimee, had undue influence on him." Pain deepened the lines around the elder Santoro's mouth. "He let her influence his decisions and then couldn't live with them.

But that's history. It has nothing to do with the bombings. In fact I called and left Aimee a message after the Market Square bombing. My wife sent her famous minestrone soup with Cris that evening. I followed up with a call to Jacqueline. Not that it's anyone's business, but we are trying."

Santoro picked up an eight-by-ten framed family photo and held it out to Avery. He took it. Happier times. Jackie looked twenty or twenty-one. Cris had his arm around her. Tosca held up two fingers behind her father's head. Aimee wore a shimmering red dress. Like her daughter, she was beautiful. No inkling of the troubles to come. "Nice-looking family."

"Thank you." Santoro cleared his throat again. "None of this has anything to do with your investigation. We're just a family that's been through hell and back. I would appreciate it if you'd give us the opportunity to move on."

"I'm truly sorry for your loss and your pain, Mr. Santoro." Avery leaned forward and clasped his hands in front of him. "Sometimes sorrow and grief lead people to do things they never would have done otherwise. You despise the city councilman who led the charge against your son and the city manager who ultimately fired him. So does your grandson, all of your family, really. Your son messed up and his bosses smeared your name all over the city—all over the state. It could be seen as motive."

"I'd say it makes my family human. I'm sure we've all said things we shouldn't have. My wife and I lost our only son. My grandchildren lost their father. It hurt, but that doesn't make us criminals." Santoro punched a button on the oversized phone on his desk. "Dana, you can put that call through now."

Scotty swooped over the desk and disconnected the call. "Human enough to concoct a plan to cover up the murders of top city officials by creating a bomber obsessed with the issue of climate control?" Santoro didn't budge. Not even his eyelid twitched. Scotty, ever the junkyard dog, tried again. "Human enough to risk killing your own granddaughter as collateral damage? Or your son's widow?"

"The idea that I would put Jacqueline in danger is ludicrous. My son and I didn't see eye to eye, but I loved him. His children are all I have left of him. I've provided you with my schedule. I was occupied the entire day Friday and Saturday." Santoro's voice turned hoarse. His Adam's apple bobbed, but his gaze didn't waver. "As was my grandson. Go find your killer and leave us to pick up the pieces of our lives and move on."

"How did it feel to need permits from the department your son oversaw for the city?"

"You're reaching. I don't pull permits. I have people who do that."

"It's been suggested you have loyal employees

who can take care of other ugly tasks for you as well, no questions asked."

"Your imagination runs away from you, Detective." His color heightened, Santoro stood. He strode around the desk and threaded his way between Avery and Scotty. "Next time I'd appreciate it if you check your stereotypes at the door. I'm a successful businessman with close ties to this community. I want to help you. If you have any constructive questions, feel free to come back. Until then, please go."

"Let's talk about your businesses—"

"Good day, Detective."

"Not until we say—"

"Let's go." Avery grabbed Scotty's arm and propelled him through the door. His partner's face was crimson. His lips twisted in scorn. Avery waited until the door closed. "Let it go. We have nothing that indicates he's lying. Nothing."

"You're buying the sad grandpa act?"

"He seemed sincere. Unless we can find evidence proving otherwise, we have nothing to tie him to either bombing."

At the car Avery stopped, keys in hand. He tossed them up and down.

"What?" Scotty pulled his door open and paused. "What's going on in that little head of yours?"

"Cris is the loose cannon, not his grandfather. He's in line to inherit the throne. He can throw his weight around too. He found his father's body. He was the most affected by his death. Maybe he's the one who's using his grandfather's money to orchestrate this operation. We need those phone records. When we get back, we'll see where Petra is on getting them."

"Chief isn't gonna be happy."

"If this turns out to be the thread that unravels the whole thing, he'll get over it."

If it wasn't, they could always get jobs as rent-a-cops.

THIRTY-TWO

The open garage door provided the first clue. Avery pulled into his driveway, turned down a Miranda Lambert song, and stared. The door was up. He hadn't left it up. Obviously. The motion-sensor security lighting glared in his eyes. If the door was up, any Tom, Dick, or Henry had access to Avery's house. He turned off the engine, slid from the truck, and laid his hand on his service weapon. Deuce and Ace made a ruckus in the backyard. They would have to wait. Even a sliver of a chance that they might get caught in the crossfire was too much. His pulse beating in his ears, he entered the garage. The door to the kitchen stood open.

Time to call for backup. For now that would be Scotty—until Avery knew what was going on.

Scotty simply said, "I'm on my way" and hung up.

The smell of dirty oil, gas, and old paint thick in his nose, Avery kept moving until he could reach the switch to the interior light. The naked overhead bulb shed tepid rays on his work space, his makeshift gym, and his backup vehicle—a '67 Chevy El Camino that sometimes started. Other times didn't. That might a blessing in this case. Thieves couldn't steal the classic.

A busted padlock lay on the cement floor next to his workbench.

He snagged it.

"Theo, you idiot," he whispered.

The cabinet where Avery had stored Theo's cache of weapons stood open. Empty.

The idiot had been in such a hurry, or drunk, or distraught, or all three, that he forgot to close the garage door.

That was one theory.

Or it was a simple burglary in which the culprits likely thought Christmas had come early. A stash of weapons would bring some serious cash on the streets. More than anything in the house.

Either way, not good.

Adrenaline revved. Despite the cool October air, sweat dampened Avery's shirt. His tie strangled him. He and Theo were friends. The closest Avery had to a best friend. On the other hand, the man's behavior had been increasingly erratic. A good guy gone sideways.

Guilt rattled Avery. He should've done more. Been there more. He laid the padlock on his workbench and eased toward the door to the kitchen.

As usual the smell of day-old coffee and dog food greeted him. From the looks of the mess on the table, the intruder had helped himself to a package of chocolate-covered donuts and a cup of coffee. The accordion file was gone. Theo had always wanted to see it. Thanks to Avery, he now had it. "Theo? Theo!"

No answer.

Cursing under his breath, Avery made quick work of the remainder of the house. No signs of forced entry. Theo had the spare house key. He didn't need to break in.

Screeching tires and squealing brakes announced Scotty's arrival.

Hand still on his S&W, Avery scanned the living room and made his way to the front door.

With a suitable litany of obscenities, Scotty shoved his way in. "What's going on? Did you find anyone?"

"Nope."

"What did they get?"

Talking and walking, Avery explained while he let the dogs in through the back door. They both let him know how disappointed they were in his failure to do so sooner. "Sorry, guys, it was for your own good."

Deuce's booming response left no doubt as to his thoughts on the subject. Avery squatted and gave him a good ear scratching. "Forgive me?"

"Don't you think you should report this?" Scotty joined the parade into the kitchen where Avery filled food and water bowls. "The guy is unstable and he's armed to the teeth."

He was also a hurting friend who'd fallen under the weight of the worst grief a parent could experience. No one could be expected to simply bounce back. No harm done. Life goes on. *"God won't give you more than you can handle. God can use everything for your good."* Sunday school answers. That's what his mother called them after Emmie died. She hadn't been back to church since.

Avery could see her point, but he wasn't a quitter. He had good days and bad days when it came to his sister's death. Church gave him a place to go where he could try to work it out. On a good day he saw the compassion and empathy her death had given him for others who suffered. On bad days he perfected his shake-his-fist-at-the-sky routine.

Today he understood that Theo's suffering went far deeper than his own. Avery might question why his sister had to die, but Theo still waited for his son's killer to be punished. He couldn't grieve and move on until the culprit was found.

Avery rubbed Ace's belly. The dog hummed with pure pleasure deep in his throat. "I need to talk to him first."

"I get that he's a friend. You have history. But try looking at the situation from a cop standpoint only." His face lined with fatigue, Scotty leaned against the door frame. "What would you do if a family member called this in and asked for a welfare check?"

Avery had made his share of welfare checks as a patrol officer. "I'd come prepared with backup."

"You wouldn't mess around trying to finesse the situation."

"He said they made him feel safe. He never said anything about hurting anyone."

"You should clean up in here once in a while." Scotty straightened and stretched. "Did you talk about the threats the bomber is making against Vogel and other city honchos?"

Avery wasn't here enough to clean, only long enough to make a mess. The conversation with Theo seemed years ago. The body count had risen since then. So had the emotional terrorism meted out by the bomber. "He brought it up one of the nights he spent here—Friday night. He said he felt bad that he dumped his problems on me without asking about my day."

Scotty helped himself to the package of donuts and slumped into a chair at the table. "What was his take on it?"

"We both know he's bitter—rightfully so— toward the city. He was no fan of Chief Little or Sandoval. And he hates Vogel's guts. But he wouldn't be stocking up on ammunition if he was the bomber."

"So he said he could relate to the bomber's desire to blow the city manager et al. to smith- ereens?"

"I believe it was something along the line

of 'Do us a favor and frag the whole bunch' or something to that effect."

"His wheels have come off the track, podner." Scotty brushed crumbs from his mustache. They showered the paper plate Avery had left on the table that morning. "You're in denial. You got any coffee? I like coffee with my donuts."

Avery unfolded his aching legs and went to the counter. He dumped the dregs from his breakfast coffee into Bluebird Café mugs from his last visit to Nashville and stuck one in the microwave. "If they have to take him in for a psych hold, he'll never get his job back. That's a big part of his problem. He feels helpless. He feels like he's being punished while the gangbanger who killed his kid is still out there living it up on the street. Probably selling meth to middle schoolers and beating up his girlfriend."

"Face reality, man. They can't give him his job back. He shouldn't be carrying a weapon. His days as a peace officer are over."

"I'm out of milk." Ignoring the desire to pour the hot liquid on his undeserving partner, Avery set the mug in front of Scotty and returned to the microwave. "I'm calling him. I'll ask him to stay with me for a while. If he refuses, I'll ask for backup to do a welfare check."

Theo answered on the first ring. "Sorry, bud. I know you're mad, but those guns belong to me."

"You broke into my house. You left my garage door open. You busted my padlock."

"Exaggerating once again. I didn't break in. I took what was mine because you refused to give it to me." The words slurred, no doubt from alcohol but also anger. They reverberated in Theo's hoarse voice, the thin veneer of amiability gone. "For a friend, you sure don't listen. I told you why I needed them."

Avery faced the window over the sink. The security lights beamed behind the live oaks in his side yard. The branches danced in the northerly wind. He breathed. "I'm sorry. I just worry about you, bro."

"Don't. I'm cool. I'm sitting on my couch watching *Diehard* and eating carryout Thai and drinking ice-cold beer. I'm good."

"I know you took Caleb's file."

"Thanks for getting it."

"I got it for me, not you. I need it back. There will be hell to pay if I don't return it."

"You're a good friend. I appreciate you making an effort."

The phone felt slick in Avery's hand. His friend was slipping away. "Give me time to look into it."

"I'm a certified peace officer. I can look into it myself. I'm good."

"You're not good."

"Don't be a Debbie Downer."

"Come stay with me. I'll even pick you up. We'll go through the files together. You can bring the weapons and keep them in the bedroom with you. I bet I can find every movie Bruce Willis has made streaming somewhere."

"Don't patronize me. I don't need a babysitter." The slur worsened. So did the anger. "Aren't you busy catching a bomber? Or not catching him?"

"I'm taking a few hours off."

"To sleep?"

Avery could hear the sarcasm in Theo's voice. He knew Avery too well. "To breathe. The funerals start tomorrow."

"And I messed it up for you by freaking you out. Sorry. Sleep."

"It's okay. I'll come get you. Scotty's here. We can get a poker game together."

"Rain check." He hung up.

Throwing the phone across the room wouldn't solve anything, but it was so tempting. Instead Avery turned and leaned against the cabinet. "He's lucid. He's eating. And drinking, but at least he's eating. He's watching movies. He didn't sound like a guy about to go on a killing spree."

"Is he on social media?"

It wasn't an idle question. Mass killers often talked trash on social media before their sprees began. "No. He and Katie used to be before Caleb died, but not since. She said it was too painful to see all their friends and families posting pictures of their kids growing up and changing. Theo was always careful not to post anything political because of his job, anyway."

"We need to do that welfare check. Or get some unis to do it if you'd rather."

"I'm not shuffling him off on someone else."

"You're up for an emergency detention? He's obviously a danger to himself or others."

The Texas Health and Safety Code gave them the authority to take Theo into custody so he could be evaluated at a mental health facility. That would give them forty-eight hours to obtain a judge's protective order to keep him longer if the San Antonio State Hospital folks decided he needed to stay. No peace officer relished the responsibility. If it saved lives—including Theo's—Avery had no choice. "Let me call Katie."

Avery's phone blared. He snatched it up. Maybe Theo changed his mind.

It was Katie. "Have you talked to Theo?"

"I just talked to him. Why?"

"He called me a few minutes ago." She ran the words together with a quiver. "He told me to come home."

"I don't think that's a good idea." Avery raced through the gun situation. "He says he's good, but it's obvious he's not. We're headed that direction. You shouldn't be there. You can meet us at the state hospital."

"He's not at home."

"What do you mean? I just hung up with him. He said he was eating takeout and watching movies."

"Then he lied to one of us." A sob punctuated her words. "He told me I could have the house. That it wasn't fair to me that I had to stay with my sister. That he should be the one to move out. He claimed he had."

"Did he say where he was going?"

"To stay at one of the hotels where he's doing security. He didn't say which one."

Did they hand out room keys to anyone with an employee ID? It didn't seem likely. "What hotel chain, at least."

"The Courtyard."

They owned several large hotels in the downtown area and near the airport. "We're on it. We'll track him down."

"He sounded upbeat—more upbeat than he has in a long time." Katie's voice faded. Avery had to strain to hear her. "He would never hurt anyone. Not my Theo. Do you really think he needs to be committed?"

"That's for the docs to decide." Thanks to a vicious animal with no conscience, the Theo Katie married didn't exist anymore. Avery tried to imbue his tone with positivity. "I just don't want to underestimate the situation and regret it later—for Theo's sake and for yours. Sit tight. I'll call you when we find him."

"Don't hurt him."

"Katie—"

She hung up.

Fifteen minutes later, Avery and Scotty parked in front of the Beretta home. The interior was dark and the driveway empty. That didn't mean Theo's Tundra couldn't be in the garage. Avery undid his seat belt and shoved open his door.

"Sure you don't want to call for backup?" Scotty held up his phone. "Or I could do it."

"Hang back for a bit. If I need you, I'll let you know."

"By then it might be too late. You're not thinking straight. You might not get so lucky this time."

Avery involuntarily touched the gauze on his cheek. The cut didn't hurt anymore, but he could add another scar to his collection. Did women find that sort of thing attractive? What a stupid question. Thank God he didn't voice it aloud. "We've known each other since high school. He gave me my first cigarette and my first beer." Not exactly stellar references, but ones Scotty would understand. Also a military brat, Avery's partner understood the never-ending process of starting over, making new friends again and again. "His dad taught me to drive while mine was deployed."

"I get that." Scotty pushed open his door. "It

was a long time ago. Now I'm your partner. Let me do my job."

Traffic hummed on I-10 in the distance. Their footsteps sounded loud on the sidewalk. Avery reached the small brick-and-cement landing first. He didn't immediately knock. Instead he picked up the accordion folder with a sticky note attached.

Avery, Sorry. Don't worry. I'm fine. Theo.

An envelope addressed to Katie had been skewered with a tack to the dark-blue door.

"Saying good-bye?" Scotty's gaze flitted across the house and the yard. "Are we facing another Las Vegas in downtown San Antonio? I wonder if his firm does security for any of the big tourist hotels. Ones that overlook the River Walk and the Alamo."

"He was wearing a Jason Aldean concert T-shirt the last time I saw him."

The country music star was on stage performing at the Route 91 Harvest festival in Las Vegas when a shooter killed 58 concertgoers and injured 413 in ten minutes using an AR-15 modified with a bump stock.

God, no. Avery pounded on the door in the off chance the notes were an attempt to throw them off his scent. "Are you in there, Theo? If you are, let me in. Come on."

Nothing. Just the whistle of a cold breeze that sent a shiver down Avery's spine.

Scotty dug his phone from his pocket. "I'm calling LT. We'll ask for a BOLO and an emergency protective order. What's he driving?"

"A 2017 Toyota Tundra, metallic gray."

That was the thing about guy friends. They knew what beer they liked. Cowboys or Texans. Cowboys, of course. Whether they liked their ribs smoked. What cars they drove. Feelings not so much. Yeah, Theo was hurting. Anyone could see that. How far he would go to assuage that pain, Avery couldn't be sure. Had he missed that point of no return?

Avery waited until his partner made the call. Together they headed to Scotty's Mustang. "We need to find him."

Before it was too late.

After a chat with the chain's security head honcho at the corporate offices, they cruised to the biggest hotel in the downtown area. Chief of security assured them hotel security personnel were not allowed to live at the hotel. Unless Theo was on duty, he shouldn't be on the premises. According to the schedule on file, Theo was not on duty.

That didn't mean he wasn't hanging out at the hotel. Maybe he took a room on his own dime. No such luck. Three hotels later Avery slid into Scotty's vehicle and managed to not quite slam the door. "Easy, bud." Scotty started the engine but didn't put the car in gear. "Let's call it a night. He's in the wind. He lied to you. He lied to his wife. Get a few hours of sleep. We'll start fresh tomorrow."

"I told Katie I'd do my best to bring him in without anyone getting hurt. If someone else picks him up on the BOLO, he may do something stupid."

"We can only control what we can control. Theo may call the shots."

Scotty had that right. Avery rolled down his window in hopes that the cool night air would wash away the sense of dread. "I was sitting by myself in the cafeteria, third day at a new high school. I didn't know a soul. Theo strolls over, slaps his tray down, plops down across from me. He starts talking like we've known each other for years. Within two weeks we were on the basketball team together. We played video games at his house all the time. I dated his sister. He teased mine. We snuck out of the house and grabbed a bus to go to a concert on a school night."

"I totally get it." Scotty lit a cigarette and took a long puff. "We moved like seventeen or eighteen times. I went to two high schools in four years. Lunch was the worst."

"My mom said I should be able to invite myself to sit with other kids who didn't know me." Avery winced at the thought—even after all these years. "I know it's hard to believe now, but

I wasn't as suave then as I am now. I was awkward."

With a hoot Scotty put the car in gear and pulled from the parking lot. "Suave? Is that even a word?"

"Like suave and debonair."

More hooting. "How did you ever snag Chandra?"

"She snagged me."

"There's no accounting for taste." Scotty turned onto Babcock Street and headed for Avery's house. "She must've had a few shots of tequila around closing time."

"We were at the Komen Race for the Cure, you idiot. I ran for my sister. Chandra ran for a friend." Memories of the humid May air, a light drizzle on his face, the electric hum of thousands of participants talking, and the searing pain in his side wafted over Avery. "Chandra was at the finish line cheering on the stragglers. She was sweaty and beautiful in shorts and a tank top. I was so crazy in love at that moment I dropped the cup of water she handed me."

"And she took pity on you." Scotty's laugh trailed off. "You never talk about your sister."

"Nothing to talk about. She got cancer at twenty-eight, had a double mastectomy, chemo, and radiation. Died at thirty-one." Even with the passage of years, Avery's throat tightened at the immediate, visceral pain in his gut. Anger, grief, bewilderment. The images of her bald head. How translucent her skin was near the end. Like he could see through it to her heart struggling to keep beating. "Nothing could kill the beast."

"That's rough." Scotty pulled into Avery's driveway and parked. "I have five brothers and sisters. We fought all the time, but if anyone tried to mess with one of us, we melded together into one big fighting machine."

"Emmie was my bestie. We always had each other in all those moves. In every new place we played hide-and-seek—just the two of us—in the new house and the new neighborhood. When Mom or Dad deployed, we still had each other. Emmie got bullied because she was small and plain like I was tall and plain. I got good at beating the snot out of kids who messed with her."

"The joys of being a military brat."

"The thing is, we could never complain about it. When your parents are serving your country, it's a noble cause. The whole family serves. My dad said we had patriotism in our DNA. He was sure I'd be a soldier too."

"No way—not me."

"Me neither." Not a popular sentiment in Military City, USA. Avery opened his door, then paused for a second. "I don't fault him, but I don't want that for my kids."

His hypothetical kids.

Thankfully Scotty let that go. "I totally get why Theo is important to you. We'll find him. We'll get him straightened out."

Scotty wasn't an optimist. Avery appreciated the effort he was making. "We have to find him. And soon."

Before he did something stupid. Something a friend couldn't fix.

"Are you headed to HQ?"

"Where else?"

Scotty saluted. "See you there, amigo."

Avery slid out, shut the door, and trudged to his truck. He'd sleep when this was over.

THIRTY-THREE

Funerals were for the living. Estrella would've hated the fuss. Jackie refused to wear black to the memorial service. Instead she chose her friend's favorite color in a red blouse coupled with a matching A-line skirt, a navy blazer, and pumps. She would save her black suit for the following week when Victoria's funeral was arranged and her children's families arrived. What did one wear to a Muslim funeral?

Sweet, scared Meher gone now, leaving behind two children and a distraught husband. The TV news broadcasted digital recordings of Adad Faheem collapsing in Jackie's yard. Avery, his partner, and Chandra tried to help him. That kind of grief couldn't be helped.

What Jackie wore to these funerals shouldn't matter, but somehow it did. Many of Estrella's coworkers chose red as well. A sea of black punctuated by splashes of red spread across the sanctuary. The program proclaimed the service a Celebration of Life.

Jackie called it a Life Cut Short.

Mateo and Mercedes sat in the front row with Estrella's half dozen siblings. Tony was wedged between her big brother Mateo Junior and her youngest sister, Luz. Many city council staffers who shared a bond with Estrella occupied the next row. The city manager and mayor sent representatives rather than coming themselves. Jackie was glad. The focus should be on Estrella and not on San Antonio public figures.

Bella had chosen to sit with the contingent of media covering the service. Sig had his arm around her. It would be nice to have that warmth. The church was freezing. Jackie shivered and pulled her blazer tighter.

Mother touched Jackie's hand with her splinted fingers and offered an inquiring glance. *Are you okay?*

Jackie nodded. No, but she would be. Estrella would expect it. Thankfully she had not been asked to do the eulogy. Not because she couldn't share a million beautiful memories of Estrella, but because she wouldn't be able to get through one without breaking down. Instead she stared at the enormous stained-glass window of a dove hovering over a flame behind the pulpit while Estrella's older sister Paloma did a beautiful job fashioning a colorful bouquet of stories from anecdotes lovingly shared by family members and friends.

Like the time Estrella and Jackie got separated from their Daisy Girl Scout troop at the San Antonio Museum of Natural History and decided to climb into a dinosaur exhibit. The troop leader found them astride a T-rex replica, riding it like a horse.

Thank You for the good times, Lord.

Or the story of how Estrella went after a UT–Austin professor who made the mistake of sexually harassing her. The campaign ended with the professor under investigation and eventually without a job.

Or her efforts to collect a blanket one winter for every man, woman, and child at Haven for Hope's campus for people experiencing homelessness.

When Estrella chose to do something, she did it with every ounce of strength she could muster and she compelled those around her to want to do it too.

Finally they sang MercyMe's "I Can Only Imagine," and the service was over. In that strange seesaw between sorrow and joy experienced when a believer leaves the world, Jackie wanted the service to last forever. Then she wouldn't have to say good-bye. It was too soon to say good-bye.

Her throat and chest hurt with the effort not to cry. Jackie sank back on the pew and let Tosca and Mom go first. After a few seconds she stood on shaky legs and moved toward the aisle. Paloma had asked her to supervise the food tables and make sure new dishes were set out when needed. A simple task she could handle on a day like today.

Don't cry. Don't cry. Don't cry.

377

She breathed in and out, in and out.

"Hey, Sis."

Cris edged his way between two of Estrella's tías. He hadn't forgotten Estrella's favorite color either. He wore a button-down collared red shirt with tan slacks and leather penny loafers. He looked so much like their father it made Jackie's heart heave against her rib cage. *Keep it together.* His cheeks were hollow and his clothes hung on him, just like Dad's had in his last days.

"Hey, Cris. I'm so glad you came."

This time she held out her arms. He walked into the hug. His arms tightened around her, then fell away. "Of course I came." He clipped the words in careful enunciation, as if he had only so much energy to expend on speaking. "Estrella was my friend."

Master of the understatement. "You were each other's first true love."

He linked arms with her and guided her through the swarm of people headed for the reception in the fellowship hall. "That was a long time ago."

"It feels like yesterday."

Only yesterday they'd taken turns dunking each other in the pool at Woodlawn Lake Park and he'd taken more time than necessary to lather sunscreen on his girlfriend's shoulders. Only yesterday they'd roasted marshmallows in the backyard with Foo Fighters on the CD player until Mom stomped out on the deck and demanded they turn it down.

"I guess I don't blame them for being leery of the USAP angle. I can't find any trace of such an organization here or anywhere in the world."

"You shouldn't be looking." His hand tightened on her arm. "Stay clear of it. Let the police do their jobs. Every applicable law enforcement agency is involved."

"This is Estrella we're talking about. You know she would do the same for me or Bella. Or you."

"Be smart. Stay out of it. They find out and they'll make up some bogus charge like interfering with an investigation and stick you in a cell."

The wave of people swept them into the fellowship hall, where tables laden with food provided by Mercedes and Mateo's Sunday school class and members of her women's group lined one wall. These women knew how to feed an army. King Ranch Casserole, lasagna, fried chicken, chicken parmesan, enchiladas, and other staples of the church potluck filled the hall with aromatic scents. The men had set up tables and chairs. The women covered the tables with paper tablecloths and placed arrangements of Estrella's favorite sunflowers on each one.

"I want to pay my respects." Cris let go of Jackie's arm. "I'm dreading it."

"They're doing fine. Better than the rest of us."

Jackie led the way. Mercedes and Mateo were standing in a receiving line with their children and grandchildren. Both wore red shirts and black slacks. Mercedes' red shoes were sparkly red *Wizard of Oz* flats. Cris hunched over and hugged Mateo and then Mercedes. They'd once thought of him as a future son-in-law. What they thought now was anyone's guess. He leaned close and whispered a few words in Mercedes' ear. The old woman smiled and patted his cheek. He moved on to Mateo, who greeted him like a long-lost son, which, in a way, he was.

"Let me get you a chair." He turned. Tears teetered and then slipped down his pale skin. "You should sit down, Mama."

Mercedes caught his hand, making him turn back. "*Gracias, mi hijo*, but I am fine. We'll sit soon. Get yourself some food. You're too thin."

"At least let me get you a cup of *chocolate caliente*." Cris leaned down and planted a kiss on her coiffed gray curls. "Your hands are cold."

"You're a sweet boy. Stay with us. You're family."

The pain on his face forced Jackie to step in. Mercedes held out her arthritic hands. Jackie took them. "Let him bring you the cocoa. It'll make him feel better. He needs to be busy."

Mercedes acquiesced with a sad smile. "You look tired, mi hijita. You sit."

That was Mercedes, ever the mami.

"It was a lovely service. Pastor Mike did a beautiful job."

"My girl walks the streets of gold." Mercedes' luminescent brown eyes warmed Jackie. "It would be selfish to want her here when she worships at the throne now."

Selfish but human. "Can I bring you a plate?"

"Later when all our guests are seated, *mis hijas* will bring food for us. You go. Sit. Eat. Try the King Ranch Casserole. Mi amiga Ida made it."

The thought of food turned Jackie's stomach. She managed a smile. "Later. When you eat."

"There's *tres leches* cake. I made it myself." Again classic Mercedes. In the midst of entertaining their entire extended family in town for the service, she would take time to cook one of Estrella's favorite desserts. "You're too thin, mi amor."

Mercedes always thought Estrella's friends needed fattening and did her best to tackle the job on her own with tamales, arroz con pollo, enchiladas verdes, chicken in mole sauce, *carne guisada* with homemade tortillas, and many other dishes in her vast repertoire. Between Mercedes' Mexican and Mom's Italian dishes, Jackie had never been in danger of wasting away. "I wouldn't miss it for the world."

"What are you doing here? How dare you?"

Jackie whirled at the sound of Cris's loud, agitated voice.

Her brother stood between Detective Wick and the family's receiving line.

How dare Avery work Estrella's funeral? Surely cops prowling at funerals was dross from TV shows and movies.

By the same token, Estrella's family didn't deserve a dustup between Cris and the detective during a time of mourning and remembrance. Jackie laid her hand on her brother's arm. "Please, Cris, let me deal with this."

"He's got a lot of gall, showing up like this." His voice full of venom, Cris jerked his arm away. "This isn't some cheap dime-store detective novel. We're saying good-bye to a beautiful soul. The police here are worthless. They go after innocent people and destroy their lives."

His voice choked, Cris closed the space between Avery and himself. "Get out, get out now, before I throw you out."

"Come on, Cris, you don't want to make a scene here." Avery kept his voice low, placating. "I only came to pay my respects."

"Don't lie to me. You're a lackey to the city manager and his cronies." His fair complexion scarlet, Cris fisted his hands. He planted his feet wide apart. "Your new boss probably sent you here to find another sacrificial lamb—"

Conversations ceased. People stopped filling their plates in the serving lines. No one moved for several seconds.

"Cris, please." Jackie stepped between the two men. "Not here."

Not anywhere. It would only give the police more ammunition for pinning the bombing on a member of the Santoro family.

Avery's pained expression met hers. Dark circles ringed his bloodshot eyes. He needed a shave and ten hours of sleep. He shook his head. "I meant no disrespect."

"I know, but Cris is right. It would have been better if you'd stayed away from this one." Jackie turned to her brother. "Mercedes needs you right now, Cris. Do you want this to be what she remembers about her daughter's funeral?"

The fury in Cris's eyes dissipated. His shoulders sagged. "I want him gone."

"Let me take care of that."

Mateo Junior slipped in beside Jackie. She squeezed his hand. It was clammy. "It's okay, Junior. Can you show Cris where the bottled water is? We need to replenish. Your mother needs some hot chocolate. She's cold."

Mateo Junior whispered something in Cris's ear. Her brother nodded, but his gaze never left Avery's. The detective's contrite expression never changed. Mateo put his arm on Cris's shoulder. Her brother nodded again. "Send him packing, sis. He doesn't belong here." He strode past Avery, his shoulder bumping the detective's, and kept going without excusing himself.

Avery's eyebrows rose, but he said nothing.

Jackie drew closer until she could speak in a whisper. "Have you no shame? Seriously, what are you doing here? Why aren't you out there catching a mass murderer?"

She stopped for breath.

"I—"

"And what happened to your face?"

THIRTY-FOUR

The look on Jackie's face told a story of assumptions. Just as Cris Santoro's had. Avery held up both hands, fingers spread as if surrendering. "I cut myself shaving. I came to pay my respects." He didn't exactly tower over this Amazon woman, but he drew himself up as tall as he could. He kept his voice low, quiet. He was far too tired for this. The unfruitful search for Theo had left Avery running on fumes. A day later and he and his arsenal were still MIA.

The scenarios ravaging Avery's vivid imagination kept his blood pressure higher than Mount Everest. His patience nonexistent. His head hurt, his back ached, and he needed an antacid. "I'd appreciate it if you'd let me do that. If you want to discuss my presence after that or kick me to the curb, that's fine. Just give me a moment first."

Jackie's creamy white skin blushed crimson. "Sorry. Of course."

It would've been easier if she'd said no. Then he could tell himself he tried and leave. With Richter and Theo out there doing who knew what, Avery didn't have time to spare. People were dying.

Gritting his teeth, he slipped past Jackie and approached Mr. and Mrs. Diaz. They both smiled, just as they had done when he and Scotty went to their house to interview them after their daughter's death. He rarely saw such strength in adversity. Usually the families of murder victims screamed, cried, and wailed—not that he blamed them. Those who showed up on TV for their thirty seconds of fame were anathema to him. They insisted their son or daughter was a wonderful human being even though the circumstances of their death clearly indicated they'd died in the middle of a gang-related incident or a drug deal gone bad.

"Mr. Diaz, Mrs. Diaz—"

"Mateo and Mercedes." Mr. Diaz's handshake was firm, his smile genuine. "Thank you for coming. It means a lot to us."

"Why aren't you out there finding out who did this to our sister?" That was one of the sons. "Or have you arrested someone?"

"Hijo, that's enough." Mr. Diaz's smile disappeared. His tone brooked no argument. "Detective Wick took time from the investigation to attend your sister's service. That is a sign of respect. Show some in return."

"Get something to eat." Mrs. Diaz pointed toward casserole-laden tables. "You're too thin, mi hijo. Try the tres leches cake."

The thought of food made Avery's stomach lurch. Too much coffee and not enough sleep. They were kind. They understood his need to be here even though he'd never met their daughter. "I'm sorry for your loss."

"She's with Jesus." Mrs. Diaz's voice held only the slightest quiver. Her husband clasped her hand. "It's selfish to wish otherwise."

Another anathema. Such faith. "I'll let you know if we have a break in the case."

"We know you will." Mr. Diaz's smile faltered. "We are satisfied that our child is in a safe place free of suffering. That doesn't mean we don't want justice for her. Find who did this and make sure he is punished."

"That's the plan."

Avery moved down the line, shaking hands with brothers, sisters, aunts, uncles, and even two eightysomething grandmas and a wizened, barely breathing great-grandpa. So many funerals to go. It was important to see firsthand the agony of the family members. To be reminded of why he did this job. To remind himself of why he never gave up. That ridiculous word *closure* didn't do justice to what these folks needed. He couldn't return to them their beloved, but he could give them justice so they could begin to heal. When they looked at that empty chair at the table, they would know that the guilty party didn't still walk around free and unpunished.

Paying his respects didn't mean Avery hadn't also scoped out the attendees in the sanctuary. Not that he could tell if anyone was out of place.

Estrella Diaz had an enormous extended family and every one of them seemed to be in attendance. All her coworkers from the city council offices were there. Several elected officials. The mayor had sent a representative and the city manager his chief of staff. Both had paid their respects to the grieving family. The media wasn't allowed into the reception—a fact that probably galled the reps. No video of them embracing the anguished parents.

Just video of them entering and leaving the church. That would have to do.

The desire to puke overwhelmed Avery. So did his own cynicism.

Finally it was done. He drew a long breath, exhaled, and slipped between the crowded tables toward the double doors. Jackie stepped in his path. She held a plate piled high with food. "I made you a plate."

He swallowed hard against the rank, foul-tasting ball in the back of his throat. "Thank you, but I need to get back to HQ."

"You can spare fifteen minutes to eat. You have to eat. The ladies at this church know how to cook."

"Did you eat?"

Jackie shook her head and shrugged. "I'm one of those people who can't eat when I'm stressed."

"I guess that's me too."

She set the plate on the table. "Thank you for

coming. It took guts. I'm sorry for the way my brother acted. He's grief stricken if that's any excuse. I'm sorry I jumped to conclusions."

"It's okay." Red was her color. It made her eyes an even deeper blue. She looked tired but determined. A strand of her dark hair had slipped from her chignon. It lay at the nape of her long neck. The desire to tuck it back in almost won out. He'd given in to the desire to hold her hand at her house. He couldn't bring himself to regret it. Nor could he allow it to happen again.

"Trauma gives people a short fuse. I'm sorry for your loss. I'm sorry about Meher too. You had a connection to her. You didn't know her well, but finding her body like that will leave deep scars."

Her chin quivered. She studied a spot over his shoulder. "Thank you. When I close my eyes, I still see her . . . there on my floor. And I ache for her children and her husband. I don't understand how you—how it could've happened. I know law enforcement can't be everywhere all the time, but she was a person of interest. She was staying with a well-known attorney, your ex-wife." She took a breath. "I'm sorry, this isn't the time for this, but it all comes welling up at the most inopportune moments."

She didn't outright accuse him. Nor was she saying anything he hadn't said to himself in the last twenty-four hours. He glanced around. No one was paying attention. They'd gone back to their grief and their food. "Walk me to my truck?"

Surprise registered in her expression. She would say no and he would go about his business. "Of course."

Together they squeezed through the clusters of people congregated in the foyer, reached the front door, and made it to the education wing's porch. Sweet silence. "I'm sorry we didn't do more. That we couldn't do more. We're all aware of our shortcomings surrounding Meher's death. I was surprised when the Feds didn't take her into protective custody, at least temporarily, but my ex is good at what she does. She also has a superhero complex. I have no doubt she thought she could keep Meher safe. She let her go grocery shopping and Meher ended up dead."

"Meher was an adult and she wasn't a prisoner."

"I know. Now that the initial shock has passed, Chandra is spitting mad. She's representing Meher's husband with Drucker's help."

"Please tell Chandra I'm praying for her and the Faheem family. I'd like to go to the funeral."

Chandra would smile and appreciate the sentiments, even though her own religion was more Unitarian and geared toward her version of social justice. "I will. I interviewed your brother and your grandparents."

"I know." Her sigh was filled with regret, uncertainty, and faint misery woven together by sadness. "Cris was the hardest hit by my father's death. I almost wish I had found Daddy's body, not him. He likes to pretend he's tough. He's suffering and it comes out in all this stupid macho-ironman-of-few-words thing."

"Chandra says it takes men a lot longer to grow up than women."

Did he just quote his ex-wife to a woman he wanted to date?

"Cris isn't the bomber. Surely you have other leads, other possibilities."

The admonition in her voice stung. He couldn't share intel with her, all the same. "We're exploring other avenues."

Including his best friend.

"What? You look so sad. I didn't expect that from a homicide detective."

"We're humans, believe it or not."

She inched a tad closer. "I never doubted that. Surely you've grown a thick shell, though."

"If you stop feeling, you stop being good at the job." It was hard to explain. Losing the ability to see victims and perpetrators as hurting, scared human beings would impede his ability to solve murders. "I actually can relate to your anger and hurt over having a family member in my crosshairs."

"Someone you know might be a murderer?"

"Theo was my friend when no one else was." He shifted from one foot to the other. A sudden hard lump in his throat made it hard to speak. He cleared it and gave her a bare-bones summary of the situation with Theo. "He picked me and stuck to me like a burr on my sock. I couldn't have shaken him if I wanted to and I didn't want to. Now he's messed up and he needs a friend. I can't find him and I can't spare time to look for him because I have nothing to tie him to the bombings but a horrible feeling in my gut."

"I can't claim to know how Theo feels." She cocked her head and stared at a flock of birds headed south for the winter, their V dark against the blue sky. "His child died in his arms. Justice hasn't been served." Her voice cracked. "It would be enough to break a strong, good man. But he's gathering an arsenal, not bomb-making materials."

"I know. So what if we have two forces at work, complementing each other, threatening to wreak havoc on this city? A horrible, uncalculated, coincidental meeting of minds unbeknownst to the parties involved. Or what if the bomber's actions were just enough to feed Theo's certainty that the ends justify the means, that vigilante justice is better than no justice, that pressure has to be applied to get the powers that be to do what you or I think is right and just?"

"What a beastly thought."

"Welcome to my world."

"The good news is you're on top of it. You

could be wrong about Theo, but if you're right, you have the opportunity to shut it down, to save your friend from himself. That's what best friends do. True blue friends are hard to come by. My circle is small and getting smaller, so I understand how you feel." Another wave of unmitigated grief washed over Jackie's face. "I lost one of my best friends to the bomber with no warning. You can save other people from experiencing that kind of pain."

She did understand, in a way that few could. Once again Avery gave in to the urge to grab her hand and squeezed. No one with a shred of humanity left could stand by and not offer comfort at this moment. "I'm so sorry for your loss. I promise to do my best to catch the sorry son of a gun who did it and bury him."

Jackie stared at his hand over hers. The grief faded, replaced by an uncertain, faint smile. "Why did you want me to walk you to your truck?"

Avery let her hand drop. He flipped through the mental Rolodex filled with reasons. "First I wanted to apologize for the way I acted at the library. It was unprofessional for me to insert myself—"

"It was sweet, actually. I was the one being a jerk." Her cheeks suddenly pink, Jackie touched the filigreed gold cross that hung from a gold rope chain around her neck. "You are right about the ball. I told Meagan the same thing right before I got on that elevator."

"So why argue with me?"

"Because I don't want you inside my defenses."

A door appeared that hadn't been there before. It opened a few inches. The feeling was mutual. Time to steer away from dangerous territory. "There is a question unrelated to the investigation that you could answer for me."

Relief mixed with a touch of disappointment flitted across her face. Then she smiled. "What's the question?"

"It blows me away how accepting Mr. and Mrs. Diaz are of their daughter's death. If I had a daughter and this happened, I'd go to the ends of the earth to kill the . . . animal who did this."

God didn't strike him down for cursing in a church parking lot. His mercy and grace really did extend to a sinner who never seemed to get better, no matter how repentant. Avery kept making the same mistakes, like a little kid who keeps saying he's sorry but swipes the cookies from the cookie jar anyway.

"When I was a kid, I wanted to be Mercedes when I grew up. Which is pretty funny considering my family is of Italian descent and Mercedes is a Mexican immigrant's child." Memories softened her face. "Both families were big and raucous and crazy and fun, but I loved being at Estrella's house. Don't get me wrong.

I love my mom and dad, but the Diazes are something special. Faith that moves mountains."

"Or accepts a child's death in a senseless act of violence." Digging his keys from his pocket, he stopped in front of his pickup. "This is me."

"How is Chandra doing?"

"She's dealing with her guilt by working harder, doing more, parenting more. She feels responsible. She wants to do something for Meher's family. She just hasn't figured out what yet."

"That's not her fault. I told Meher she could come to my house. I didn't get there fast enough."

"If you'd arrived sooner, you would be dead too." And his chance to have something with her would be gone. What a selfish thought. "You're both wrong. It's not your fault. A psychopath did it."

"Chandra's nice. Empathetic. She also speaks highly of you."

"She *is* nice." And far too perceptive. Heat washed over Avery. Was Jackie interested in him or was it wishful thinking on Chandra's part? She'd found happiness with a new partner and she wanted the same for him. "Her kind words notwithstanding, she divorced me."

"Sounds like it still rankles."

"Only my pride hurts."

Jackie surveyed his old beater with obvious interest, then turned and leaned against it. "Do you have faith?"

She did like to get down to the nitty-gritty. Avery tried to gather his thoughts. "I don't know how to answer that. Sometimes I try, other days I don't. It's the nature of what I do for a living."

"That's fair. I think we all have our days. You don't have a daughter. What about a son?"

Again, the nitty-gritty. He gave her props for being a good interrogator. "No. Chandra and I never could agree on the right time, and then we ran out of time."

"That doesn't mean you don't still have time."

Men didn't have the same powerful biological clocks ticking that women did, but Avery could still feel the wind on his face as time flew by. To have children required the right woman. No such woman had appeared in his life. He didn't know Jackie well enough to know if she was that woman. He'd like to find out.

He turned so he could memorize her face. He was a detective in the middle of a massive multiagency investigation in which she played a major role. Then again, he'd never played by the rules. Why start now? "I don't know. I'm not convinced I'd be good at it. My dad was deployed a lot when I was growing up. My mom took her turns as well."

"Do you like basketball?"

"Who doesn't like basketball? I attended UTSA on a basketball scholarship."

"Same for me, only it was UT–Austin."

Avery whistled. "Maybe I should genuflect."

"Don't you dare."

"I also like baseball and football. I bowl a mean game. I'll even play badminton or ping-pong. I guess I'm competitive. The only sports I don't like are golf and soccer."

"Do you have pets?"

"Two rescue dogs."

"Were you a Boy Scout?"

"I was." Probably not a good time to share that he'd been kicked out for smoking cigarettes on a campout. "A long time ago."

"You're hardworking in an honorable profession. You're kind and compassionate—I've seen that firsthand. You like sports, especially basketball, and you rescue dogs. Cats would be better, but dogs are good. You'll do fine."

"It's strange how events like the bombings make us think about our lives in the bigger picture. Most of the time I'm too busy just trying to keep up. I don't stop to think about the mark I'm making on the world."

"I do DIY projects at my house and read a lot of books when I'm not working." Jackie contemplated the cloudless sky. "We're all guilty of believing we have plenty of time."

"What about you? Do you want children?"

"Several would be nice. I'd like to read them bedtime stories and make cutout cookies on Christmas Eve morning so we can leave some out for Santa that night after we attend the candlelight service at church. I want to play ring-around-the-rosy and teach them to tie their shoes. I'd like to teach them my jump shot and my left-handed hook and take them to Spurs games and coach their baseball teams. And teach them to swim, of course, and to dream big."

"You've given this a lot of thought." Avery filed those images away with the one of her face raised to the sun. "You've never been married?"

"My life imploded when my dad killed himself. I had a friend at the time, but he headed for the hills when the dung hit the fan." She was brutally transparent. It was nice. He didn't have to read between the lines. Jackie removed her blazer and slung it over her shoulder. "I've been burned, so I tread carefully."

"Been there, done that."

"So I gathered."

"I really have to go." What he really wanted to do was thoroughly kiss her until that sad look disappeared. It would be totally wrong. And presumptuous. He was the beast to her beauty, and old. "Work calls."

"Chandra says you don't read."

Would this be her hill to die on? He couldn't lie. What if she asked him to name the last book he read? He couldn't remember. "I don't."

"Never?"

"Do the backs of cereal boxes count?" He went

for humor. Her eyebrows lifted. He fell back on more humor. "I feel like you're judging me. Like I just admitted to being something worse than a murderer."

"Did you ever read?"

"Comic books when I was a kid." His parents weren't readers. He'd never even had a library card. She might faint if he told her that. "Whatever I had to read to get through my criminal justice degree at UTSA. The funnies."

"That's better than nothing, I guess."

"Thank you."

"I'm going to find a book you'll like and get it for you. You'll see. It's never too late."

A cricket chirped. Which meant he had a text from Scotty. "I really do have to go."

"Take care of yourself."

"You too."

Neither of them moved.

"I'll . . . I'll call you if anything breaks on the case."

"You have my number."

He did. He would solve this case for the sake of the victims, but also so he would have another reason to call her. And then kiss her. If she deigned to let a guy like him kiss a girl like her.

THIRTY-FIVE

Dead as an armadillo decorating the middle of a Texas highway. Avery had to concur with Scotty's pronouncement that Ethan Richter wasn't just dead. He was DRT. Dead Right There. Splattered on the hard South Texas earth.

Their one good lead hadn't stuck around long enough for them to redeem themselves and solve this case. Which left them with the Santoros. And/or Theo.

Not Theo.

The fake security guard's body lay at the bottom of a Friedrich Wilderness Park canyon where he had fallen—or been pushed—from a trail that followed the narrow rock ledges that snaked along the edge of the canyons on either side of the ridge.

There were worse places for a crime scene, but Avery couldn't think of one offhand. Friedrich was a nature preserve, which meant minimal development away from the main entrance. Vegetation was left in its natural state. Lighting, bathrooms, and water fountains were confined to the area near the offices and outdoor classrooms. The park normally closed at sunset. In the final days of October, the gates swung shut after the last park patron left, around six forty-five—ten minutes ago.

Scaling down the steep rock face, outfitted in harnesses attached by the fire department, had been the icing on the cake after a three-mile jaunt from the main entrance, the last mile of which involved a narrow ledge called the Vista Loop Trail.

Scotty had cussed, coughed, and complained the entire three-mile hike to the spot where park employees had discovered the body. Avery didn't have the lung capacity to join him. Plus he was too busy making sure his slick leather loafers stayed on the narrow ledge they laughingly called a trail. The CSU folks weren't much happier. They had to bring in generators and lights. The entire cadre of LEOs and the ME investigator crawled down the steep rock face in harnesses.

Park naturalist Jamie O'Neill had entertained all of them with a nature guide monologue on the vegetation—lacey oak, red oak, cherry, and walnut—and the geography and history of the trail—it climbed to the crest of the ridge that divided the park into its east and west valleys. The upper portion paralleled an old stone fence that ran north-south along the highest part of Friedrich. The high part was apparent. The steady stream continued until they stood a few yards from where Richter had landed facedown. Then O'Neill spun around and managed to stumble a few yards before vomiting under one of those lacey oaks.

Avery waited until the park naturalist composed himself to start from the top. "Tell us about the guys who found the body and what they were doing up here."

"A hiker reported some debris blocking the trail after that rainstorm we had the other night." O'Neill wiped his mouth on his sleeve. He hadn't broken a sweat on the hike. Even in October he had the ruddy complexion of a man who spent all his time outdoors. And a future candidate for skin cancer. He faced Scotty as if to keep his mind off Richter's mangled body. "So a couple of our guys came up to clear it. Some of these old trees at the end of their life cycle will fall in a brisk breeze."

"So they looked down and saw the victim?"

"They could see the vultures circling, so they checked it out. They figured it would be a deer or a rabbit or even a raccoon. We occasionally have sightings of bobcats and mountain lions, but they're at the top of the predator chain, so . . ."

Scotty held out his phone, displaying the photo the park police officer who handled the initial contact had texted to the PD dispatcher, along with one of his driver's license. It was easier than making O'Neill get up close and personal with the corpse. Besides, the ME investigator didn't like the intrusion on his space. "Do you recognize him?"

O'Neill studied the photo and shook his head. "Sorry. Hundreds of park patrons go through here on a weekly basis. The park's so popular we have trouble protecting the vegetation and wildlife even though people mean well."

"You don't check in or pay or register or anything?" Scotty sounded dumbfounded. He was allergic to clean air and exercise on principle. "How do you know how many people are here?"

"We have a general idea when the parking lot is full. City parks are free, unless you count your taxpayer dollars, which, believe me, our patrons do. They have great ownership in the park."

"I'm sure they do." Scotty hawked up a loogie and swallowed. He knew better than to contaminate a crime scene. "What about his car?"

"There's one vehicle left in the lot." O'Neill took his turn and held out his phone. "The park education gal sent me this."

A photo of a blue Chevy Silverado.

"We could go back with one of the CSU guys so they can toss it. The Feds can handle this." Scotty sounded hopeful. "It'll take us another hour to get there."

"The parking lot is lighted," O'Neill offered.

"We're not close to being done here. Hang tight." Avery intervened. He, too, would like a gallon of water, a toilet, and three ibuprofen. "Let me see what Pogue has to say."

Pogue being the investigator who drew the

lucky number to scale down the side of a cliff to examine Richter's body. Avery squeezed in next to Jantzen, who had donned her FBI jacket as if cold. She knelt as close to the body as she dared, given Pogue's tendency to lash out at those who invaded his work space.

Avery squatted next to her. Richter's legs were twisted in an unnatural pretzel. He'd landed on one arm while the other was flung outstretched. His head faced the other direction. "So, Pogue, cause of death is the fall?"

"Won't know until the autopsy."

It was an automatic reflex response. "Nothing else jumps out at you?"

"The kill shot between the eyes is a dead giveaway, if you'll pardon the pun."

Nothing like a delayed punch line. "Thanks for getting right to the point."

"You're welcome."

Avery rolled his eyes at Petra, who rolled her jasper eyes like a teenage girl. Avery stood and approached the CSI in charge, Connie Kappel. "Did y'all find any casings up top or down here?"

"Nope."

"Blood spatter up top?"

"No, but if he was shot and the force of the hit knocked him backward off that narrow trail, there wouldn't be any to find. Either way, we need to get a better look at both locations in daylight."

Kappel squatted next to a thick juniper and

waved her flashlight around the base. "What do we have here?" She reached under the shrub and brought forth a pistol grasped by her gloved thumb and index finger. They combined their flashlights for a closer examination.

"A Heckler & Koch HK45." Keppel whistled. "Nice."

Mercenaries favored the German-made pistols. "You said earlier he had an empty holster strapped to his body."

"I did. I assumed the shooter took it. Guess I was wrong."

Avery turned to study the body. Someone had gotten the jump on Richter. That took some doing. Somebody Richter knew? "He either drew it and got the raw end of a gunfire exchange or he didn't have time and the gun fell from his holster."

"No casings of any kind, so it's hard to say if more than one weapon was fired."

"I'm thinking he knew his assailant," Petra piped up. "Why else would he meet someone out here in the middle of the boondocks? He's not dressed for hiking."

"We need to close up shop. Come back tomorrow in the daylight." Avery shone his high-powered flashlight on the sheer rock wall. Scaling up would be far less enjoyable than coming down. He'd felt like a champion rock climber for about two seconds, until he lost his footing and swung like Tarzan and then hung in the air like an awkward monkey. "It's impossible to do a thorough examination of the site in the dark. Let's get SAFD to bring up the body. We can finish up in the morning."

"Agreed. Tell the park staff to get the word out on social media that the park will be closed tomorrow. Possibly longer." Petra's flashlight joined his on the wall. She didn't look any happier than Avery felt. "We need to interview every employee. If they can identify any park patrons who were here today, we interview them too. Somebody saw something."

Maybe. In a sixty-acre nature preserve, maybe not. "On it, ma'am."

She grinned. "Thanks."

"You're welcome."

Despite the powerful lights provided by SAFD, the trek back was even more adrenaline laced. Maybe he should call Jackie and tell her how he felt about her before he fell into a canyon and never had the chance.

So much for staying on task. He entertained himself—and kept his mind off the deadly heights from which he would fall when his slick loafers slipped from the rocky ledge—by reviewing images of her from the church parking lot. Soaking up sun. Sad. Happy. Frowning. She looked good no matter how she felt.

Finally they straggled into the parking lot.

SAFD delivered Richter's body to the ME's van. The victim's truck was parked in the last space in the last row closest to the gate. In other words he had been one of the last to arrive to the park. No bomb-making manual in the glove box. That would be too easy.

Keppel, who perked up once she partook of water from an oversize Igloo O'Neill brought out to them, used bolt cutters to break the padlock on the oversize toolbox in the truck's bed. A cache of weapons that made Theo's collection seem like child's play nestled under a thick Army surplus store blanket.

O'Neill, who balanced his worn hiking boots on the curb, almost fell off. "Are those assault rifles?"

Nodding, Avery stuck his hands behind his back in case they decided to break the rules and get grabby. One of Keppel's colleagues spread a plastic sheet atop the pattern of rectangular cement blocks alternating with grass that formed the preserve's ecofriendly parking lot. A fountain of information garnered from Google searches over the years, Scotty announced each weapon like an auctioneer as the two CSIs laid them out.

"Sweet. An AK-47 with a nice 100-round detachable box. The semiauto rate is 40 rounds a minute. Full-auto burst rate of fire is 100 rounds a minute. This baby is a favorite of mercenaries, terrorists, and militaries for its low cost, ease of use, and durability. Originally made in Russia and known as the Kalashnikov. Now it's made everywhere."

Next came two HK416s. Scotty shared a low whistle with Keppel. "This beauty is used by armed forces around the world, including U.S. Special Forces. It has an AR-15 platform and uses standard NATO ammunition, 5.56 x 44mm. Rate of fire is 700 to 900 rounds a minute."

Finally two M4 carbines. Apparently Richter liked pairs. Avery, Petra, and Scotty joined the CSIs in squatting next to the plastic. They were beautiful killing machines. Scotty's running commentary turned into a mutter. "The M4s are the current weapon of choice in the U.S. armed forces. Fire options include three-round burst, semiautomatic, and fully automatic. They can also be fitted with grenade launchers. The rate of fire is 700 to 950 rounds a minute. The effective range is 500 meters for a point target and 600 for area targets."

Finally a series of packages containing the corresponding ammunition for the weapons. Dozens of packages.

No one in peacetime had any reason to own any of these weapons, Second Amendment or not. They were a mass murderer's dream and law enforcement's nightmare.

"We'll get them into evidence ASAP." Keppel tugged on her glove and let it snap against her wrist. "It's hard to imagine what the guy planned to do with these. It's not PC, but whoever punched his ticket did us all a favor."

Avery couldn't disagree. Except they really needed to interrogate him first. The weapons told them little. What they needed were bomb-making materials. "No trace of gunpowder."

"No. Dust, dirt, garden-variety vegetation on the bed liner, that's about it." Kappel rose and stretched. "You saw the interior. Clean as a whistle. Just like his duplex. The guy is a neat freak."

Par for the course on this case. Avery dragged himself to his feet. "If you find anything else, let us know, please?"

"You know I will."

They needed a break. The clock was ticking. Any second the bomber would make good on his threat and more innocent people would die.

THIRTY-SIX

The sound of a tap on the Rogue's window jerked Jackie's eyes open. She straightened in the driver's seat and blinked away renegade tears that had sneaked up on her. Back-to-back funerals were the final straws on this Friday afternoon that finally would end a hellish week. She simply wanted two seconds with her eyes closed. Just two seconds.

Bella tapped again and motioned for Jackie to roll her window down. She obliged.

"My car is dead." The level of frustration in Bella's voice suggested she might kill the VW Bug if it wasn't already dead. "Of all times."

"Should we try to jump it?"

"The jumper cables are in Sig's car. It's more decrepit than mine, if that's possible. Do you mind? He got called out for a triple homicide in Lytle. Tony has to accompany Sandoval's family to the reception or I'd ask him. I have to get back to the newsroom and write my story."

The story would chronicle the service for a dedicated councilman who left behind a wife and three children, eulogized by the mayor and the county judge, followed by the less flashy but equally well-attended funeral of the library foundation board chairman. He, too, left behind a wife and three children plus half a dozen grandchildren. Cute, sweet little kids who would miss their grandpa. "Let's do it."

They were both dressed in funeral finery, but neither would admit to not being able to jump a car. Daddy had made sure Jackie could change a tire and jump a dead battery. In this case, it didn't matter. The ten-year-old car had 105,000 miles on it and no intention of moving.

A crowd of men gathered around to offer help and advice. Nothing helped. Bella thanked them effusively, grabbed Jackie's arm, and propelled her back to the Rogue. "My editor just texted. Park police found a black backpack on the River Walk, near one of the barge stations. They're evacuating the entire area, including Alamo Plaza and Hemisfair Park."

So much ground to cover. Fighting nausea, Jackie waited for Bella to run around the Rogue and dive in before she jammed the SUV in Drive and took off. The church was only five or six miles from downtown. She could jump on 35 South from 281 and exit onto Houston Street.

Please, God, don't let him do it. Work on his heart. Save those innocent people. Please.

"Faster." Bella snapped her seat belt tighter. "Floor it."

"This is a Rogue, not a Ferrari." Jackie stomped on the accelerator. The abused six-year-old SUV crossover lurched forward. "Hang on."

"Don't mind me." Bella stuck her phone to her ear, then punched the speaker button.

The city desk editor's deep voice rattled the Rogue's interior. "They're evacuating surrounding businesses, that building that used to be the post office, the Emily Morgan Hotel, the Crockett, the businesses across the street from the Alamo. Even Rivercenter mall."

"If it's a bomb like the other ones, it won't have that kind of reach."

"They're not taking any chances. They've cordoned off the area. The bomb squad is standing by to use the bomb-disposal robot to clear them."

"We won't be able to get close."

"Do your best. The police PIO is on-site with Chief Ruiz. They're posting updates on social media urging people to stay away from downtown until the incident is resolved."

"Got it. I'll be in touch."

Bella disconnected and hopped on social media. "Houston, Alamo Street, Crockett, Commerce, and Bonham are all closed with manned PD vehicles in the vicinity of the Alamo." She stared at her phone. "I think our best bet is Avenue E and Third Street. We can park in the newspaper lot and I can hike in from there."

Jackie exited the highway still going the speed limit. The Rogue took the curve like a champ. "*We* can hike in."

"There's no reason for you to get closer." Bella

grabbed the hand grip over her head and hung on. "Why put yourself in danger? Your family has been through too much already."

"I'm going."

End of discussion.

Jackie parked, pushed her door open, and ran. Shades of Saturday's desperate race from the library to Market Square enveloped her. Blood pulsed in her ears. Her muscles ached. Her heart clobbered her rib cage. *Please, God, let no one be hurt. Stymie this madman's efforts. Let there be no more deaths at the Alamo, no more need of a memorial on top of a memorial.*

The words spun from her heart into every tortured breath she took. *God, God, God.*

They hit the first blockade at Houston Street. Gasping for breath, Bella stopped long enough to flash her newspaper press credential and try to get information from the uniformed officer who had his cruiser parked cockeyed in the middle of the street. Curious onlookers crowded the sidewalks but mostly heeded the cadre of officers who used bullhorns to order them to back off, to disperse, to stay out of harm's way.

"I'm not authorized to speak to the media." The officer didn't make eye contact, as if that, too, was verboten. "You need to speak to the PIO."

"I'd love to. How do I find him?"

"Call HQ. I'm sure you have the number."

"I heard he was here with the chief. Where's the chief?"

"I don't know." He turned his back and chased off a young kid who had one hand on his scooter and another on his phone, recording the scene.

Bella shook her head. Jackie nodded toward the west. "Let's see if we can get through on Presa or Navarro."

Jackie's phone vibrated in her hand. She didn't recognize the number. No time for spam right now. She kept going. The caller hung up and rang again, a second, then a third time. Irritated, she answered. "Stop calling or leave a message—"

"That's no way to talk to a person who holds your life in his hands."

Jackie plowed to a stop. What little breath she had left fled. Light-headed, she bent over and tried to suck in air. No dice. Bella slowed, looked back, then backpedaled. Jackie pointed to the phone and mouthed, *It's him.*

Bella stumbled toward her. Jackie put the caller on speaker and hit Record. Together they continued down Presa. "How did you get this number and why are you calling me? I thought you were afraid of your calls being traced."

"That's for me to know and you to find out." He-She sounded like a snotty kid. Still using the voice changer. "We're using burner phones. No tracing those, right?"

We. So the bomber was still hanging on to

anticlimate-control persona. "Why are you calling me?"

"To instruct you to tell your bosses that they brought this on themselves. They are such bloated egocentric blowhards they think the city can't survive without them. What happens next is on them."

"No, don't—"

"We can and we will. We can keep doing this over and over until the mayor and his lackey city manager give it up and step down. In fact, our demands have changed. We want the entire city council to step down. We want new elections with new candidates in each district. No one who has served or run before."

"Why do you keep saying 'we'? It's just you, isn't it? Just you murdering innocent people for your own psychotic reasons."

"Believe what you want. We will gain control of city government and our issues will be addressed."

"So why not work through the system to start—?"

He-She hung up.

Jackie punched in 911 and told the operator what she could. Which wasn't much. The dispatcher directed her to stay put until an officer could get to her.

"That doesn't make sense. I'm within three blocks of the Alamo. Where's the chief?"

"They'll get to you, ma'am. Stay put."

Jackie hung up. With Bella in hot pursuit, Jackie sprinted to the corner and hung a left on Crockett. Cop cars blocked the street at Broadway.

An officer stepped directly in her path at the intersection. "Back off! Back off now!"

"He's going to detonate—"

Boom, boom, boom, boom.

The blasts shattered the air in tandem. The now unmistakable sound hurt Jackie's ears. Bella grabbed her. They hit the ground. The officer hunkered down, his body shielding them.

Time slowed to a nightmarish trickle.

Nothing more. The bombs were too far away to wreak havoc on them.

Four blasts.

Jackie struggled against the officer's weight. He rolled away, came up on all fours, then scrambled to his feet. His hand went to his weapon. "Stay down. Don't move." He shot toward Alamo Street.

"Are you okay?" Bella scrambled up. "My ears are ringing again."

"I'm fine, except for where my head hit the cement." Jackie rubbed her forehead. "Did you hear four explosions?"

"Yes. Stay here or get back to the car." Bella bolted in the same direction as the officer had. "I have to get the story."

Jackie followed. *Thank You, God, for the bomb-*

disposal robot. No officer would've been close. But where were the other bags located? In areas that had been cleared?

Officers had abandoned their street blockades when the bombs detonated. The evacuated businesses and streets were empty. Law enforcement, on the other hand, filled Alamo Street in front of the Alamo in organized chaos. HSI, FBI, SAPD, ATF—alphabet soup prevailed once again. Bella dodged a sawhorse barricade and waded into the fray. Jackie followed.

The hulking sixty-foot-tall Cenotaph a few hundred yards from the Alamo itself had been ground zero for one of the bombs. Hallowed ground for Texans. It was scarred, but the gray Georgian and pink Texas granite had withstood the direct blast. Pieces of the sculpted bodies of Alamo defenders like James Bowie, Davy Crockett, and William B. Travis had been torn away. But still *The Spirit of Sacrifice* created by sculptor Pompeo Coppini in the late 1930s had survived.

The Alamo itself, built in 1716 as part of the Spanish Catholic mission, was untouched. It was the most visited tourist attraction in the state of Texas and the bomber had spared it. A Texan?

The beautiful gazebo restored with parks foundation funds was in shambles—destroyed. Ironic, considering the latest plan to "reimagine" Alamo Plaza involved removing it. Proponents of the changes would get their way thanks to the bomber.

"Hey, you can't be in here."

Jackie recognized the officer who trotted toward them, fire in his dark eyes. Lieutenant Carmichael often attended event security meetings for library events. Bella waded in before he had a chance to herd them away from the blast zone. "There were four blasts. What else did he hit besides the Cenotaph and the gazebo?"

"You work at the library, right?" He didn't acknowledge Bella's presence. He also knew who she was. "What are you doing here?"

"The bomber called me." Jackie played the recording on her phone before he could speak again. Carmichael's expression changed as he listened. "I'll get you to the incident command center. They're setting up on Bonham Street."

He jerked his head toward Bella. "You need to get back. They'll have a media briefing as soon as they assess the scenes and the damage. They're kind of busy right now."

"Scenes? Which are?" Bella doggedly kept pace. "The bomber called me first. I'm a witness to the bombing at the Tobin. The newspaper has been collaborating with city officials since the beginning."

Carmichael didn't argue with her. Either he didn't want to waste his breath or he figured his bosses would kick her out with more authority.

Without answering her questions, he skirted Alamo Plaza and led them east on Houston Street.

Practice, it seemed, did make perfect. An overwhelming sense of déjà vu enveloped Jackie. The ATF's mobile unit was parked behind the Alamo near the intersection of Bonham and Crockett. Law enforcement in every flavor worked feverishly setting up the incident command center. A Victim Assistance area took shape with tables, chairs, and pop-up canopies. EMS and Fire personnel dispersed behind the bomb squad members who would search for victims, allowing them to start the triage process immediately.

Jackie and Bella stayed close to Lieutenant Carmichael. He squeezed through the steady stream of first responders without looking back. No one took time to question their presence. Finally they reached the inner circle in front of the ATF RV van. Chief Ruiz stood talking to several familiar faces.

"Chief, we've got something you'll wanna hear."

Chief Ruiz swiveled. So did the man next to him. Wick. The detective's scowl deepened. "What are you doing here? Are you nuts? Do you have a death wish?"

He peppered the question with the usual obscenities. Ruiz frowned. "Detective, that's not the way we talk to civilians."

Even in the middle of a horrific disaster, certain niceties had to be preserved. Or the events were so surreal even Chief Ruiz couldn't fathom the reality.

Wick's face went red. His jaw worked. "Fine. What are you doing here, Ms. Santoro?"

"She didn't do this. I'm a witness. She's been with me the whole day. And the bomber called her. She has another recording to prove it." Bella jumped in. "He called right before the bombs exploded. There were four that exploded, weren't there?"

Wick gritted his teeth. A muscle twitched in his jaw. It wasn't his place to answer questions from the media.

"There were four. It looks like the River Walk bomb was meant to be a distraction. The disposal robot took care of it without detonation. The Cenotaph, Alamo Plaza, one inside Rivercenter mall entrance, and a fourth in the wax museum lobby exploded." Chief Ruiz motioned to Special Agent Jantzen and her colleagues from the ATF and HSI. Everyone crowded around while Jackie played the digital file.

No one spoke for a few seconds.

"He had to be close by to detonate the bombs. He knew the area was being evacuated." Wick spoke first. "He wanted to detonate the bombs before everyone was out. He's a psychopath."

They could all agree on that. Jackie shivered.

She rubbed her aching forehead. "Did he succeed? Were there fatalities?"

"A park police officer was killed. He was out of position at the time of the blasts." Chief Ruiz's voice turned hoarse. Another one of their own. "A janitor at Rivercenter who failed to evacuate. A vlogger who sneaked past a barricade to try to get video. That's what we have so far. There likely will be more, but all things considered, many less than would have been killed had the park police officers not found the first bag."

"How did he manage to leave the bags without being seen? How bad were the damages at the Alamo and the Plaza?" Bella had her phone out, recording. "People are going to be up in arms. Vigilantes will come out of the woodwork if you don't get this guy."

"We're collecting recordings from cameras in the area." Ruiz glanced at a text, then went on. "The working theory is he disguised himself as a park maintenance man, a park police officer, or maybe one of the Centro San Antonio ambassadors who help visitors, pick up trash, and clean up around the bus stops."

Hit by another wave of chills, Jackie clutched her jacket to her chest. "This is crazy. Are you any closer to figuring out who this monster is?"

"We're making progress. That's all I'm willing to share at the moment." Ruiz glanced at his phone again. "We'll need a copy of that recording. There will be a news conference in one hour at Hemisfair Park. Lieutenant Carmichael can escort you, Bella. Ms. Santoro, Detective Wick will get you back to your car. I don't want to see you around here again."

"Is that just here or all of downtown?" Adrenaline coursed through Jackie's veins. She couldn't restrain her annoyance. "I work downtown, as you know."

"Confine yourself to the library or I'll have you taken into protective custody as a material witness. The perpetrator has been tying up loose ends. He may decide you're one."

"Protective custody is a good idea." Wick whipped out his handcuffs. "I'd be happy to take care of that."

"Take it easy, Detective." Ruiz moved toward his black SUV where his Protective Services driver stood. "Just get her out of here."

"I don't need an escort."

Wick grabbed her arm. "You heard the man."

She had no choice but to comply. "Bella, call me as soon as you can."

Her cohort, already headed in the opposite direction, yelled her acquiescence.

Jackie broke free of Avery's hold. "You can let go of me now. I promise not to try to escape."

His grim expression darkened. "Move."

"You don't even know where I'm parked."

Avery picked up his pace, took a left on

Houston Street, and headed toward Avenue E. "Has to be the newspaper."

"No wonder you're a detective."

"Sarcasm will get you nowhere."

"What are you so mad about?"

"If you don't know, I'm not telling you."

Jackie picked up her pace to match his. "Look, I'm sorry if I did something to make you mad—"

"Is it necessary for you to run into the burning building every time?"

A lightbulb went on. Something like affection inundated her. Not affection. No, it was stronger than that. Warmer. Toasty. "I'm fine. I'm not hurt."

A string of obscenities greeted her statement.

"You really know how to sweet talk a girl."

More obscenities.

"I like you too."

Wick jerked her around, planted a hard kiss on her lips, then let go of her arm.

"Hey." Sputtering, Jackie halted. "That's no way—"

"Keep moving." He ducked his head and followed his own command. "This isn't the time or the place."

As first kisses went, it left much to be desired.

Jackie broke into a trot. There would be more where that came from, and she fully intended to be ready when the right time and place materialized. "Hey, stop, would you just stop?"

He slammed to a halt. "This can't be happening."

"What can't be happening?"

"You. Me. You and me."

"You have a funny way of demonstrating that it can't happen."

He threw his hands up in the air and stormed into the parking lot.

"Avery. Avery! It's okay." Jackie caught up to him in the open space between her car and a rusted Ford Focus of indeterminate color with hail damage. "I don't know what's going on either, but whatever it is will wait until you do your job. It's crystal clear that we're in the middle of a full-blown crisis. Not the best time to even consider having feelings for each other. So no feelings. And you're off the hook for the kiss. Okay?"

Avery studied her Rogue for a few more seconds. Finally his gaze met hers. "Sorry about that." His deep voice turned even gruffer. "It was uncalled for. Stupid."

"Don't apologize. Don't be embarrassed. Don't regret it."

"But I shouldn't have done it."

"It was the nicest thing that has happened to me in a very long time." The desire to look anywhere but at Avery's face overwhelmed Jackie, but she dug in her heels and met his gaze. "My only complaint? Too short."

"Get in the car."

"What?"

"Get in the car." He unlocked the SUV, strode around the Rogue, and climbed into the passenger side.

Engulfed in a world so surreal she might be dreaming, Jackie complied. She put down the windows and let a humid, semicool breeze bathe her face.

"I'm a divorced cop at least ten years older than you."

"What does any of that have to do with anything?"

Jackie scooted around in the seat so she could get a better look at him. Wick's face was a deep scarlet hue. He drummed the fingers of one hand on her dashboard. She reached over to still them. He grabbed her hand and held on.

"I'm in the middle of a case." He cleared his throat, his gaze on her hand. He smoothed his fingers over hers. "I may not be entirely objective when it comes to your involvement. That's not a good thing."

"After everything that's happened, you still think I'm involved?"

"No."

"That's a start."

"But I have to follow the leads where they go— no holds barred."

"I know." He still thought a member of her

family was involved. Jackie buried the caustic comments that billowed to the surface. He was being honest. He was doing his job. "Do what you have to do. I want the guilty person stopped as much as you do. More. For Estrella. For Victoria. For Meher. I'll be around when it's over."

"You say that now—"

"I want justice for the victims. Whoever did this—whoever it may be—can't continue to walk around free."

"I know. That's what's killing me."

"You're still worried about Theo."

"We still haven't located him. The longer he's out there on his own, the more worried I get. Plus, he was a park police officer. He patrolled the River Walk District. He knows where the cameras are. He knows the officers' patrol schedules. He knows the routines followed by businesses on or near Alamo Plaza."

"A park police officer died. Would he have placed fellow officers in harm's way?"

"Until a few days ago I would've said no. But I also wouldn't have thought a member of your family would put you and your friends in danger either."

"Now you're not sure."

"I'm not sure of anything."

Neither was Jackie. "You're good at what you do. You'll figure it out. And when you do, I'll be thankful—regardless of who it turns out to be."

Wick's gaze lifted. "Just so you know, I'm bad at this dating thing. I've tried a few times since the divorce and it sucked."

"Maybe you weren't dating the right woman."

His forehead wrinkled, Wick's gaze returned to her hand. He nodded once and then gently kissed her fingers and let go. "To be continued."

"To be continued."

He shoved from the SUV and took off in an easy lope.

Jackie sat, not moving, her hand nestled in her lap, for a long time.

THIRTY-SEVEN

*I*diot.

Kissing Jackie in the aftermath of four bombs that rocked the site of the most important battle in Texas history had to be the stupidest thing Avery had ever done. And that covered some doozies. Still, the feel of her lips on his, the soft skin of her fingers, sent waves of heat through him every time he replayed the moments. Which he'd done repeatedly as he raced back to his vehicle and drove across town to HQ.

A text from LT had ordered him to return to base. With the help of business owners, tech support had pulled the digital recordings for the entire day from cameras in the vicinity of the Alamo. All hands on deck were needed to comb through them for a glimpse of the person who'd managed to drop off five backpacks under the noses of park police, bicycle patrol, and beefed-up SAPD vehicle patrols in the downtown area.

Still no sign of Theo. Bill Little's funeral had taken up most of the morning. Law enforcement from across the state descended, many to assist with covering patrol while SAPD personnel attended. Bill's wife had arrived in a wheelchair. Her cheeks were sunken and her eyes ringed with bruises.

Three long hours of procession, honor guards, music, flyovers, accolades, tears, and, surprisingly, laughs as friends and colleagues remembered the chief.

Then this. No time for grief. No time for kissing, certainly.

More death. More loved ones grieving.

It had to stop.

Propelled by his own thoughts, Avery bounded from the elevator and grabbed a chair at the bank of computers. Scotty leaned back in his chair and shot Avery a curious glance. "Look what the cat dragged in. I hear you got dinged for cussing at your lady friend."

"Not my finest moment."

"Why so sheepish, podner? You look like you just bit into a red-hot serrano."

"Mind your own business. What was the final body count?"

"Four killed. Six injured. It could've been so much worse."

"Tell that to the families of the dead."

"Singing to the choir, bud." Scotty stuck an ink pen behind his ear. He held up a stack of papers for a second, then let them drop onto his desk again. "Petra's guy did a detailed review of Cris Santoro's phone records. Nothing unusual. He calls his grandma a lot. Is it possible to be a grandma's boy?"

"I suppose." Another dead end. Avery's head

throbbed. He rubbed his temple. "What we need is a break."

"I might be able to help you with that." Scotty scooped up another sheaf of papers. This time he held them out. "Ethan Richter's phone records for the past thirty days."

Avery accepted his offering. Yellow highlighter had been used numerous times, all the same number. A 210 area code. "Whose number?"

"Burner phone."

"That's no help."

If this were a TV show, a box of burner phones would miraculously turn up, allowing detectives to trace the phones back to their point of sale, where the seller would magically come up with a credit card receipt and the name of the buyer or even have store camera recordings of the bad guy. Real-life investigations rarely followed the easy path.

"It's the same number that the bomber used to call not-your-lady-friend Mizz Santoro today."

Avery pumped his fist. They had a firm connection between Richter and the bomber. "Way to bury the lead, Brother. What about his financials?"

"Some big money dumps into his account in the last month. Big even for a mercenary. He moved most of it into offshore accounts."

"Where did it come from?"

Scotty shrugged. "The FBI's forensic accountants are working on that. Apparently it's a tangled mess involving a lot of transfers and international accounts and bogus companies."

"So we know Richter was doing somebody's dirty work and that somebody got cold feet. Maybe he wanted more money. Maybe he decided to play the blackmail card."

"The bomber snipped that loose end. That means it's very likely he did his own dirty work today. We could see him in one of these recordings."

"He's not stupid. He likely knows where the cameras are and avoids them. Or he's dressed in a way that keeps us from seeing his face."

Avery's words turned out to be prophetic. A few hours later one of the FBI's tech support guys called them into the conference room for a viewing. Cameras in front of the wax museum captured a man dressed in a bright-yellow Centro San Antonio ambassador polo and khaki pants sweeping up trash in front of the museum around 10:00 a.m. The required straw hat's brim hid his face. The man was tall, medium build, and white. That was it. Scotty groaned. Avery sucked in air and held it to keep from joining him.

The maintenance ambassador pushed the usual trash receptacle on wheels. After a few seconds he disappeared from the screen, then reappeared on the lobby camera's feed. There he nonchalantly pulled a backpack from the trash

432

receptacle and set it behind the museum's trash can near the front door. No one would see it until museum maintenance emptied the trash later in the day.

"So we know how he got the bomb into the museum." Petra rubbed her red eyes. Dark circles around them made her look like a silver-haired raccoon. "But we still have no idea who he is."

"Centro San Antonio does an extensive background check on potential ambassadors. It takes weeks." Scotty tugged on his mustache. "How long has this guy been planning this?"

"He didn't walk in the door and get hired on," Avery theorized. "He made a slot for himself."

Similar footage existed of the ambassador cleaning around the Alamo Street entrance to Shops at Rivercenter mall. Once again he popped inside and deposited the bag out of sight. The techs were still viewing camera recordings for the other locations.

Sometimes Avery hated being right. Juan Garza, sixty-one, a six-year employee of Centro San Antonio, was reported missing by his wife of forty years when he failed to return home from work on Thursday night. A bicycle patrol officer found his bludgeoned body, clad only in underwear and socks, hidden behind a downtown Dumpster at 8:00 a.m. Friday. Now they knew why he'd been killed.

Avery and Scotty made it to the ME's office

in the medical center area in less than twenty minutes. The body was still in the queue for an autopsy, which was fine. It gave them a chance to view his battered corpse before cutting began.

"How tall do you think he is?" Avery sized up the victim. He was slim and muscular. Eight hours of walking San Antonio streets pushing a trash can had kept him trim and fit. "Six two, six three?"

"That's about right." Scotty leaned in for a closer look. "Maybe 175 or 180 pounds. Seems like the killer caught him from behind."

"It's easy to catch these guys off guard. They're trained to stop and answer any and all questions. It's their job to be the face of San Antonio for visitors. It wouldn't occur to them to be afraid."

No good deed went unpunished.

The clothes worn by the bomber had fit him perfectly. So he was tall and didn't have a lot of body fat. He could be skinny or muscular. Hard to know. Did he pick his victim based on body size and height? "He's one stone-cold killer."

Avery let Scotty drive them back to the station. He leaned his head back and closed his eyes.

"You should ask her out. She's not a serious person of interest now. We're zoomed in on Richter. We know she didn't kill the ambassador guy. The killer called her. Bella Glover witnessed it. She was at funerals in the hours leading up to today's bombings."

Scotty was way too perceptive for a middle-aged guy whose favorite pastime was watching Fast and Furious movies. Sometimes he was more like a granny than a partner. "No way. This is an active investigation in which she's at the very least a material witness and a member of the Santoro family."

"Just saying, it's obvious she's gotten under your skin. You're a love-at-first-sight kind of guy, as history shows. And you're a one-woman man, unlike some of the players around her. Stop torturing yourself and go for it."

"Can we just not discuss my love life, seriously?"

"As if you had one."

Avery squeezed his eyelids shut tighter. "I'm sleeping."

Scotty's phone dinged. "You might want to wake up." His playful tone disappeared. "Something's going on at city hall. LT says we should check it out and report back."

Avery opened his eyes and straightened. Sure enough. Mayor Cavazos stood at a portable podium on the city hall steps that faced the Municipal Plaza building. Vogel and several council people milled around behind him. Media clustered below, along with a crowd of city staff and citizens rubbernecking the media.

They pulled into the Plaza de Armas lot and double-parked. Cavazos boomed over the mic by the time they rushed around the side of the building.

"I can't stand by and let this go on." Cavazos's voice shook with emotion. "It's unconscionable what this criminal is doing to our city. If you're listening, USAP, or whoever you are, you win. I can't stand idly by and let you destroy our most sacred history. I can't let you endanger the innocent residents and visitors who deserve to be able to walk our streets safely and without worry. You win."

"What's he doing?" Avery squeezed in between Bella and a KENS 5TV reporter. "Is he doing what I think he's doing?"

Bella nodded. "It looks like it. We got a media advisory about an hour after the chief's briefing at Hemisfair. It just said the mayor would make an announcement."

"He can't quit. It sets a horrible precedent."

"We have relied on law enforcement—both local and national—to stop this monster. They have been at best ineffectual." Cavazos's voice rose. "They must do more. They must capture this monster and send him to death row."

Great. Playing the blame game was so helpful.

"In the meantime I must do my part. I'm officially announcing my resignation from the office of mayor of this great city of San Antonio. God, have mercy on us."

He lowered his head for a full second, then

looked up. "Furthermore, I call upon my colleagues on the council to do the same." He wiped tears from his face with a white handkerchief. "I urge City Manager Jason Vogel to tender his resignation. Let us start anew. I, for one, will focus all my future endeavors as a gun-control advocate and Peace Coalition member. Thank you."

He stepped away without taking questions. The reporters weren't having any of that. They shouted questions over each other. No one answered. None of the other elected officials came to the podium. Vogel slipped through the double doors and disappeared.

The media surged up the steps.

Avery looked at Scotty. Scotty shrugged. Did their job just get easier or harder?

That depended on how the perpetrator took the news.

THIRTY-EIGHT

Tick-tock. Tick-tock.

Jackie beat back worries about the bomber, instant replays of Avery's kisses, and grief over so much loss. She locked them all in a closet for the day. Nothing else could matter but the Catrina Ball. Mayor Cavazos's shocking resignation the previous day couldn't be allowed to matter. Saturday—one week since Victoria's death—had been filled with the final preparations. In a few minutes the costumed guests would pour through the Central Library's front doors, expecting to be wined, dined, and entertained. Every detail had to be perfect.

Hanging on to her fourth espresso of the day like a woman dying of thirst, she threaded her way through the first floor ofrendas behind Meagan and the library director. He never involved himself in the details, but this ball was different from any other. The former mayor would not attend. The mayor pro tem would take his place during the official ceremonies, which included unveiling the altar built to honor their dead foundation board chairman. The ball was also different because one of the other ofrendas honored Jackie's best friend.

A gaggle of undercover officers dressed in

black tuxedos and top hats, skeleton faces painted on with black and white grease pencils, would mix with the donors in search of any hint of something out of the ordinary. The slightest hiccup and the ball would end in an evacuation. The foundation had agreed to the plan—under threat of cancellation if they didn't. The security firm and the alphabet soup of law enforcement agencies had hashed and rehashed their plans to keep guests safe until finally they'd gone away to dress for the occasion.

This was not business as usual. This was personal.

Tosca and Lee would attend. So would Cris and his plus-one. Who would that be? Jackie brushed the question aside. It didn't matter as long as he had a good time. Nonna and Nonno would attend for the first time. Nonno in a Día de los Muertos costume was hard to imagine. Not so with Nonna. She had grace and style no matter what she wore.

Avery would also be here somewhere. He'd kissed her. Surely she could call him by his first name now. Would he recognize Jackie in her full-length emerald-green-and-red-rose-print dress? Borrowed from her mother, it had a princess neck and flowing, lacy sleeves. She'd decided to leave her hair down and selected a headpiece made of silk roses in red, purple, and green. Her sister made up her face in white with black "stitches" across her lips. A mask in red, green, purple, and blue sequins surrounded by gold glitter around her eyes completed her ensemble.

"Jackie, those tables are crooked." Meagan bustled toward the registration area with its tables covered in teal silk tablecloths. "I've told you that twice."

And twice Jackie had adjusted them. She repositioned the gold skull vases a third time between one black and one white candle, then fluffed the floral bouquet of orangey-pink roses and marigolds once again.

"And what about the street tacos and appetizers? Will the meat and tortillas be hot and the toppings cold?"

For the third time, yes. "The caterer has everything under control."

Which immediately brought to mind Meher. The caterer and chef would never concoct another culinary delight. Never bake another soufflé or grill salmon. Never teach her little ones to make bread. *Don't think, just keep moving.* "The musicians are all here as well. The guitarist, the mariachis, the jazz trio, the Tejano band, everyone."

She had checked and double-checked that the audio folks were set with every sound system working. Every musical group and all the dancers were present and accounted for.

Check off every box next to every task before the event starts and it will take on a life of its own. Jackie had learned this maxim long ago.

Meagan's face blanched. "What about the speaking remarks for the mayor pro tem?"

"The PR folks coordinated all those details. The media advisory has gone out as well."

"The—"

"Everything is done, Meagan." Jackie called upon her last ounce of patience. "All we can do now is go with the flow. It's too late to change a thing."

Meagan's hand went to her mouth. Her eyes widened. She whirled and headed toward the restrooms.

Not everyone had the stomach of steel it took to do megaevent planning.

Jackie touched the beautiful yellow marigolds in baskets that lined the front of Don Pedro's ofrenda. He offered her a suitably macabre, toothy grin. So did his Catrina. Jackie glanced at her watch. "T-minus ten, nine, eight, seven, six, five, four, three, two, one."

Please, God, don't let there be a blastoff.

Right on time, the first guests sauntered through artist Stephen Antonakos's neon Blue Room and into the lobby where they checked in at the registration desk manned by foundation volunteers dressed in black lacy dresses and red silk shawls. The race to get through the night without death and destruction had begun. Five hours. Just five hours.

Jackie plunged into her duties, which included making the rounds to food and drink stations to make sure the caterer's waitstaff kept up with the steady flow of beverages and food. She was to point out spills and trash, direct guests to the bathrooms, answer questions about the ofrendas, and encourage patrons to participate in the silent auction. And check on the musical groups again. Jill-of-all-trades, in other words.

Within half an hour her head pounded and her cheeks ached from smiling. So far she hadn't seen a single family member. It seemed strange. She might not immediately recognize them, but surely they'd recognize her.

And Avery. What about Avery? She glanced at her watch for the hundredth time: 7:05. She heaved a breath and said yet another prayer.

"Where's the closest drink station?" A woman who sounded like she'd had a few drinks before the ball opened teetered on stiletto heels. "And the bathroom?"

Jackie stared over the petite woman's shoulder. Was that Avery striding past Selena's ofrenda? He might want to blend in, but it seemed doubtful he would put that much effort into a costume. Yet something about the way he walked seemed familiar. The man wore a black suit with a "dead" raven on his shoulder. He wore a top hat. A skull mask covered his entire face and skeleton gloves hid his hands. The red band on his hat offered the only hint of color.

He lifted a bottle of sparkling water in her direction.

He knew her or he simply knew she was watching him.

"Hey, I really have to go." The patron came close to crossing her legs standing up. "Hello?"

"Sorry." Jackie made up for her inattentiveness by leading the woman to the nearest restroom.

By the time she returned, Raven Man was gone. She threaded her way through the tables on the second floor near the Chihuly sculpture and saw no one she recognized. The Spanish guitar soloist wowed the patrons while they ate street tacos, stuffed avocados, and ceviche and sipped their choice of high-end microbeers or wine. Everyone seemed happy. No one seemed worried by the events of the past week.

The nausea in Jackie's gut didn't abate.

"Hey."

A finger tapped her shoulder. Jackie shrieked and jumped.

"Good grief, Sis, it's just me."

Tosca wrapped her arm around Jackie's shoulders. She was unrecognizable but beautiful in her strapless, red-flowered dress. A rhinestone dragonfly pin decorated the dress while heavy rhinestone snowflake earrings dangled from her ears. But her face and hairpiece were the head turners. She'd covered her face in white, then added red flowers on her cheeks and across her forehead. Blue sequins surrounded both eyes. Her hairpiece consisted of white and pink roses interspersed with pink carnations and topped with a gorgeous monarch butterfly.

"You look stunning." Jackie hugged her little sister. A friendly face. "Just amazing. Where's Lee?"

"Probably talking shop. Half the attorneys, assistant district attorneys, and judges in town are here."

"Half of San Antonio is here."

"Which should make you happy. A successful fund-raiser pays for all those fun programs you thrive on." Tosca frowned and patted Jackie's cheek. "I know it's been a horrible week, but try to enjoy this. Estrella would want that. So would Victoria."

"I can't believe we're doing this. With so much loss of life and destruction, it's disrespectful." Jackie drew a long breath. "Plus he's still out there. Avery—"

"Avery? Now you're calling the detective Avery?"

"That's beside the point." What would Tosca think if she knew about the kisses? Jackie swatted away the thought. "Avery is sure he'll strike again, maybe even tonight, here."

"It's his job to worry. I imagine he and his cohorts have this place blanketed."

"I know. I know, but I wish I could see him. It would make me feel better." Jackie tried to tamp down that burgeoning sense of dread. "By the way, have you seen Nonno and Nonna? Or Cris? They're supposed to be here."

"Probably fashionably late. You know how they love to make an entrance."

They certainly did. But Nonno also liked to get his money's worth. He would want to be here for every bit of the moving dance, the entertainment, and the speechifying. He was a social animal. He would be in his element here. "I wonder if Cris is bringing a date."

"With him it's hard to say." Tosca's face softened. "Poor baby is so busy burying his pain, he works all the time instead of finding solace with people who love him."

Always the perceptive one, Tosca could be relied on to sum up a situation best. "You are the best one to try to reach him."

"I'll keep trying." Tosca's gaze flitted over Jackie's shoulder. "Don't turn around. There's a man standing by the drink station. He's staring at you."

Jackie started to turn.

"No, no, don't look." Tosca sipped her wine and leaned closer. "Maybe it's your friend Detective Wick—Avery, I mean."

"What does he look like?"

"How do I know? He's wearing a black suit,

top hat, and a dead raven on his back. And, of course, the obligatory skull mask."

The same man as before. "I saw him earlier. It's not Avery. He wouldn't wear such an elaborate costume."

"Yeah, but he has eyes for you only."

"You're dreaming." Jackie snatched a stuffed and overloaded nacho from a tray and nibbled it as she turned slightly to gaze over her shoulder. "Where? I don't see anyone."

"He's gone. He saw you leering at him and ran away."

"You're such a goober."

"Here comes Lee. I have to be a good girl and trail about on his arm for a while."

Lee had paid minimal homage to the evening's theme. Still, the man looked sensational in his fitted tux. Jackie sighed. Her sister was blessed. "If you see our grandparents or Cris, tell them I'd like to at least say hello."

"Will do. You do the same with me."

Jackie glanced at her watch. Seven forty-five. Four hours and fifteen minutes to go.

Tick-tock, tick-tock.

"Cinderella, you're late for the dance."

Ignoring Scotty's remark followed by a wolf whistle, Avery grabbed his top hat from his desk and headed for the elevator. The rented tux chafed his neck, and the trousers were too long.

"I have Daniel Santoro's financials on my screen. I printed his phone records. Go through them, will you?"

"No problem. Don't forget the carriage turns into a pumpkin at midnight."

"Good thing I'm driving my truck."

"That old clunker? What if it dies on you after she agrees to a nightcap?"

"This is not a date and just shut up." He let the elevator door close before Scotty could respond. Immediately his phone rang. Theo's wife. "Hey, Katie. Did he show up?"

"No, but he called. Finally. I tried to talk him into coming home. He says he can't." Her voice quivered. "I hate this, Avery, I just hate it. I hate being in our house alone. I hate worrying about him all the time. I can't do it anymore."

"I know. I'm so sorry." Avery wanted to kick Theo's rear all the way to Montana, then arrest him and throw away the key. "Did he give you any idea where he's staying? Is he still working security for a hotel?"

"He didn't say where he's staying, but he did tell me not to worry about money." Katie's half-stifled sob ramped up Avery's anger with Theo. "He said he got a new job with a security firm. In fact he said it's the one that did security for the Tobin. He said it was ironic that they had openings because they lost some guys after the first bombing."

Alamo Security would provide extra bodies in addition to the library's regular security at the ball tonight.

Which gave Theo access to the event where he would be within spitting distance of the city manager, the interim chief of police, and various city council members. As a security team member he would have access to the entire building. No one would see him as a threat. He wouldn't be subject to search.

Avery exited the elevator and broke into a trot. "He shouldn't be working security. He shouldn't be carrying a gun."

"I know. I can't believe they hired him. I tried to tell him that." Katie's voice dropped to a near whisper. "I told him I thought he needed help. That you were searching for him to help him. He didn't take that well. He said to tell you to back off."

Avery shoved through the exits and picked up speed. He'd parked illegally on a side street. He slid into his truck and grabbed the PD placard from his dashboard. "There's an event at the library tonight. I'm headed there now. It's possible he's working it. I'll talk to him."

"Take it easy, please. He wouldn't hurt a soul. Only himself. You know him. You know he wouldn't hurt anybody."

No point in worrying her more. She didn't need to know about Avery's suspicions. He reached deep for a convincing tone. "I'm just going to talk to him. I have to go."

"Call me as soon as you talk to him. Please."

"I will."

"Promise me nothing will happen to him."

"I promise I'll do my best." That was the best he could do. An officer who promised a happy ending set himself and loved ones up for heartache. "I'll call you as soon as I can."

After a few more reassurances, Katie allowed Avery to hang up.

He spent ten seconds pounding on the steering wheel. Katie didn't want to admit Theo had changed. That was understandable, but her husband's erratic behavior and the stockpiled weapons screamed danger to others as well as to himself.

Avery called Alamo Security to demand Hausman pull Theo off the job. Theoretically that would end the threat. If Theo hadn't already smuggled some part of his arsenal into the building.

Voice mail.

Avery left a pointed message. He hung up, pounded on the wheel some more, and cussed. For two seconds. Then he called LT.

His boss picked up on the first ring. "Where are you, Wick? You should be here by now."

Avery pulled into the delivery drive behind the building and parked. He explained the situation.

Lieutenant Carmichael joined him in hurling obscenities. "You didn't try calling him, did you?"

"No, I didn't want to tip him off that we're onto him."

"I'll grab the Alamo Security guy in charge. He'll have comm contact. I'll direct him to call Beretta to their base of operation in the administrative offices on the fourth floor. We can take him down there. No fuss, no muss."

Yeah, in an alternate universe filled with unicorns, rainbows, and perpetual holidays on sandy beaches it might be that easy. "I'd like to see him taken into custody without anyone getting hurt. He needs a psych eval, not a prison cell."

"It's possible he's the bomber. If he is, he'll get his psych eval and the prison cell—on death row. He's been jerking you around this whole time, pumping you for information."

"Anything's possible." Avery couldn't imagine a world where this guy he'd won a state basketball championship with was also a mass murderer. "I can't see it, but I never thought he would stockpile weapons and talk smack about city officials. His son's murder unhinged something in him."

If he wasn't the bomber, then they had competing psychotic murderers bent on revenge, converging in one building filled with innocent people.

"The mayor pro tem and the city manager are scheduled to speak in the atrium in thirty minutes. That can't happen. I'll let the chief know they need to leave ASAP."

"If they leave the bomber will know something is up. We won't have a chance to flush him out."

"They're in costume. We can have officers take their places. He'll never know."

"Let me do it."

"Your job is to find Beretta. You pick up a comm from Jantzen on the way in, but don't use it unless you absolutely have to. Beretta will have access to one. I'll brief her on the situation. She has agents posted on every floor. If you need help, reach out. Search for him. If he doesn't respond to the order from his supervisor, your job is to neutralize him without creating a scene."

"By talking him down."

"By any means necessary."

Adrenaline pulsing though him, Avery slid from the truck. He stuck the skull mask on his face, placed the top hat on his head, and ran.

God, please don't let me have to shoot my oldest friend.

THIRTY-NINE

*Q*uoth the raven, 'Nevermore.' "
    The famous words of Edgar Allan Poe waltzed on repeat around Jackie's head. Every time she glanced around, she saw the man with the fake bird on his back. When she started toward him, he disappeared into a crowd that grew more jocular and raucous as the night wore on. Maybe like the famous author of Poe's narrative poem, she, too, descended into madness. Who was this man and why did he seem to be following her yet dodging her?

She double-checked the tables around the Chihuly Tower. Patrons packed them. The waitstaff valiantly attempted to keep up. The mariachis, who'd added skull makeup to their *trajes do charro*, regaled the crowd with their version of "*Volver, Volver*," and then launched into "*El Mariachi Loco*." The onlookers immediately spread out on the temporary dance floor. Her foot tapping, Jackie checked her watch. Two and a half hours to go. Her feet hurt, her eyes burned, and the headpiece crushed her brain. A week without sleep did that to a person.

Maybe the face behind the mask belonged to Cris. It suited his sense of humor. The man stood about the right height and had a similar build.

"Jacqueline!"

Only Nonna and Nonno called her by her given name. Jackie spun around and found herself in her grandmother's warm embrace. She smelled like roses. Memories flooded Jackie. Searching for Easter eggs in the enormous yard behind Nonno's house. The smell of sunscreen and chlorine when they paddled around in the pool. Her grandmother taught all three kids to play "Twinkle, Twinkle, Little Star" on the piano.

The days before Daddy and Nonno stopped talking.

"You look smashing, my girl." Nonna had to shout to be heard over the trumpets, violins, guitarrón, and vihuela played by enthusiastic mariachis. "Why do they have to play so loudly?"

Laughing, Jackie tried to see the band through her grandmother's eyes. Jackie loved the Mexican cowboy suits comprised of bolero jackets and, for the women, full-length skirts. The jackets were decorated with gold buttons and metallic embroidered designs of plants and flowers. As a child she wanted to learn to play a vihuela—the high-pitched five-string guitar— so she could wear the outfit. Mom had insisted she master the piano. "One thing I've learned in event planning—never mic the mariachi."

Nonna nodded, but her raised eyebrows suggested she couldn't hear Jackie. "You and Tosca must get your photo taken with me when you have a moment."

"What about Cris and Nonno?" Jackie leaned close and shouted in her ear. They hadn't taken sibling photos since before Daddy's death. "Where are they?"

"Your grandfather was glad-handing last time I saw him. You know how he is. Everyone is a potential business contact." She waved a fancy silk fan in front of her perfectly made-up face. "Cris said he'd meet us here. You haven't seen him?"

"No. I'm curious to see his costume."

"I suspect he chose to go with the traditional tux. He said he couldn't see making a holiday out of . . . your father's death."

The catch in Nonna's voice caused the knot in Jackie's throat to swell. "I'm sorry, Nonna, I know it's hard. I'm so glad y'all reached out to Mom with the soup. She really appreciated it."

"We're trying, but it's still hard, knowing your mother encouraged him." She straightened Jackie's headpiece. "Your nonno puts on a strong front, but inside he's hurting."

"Did he tell you he stopped by my house the day of the first bombing?"

"He didn't." Nonna's free hand flitted to the string of emeralds around her slim neck. "It doesn't surprise me, though. He worries about you the most."

"Why me?"

"You're so determined to be independent. He's

afraid you'll never find a good man and settle down."

What would he say about a homicide detective ten years Jackie's senior? *"The horror, the horror"?* Jackie suppressed her smile and studied the mass of gyrating people doing their version of dances such as the salsa, cumbia, merengue, and *zapateados*, none to the beat of the music.

There he was. Raven Man. He sidestepped a couple doing their own personal version of the tango and melted into the crowd.

"Nonna, I have to go check on something. Why don't you call Tosca and get her to meet you on the first floor by the Don Pedro ofrenda? I'll find you and we can get our photos taken together."

"Good idea. My voice is getting hoarse and this music is giving me a headache."

Jackie waved and darted into the crowd. She had no choice but to dance her way through the hordes. She scooted around the corner just in time to see Raven Man slip into the elevator. It stopped on the sixth floor. Jackie punched the button repeatedly, but the elevator took its time returning.

The sixth floor housed the Texana-Genealogy Collection, one of the most popular in the library. With its vast collection of microforms, seventy-five thousand books, and archival files, it was one of the most visited locations in the library. Funds raised from the ball would be used to renovate the ten-thousand-square-foot space. To destroy it would be to destroy family histories that went back three centuries or more.

Jackie's phone buzzed as she stepped off the elevator. Ignoring it, she slipped into the room where the long tables with their individual reading lamps had been replaced with round high-top tables covered by teal silk tablecloths with the requisite floral arrangements.

A jazz trio waxed poetic with a mellow version of a Miles Davis tune. The clusters of patrons were more sedate than their Chihuly counterparts, but the hum of alcohol-fueled conversation still filtered out into the hallway.

No Raven Man.

The phone rang again. Irritated, Jackie slipped it from her tiny sequined bag. Avery.

Suddenly breathless, she dashed into the stacks as far from the music as possible and stood with her back to the party. "Hi."

"Where are you?"

His tone sounded accusatory. No greeting. What did she expect? A declaration of love? Jackie donned her professional voice. "Sixth floor. Texana and Genealogy. Where are you?"

"You need to leave."

She placed her hand over her other ear to better hear him. "What's going on?"

"I don't have time to explain. Get your grandparents, Tosca, and Cris. Leave."

"I can ask them to leave, but I'm working." Her professional mask slipped. She gulped air and counted to five. "We've had this discussion. What's going on?"

"It's a long story. Go."

"I don't work for you. Is the bomber here? Do we need to evacuate? If we do, you need to tell me."

"It's not just the bomber. Theo's here. We're searching for him floor by floor. We don't want to spook him. If we don't find him in the next ten minutes, we'll quietly start an evacuation. I have to go." His tone had gone from accusatory to desperate. "Leave. Find your family and go."

"I'm so sorry, Avery. I'll pray you bring him in without hurting him. And I'll evacuate when you do. There's something else you need to know—"

"Thank you." He hung up.

"Avery?"

Jackie fumbled with the phone. She needed to tell him about the Raven Man.

A skeletal gloved hand ripped the phone from her grasp. "I'll take that."

The voice sounded familiar. She whirled. A grinning skull's face loomed over her. The skeletal hand closed over her mouth.

"Quoth the raven, 'Nevermore.' "

FORTY

The Central Library was a nightmare. Too many hiding places. Avery pulled his mask down. It kept sliding up, obstructing his view. Evacuating meant Theo and the bomber—Avery refused to believe they were one and the same—could slip out the exit with hundreds of patrons unaware that a mass murderer and an unhinged father—both bent on revenge—might be nearby.

Rivulets of sweat trickled down Avery's face. His armpits were soaked. His mouth was so dry his tongue stuck to the roof of his mouth. The surreal scene filled with walking dead creatures with grinning skulls dancing like zombies fueled the nightmare.

Only he couldn't wake up. He needed to wake up. He had to catch the bad guy.

In his dreams he never did. They were always a few yards ahead, hidden in shadows or behind overflowing Dumpsters.

Here they were hidden in plain sight. At any second the bad guy could set off an explosion that would kill Jackie and hundreds of other innocent people.

Not Jackie. Please, God, not her.

Get it together, Wick.

Was that God or his own conscience talking?

No time to figure that out.

Gritting his teeth, Avery adopted a slow stroll. He grabbed a glass of wine from an eight-foot-tall skeleton dressed in a wide-brimmed hat, black blouse, and a wire skirt that provided at least fifty glass holders. Squinting through the mask's eyes, he mingled with partygoers on the first floor.

Please, God, get Jackie out of here. Overcome her stubborn self and make her just leave.

As much as he wanted to haul her out of the library on his back, he couldn't. He had a job to do.

Focus.

Connect with the city manager and he would connect with Theo.

Spanish classical guitar music wafted from the art gallery where the celebratory remarks were set to begin any second. Avery followed an artist's rendition of a spiky snake made of cloth and some kind of green plant as it meandered through the gallery in shifting shades of green. A sign at the door explained the art installation was called "Digging." The green stuff was dried nopals.

Avery wasn't a fan of snakes, dead or alive. Petra stood near a microphone stand at the back of the gallery. She engaged in a fierce whispered argument with City Manager Vogel. The mayor pro tem sipped wine. From the way he swayed, he'd had a few. Acting Chief Ruiz raised his index finger and punctuated a comment. Only Tony Guerra, who'd chosen not to wear a costume, stood slightly apart, his somber gaze focused on the swarm of people.

Library patrons crowded the room. The women sipped wine and circulated, their heels clacking on the slick beige tile. The men clustered in the middle, their deeper voices adding to the din. Avery set the wine glass on a tray and plunged forward. The sea did not part for him. Examining each face for familiarity, he reached the microphone with no sightings.

"What's going on, Chief?" Protocol dictated he started with Ruiz. He assumed LT had brought him up to speed on the Theo threat. "Why are y'all still here?"

"The mayor caved. I don't plan to do that." Vogel's whisper held fury. "I plan to stand next to our mayor pro tem while he unveils this altar honoring a good man."

"I appreciate your resolve." Ruiz, dressed in a tux but no costume, spoke in a reassuring tone. He served at the pleasure of the city manager and the council. "But you're endangering the people in this room and beyond. It's not the bomber we're worried about."

"I know, I know. Theo Beretta is crazed with grief. I get that. He's not going to hurt me. If he was, he'd have done it a long time ago."

As in the case of Jackie's father, Vogel accepted no fault for the way events unfolded. Surely he saw how cutting park police positions to bolster regular PD officer slots had a ripple effect. Gun and gang violence threatened the entire community. Drive-by numbers had dropped in the last few years, but that wouldn't bring back Caleb.

"I've spent time with Theo in the last few weeks, Mr. Vogel." Avery ignored Ruiz's pained expression. A detective shouldn't speak unless spoken to in these rarified strata. "He has amassed an arsenal. He believes you are responsible for his son's death. You, Councilman Sandoval, and Chief Little. I'm sure he won't mind taking out a few more of your colleagues as well."

"He's lost his mind."

"That's what I'm telling you." Avery employed the soothing voice he used with Deuce during thunderstorms. "We need to get y'all to a safe place. We can have our officers sub for you in costume so he won't know you've left."

Random movement caught the corner of his gaze. A man in an overcoat made of a shiny black material and a top hat decorated with marigolds edged along the wall, following the snake's trail. His face was hidden, of course, but something about him seemed familiar. And why wear an overcoat when a tux jacket would do?

"Get them out of here." Avery leaned closer

to Petra, who had stood silently by during the conversation. "Arrest them if you have to."

She tensed. "You got something?"

"Maybe."

"You need backup?"

"Just get them out of here." He broke away and headed for the overdressed patron. The man immediately edged the other direction. Avery followed. Overcoat plunged into the crowd.

Again no one moved out of Avery's way. "Excuse me, excuse me, coming through." He dodged, pivoted, and two-stepped, still yards behind his quarry. "Let me by, please."

They might be genteel drunks, but they were still drunks. Two spilled drinks and several well-placed pointy heels to his feet later, Avery made it to the hallway outside the art gallery. The new book section was empty. He cut left. Another crowd. More music—this time loud ranchera. An altar. But no Overcoat.

Avery whirled and retraced his steps. He stopped at the fat horse sculpture next to the checkout counter. No sign of Overcoat. He couldn't have gone far.

Did he leave? Not without accomplishing his mission.

The escalators. Avery smacked into a woman dressed in traditional Mexican campesino clothes. She jolted back, then kept going. He danced around her and did the same.

At the bottom of the escalators, he glanced up in time to catch the back of Overcoat and his hat with red flowers. Avery scaled the steps three and four at a time. "Theo!"

Overcoat disappeared.

Winded, Avery paused for one second at the feet of an enormous glass sculpture. Right or left? People swarmed the tables for drinks and food while mariachis serenaded them. Not even the thick black carpet with its red, blue, and gold squares could absorb that much noise. The elevator dinged. His feet complaining in his stiff black dress shoes, Avery shot toward it. Overcoat punched a button and the doors closed.

Blood pulsing in his ears, Avery cussed under his breath. He pounded on the button. According to the numbers overhead, the elevator stopped on the third floor.

If Overcoat was Theo, he didn't dare play this game much longer or he would lose his chance to take down Vogel and the others. He knew that and Avery knew it.

An eon later, the doors opened. Avery lunged forward and banged on the buttons some more. A couple tried to hop in with him. He flashed his badge and shook his head. They backed off.

On the third floor the party was confined to the area that normally served as the children's story room. Avery raced down the hallway toward the bright-yellow balcony that overlooked the atrium below. Overcoat leaned over as if surveying something beyond Avery's line of sight.

Only one man he knew would wear black Lucchese ostrich cowboy boots with a tux.

"Theo, amigo, you should've left the boots at home. I know it's you. Stop. Let's work this out. Don't do this to Katie."

"I'm doing this for Katie." Theo whirled. His coat hung open. An M4 carbine hung from loops sewn inside it. His top hat lay crushed on the carpet. He ripped off his mask and pulled the weapon from the Velcroed loops. "Oh man, you should've stayed away from me, dude."

Avery couldn't do that. "Sorry, buddy." He launched himself into the air. His body slammed against Theo's. Air whooshed from his lungs. Theo had a body like a hundred-year-old sequoia. They both went down.

"Are you nuts?"

Mariachi trumpets and Mexican *gritos* that sounded like "eye-eye-eye-eye" swallowed up Theo's outraged shout.

"I'm saving your life." Avery fought to pin his friend to the floor. Fueled by rage and desperation, Theo bucked and heaved Avery to one side. His arms free, he landed a hard right to Avery's head.

Ears ringing, Avery grappled for the M4. It lay just beyond his outstretched arm. *Come on, come on.*

Please, God, please. I don't want to shoot my best friend.

In his sixteen-year career Avery had never shot anyone.

Could he do it now? *God, please no.*

Theo rolled left. Avery scrabbled to his feet. Theo did the same. He scooped up the rifle before Avery could get to it. They danced around for an eternity of seconds. This was the moment. Avery's life would end at the hands of his closest friend.

He daydreamed many scenarios. Dying quickly in the line of duty was his first choice. Killing him would end Theo's life too. He couldn't let that happen.

He lunged. Theo smacked him with the butt of his weapon. Avery pitched backward against the balcony bars.

Theo could've shot Avery but he didn't. Hope flamed.

"Give it up. It's not too late." The scant air in Avery's lungs escaped with the words, giving them a wheezy asthmatic squeak. "Why are you doing this? Why destroy your life?"

Theo shoved the rifle under Avery's neck and pushed him against the balcony railing. One more shove and he would send Avery crashing into the second-floor revelers.

Avery flailed and landed a punch to Theo's temple.

The man flinched but didn't let up. His blue eyes, huge and bloodshot, stared down at Avery. "It's already been destroyed and you did nothing to help."

"Please . . ." The crushing weight on Avery's chest made it impossible to breathe, let alone speak. Unbearable pressure threatened to break his spine. "Don't. . . ."

"You should've helped me. You got the files, but you did nothing. Nothing."

The pressure increased. Avery flailed his arms, desperate to connect with the railing. His hands brushed air, nothing more.

Jackie.

"Pull him in now. Now. Before I blow your brains out."

Petra. Thank You, God, for Petra.

The pressure let up for a split second. Theo looked back.

Avery heaved himself forward and slammed into a man he no longer recognized. They toppled over backward.

Sucking in deep breaths of sweet air, Avery scrambled to his feet. His spine screamed with pain. He ripped the M4 from Theo's grip and landed one foot on his oldest friend's chest. "Don't move. Don't you move."

Theo's face crumpled. He stopped struggling. "I'm sorry. I'm so sorry."

"Me too."

"I told you to stay with Vogel and the others." Avery handed the weapon to Petra. He knelt next to Theo to handcuff him. "Not that I'm complaining."

"Assisting means assisting." Petra directed the rifle at Theo. No doubt from her expression she was contemplating using it. "You needed backup."

"Tell Katie I love her." Theo moaned, but he rolled over without help to allow the handcuffs. "Tell her I'm sorry."

"You can tell her yourself. We're gonna get you some help." Avery helped him stand. "I'll be there with you. I promise."

Petra holstered her weapon. She helped Avery walk Theo through a cluster of rubberneckers to the elevator. "Your partner called me when he couldn't get to you."

"What did he have?"

"We know who the bomber is and you're not going to believe it."

Avery helped Theo into the elevator. His shoulders sagged. Tears streamed down his face.

Adrenaline faded, leaving Avery bone weary. He'd done his job. Attaboys were not in order.

One down and one to go.

FORTY-ONE

*D*on't *go into the basement.*

How many times had Jackie and her friends shouted those words at the TV screen while watching a horror movie?

She had no choice. Raven Man smacked the elevator button for the library basement and it hummed in the affirmative. The pistol in his hand looked small but deadly, nevertheless. Without moving her head she let her gaze travel to his face. Nothing but his blue eyes showed. Her assailant was slightly taller than she was. His eyes were sapphire like her own.

"Cris?"

Raven Man laughed softly, almost to himself, but he didn't speak.

If not Cris, who? "Tell me why you're doing this."

The pistol moved until it pointed at her face. Still, he said nothing.

The elevator doors opened. "Move."

The Central Library's basement might not be the stuff of horror movies, but Jackie had never visited the Friends of the Library's used bookstore The BookCellar late at night with a masked gunman. "Why are you doing this?"

"You never were good at obeying."

An iron band of disbelief and disappointment tightened around Jackie's neck. It couldn't be true. Not possible. "Nonno?" Her voice squeaked. "Please, is that you?"

Raven Man took her arm. His gentle touch filled Jackie with dread. "Come along."

"Don't touch me." She jerked away and plunged into the dark hallway. Security lighting popped on, bathing her kidnapper in a blinding light. "Tell me you weren't the one who set off the bomb at the Tobin. You didn't kill Estrella. And Market Square. Victoria. You couldn't have."

"You're the stupid one. You always were."

His scorn burned like acid eating through her skin to the marrow in her bones. Jackie stumbled toward the doors that led to the bookstore. *Think, think.* Why bring her here? Not to save her. He didn't care about her. She could've been killed in the Tobin blast.

Nonno couldn't have known his daughter-in-law would be at Market Square on Saturday. Were she and Victoria simply the collateral damage the caller mentioned? And the Alamo? Only blocks from one of his jewelry stores?

None of it made sense. He might not have been the kind of grandfather who doled out endless hugs and kisses when she was a child, but neither had he been cruel and vicious. Nonna said Nonno spent more time with Cris because he was more comfortable doing boy things. *"He doesn't know what to do with little girls."* It wasn't because he played favorites.

Jackie and Tosca had accepted her explanation because they didn't know any better. "Take off the mask."

"What difference would that make, my dear? I know you recognize my voice." He lowered the gun and pointed to his eyes. "My eyes are your eyes. I know you failed your first driving test. We both remember when I offered all three of you kids quarters to eat your brussels sprouts and you were the only one who managed to do it. You gagged and threw up, but you still insisted I give you the quarter."

"You know better than anyone that reneging on a deal is bad business." Jackie struggled to tame the quiver in her voice. Blue dots speckled her vision. This would be a bad time to bend over and put her head between her knees. "Bombing historic sites is bad for business in this town. You're hurting your own bottom line. Why, Nonno, why?" Despite her best efforts, her voice rose.

"Don't get so excited. You'll accomplish nothing by stressing yourself out."

"How can you be so blasé about being a mass murderer?"

"How can you work for the man who killed your father—my only son—my only child? How can you take money from a corrupt business run by corrupt politicians who sacrifice employees at the altar of a good sound bite?"

Vomit rose in Jackie's throat. She swallowed against it. The ignominy of throwing up on her grandfather's shiny black shoes would be too much. She inhaled through her nose and exhaled through her mouth. *One . . . two . . . three . . . God, help me. Please help me help him. Make him stop. Show me what You want me to do. Don't let those innocent people upstairs die.*

"I know what you're doing." Sarcasm soaked Nonno's words. "You're praying. I stopped doing that the day your father died. I'm afraid I contributed to my only son's demise."

"What do you mean?"

"Your father was swimming in debt." Nonno's voice cracked. "He came to me and asked for a loan. Of course I agreed. I wanted him back, as my son and as my heir apparent. And he was in the unique position to help me out with certain aspects of my business. He shared with me information on who planned to build what and when and where far before it became public knowledge. Sure, by the time permits are pulled, plats are a matter of public record, but he knew so much insider information far before the general public did."

The truth dawned in a slow, painful wave that took Jackie's breath. Her hands went to her throat. She sucked in air but her lungs refused to inflate. "You didn't . . . you wouldn't . . . he wouldn't. Why would he do it? He broke away from you to live his own life."

"Your father thought highly of himself. It turns out he wasn't the businessman he thought he was. He made bad investments. He spent money he didn't have. He came crawling back to me."

"You're responsible for his death."

"No. If that cretin Vogel hadn't decided to toss him in a ditch, he'd still be here. I would have hired him the best defense attorneys in the country. They would've made mincemeat of those public servant ADAs. I told him so that night—"

"You spoke to Daddy the night he died?"

"He called me. He asked me to take care of you and your siblings. Your mother." Nonno spit out the last two words. "I tried to convince him he could still have a future. He could still be my second in command. He made stupid, stupid mistakes. He got caught, but I could fix it. I told him suicide was for cowards."

"Not even that stopped him?"

"No, he couldn't live with himself, so he took the easy way out."

Nothing about suicide was easy. Nonno was a psychopath. "You killed him."

"No. He killed himself because Vogel, Sandoval, and the others exposed his mistakes

473

to the world. Like they haven't broken laws, pandered to politicians, taken bribes, slandered others, all to get where they are today."

"You murdered all these people to assuage your own guilty conscience. You killed Meher, an innocent woman with small children."

"No, imbecile, that was Richter."

"The security guard from the event at the Tobin?"

"Yes. He was a useful operative—especially when he realized the backpack had been moved. He returned it to its rightful place. But he couldn't leave well enough alone. His paranoia got the best of him. He was sure she could identify him in a lineup."

"So you had to kill him?"

"I did. When he began to act autonomously, he gave me no choice."

"You always have a choice."

"You are a naive twit."

"Did he leave the letter in my mailbox or was that you?"

"Does it matter?"

If the questions kept him talking, it gave Jackie time. Gave Avery time to find her. *Please, God.* "Yes, I want to know how depraved you are."

"Depraved? Me leaving a note in your mailbox isn't depraved. That's Vogel, Cavazos, and Sandoval, those who tossed my son to the wolves. Are you so dense that you can't understand that?

Your God doesn't exist. There's no one 'up there' who will help you."

Yes, there was. God in heaven and Avery upstairs in the library. She had to find a way to get to him. To tell him. To save him. Nonna and Tosca. And all the others. "Surely you won't hurt Nonna, Cris, and Tosca. Cris is your heir apparent now. You might not love Tosca the way you do Cris, but she's still your granddaughter."

"I sent Cris to Houston on urgent business a few minutes before he was supposed to arrive at the ball." Nonno sounded proud of his ingenuity. "I slipped a Mickey in your grandmother's drink. Not enough to hurt her, just enough to make her woozy. She was so 'tired' she went home shortly after you spoke to her in the atrium. Tosca doesn't rate an invite to the VIP after-party so she was never a concern. It was never about quantity, but quality. I wanted to send Vogel and his comrades to hell where they belong. Waiting until later had the added benefit of letting our friends in law enforcement think they'd kept everyone safe from the boogie man tonight. Then *boom*—their smug faces are blown up with the rest of the sheep."

Avery blown up. The image of Estrella's mangled body floated in Jackie's mind. A spurt of anger blew through her. Not again. She wouldn't lose another person she cared about. *Number one, keep him talking. Number two, get past him. No, number one, pray, then do the rest.*

Nonno began to pace in mincing steps, but the gun remained pointed at her face. "Everything was going like clockwork. Then you and your detective friend started talking about evacuating. You were about to tell him about the man with the raven. You thought you were so smart."

"Why follow me around?"

"I was having a little fun at your expense before reeling you in."

"And in the process gave yourself away."

"No, it's not too late. I can still make it work."

"Avery—Detective Wick is looking for me right now."

"No one is looking for you." Nonno shoved her into a storage room filled with boxes of books. "This is a perfect place to muzzle you while I modify my plan."

She took a quick look around—books on the floor, cleaning supplies on the shelves, mops, a vacuum. A first aid kit. Handy. She summoned all the bravado left in her shaking body. "Why not kill me now? You hate me so much."

"If you must know, the plan was for you to be the culprit. Your buddy Wick and all those library patrons would be dead. The Chihuly sculpture blown to smithereens. And you would never be able to convince them you didn't do it. I would disappear and only my watch would be found in the debris." He shifted so the gold Rolex, worn only on occasions such as this one, showed. "The plan was for them to find the materials in your house and traces in your Rogue."

"They would never believe it. Why wouldn't I run away after detonating the bomb—?"

"Bombs. I've spread my largess about for maximum damage to your beloved library. You loved it more than you loved your father. You're a traitor to the Santoro name."

"How did you get the bombs inside?"

"I went through the machine the first time. After that I had to run out to the car for the purse your grandmother allegedly forgot. I stuck the backpack underneath my overcoat when I came back. Then in my rush to get back, I allegedly forgot to lock the Mercedes. Can't have that. The guy checking invitations waved me through—after all, I'm a patron and a donor who'd already been through the screening. All he saw was an addled, forgetful old man."

"You thought of everything." Ignoring legs like puddles of water, Jackie strode toward him. "But you couldn't resist toying with me. You spoiled your own plan."

"Believe me, I'm flexible, my dear. I can still make it work. First, I must reconnoiter before I make a final decision. A good event planner always has a plan B. You of all people should know that."

He held up a ring of keys. "The cleaning crew supervisor didn't mind handing over the keys to his kingdom once he saw my little firearm. Of course he probably thought it would save him. It didn't. Sit tight while I do my reconnaissance. It'll give you time to meditate on your sins."

He snapped the door shut.

Jackie rushed to the door. It didn't budge. She spun around in the closet.

Nonno underestimated her. He always had.

The time for meditating on her sins would come.

This was not it.

FORTY-TWO

On the upside, Avery hadn't killed his best friend. He studied the Catrina Ball–goers as they exited the library. Agents escorted them to nearby Madison Square Park where they would be screened, interviewed, and released one by one. No one looked happy. Some people complained. One woman fainted. A few cried. But for the most part the genteel crowd moved, wine glasses in hand, toward the exit in a tense, quiet effort to get out as quickly as possible.

Without the music the lobby was eerily quiet. LEOs from the task force surveyed each person as he or she left. Guests had been ordered to remove hats, masks, and hairpieces. It didn't help with those who wore makeup. To check IDs would slow the process too much. In the meantime the bomb squad had begun the meticulous process of sweeping each floor. So far, nothing.

Uniformed officers had escorted Theo to the jail, where he would be held on suicide watch until morning. Then he would go to magistrate's court for a bail hearing. With any luck a decent attorney would argue for a psych eval at the state hospital. Bail would be out of the question.

On the downside, Ethan Richter's phone records had revealed a steady stream of calls between the dead mercenary and Daniel Santoro. The FBI's forensic accountant uncovered financial records that showed the beaucoup bucks in Richter's accounts had come from a Santoro shell company. Richter had been on Santoro's payroll for at least two years with regular bonuses for services rendered.

Dead men told no tales. Avery theorized Santoro had been tying up loose ends when he shot Richter to death on that ridge in Friedrich Park. He might be seventy-three, but he looked fifty. He worked out with a personal trainer and ran half marathons. He could climb that trail without breaking a sweat. He then killed the Amigo Ambassador and set the bombs around the Alamo. They simply had to prove it. Were Cris and Lucia Santoro part of the grand revenge scheme? Avery couldn't rule it out.

"See anybody you recognize?" Petra had her phone out, recording faces as they passed by. "I know. It's a stupid question."

"No."

Jackie would be devastated. He had to find her. He punched in her number for the third time. Voice mail for the third time. "Where are you? Evacuate. I'll meet you at Madison Square Park when this is over. Don't go alone. Take Tosca and Drucker with you. Call. Me. Now."

Petra lowered her phone for a second. "Isn't that the supervisor Jackie works for?"

Meagan Nobel stood in line between two couples dressed to the max in expensive costumes. Avery squeezed in front of her. "Step out of the line, please."

"We're supposed to evacuate."

"I'm aware. We'll get you out of here as soon as I ask a couple of questions." He drew her aside. "Where's Jackie?"

"She's never where she's supposed to be." Nobel sounded like a bad imitation of Queen Elizabeth. "Ask her sister. She's around here somewhere."

"You don't have comms or radios to communicate during events?"

"We just text each other. It's cheaper. Of course she's not responding." Nobel's thin upper lip covered with a peculiar shade of purple curled in disgust. "I tried to call her when the evacuation order came down. Nothing."

"How is Tosca dressed?"

At Nobel's blank look, Avery swallowed an obscenity. "Her sister."

"I haven't seen her. Can I go now?"

As much as he'd like to strap Nobel to the bomb, Avery knew better than to let his baser instincts take over. "Go."

"Detective Wick!"

A familiar voice called from across the lobby. It wasn't the voice Avery wanted to hear, but it would do. He squeezed through the crowd and strode toward Tosca Santoro and Lee Drucker. She looked stunning in a strapless, red-flowered dress. "Where's Jackie?"

"That's what I was going to ask you." Avery hated to disappoint her. "I've called her several times, but she doesn't answer."

"Me too." Tosca sounded tearful. "I'm worried. She's all about her job. It's not like her to disappear in the middle of an event, especially one where people are being evacuated."

Avery wouldn't tell her about her grandfather's crimes until they had him in custody. Until they were absolutely sure. "Where's your grandfather and the rest of your family?"

Tosca glanced around as if searching the lobby. "I haven't seen him all evening. Nonna wasn't feeling well. She went home. Cris never showed up."

"Take her and get out of here." Avery directed the command to Lee, who released Tosca's hand and slid his arm around her. "You can't wait around for Jackie."

"I'm not leaving without her." Tosca drew away from Lee. "What aren't you telling us? Where is she? Is she with my grandfather? Are they okay?"

"There's no time to explain." Avery locked gazes with Drucker. "Lee, get her out of here."

Petra hot on his heels, Avery loped to the elevator. "The last time I spoke to her she was in the Texana Genealogy Section on the sixth floor.

That was at least half an hour ago, but it's a place to start. The bomb squad has already cleared it."

"You don't think Santoro will hurt her, do you?"

Her expression said the rest. Already hurt her. Or killed her.

A man who would commit such an atrocity wasn't a human being anymore. Even the needle would be too good for him. A few minutes alone with Santoro would be all Avery needed. He quashed his anger into the vault next to the one for the animal who killed Theo's son. "He knew she'd be in the Tobin last week and he blew it up with her in it."

They exited on the sixth floor. "You go left, I'll go right." His S&W in one hand, Avery ducked into the stacks. He eased down the first aisle, then the second.

Nothing.

Come on, come on. His pulse banged in his ears. Adrenaline surged through him. *Come on, come on.*

A phone lay under a reading alcove chair. Avery darted forward and squatted next to it. The cracked face revealed a photo of Jackie's cats snuggled together, sleeping on her couch.

His stomach bucked with nausea. Apprehension formed a tight knot in the back of his throat. "Where are you, Jackie?" he whispered.

"I didn't find anything." Her weapon in one hand, Petra trotted toward him. "You?"

He pointed to the phone covered with a yellow facsimile of an old-fashioned library card. "It's hers."

"If we had her pass code, we could see if she got any phone calls from Santoro." Petro knelt next to Avery. "I know you're thinking the worst. Don't."

Avery had seen too much in his career to delude himself. The worst happened every day.

Mostly Jackie's call history would reveal his profanity-laden voice mail messages. He snapped several photos of the phone from different angles, including the table and chair. Then he picked it up with two fingers and laid it on the table. "Maybe Tosca knows."

Using his own phone, he called Tosca at the number she'd given him after her interview. She picked up on the first ring and launched into a tirade. "We're waiting for you. Where is she? Where's Nonno—?"

"Working on it. What's your sister's pass code for her phone? Do you know it?"

"You found her phone but not her?" Tosca's voice rose. "What about Nonno? Never mind, I'm coming back."

The agents at the park would never let her back into the building. "Do you know her pass code?"

"She uses Mom's birthday for everything. 0120."

"Stay put."

"Seriously—"

Avery hung up. Donning the handy gloves he'd stuck in his back pocket, he punched in the four numbers. They worked. He breathed again. Nothing. No calls this evening other than his own. Santoro hadn't used a phone call to lure her away from the party.

Santoro's cell number was in her contacts. Avery held his breath again while he accessed the number.

Daniel Santoro answered on the second ring. "Jacqueline, I was just looking for you."

"This isn't Jackie and you know it."

"Detective Wick. How did you get Jackie's phone? Is my granddaughter all right?"

"I found it where you left it." Avery closed his eyes and pictured the Spurs playing the Los Angeles Clippers and that traitor their former teammate Kawhi Leonard. Anything to keep from screaming what he really wanted to say. *You hurt your granddaughter and I will kill you without batting an eye.* "Are you enjoying the ball?"

"It's been lovely. Unfortunately my better half wasn't feeling well so she went home early."

"Surely you realize the library is being evacuated."

"Yes, I know, but I can't leave without my dear granddaughter, Jacqueline. You haven't by any chance seen her?"

"I know you're concerned for her. So am I.

Maybe we could meet in the lobby and combine forces." Nothing like calling a psychopath's bluff. "The bomb squad is sweeping every floor. They may have found her by now."

"That sounds like an excellent plan, Detective. I'll meet you there." He disconnected.

"They'll serve ice water in hell when that happens." Avery avoided Petra's concerned gaze. He set the phone on the study alcove table. There was no time to get a CSU to their location. "Do you have any evidence bags with you?"

Like a good case agent, she did. He slid the phone into the bag and headed to the elevator.

"What's the plan?"

"I have a feeling if we find Jackie, we'll find Daniel."

They rode the elevator in tense silence. Back on the first floor, Avery hesitated. Combine with the other task force members to spread out, or see what the bomb squad came up with? The second elevator hummed. He glanced up. The other elevator passed the first floor and kept descending. The only floor left was the basement.

"Nobody should be headed to the basement." Avery jabbed the button.

Petra beat him into the elevator. "You think it's him."

"I'm praying it is. I'm sick of his games." He didn't tell Petra his heart beat so hard he might drop dead of a heart attack before they descended one floor. "I'm ready to read him his rights and bury him on death row."

Or in the ground. Either would be fine.

FORTY-THREE

A distant *ding* told Jackie everything she needed to know.

He was back.

Would she have heard or felt an explosion on the first floor? The building was solid. Maybe not. What was Plan B? *Please, God, guide all those innocent people from this building. Foil evil. Give me the strength to do what I need to do.*

She refused to be his victim. Mom, Tosca, and Cris had been through enough. No more deaths. No more grief.

Galvanized by a massive wave of anger mingled with an equal dose of fear, Jackie grabbed another bottle of toilet cleaner from the shelf. She ripped off the lid and poured the liquid into a bucket already half full of bleach and glass cleaner. Drops splashed on her hands and her dress. The fumes made her eyes water.

Such a small room might not have enough ventilation to keep her from passing out.

Please, God, don't let me faint. I can't die. They don't need more tragedy and pain in their lives. Please keep them safe. Put Your bubble of protection around them and all the people in the library now. Including Avery, please.

Jackie didn't want Nonno to die either. She only needed to incapacitate him long enough to escape. She needed a direct hit. Only his eyes and mouth were exposed. If she could hit him in the face, in the eyes, he wouldn't be able to see her.

Or shoot her.

Once he reached the bookstore, the carpet would muffle the sound of his feet. Was he close?

Jackie dragged the bucket across the tiled floor. She turned off the light and leaned against the door. Scraping sound. A click.

Backing up, she grabbed the bucket and stationed herself in front of the door.

The door squeaked. Light from the bookstore flooded in.

"You ruined everything. You spoiled it. Vogel is gone, all his cronies are gone. Everyone is leaving. Everyone!" Gun in hand, Nonno charged into the room. "You're just like your mother. You both should've died in the bombings."

Jackie hurled the caustic cleaning solution at his face.

Nonno screamed. Praying he couldn't see her, Jackie dropped on all fours and crawled past him.

Groaning, the gun still in position, he whirled.

The gun blast reverberated in the basement's silence.

Jackie's ears rang. The liquid burned her hands and knees. The fumes burned her nostrils and eyes. Vomit rose in her throat. The bizarre reality ricocheted inside her head.

Her grandfather truly wanted to kill her.

She scrambled to her feet and ran. Straight into Avery's arms.

He grunted and held on. "Where is he?"

"Gun, gun," she yelled. "Behind me."

Avery shoved her aside. She stumbled, regained her balance, and turned.

Nonno staggered from the storage room. His right arm swung widely.

"No, please, Nonno, no." Jackie rushed forward. He would shoot Avery or Avery would shoot him. She couldn't let that happen. "Stop. It's over."

"No, it's not." Nonno fired. The shot went wide and pinged in the wall.

Avery knocked Jackie to the floor and shot in one sweeping motion. Nonno returned fire.

A barrage of shots ringing over her, Jackie crawled behind a mobile book rack. *God, God, God.*

Then it stopped. Silence reigned.

Her lungs didn't work. Her feet wouldn't move. *Get up, get up.* "Avery? Avery, are you all right?"

"It's over."

Jackie forced herself to look up at his outstretched hand. It shook. His chest heaved. "I'm sorry. I had to do it."

"He gave you no choice." Her voice sounded

distant and unrecognizable in her own ears. "He gave me no choice."

The muscle in Avery's jaw twitched. His Adam's apple bobbed and he nodded. "Still, I'm sorry."

Jackie took his hand and he pulled her to her feet. She let go and wobbled around his solid frame. A second later his voice echoed behind her. Words burbled to the top. Shots fired, suspect fatally shot. CSU, medical examiner, officer-involved shooting teams—both PD and FBI.

In a few seconds the horde would descend. The silence would be broken and the opportunity to confront the reality of her loss would disappear. Jackie forced herself forward.

Special Agent Jantzen squatted next to Nonno. He lay on his back, arms and legs splayed. Blood pooled under him in a widening puddle. The FBI agent slid the gun beyond Nonno's reach. An automatic reaction, no doubt, even with a dead suspect. She slid a toy car remote from the inside pocket of his tux and gently laid it on the floor. Finally she looked up. "I'm sorry. He's gone."

Nausea gripped Jackie. She clasped her hands in front of her and nodded. "I want to see his face."

"I'm sorry. We need to leave him as is until the CSU folks get here. They'll remove his mask."

"Just for a second." Jackie looked back at Avery. "Please."

He moved past her, snatched a tissue from a box next to the cash register, and knelt next to Special Agent Jantzen. With two fingertips he lifted the mask.

Jackie edged closer. It was Nonno. She'd known that, but somehow it still didn't seem real. Didn't seem possible. The skin around his eyes and mouth bubbled where the cleansers had hit. A thin line of blood dribbled from his slack mouth. Blessedly, his eyes were closed.

Her grandfather lay on the floor in the basement of her favorite place in the world. He'd died a serial bomber, a mass murderer, responsible for twenty-one murders, 165 injured, and hundreds of thousands of dollars in property damage. Her nonno, who showed her how to find the Big Dipper in the night sky, killed Estrella and Victoria and intended to kill Jackie.

Shivering, she tore her gaze from his lifeless form. "I needed to see his face in order to believe he did all this. He killed Estrella and Victoria. He fully intended to kill me. How is it even possible? I don't understand how he had time to perpetuate these horrible attacks."

"He had help." Avery slipped the mask back in place and stood. "A man named Ethan Richter did most of the dirty work. Your grandfather learned what he needed to know from Richter and then killed him. Your phone is evidence. Sorry about that. Do you want me to call Tosca? You won't be allowed to talk to her until the preliminary interviews are done—by someone besides me and Special Agent Jantzen."

"I should be the one to tell Tosca about Nonno. We'll tell Nonna together."

"I'm sorry this isn't over yet."

"Please stop apologizing. I'm probably under suspicion all over again. He planned to frame me for the bombings. He said he planted bomb-making materials in my house. He planned to say he killed me before I killed him."

"Given how things played out here, no one will believe you had anything to do with it."

Jackie turned so she had her back to Special Agent Jantzen. Regret and pain etched Avery's face. Likely it mirrored hers. "Just know I don't blame you for his death. I can't believe I didn't see this coming. My grandfather was a criminal who led his own son astray. He was also a serial bomber. With my pedigree I wouldn't blame a person for shying away."

"You aren't them. Never forget that. You're a kind, compassionate . . ." His pale-blue eyes closed for a second, then opened. "I'll be around if you need to talk."

Would he or was he just being nice? His parents served their country honorably. Her father defrauded the citizens of San Antonio. Nonno was a psychopath. Any person in his right mind would run the other direction.

The elevators dinged one after the other. Wave upon wave of law enforcement types inundated the bookstore. They came between Jackie and Avery. Still, she could feel his gaze on her back as an FBI special agent led her to the elevator.

The red enchilada library, a monument to free exchange of information, still stood. The rest of her family had survived. Jackie lived. God answered her prayers.

Just not the way she had hoped.

FORTY-FOUR

Time stood still. So exhausted her body refused to respond to simple commands, Jackie tottered into the library's first floor lobby. The interminable interview by a host of law enforcement people who asked questions in a ping-pong approach had ended. They were alternately sympathetic and compassionate. Hot coffee, a blanket, more hot coffee. Jackie would never sleep again. She stumbled. An FBI agent took her arm. She was too numb to feel his grip.

"Jackie!"

"Tosca!" Her sister, accompanied by Lee, stood by the exit. Tosca's makeup was a smeared mess and her headpiece long gone. Jackie shook loose and darted across the tile floor into her sister's arms. "I wanted to be the one to tell you."

"I know." Tosca's voice was muffled against Jackie's shoulder. "I'm so sorry you had to go through this. I can't believe it. I just can't believe it."

"He tried to kill me and I still can't believe it." Jackie stroked Tosca's tangled hair. "He wasn't the person we grew up with. He held all that pain and bitterness inside until it turned into a vile, spewing rage."

"I called Cris. He's trying to get a return flight.

I'm glad he's not driving. He could barely put two words together. Telling him was awful." With a shuddering sob, Tosca broke away. "How will we tell Nonna?"

"Together." They needed to do it quickly, before the media started hounding her. Before she saw it on TV. "I'm so sorry you had to be the one to tell Cris. I know he's in shock. He's numb. I am. Does Mom know?"

"No. She would still be asleep. Why wake her? Morning is soon enough. I vomited in a trash can during the interview." Her face scarlet, Tosca whispered the admission as if someone would think less of her. "How could he do this to us, to Nonna? How could he? After what we went through with Daddy, to have a grandfather like him? It doesn't make sense."

Nothing did. It wouldn't for years to come. "It's okay, Sissy. We'll get through it. We did the first time. We will again."

The famous Santoro stiff upper lip held Jackie in good stead once again.

Arms locked, the three of them pushed past the officers at the exit and into the cold air of an October day just dawning. Jackie took a long breath. Cool, sweet oxygen filled her lungs. In spite of it all she could be thankful. She was alive. Tosca, Cris, and Nonna were alive. Mom was alive. *Thank You, Jesus.*

Their father's death had taught them they could

survive anything. They would survive this too. Even if it didn't feel that way right now. The scent of cigarette smoke wafted over Jackie. She glanced back.

A cigarette in one hand, Avery stood on the grass several yards from the entrance. He looked up. Jackie slowed. She squeezed Tosca's shoulder. "I'll catch up with you."

Lee followed her gaze. "I'll bring the car to the street. You can get in there."

In the dusky light Avery's face was drawn. He took a long pull from the cigarette. The lit end throbbed red.

Jackie paused on the sidewalk a yard or two from him. "I didn't know you smoked."

"I don't. Not since I married Chandra. She drew a big fat line there." He took another puff and let the smoke stream through his nostrils. "A moment of weakness."

"It's understandable. I wish I smoked or drank or something."

"Look, I—"

"You did what you had to do."

"I killed your grandfather. I've never shot or killed anyone before." His hoarse voice deepened. "Why did it have to be your grandfather? Or anyone for that matter?"

"I don't know. I wish I did."

He dropped the cigarette on the cement and ground it under his heel. "I know it's an awful habit. If I had something to put it in, I'd pick it up."

Of all the horror of this evening, he was worried about how she'd react to a cigarette butt? "I don't blame you for anything. You saved my life."

"You saved mine and Petra's by alerting us to the gun and by blinding him."

"I was running on instinct."

"Me too."

She should say something. Anything. "At least it wasn't Theo."

"It was Theo too." Avery pulled a package of cigarettes from his jacket. He stared at them as if he didn't know where they came from. "He planned to shoot up your dance."

"I'm so sorry."

"So am I," he whispered. "I thought I might have to kill him tonight. But I didn't. So there's that. He's in jail. I'm hoping he'll get the help he needs now."

"You'll make sure of it."

"I know you need time." He rubbed his eyes with both hands. "I know you can't tell me how much. But I'm hoping you'll forgive me."

Jackie scraped the bottom of the barrel in search of a way to make him understand. She didn't blame him. She needed him. She wanted him. The events of the last few hours hadn't changed that. In fact they only underscored how much she wanted to find out how deep her feelings for him might one day grow. "There's nothing to forgive. You did your job. You're good at it. Because of that, I'm still here. Now we have unfinished business."

"We do?" Confusion laced the two syllables. His expression lightened. "Oh, you mean that."

"Yes, that. The kisses you stole in the aftermath of a series of bombings."

"That was ill advised."

"Even so. Your actions spoke louder than words that day. But you caught me by surprise. Our timing seems to be lousy. All I know is I'd love the chance to do it properly."

Avery's tentative smile warmed her. He shook his head. "I want to make a good impression the next time. I stink of sweat and cigarette smoke. My breath is bad. I'm wearing a stupid tux that doesn't fit."

"I'm a mess too." Not just physically. He was right. They needed a fresh start. She met him halfway. Their hands touched. Jackie kissed his cheek. "You know where to find me when you're ready."

Two short horn beeps announced that Jackie's ride had arrived.

Avery leaned down. His lips brushed hers. He did smell of cigarette and sweat. It didn't matter. His somber gaze mesmerized her. "I was going to say the same thing to you."

Only the thought of what still lay ahead—

telling Nonna—forced Jackie to move. At the car door she looked back. Avery had lit another cigarette.

Healing would take time—for them both.

FORTY-FIVE

*H*ere *I go.* Jackie parked in front of Avery's house and turned off the Rogue's engine.

His old pickup truck sat on the street rather than in the driveway. The garage door was up. He was home. A basketball hoop adorned the garage above the door. Always a good sign. She rolled down the window and let the brisk December breeze cool her face. She couldn't wait another day.

Would Avery feel the same way?

Time to find out.

She flipped down the sun visor and checked her makeup. She wasn't wearing much. She tugged lip balm from her bag and used it. In her fierce, ongoing desire for a fresh start, she'd gone through her entire house, throwing out stuff. Including all her lipstick. She hadn't returned to work yet. Meagan was gone for good. Jackie's colleagues reported she'd left San Antonio for Florida after announcing to the entire staff she planned to sell real estate in the Sunshine State. It was safer, she said.

Jackie had woken up each day for the past two months with a painful aversion to any thought of entering the building where she'd faced death and walked away only because her grandfather died. Her therapist said to give it time.

Her grandfather the serial bomber. The mass murderer. The crooked businessman who led his only son astray.

Tosca was designing a garden for Mom's yard. They'd plant it in the spring. With Lee's encouragement, she went to a therapist twice a week. Like Bella and Sig, they'd set a date for their wedding. Nonna was decorating the modest home she'd purchased in Kerrville. The house she shared with Nonno had only been on the market for a month before a wealthy couple from Guadalajara purchased it. Cris had taken over running Nonno's business empire. His first order of business was to clean up Nonno's below-board business practices. He chose to live with Mom, who was helping him look for a new house he could make his own. He'd chosen not to seek therapy—for now. He did acquiesce to Mom's quiet request that he attend church with her. Whether that meant he'd reconciled with God remained between him and his Creator.

He also dealt with a multitude of civil lawsuits brought by injured bombing victims and the families of those who'd died. They were also suing the city of San Antonio for failure to keep them safe. Lee was helping Cris with that—or trying to help. Cris refused to settle.

Reading one book after another served as

Jackie's escape. Nonna didn't think it was healthy. Mom disagreed. She encouraged Jackie to volunteer as a basketball coach at the YMCA. She had cleared the background check and started the previous week. She had also joined her own adult league team and played regularly now.

Sprigs of hope burst from the tragedy-scarred soil each day.

They all gathered, including Nonna, at Mom's every Sunday now for supper. No excuses.

Two months.

What if Avery wasn't ready? Why hadn't he come looking for her? He knew where she lived. Chandra had stuck a business card with Avery's address scribbled on the back in Jackie's bag after Nonno's funeral. It had been kind of her to attend. A smattering of the Santoro family, along with Bella and Sig, had filled a dozen seats in a brief service officiated by Nonno's pastor. Then his ashes were interred without fanfare in a Santoro family mausoleum. Not the grand finale he'd once imagined, no doubt.

From there Jackie and Chandra had struck up a sturdy friendship that started with a bond over Meher's death and bloomed into sporadic lunches in Madison Square Park and game nights with banana splits with the kids.

Avery didn't attend the funeral. Jackie still wondered what the proper etiquette was for such a bizarre situation. Should a homicide detective who shot to death a serial bomber attend his funeral in light of the detective's alleged interest in the bomber's granddaughter?

According to Chandra, her ex-husband had been cleared by the shooting team and had made the requisite visits to a department shrink. His friend Theo remained in San Antonio State Hospital. His son's killer remained at large. Avery spent his free time working out and thinking.

Chandra's exact words had been, *"Avery wants to make the pieces fit together and he can't. That bugs him. But he'll get there. He just needs time."*

How much time? If Avery wasn't ready to contact her, should she contact him first?

She rubbed her forehead. It didn't help. The real ache was lodged in her heart. She couldn't wait another day. Not another minute.

Santoros didn't back down.

A familiar sound of a basketball smacking against pavement drew Jackie back to Avery's driveway. He stood on the cement, dribbling the ball, his attention on the hoop. After a few bounces, he drove to the basket and laid the ball up in a nice, fluid motion. He caught his own rebound, executed a quick pivot, and scored again.

So the guy had game—unopposed of course.

Jackie slid from her car, tucked her purse strap on her shoulder, and picked up the small package from the seat. She came bearing gifts—a gift.

A large, elderly German shepherd and a smaller dog of the mutt variety emerged from the open garage door. They accompanied their vociferous barking with much tail wagging, suggesting their bark might be worse than their bite.

Avery paused below the basket, rolling the ball from one hand to the other. Staring. He wore a tank top that showed off stellar biceps and pecs. His long basketball shorts didn't hide muscle-bound legs. He'd definitely been working out since the bombings. He bounced the ball once. "Ace, Deuce, that's enough. Can it. Friend, not foe."

Good to know which camp she fell in. "Hello, Avery."

"You came."

Her heart beating so fiercely Jackie could hardly hear over its pounding, she kept walking.

Avery took two steps forward and stopped. "It's good to see you."

Jackie set her purse in a ratty lawn chair parked in the grass and laid the package next to it.

"Jackie?"

No turning back. She strode to him, placed both hands to his cheeks, and stared into his pale-blue eyes. "Are you ready?"

The ball dropped from his hands and rolled away. His sharp intake of breath was audible. He came the rest of the way.

His kiss left no doubt. Pent-up white heat

exploded and shot through Jackie's body. Fears and hurts dissolved. Uncertainty disappeared. Scars smoothed. Only the fact that Avery had his arms wrapped around her waist and her body tight against his kept Jackie from sinking to the ground. Her body decided to go limp the second his lips found hers.

Mercifully, his lips moved to her cheek. Then he nuzzled her neck. Chills traveled from her head to her toes. She had years of experience dating—and kissing—but the secret was only now being revealed. Kissing the right man was monumentally better.

Please don't stop.

Avery raised his head an inch and whispered in her ear, "Just a reminder, I did tell you I'm not good at this." His warm breath tickled her ear and he sighed. "I'm really bad at it."

"I beg to differ." Struggling to draw another breath, Jackie leaned against him. "You do it very well."

He ducked his head and ran his thumb along her collarbone. The sensation made it much harder to think, let alone understand his words. His gaze locked with hers. "You know what I mean. My track record sucks."

Her turn. Jackie raised her head and kissed his chin, then his cheek. "I suspect you learned from your mistakes. I'm not worried about your track record." Her lips moved on to his nose. He leaned down as if seeking more. She obliged with kisses on his forehead and his other cheek. "I'm more worried about knowing who you are."

Telling him her deepest, darkest secrets so soon in this fledgling whatever-it-was seemed perfectly normal. "I'm trying not to shy away from this . . . thing with you because I find I can no longer be sure a person—even one I know well—is showing me his true self. My track record with men is abysmal."

"With me, what you see is what you get."

"I doubt that. People who say that are usually hiding something."

His hands cupped her head. Eyes filled with fire, he held her there, staring into her face. He seemed to be deciding something, something important. Jackie waited. A door might close here or he would decide to go through it. "I'm not always sure what I believe or if I do believe."

"Everyone feels that way at one time or another." She eased away from him. Her body protested. She grabbed his hand and entwined her fingers in his. "I ask God to help me in my unbelief."

"And He does."

"Always."

"Good to know. What about the fact that I'm divorced? I may attend church sporadically, but I remember it being a no-no."

"Haven't you heard? 'All have sinned and fall

short of the glory of God.'" She'd talked to her own pastor about this issue—among others— in the past two months. "Besides, Chandra says you wanted to go to counseling. She's the one who walked away. You had no control over her actions."

"You've been talking to Chandra."

"I spent Friday night eating Thai food with her family and participating in game night. I'll have you know I'm crushing it with Uno these days."

His expression bemused, Avery shook his head. "As if life could get any weirder."

"I'm impressed at how adult, how civilized you are toward Chandra. It says a lot about you as a person. She hurt you. We both know it takes courage to allow ourselves to get drawn into a relationship where we could end up hurt."

She picked her words with care. *God, don't let him be scared away. Let him hear the intent behind the words.* "I'm willing to risk it. Are you?"

"I wanted to ride in there on my white horse, grab you up, and carry you home to my castle. If I had one. A horse or a castle." His tone was self-mocking. "But I'm positive you don't need a white knight in shining armor. Which is good, because it's not me. You need a man who will love you for who you are. An independent woman who knows what she wants and isn't afraid to go after it."

"I am."

"I'm too old for you. I'm too old to change."

The age thing deserved no response. "Change what?"

"Like the thing about books. I don't read books."

"Actually I found one I think you might like." Jackie smiled at his disbelieving look. She let go of his hand and went to the lawn chair to retrieve the gift. She held it out. "Don't underestimate me. I've lured more people into reading than I can count."

Pleasure replaced the disbelief. He took it and ripped off the plain blue wrapping paper. "*Call of the Wild* by Jack London."

"You'll love it. I promise. It's about a dog named Buck. And it's short."

"It's possible." He rubbed his hand over the cover. "But I hope this doesn't mean you think you can change me. You can't."

"It's not about changing you. Reading is a gift. I read when I can't sleep. I read when I'm sad. I read when I'm happy. Reading gives me joy, takes me places I've never been, and I learn things. What person wouldn't want that gift?"

"When you put it that way, it does sound good." He turned the book over and read the back-cover blurb. "I'll let you know how it goes. I have something for you as well."

He disappeared into the garage. Jackie retrieved

511

the basketball from its resting spot on the street by Avery's truck. The ball felt good in her hands. Her body relaxed and fell into a rhythm that had soothed her since childhood. Her left-handed hook fell effortlessly into the basket.

"Nice." Avery emerged from the garage in time to stick out his hand and collect the rebound. He held up her journal. "This belongs to you."

Her journal. Heat seared Jackie's cheeks. She took the thin moleskin book and clutched it to her chest. "Thank you."

"I didn't read it. I promise."

The wave of embarrassment receded. Avery was an honorable man. And thoughtful. And kind. "I appreciate your restraint."

He took up a spot that would've served as the free throw line and lofted the ball into the air. It rolled around the rim twice and finally decided to drop in. "I also work too much. I don't sleep when I'm working a case. I'm all in. In fact, I don't sleep much period."

"I'm the same way when I'm working an event. It's not the same as finding killers and giving justice to victims, of course, but I understand dedication to the job." Jackie tucked the journal into her purse while he retrieved the ball. "I don't have a ton of experience in relationships, but I'd like to try to find some kind of balance. With the right person I believe it's possible. I also think it's possible to find peace in a relationship, in another person's presence, that allows you to finally relax and sleep. At least that's what I think."

Avery bounced the ball back and forth between his hands. His gaze remained on the basket, but he nodded. "I'm a slob. I like plain, simple coffee and fake creamer. I eat fast food three or four times a week. I've never had a cat. I don't do litter boxes."

"My cats, my litter box." Jackie studied his dogs, one big and one small. The big one eyed her with a hungry look. The small one's tail beat a steady thump-thump on the driveway. "Introduce me to your friends."

Ace warmed up immediately. It took longer for Deuce to succumb to her charm. He sniffed her fingers, studied her with ancient, knowing eyes, and finally deigned to let her pet him. "They're sweet."

Avery laughed. "They're guy dogs. They like the ladies."

"How do you think they feel about cats?"

"As long as they don't eat them, I think we'll be fine."

Jackie opened her mouth. Avery shook his head and tossed her the ball. "I'm kidding. They haven't eaten any of the cats in the neighborhood—that I know of."

Their laughter spilled out over his yard and their lives. Jackie couldn't remember the last time she'd laughed. "I don't want to change you. I want to get to know everything about you. Starting with whether I can beat you at one-on-one. That's critical, you know. I don't like to lose."

"Me neither." Avery grinned, swiped the ball from her hands, feinted, and slipped past her. "Game on."

Whooping, Jackie charged after him. "Challenge accepted."

Sunshine, a game of basketball, and two grinning dogs as spectators proved life could be good again. Joy had a way of finding people who dared hope for its return.

Jackie reached under Avery's long arm, tapped the ball away, dribbled twice, and lofted it into the air. *This one's for you, Estrella.*

Nothing but net.

A NOTE FROM THE AUTHOR

I love libraries and I love books. Growing up, I thought I might become a librarian. Instead I chose journalism, but my lifelong love of public libraries hasn't faltered. So it shouldn't be surprising that I've written a novel in which the main character is a strong, capable, and brave librarian. Yes, I know the bad guy almost blows the place up, but he doesn't succeed. San Antonio's Central Public Library is a beautiful piece of functional art. I loved being able to feature it in this story, along with some of the art located there. Being a member of the public relations team that planned and executed the building's grand opening in 1995 is one of the highlights of my PR career with the city of San Antonio. Visiting the building with my children, who called it the red enchilada library, is among many good memories from their childhoods.

My thanks to Morgan Yoshimura, the interim adult services coordinator for the San Antonio Public Library system, for patiently answering all my questions about being a librarian in today's high-tech world. I also want to thank former librarian and full-time author Amanda Flower for giving me some of her precious time for a phone interview. Both women helped me understand how vital and relevant libraries remain for all of us.

As always, none of this would be possible without the entire HarperCollins Christian Publishing team. A special heartfelt thanks to my editor Becky Monds for managing to read the manuscript and provide valuable feedback in the midst of preparing for maternity leave and the arrival of a precious new baby. Thanks also to Julee Schwarzburg, for jumping in to fill the gap in Becky's absence, with additional observations and her usual fine-tooth comb approach to line editing.

I'm blessed to have unwavering support from my family, especially as I deal with new, unexpected health challenges. I couldn't have completed this story without the support of my husband, Tim, my daughter, Erin, and my son, Nicholas. Love you guys.

Last, but not least, thank you to my readers. You're the best. Keep reading!

DISCUSSION QUESTIONS

1. A terrible tragedy rocked the Santoro family. As a result of her father's suicide, Jackie drew closer to God. Cris and Daniel were angry with God and abandoned their faith. Why do you think people react differently in the face of terrible trials? How have you reacted and why? What does Scripture tell us about these trials?

2. Daniel blames the city manager and other city officials for his son's death. Do you think he's right? Who do you believe is to blame and why? Have you ever done something you know is wrong and then tried to blame others when you're found out?

3. Avery and Jackie are two very different people. Avery lists the ways they are different. Yet they're falling in love. Do you think it's possible for people who are fundamentally different to find ways to build a satisfying, loving, long-term relationship? Why or why not? If you do, how would you go about it?

4. Jackie's mother encouraged her father to leave the family business and strike out on his own.

It ended badly. We don't have her firsthand account of why she did that. Do you think she was wrong to support his desire to be independent of his father? Why or why not?

5. Jackie and Avery both have jobs that go beyond the regular nine-to-five routine. They're deeply invested in their work. Avery's first marriage ended in divorce because both he and his wife were focused more on their jobs than their marriage. Is it possible to find a balance between the two? If you had a friend considering a relationship in these circumstances, what would you recommend she or he do?

ABOUT THE AUTHOR

Bestseller Kelly Irvin is the author of nineteen books, including romantic suspense and Amish romance. The *Library Journal* said her novel *Tell Her No Lies* is "a complex web with enough twists and turns to keep even the most savvy romantic suspense readers guessing until the end." She followed up with *Over the Line* and *Closer Than She Knows*. The two-time ACFW Carol finalist worked as a newspaper reporter for six years writing stories on the Texas–Mexico border. Those experiences fuel her romantic suspense novels set in Texas. A retired public relations professional, Kelly now writes fiction full-time. She lives with her husband, photographer Tim Irvin, in San Antonio. They are the parents of two children, three grand-children, and two ornery cats.

Visit her online at KellyIrvin.com
Instagram: @kelly_irvin
Facebook: @Kelly.Irvin.Author
Twitter: @Kelly_S_Irvin

Books are produced in the United States using U.S.-based materials

Books are printed using a revolutionary new process called THINKtech™ that lowers energy usage by 70% and increases overall quality

Books are durable and flexible because of Smyth-sewing

Paper is sourced using environmentally responsible foresting methods and the paper is acid-free

Center Point Large Print
600 Brooks Road / PO Box 1
Thorndike, ME 04986-0001 USA

(207) 568-3717

US & Canada:
1 800 929-9108
www.centerpointlargeprint.com